Shattered Hearts and Silent Whispers

KATHY WINSLOWER

DEDICATION

To those who have faced darkness and emerged stronger, to the friendships that light our way, and to the unwavering resilience of the human spirit.

May this book serve as a tribute to the power of unity, the pursuit of truth, and the enduring strength of love and connection.

CONTENTS

CHAPTER 1: WHISPERING SHADOWS

The crisp scent of pine trees filled Olive Adams' lungs as she stood on the cliff, gazing out at the charming town of Serenity Falls. The morning sun cast a warm glow over the rolling hills, the lush forests, and sparkling rivers flowing through the valley. The sight brought a glimmer of hope to Olive's weary heart. With her eyes fixed on the never-ending horizon, she inhaled the refreshing salty breeze.

Nature had always been Olive's safe haven. The gentle rustling of leaves and the melody of the wind spoke a language that touched her soul. As she stood there, surrounded by the beauty of nature, a sense of calm and belonging washed over her—an elusive peace she had been seeking for far too long.

After days of searching for a place to heal her broken heart, Olive was drawn to Serenity Falls, a quaint town nestled among giant mountains and serene valleys. It exuded calmness and charm, as if calling out to her weary spirit, offering a chance to start anew, a chance to rediscover herself.

Since her childhood, Olive had been enchanted by photography. Capturing fleeting moments, freezing emotions and stories in a single frame, brought her comfort and purpose. Through those preserved memories, she sought refuge from the painful past that haunted her.

In Serenity Falls, amidst the awe-inspiring landscapes, Olive decided to find a way to stay. Here, she could find solace in nature's beauty and, just maybe, find the sense of belonging she had long yearned for.

Suddenly, her phone rang, showing the name 'Tony'—a reminder of the painful past she had desperately tried to leave behind.

"Not fucking today, not fucking ever again." Olive whispered, determined to embrace the beauty of the present and leave the shadows of the past where they belonged.

Overflowing with rage and frustration, Olive let go of the phone, watching it soar through the air as if it carried away all her burdens.

As it plunged toward the crashing waves, Olive

felt an empowering rush. Tossing that phone into depths of the water, symbolized her escape from a poisonous past, a new beginning for her life. She wouldn't be trapped by those haunting shadows any longer.

The phone vanished into the river's embrace, and Olive experienced a mix of relief and nervousness. It was a moment of release, bidding farewell to all the pain, heartache, and haunting memories that had weighed her down.

The sound of the water crashing resonated in her ears, reminding her of the importance of living in the present. Stepping back from the cliff, Olive's heart felt lighter than it had in years, her past finally relinquished.

"This is my fresh start," she whispered, determination gleaming in her eyes. Serenity Falls meant more to her than just a town; it was her sanctuary, a place to heal and rediscover herself.

Surrounded by the ocean's scent, Olive vowed to embrace life's beauty, capturing moments of joy and love through her photography. Every click of the camera would weave a tale of strength, hope, and the art of letting go.

But what she didn't know was that, Serenity Falls held its own secrets, mysteries that would interweave with her journey of self-discovery. The shadows from her past would resurface, challenging the fragile happiness she had found.

Yet, at that moment, on the edge of the cliff, Olive felt a newfound strength. She had confronted her demons, broken free from their grasp, and now she was prepared to face the unknown. The road ahead might be filled with twists and turns, but she was unafraid to confront them head-on.

Olive turned away from the edge and started back towards her car, a smile pulling at her lips. Serenity Falls awaited her, ready to unveil its secrets and surprises. And she, armed with her camera and a newfound resilience, was prepared to capture every moment, both the light and the shadows, as she embarked on a journey of love, thrill, and self-discovery in this town of serenity and secrets.

***

The road stretched out before Olive as she drove into the charming town of Serenity Falls. The town had a quaint, welcoming feel to it, and she couldn't help but feel a sense of anticipation as she navigated its streets.

After what seemed like ages, she finally spotted the town's local diner. She parked her car and took a deep breath before stepping inside. The scent of freshly brewed coffee and the sound of friendly chatter enveloped her as she entered.

The diner was cozy, with its red booths and checkered floors. Olive hesitated for a moment at the entrance, taking in the atmosphere. She spotted a vacant seat at the counter and headed over, sitting down on one of the worn-out stools.

The waitress, a friendly woman with a warm smile, approached her. "Morning, hun! What can I get you?" she asked with genuine kindness.

Olive returned the smile and replied, "Just a cup of black coffee, please."

As the waitress filled up her order, she struck up a conversation. "You're new around here, ain't ya?"

Olive nodded, taking a sip of her coffee. "Yeah, I just arrived. Thought I'd take a little road trip and ended up here."

The waitress chuckled. "Well, you picked a good spot, dear. Serenity Falls is a nice little town with a lot of character."

Olive appreciated the warmth in the woman's words. "I'm Olive," she introduced herself.

"Nice to meet you, Olive. I'm Betty," the waitress replied, wiping her hands on her apron.

They continued chatting, and Olive found herself opening up to Betty. "I'm actually a photographer," she said, a thought that had popped into her head. It wasn't entirely untrue – she never worked as a professional photographer, but she had always been interested in capturing moments through her camera lens.

Betty's eyes lit up. "Oh, that's interesting! You know, there's a vacant space down the street, used to be an old bookstore. They've been trying to find someone to rent it. Would make a perfect studio, I reckon."

Olive's interest was piqued. "A studio, huh? That sounds like a great idea."

Betty nodded enthusiastically. "You should definitely check it out. It's just a couple of blocks down. You can't miss it."

As Olive finished her coffee, she felt a spark of excitement. Maybe this was the fresh start she had been looking for. "Thank you, Betty. I'll definitely take a look."

"Anytime, hun. Good luck with your photography gig!" Betty said with a friendly wave as Olive got up from the counter.

Walking out of the diner, Olive felt a renewed sense of purpose. Serenity Falls might just be the place where she could turn her passion into something more. As she strolled down the street, her thoughts drifted to the vacant space Betty had mentioned, and a small smile tugged at her lips.

***

With just enough funds tucked away in her savings account, Olive found herself making a life-altering decision to move to Serenity Falls. The cost of living in the small town was a welcome relief compared to the financial strain of New York.

The lease for her new studio shop was a fraction of what she would have paid back in the city, allowing her to allocate her resources more sensibly. She had even managed to secure a spacious house for half the rent she paid for her modest New York apartment. Though nostalgia tugged at her heartstrings for her old one-bedroom apartment, she knew it was time to embrace the change.

As the first rays of sunlight peeked over the horizon, casting a golden hue upon Serenity Falls, Olive stood in front of her freshly established photo studio. The space exuded a sense of novelty, with clean lines and an inviting ambiance.

Its large windows welcomed the sun's warm embrace, filling the studio with the gentle promise of a new beginning. A sign, elegantly hanging above the entrance, bore the words "Olive Adams Photography" in proud, bold letters.

Weeks after thorough renovations, Olive was ready to unveil her newly transformed studio. The kindness of her landlord, an elderly gentleman with a generous spirit, had led him to personally oversee the repairs and enhancements before she embarked on her grand opening. As she stood before the entrance, she took a deep breath, savoring the blend of the fresh paint's fragrance and the lingering scent of coffee wafting over from the neighboring café.

Stepping across the threshold, a rush of emotions swept over her. The studio, though compact, radiated a sense of coziness and warm hospitality. It had been meticulously arranged, thoughtfully adorned with photographs that bore her unmistakable mark.

These were snapshots she had captured during her journeys, each image telling a unique story and collectively showcasing her boundless passion and artistic prowess. The studio wasn't just a place; it was a reflection of her dedication and the realization of a dream that had taken root and blossomed into reality.

Busy arranging her camera gear, she couldn't help

but get lost in her thoughts, memories of a past she wanted to leave behind. Serenity Falls was her escape, a chance to start anew amid the beautiful mountains and valleys.

Time seemed to slip away as the gentle chime of a bell filled the air, tugging Olive's focus from her thoughts. Her anticipation grew, knowing that her very first customer had arrived. With a racing heart, she lifted her gaze, and a rush of intrigue coursed through her veins as her eyes met those of a captivating stranger.

Tall and possessing a rugged charm, the newcomer exuded an air of mystery that was impossible to ignore. His messy mane of dark hair and the faint shadow of stubble accentuated his allure, as though he bore the essence of an artist seeking inspiration or solace—much like herself. In that moment, their gazes locked, and the connection felt as though fate had intervened, weaving their paths together in a delicate dance of curiosity and possibility.

"Hey there," he greeted, his voice a deep, rich melody that sent a shiver down Olive's spine. "I noticed your studio while passing by. I'm Vaughn Knight."

Her hand met his, and she couldn't help but feel a spark in that simple touch. "I'm Olive Adams.

Welcome to my photography studio, Vaughn."

Their eyes lingered, and something unspoken passed between them—a shared understanding of pain and healing. It was as if they connected on a level beyond words.

"So what brings you to Serenity Falls, Olive?" Vaughn asked, his curiosity evident in his voice.

Olive hesitated, her heart pounding with nerves, before deciding to open up a little to this intriguing stranger. "Honestly, I came here searching for beauty and peace," she confessed. "Serenity Falls seemed like the perfect escape, a chance to start anew."

Vaughn nodded, a hint of a smile playing on his lips. "I get that. Sometimes life gets too confused, and we need to seek comfort in quiet corners of the world."

Curiosity got the better of Olive, and she couldn't help but ask, "How long have you lived here?"

Vaughn's eyes shifted to the ground, and he hesitated for a moment. He wasn't sure if he should reveal his emotions to this newfound connection, but something about her made him want to share. "All my life," he finally said, his voice tinged with nostalgia and vulnerability. "Leaving Serenity Falls has never been easy for me."

Intrigued, Olive leaned in, eager to know more. "Why is that?" she inquired, her eyes wide with interest.

Vaughn grappled with whether to share his deepest feelings with someone he barely knew. But there was a connection between them that drew him in, urging him to be honest about his emotions, even if it meant exposing his vulnerabilities.

After a moment, Vaughn decided to keep it vague, skimming the surface of his emotions. "You know what they say, 'Home is where the heart is,'" he replied, a small smile forming.

Olive sensed that there was more to his story, but she respected his boundaries and chose not to press further. She knew the pain of a wounded heart and the search for a place to belong. Vaughn intrigued her with his complexity, and she hoped to learn more about him as time went on.

"It's true, home is where the heart finds peace," she said, empathizing with him. "And sometimes, a new place can bring the healing we need."

The world around them fell into a hush, leaving Olive and Vaughn lost in their own musings. The air seemed to crackle with an intangible connection, understanding the complexities of life without uttering a word.

As they basked in the sun's warm embrace, a gentle breeze from the wide-open door, playfully tousled Olive's hair, hinting at fresh starts and the prospect of healing.

"I've always felt something magical about Serenity Falls," Olive broke the silence, her voice carrying a hint of wonder. "It's like a sanctuary of quietness that lures people in, making it hard for them to leave."

Vaughn looked up from his shoes, his eyes meeting Olive's with gratitude. He appreciated her genuine curiosity and empathy, feeling a sense of comfort in her presence. "You're right," he admitted, speaking softly. "This place holds an inexplicable beauty—a serenity that touches your soul and makes you want to stay."

In that moment, their eyes locked, and a silent bond formed between them—a connection built on shared understanding and the scars they carried.

As their conversation continued, a gentle breeze swayed the leaves outside, casting playful shadows inside the studio. The past whispers were carried away by the wind, replaced by hope and optimism for what lay ahead.

"Vaughn, what do you do for a living?" Olive inquired, genuinely interested in his life.

Vaughn's expression shifted, his cheeks tinged with a touch of embarrassment. He pondered whether he should reveal his truth. "Well, it's a bit embarrassing," he began hesitantly, "but I used to be a writer."

Olive's eyes sparkled with intrigue. "Really? Have you published any of your work?"

A soft, reminiscent grin curled up Vaughn's lips. "You know, I used to have a couple of things published. But lately, writer's block has been haunting me."

Olive's compassionate side kicked in. "Oh, Vaughn, I hope your creativity comes back soon. The world needs more artists like you."

Vaughn's eyes softened as he met Olive's understanding gaze. "You're right," he said, his voice tinged with appreciation and a hint of longing. "Well, I should let you get back to work. It was a pleasure meeting you, Olive."

Their connection lingered in the air as Vaughn prepared to leave. A thought crossed Olive's mind, and she couldn't resist sharing it.

"Likewise, Vaughn," she teased, a touch of mischief in her tone. "And if you ever need candid photos for your author's page, you know where to find me."

Vaughn let out a genuine laugh, filling the room with warmth. "That's sweet of you," he replied, enjoying the humor she brought to their conversation. "Anyways, I just wanted to say, welcome to Serenity Falls."

"Thank you," Olive replied, her eyes sparkling with gratitude.

As Vaughn headed for the exit, Olive watched him through the glass windows, her gaze fixed on his figure as he hopped into his red pickup truck. He waved goodbye, leaving an air of anticipation behind.

With Vaughn's departure, Olive couldn't shake off the mysterious encounter they had shared. Adrenaline surged through her veins, wondering what the future held.

Little did she know that Serenity Falls held more than just beauty and peace. It held secrets—secrets that would entwine her fate with others, forever altering their lives. Her arrival had set in motion a chain of events that would test her resolve, leading her down a perilous path where danger and love would collide.

But for now, as the sound of Vaughn's fading

truck echoed in the distance, Olive returned to her work, her mind brimming with the possibilities that lay ahead.

As the day went on at Olive's new photography studio, she brimmed with excitement and nervous anticipation. But alas, the day had started slow, without the delightful jingle of the doorbell welcoming customers. The clock seemed to mock her, ticking away the hours without any sign of a visitor. It was disheartening, to say the least.

By 4 pm, Olive faced a tough decision – to close up shop or keep her dream alive. Her purpose won, and she locked up, determined not to be discouraged by a slow start.

Walking towards her trusty second-hand car, Olive paused for a moment, caught in the crossroads of her emotions. The allure of a change of scenery tugged at her, an irresistible pull that promised to momentarily eclipse the disappointment that lingered within. It was then that the lively ambiance of the nearby town market caught her attention, like a summoning bell promising a break from her thoughts.

Her direction shifted in an instant, her steps leading her away from the car and toward the bustling market.

The air was infused with the vibrancy of the stalls, their colorful displays and cheerful chatter offering a stark contrast to her own subdued mood. As she strolled through the market's aisles, the simple act of grocery shopping held the promise of easing her spirits, if only for a while. And who knew, among the crates of fresh produce, perhaps destiny had an unexpected encounter waiting to unfold.

Inside the market, life pulsed through every aisle. The sweet aroma of fresh produce filled the air, and the hum of conversations surrounded her. Olive moved through the aisles, lost in thought, seeking some comfort in her favorite snacks.

Then, she noticed a vibrant display of freshly baked goodies. The smell of cinnamon and sugar was irresistible, bringing a smile to her face. She couldn't resist the temptation and added a small bag of pastries to her cart.

As she approached the checkout counter, her attention was caught by a young girl carefully picking fruits. There was something about the girl's curious eyes that drew Olive in, forging an instant connection.

"You seem to have a knack for choosing the juiciest fruits," Olive remarked, her voice warm and welcoming.

The girl glanced up, caught off guard by the surprising encounter. Her cheeks flushed, and a bashful grin adorned her lips. "I've been helping my grandma with grocery shopping forever. She's taught me all the secrets to finding the juiciest oranges and the sweetest berries."

Olive couldn't help but let out a soft chuckle, touched by the girl's enthusiasm. "Well, you'll have to spill those secrets one day. I could really use some tips on picking the perfect fruits."

Excitement sparkled in the girl's eyes. "I'd be thrilled to! Let's meet up at the park sometime. I'll show you how to spot the ripest watermelon."

Warmed by the girl's gesture, Olive felt a sense of comfort in these unexpected acts of kindness. "That sounds like a deal," she responded, her voice brimming with genuine appreciation.

As Olive paid for her groceries, a sense of contentment filled her heart. The day at the studio had been slow, but it didn't matter anymore. Serenity Falls, the charming town she had just moved to, had a way of making her feel at ease.

With her bags in hand, Olive strolled back to her car, feeling a newfound hope. This place held so much promise, and she was excited to uncover its hidden gems, one encounter at a time.

Driving home through the pretty scenery, Olive couldn't help but feel a flutter of anticipation. Serenity Falls had secrets waiting to be revealed, and she was eager to embrace them all, one grocery shopping trip at a time. Soon, she arrived at her modest suburban house, her sanctuary from the chaos of the world. Its affordable rent was a stroke of luck that put her mind at ease.

After parking her car, Olive gathered her groceries and headed towards her front door, but a peculiar sense of being observed sent a shiver down the nape of her neck.

A quick scan of her surroundings revealed nothing amiss, yet the feeling persisted, like an imperceptible presence lingering just out of sight. Shaking off the unease, she redirected her attention to the task at hand, determined to reach the safety of her home.

As she unlocked the door and stepped inside, the sensation of being watched began to fade. It was a mystery that she couldn't unravel at the moment, but she pushed it to the back of her mind. The fact that she had kept her move to Serenity Falls a secret from everyone in her past life, only added to the mystery of the situation.

Her rental house, settled in the heart of Serenity Falls, exuded a sense of inviting warmth every time Olive stepped inside. The comfortable living room greeted her with its plush furniture and soft lighting, an ambiance that gestured her to unwind. The spacious master bedroom, adorned with neutral colors and tasteful décor, awaited her like a sanctuary.

The kitchen and dining area on the first floor boasted modern appliances and an open layout, providing an ideal space for Olive to explore her culinary inclinations. Upstairs, there were two spare bedrooms that held the promise of potential. While undecided about their purpose, the idea of transforming one into a dedicated space for her photography work was a promising prospect.

The house had been thoughtfully furnished, a relief for Olive who had embarked on her journey with minimal belongings. Each piece of furniture seemed to fit perfectly, creating a sense of coherence and belonging. Stepping further into the house, Olive was struck by the simplicity that enveloped her. Fresh coats of paint adorned the walls, giving a sense of renewal and a blank canvas for her new life.

As she unpacked her groceries in the kitchen, a flicker of movement caught her eye. Her heart skipped a beat, and she turned to the window, spotting a dark figure lurking behind the neighbor's bushes, watching her intently.

Breathless, she strained to make out the details, but the figure disappeared as quickly as it had appeared, leaving her uncertain if she had imagined it all. She tried to convince herself that it was a trick of the fading light, but a small voice urged her to stay vigilant, to remain aware of her surroundings.

Determined to shake off the unease, Olive focused on the task at hand, the clinking of jars and rustling of bags soothing her nerves. She refused to let fear taint the peace she sought in Serenity Falls. This place was meant to be her home, a refuge from her haunted past.

As the day turned to dusk, Olive couldn't help but steal another glance out the window. The neighbor's yard remained serene, the swaying grass and bushes providing a calming sight. She let out a breath she didn't know she was holding, relieved to find no lurking figures.

Drawing the blinds shut, she allowed the warm, dim light to bathe the room, embracing the peacefulness that washed over her. Serenity Falls held promise, and Olive was determined to embrace it, undeterred by any mysterious shadows that might linger at the edges of her new life.

With the warm sun streaming through the windows of her cozy little house, Olive felt an inexplicable sense of contentment. The scent of fresh ingredients filled the air as she moved around her kitchen, preparing a simple yet delicious meal. The rhythmic chopping of vegetables and the sizzling of the pan created a soothing melody that echoed in the room.

As she worked, Olive decided to add a touch of her favorite music to the mix. She grabbed her phone and connected it to a small speaker on the counter. The lively notes of a familiar song filled the room, and she couldn't help but sway her hips to the beat.

With each movement, Olive felt a weight lifting off her shoulders – a weight she had been carrying for far too long. The music resonated with her newfound sense of freedom, and she twirled around the kitchen, her heart feeling lighter than it had in years.

The aroma of the food mingled with the music, creating an intoxicating blend that seemed to infuse every corner of her home. Olive's laughter filled the space as she danced between the counter and the stove, her movements becoming more energetic with each passing second.

For the first time in a long time, Olive felt truly alive. She had escaped the clutches of a toxic relationship, and now she was embracing her newfound independence with open arms. The vibrant energy of the music coursed through her veins, and she let herself be carried away by the sheer joy of the moment.

As the song reached its peak, Olive spun around one last time before finally coming to a stop, breathless and exhilarated. She leaned against the kitchen counter, a wide grin on her face as she caught her breath. The meal she had been preparing was nearly ready, and the aroma wafting through the air made her stomach rumble.

With a satisfied sigh, Olive turned off the stove and plated the meal. As she sat down at her dining table, she couldn't help but reflect on how far she had come. The dance in her kitchen wasn't just a simple act of joy – it was a celebration of her newfound freedom and the courage she had mustered to start over.

And as she savored each bite of her meal, the music still playing softly in the background, Olive couldn't help but feel grateful for this moment of pure bliss. It was a reminder that she was in control of her life, and that she could find happiness in the simplest of pleasures – like dancing in her own kitchen, with music and freedom as her partners.

***

As Vaughn drove back from Olive's photography studio, his mind was a whirlwind of thoughts and emotions. The encounter had stirred something within him – a mixture of curiosity, nostalgia, and a growing attraction to the woman he had just met. He glanced at the road ahead, his grip on the steering wheel tightening as memories of another woman flooded his mind.

He remembered the way her eyes would light up when he surprised her with a small gift, the way she would playfully swat his arm when he teased her, and most vividly, the sound of her laughter. Her laughter was like music to his ears, a sweet melody that could brighten even the darkest of days.

A bittersweet smile tugged at the corners of Vaughn's lips as he recalled the times they spent together. He remembered how she would curl up on the couch with a book, her legs tucked under her, lost in the pages. And then there were those lazy Sunday mornings when they would make breakfast together, filling their home with the aroma of pancakes and coffee.

His mind wandered back to one particular memory – a memory of a playful tickle fight that had escalated into a fit of laughter. Her giggles were infectious, and Vaughn couldn't help but smile at the memory of her squirming and laughing uncontrollably as he tickled her. It was moments like those that made him realize just how lucky he was to have her in his life.

But his smile faded as the reality of the present set in. She was gone now, and there was no way to bring her back. His heart ached at the thought of all the moments they would never share again. The pain of losing her was a constant presence in his life, a wound that never seemed to fully heal.

As he drove on, Vaughn's thoughts began to shift to the present moment. He realized that he wanted to get to know Olive, a woman who was so uniquely herself. He felt a connection to her, and while it was different from what he had with his ex, it was still meaningful in its own way.

With a sigh, Vaughn turned up the radio, allowing the music to fill the car. He needed to focus on the road and the present, rather than getting lost in memories of the past. As the miles passed, he found himself looking forward to the future, to the possibilities that lay ahead, and to the chance to create new memories with someone who was breathing life back into his heart.

Soon, he reached his modest house, a mix of relief and exhaustion washing over him. Upon stepping inside, he couldn't help but notice the disorder that surrounded him.

"Could use a woman's touch in here," he said with a small smile to himself.

Needing a moment to unwind, he headed to the fridge and grabbed a cold drink, savoring it's refreshing taste with each sip. A familiar pull drew him down to the basement, where memories and secrets were kept hidden. Flicking on the light, the room glowed warmly, revealing his personal haven. In the dim light, he found himself standing before a large board covered in photographs.

These women all had captivating dark hair, their allure and mysteries intriguing him deeply. They weren't just random faces; they were parts of his past, reminders of a puzzle he was yet to solve. With a soft sigh, Vaughn studied the board. It wasn't merely about the women themselves; it was about the untold stories, the journeys they had taken, and how their paths had crossed with his own. His heart yearned for that unexplainable connection, that one person who would fill the voids in his soul.

Unbeknownst to him, fate had a plan in the works, a destiny that would lead him to a woman holding the key to unraveling this mystery. As he traced his finger over the photographs, an electric current surged through him, a spark of excitement for the possibilities that lay ahead.

***

CHAPTER 2: THE MYSTERIOUS CASES

Nina Santos stepped out of her rented car, her petite figure adorned with an air of fierce purpose. Her auburn hair cascaded in waves, catching the sunlight like strands of fiery gold, a vibrant contrast to her olive skin that reflected her Latin heritage. Serenity Falls had always held a special place in her heart, but today, it felt different. The last time she had been here was fifteen years ago, which was a lifetime ago, when she and Daniel Turner were just teenagers in love. They had drifted apart after high school, their paths leading them in opposite directions.

As she made her way through the small town, memories of their stolen moments together flooded her mind. Nina couldn't help but smile as she recalled their secret meeting spot by the waterfall, where they would talk about their dreams and aspirations. Back then, they had thought their love was invincible, that nothing could come between them. But life had a way of changing things, and they eventually lost touch.

Now, she was back, but not for a nostalgic trip down memory lane. Nina had a purpose—to find her sister, Elle, who had disappeared without a trace several months ago. The police investigation had yielded no results, and that's when Nina decided to take matters into her own hands. As a seasoned journalist, she had a knack for uncovering the truth, and she was determined to bring her sister home, no matter the cost.

Her first stop was at the local cafe, a quiet place where she hoped to gather some information discreetly. Nina adjusted the strap of her messenger bag, which held her trusty notebook, camera, and a few essentials for her investigation. Her journalistic instincts told her that the cafe might be a good place to start gathering information discreetly. Serenity Falls may have been her hometown, but she knew that there were secrets lurking beneath the serene surface of the town.

As she entered, the familiar smell of coffee and freshly baked pastries enveloped her, evoking more memories of her past. She found an empty table near the window, the perfect vantage point to observe without drawing too much attention. As she settled in, her eyes scanned the room, taking note of the locals engaged in hushed conversations.

Just as she was about to pull out her notebook and pen, a voice interrupted her thoughts, and her gaze snapped up to meet a pair of warm, familiar eyes.

"Is that you Nina?," the voice said, tinged with a mix of surprise and excitement.

Nina's heart skipped a beat as she recognized the ruggedly handsome face before her. It was Daniel Turner, the boy who had stolen her heart in high school. He hadn't changed much since then, still emanating the same charm and charisma that had captivated her all those years ago.

"Danny," she said, using the nickname she had given him back in their school days. "I didn't expect to run into you so soon."

Daniel chuckled and slid into the seat across from her. "You know Serenity Falls, it has a way of pulling people back in," he replied. "It's good to see you again, Nina. Fifteen years is too soon for a reunion."

For a moment, they simply stared at each other, both lost in their thoughts. They hadn't seen each other in years, and the memories of their past hung heavy in the air. A blush crept up Nina's cheeks, though she tried to hide it behind a composed smile. She couldn't help but feel a flutter of excitement at seeing Daniel after all these years. As they exchanged pleasantries, she noticed how his eyes lingered on her, studying her intently, as if trying to uncover the secrets she carried.

"You must be back because of Elle," Daniel finally said, his voice soft with sympathy. "I'm sorry, Nina. If there's anything I can do to help..."

Nina appreciated his empathy and support. She had always admired Daniel's genuine kindness, even back in their high school days.

"That's exactly why I'm here," she confessed. "I couldn't just sit around waiting for the police to solve the case. I need to find her, Danny."

He reached across the table and placed a reassuring hand over hers. "We'll find her together," he said firmly. "I've been looking into the missing persons' cases in Serenity Falls, and there's something strange going on here. I think it's connected to Elle's disappearance."

Nina's eyes widened with surprise. She hadn't expected Daniel to be involved in this investigation as well. "You're investigating the missing persons too?" she asked.

He nodded, his expression serious. "Yeah, I started looking into it after a close friend of mine asked me a few months ago. The police seemed indifferent, so I decided to dig deeper."

Nina admired his dedication and felt a renewed sense of hope. With Daniel by her side, she knew they could uncover the truth. "Let's work together then," she said, a newfound determination in her voice.

Daniel smiled, his eyes lighting up with excitement. "Deal. We make a good team, remember? The infamous teenage detectives of the town."

She couldn't help but smile back, her heart fluttering at the memories of their past adventures. "Yeah, we always did," she replied softly.

As the hours passed, Nina and Daniel found themselves engrossed in each other's stories, reminiscing about their shared memories from high school and exchanging tales of their separate journeys since then. Nina learned that Daniel had stayed in Serenity Falls, following in his father's footsteps as a private detective.

He had built a reputation for being the go-to person whenever someone needed help, but his involvement in missing persons' cases had intensified in recent months, driven by a personal tragedy that had hit close to home, the missing case of Elle.

"I know it's not easy," Daniel said, his eyes clouded with sorrow. "When you lose someone you care about, and the authorities don't seem to care enough to find answers, you have to take matters into your own hands."

Nina remembered the grief she felt when she heard her sister Elle had gone missing. It had torn her apart, leaving her in anguish, and the lack of progress from the police had fueled her resolve to uncover the truth.

"I completely understand, Danny," she replied softly, reaching out to squeeze his hand in a gesture of comfort. "Losing someone you love is a devastating experience, and feeling helpless only adds to the heartache. We'll find Elle, and we'll find out what's happening in this town. I promise you that."

Daniel gave her a grateful smile, his rough exterior momentarily softened by her words. "Thank you, Nina," he said. "Having you here, working on this with me, means more than you know."

The sincerity in his eyes and the warmth of his hand in hers sent a tremor over Nina's skin. It was as if no time had passed between them, as if they were still the young couple in love from their high school days. But the reality of their situation quickly pulled her back to the present. They had a serious task at hand— a mystery to solve and lives to protect.

As they continued to delve into the details of the missing persons' cases, Nina noticed a pattern emerging. "Danny, have you noticed that all the disappearances happened around the same time every year?" she asked, her brows furrowing in contemplation.

Daniel leaned forward, his expression serious as he studied the evidence before them. "You're right," he said, nodding. "It's like there's a pattern to these incidents, as if someone is following a schedule."

Nina tapped her pen against the table, lost in thought. "But why would anyone want to target people with connections to Serenity Falls?" she mused. "There has to be a reason behind it."

Daniel's eyes sparkled with determination. "I have a feeling there's more to this town than meets the eye," he said. "Something hidden beneath its surface. And I think Elle stumbled upon it, which might be why she went missing."

Nina's heart skipped a beat at the revelation. "Do you think she found something incriminating?" she asked, her mind racing with possibilities.

"It's possible," Daniel replied. "But whatever it is, it's dangerous enough to make someone want to silence her."

As the weight of the situation settled on Nina's shoulders, she couldn't help but feel a combination of fear and determination. Fear for the danger they were getting closer to and determination to bring the truth to light, no matter the risks.

"We're gonna have to be careful," she said, her voice resolute. "Whoever's behind this is not going to let us dig too deep. We need to be one step ahead and protect ourselves."

Daniel nodded in agreement. "I won't let anything happen to you, Nina," he vowed. "We'll watch each other's backs, just like we used to."

His words brought a surge of emotions to the surface—memories of their tireless support for each other during their teenage years. Back then, they were inseparable, a team that could conquer any challenge. And now, fate had brought them back together, reunited by a shared purpose.

As the afternoon sun dipped below the horizon, casting a warm golden glow over Serenity Falls, Nina Santos decided to follow Daniel Turner to his office. She had to admit, being back in this town after fifteen years brought a blend of emotions she hadn't anticipated. But there was a newfound sense of purpose and resolve that fueled her as she trailed behind Daniel's car.

Once they arrived at Daniel's office, Nina noticed how it perfectly reflected his character—modest and unassuming, yet with an air of competence. The dimly lit space was filled with old case files, photographs, and souvenirs from his previous investigations. It felt like stepping into a noir detective movie, and Nina couldn't help but feel a sense of excitement and intrigue.

"So, this is where you've been cracking all those mysteries?" Nina teased, giving the cluttered room an appreciative look.

Daniel chuckled, looking slightly embarrassed by the mess. "Yeah, it's not the neatest place, but it gets the job done," he replied with a shrug. "Please, have a seat. Let's get down to business."

Nina took a seat in an old leather chair, her eyes scanning the room once more. It was clear that Daniel had dedicated his life to this work, and she couldn't help but feel a deep sense of respect for him.

He handed her a file filled with information about the missing persons' cases in Serenity Falls. "Here's what I've gathered so far," he said, his voice serious.

"It's not much, but I thought we could start by going through these together."

Nina nodded, taking the file and opening it carefully. As they began to sift through the documents, photographs, and witness statements, their conversation flowed effortlessly, just like in the old days. It was as if the years apart had never happened, and they fell back into their rhythm of friendship and trust.

In Daniel's dimly lit office, they spread out the files and photographs, trying to piece together the puzzle of the missing persons' cases. The more they dug, the clearer it became that something sinister was lurking in Serenity Falls.

"I think there's a pattern here," Nina said, her brows furrowed as she studied the evidence. "All the victims had some connection to this town, whether they were born here or had lived here at some point."

Daniel nodded in agreement. "That's what I've been noticing too," he replied. "It's like someone is targeting people with ties to Serenity Falls."

"But why?" Nina wondered aloud. "And how does Elle fit into all of this?"

As they delved deeper into their investigation,

they knew they were treading on dangerous ground. Whoever was behind these disappearances was cunning and elusive, and they had to be careful not to become the next victims.

The hours passed swiftly as Nina and Daniel worked together, reigniting their trust in each other. Despite the seriousness of the situation, Nina felt a twinkle of hope that they were making progress towards uncovering the truth.

They became engrossed in their investigation, losing track of time and the outside world. The office was bathed in a soft glow from a desk lamp, their heads bent over files, their purpose binding them together.

Suddenly, Daniel broke the silence. "Nina, I know this must be tough for you, being back here after all this time. But I want you to know that you can count on me. I'll do everything in my power to find and bring back your sister."

Nina looked up, touched by his sincerity. "Thank you, Daniel," she replied softly. "I don't know what I'd do without you. You've always been the one who made me feel safe."

Emotion flickered in Daniel's eyes, and he reached out, placing a comforting hand over hers. "I'll always be here for you, Nina," he reassured her. "No matter what happens, you can lean on me."

Her heart warmed, and she smiled gratefully. "I believe you," she said. "And I'm here for you too, Daniel."

Their eyes locked for a moment, the unspoken depth of their connection hanging in the air. But they knew now was not the time to delve into the complexities of their past or their possible future. They had a mission—to uncover the truth and save lives.

As night fell over Serenity Falls, they decided to call it a day, both exhausted but determined. Nina felt a sense of gratitude for having Daniel back in her life and hopeful that, together, they would unveil the mysteries of Serenity Falls. Their bond, stronger than ever, gave her the courage to face whatever challenges lay ahead.

Before she left his office, she turned to him and said, "Thank you, Danny. For helping me with this, and for being here for me."

Daniel gave her a gentle smile, his eyes reflecting the sincerity of his feelings. "Always, Nina," he said softly. "I'll always be here for you."

And with those words, Nina knew she wasn't alone in this daunting quest. Together, they would unveil the mystery of Serenity Falls and bring Elle and the other missing souls back to where they belonged.

Before Nina left Daniel's office, she couldn't help but feel a sense of relief and comfort in knowing that she had someone like Daniel on her side. As they wrapped up their investigation for the day, she decided to share her current whereabouts with him, a gesture of trust and a reminder of their newfound partnership.

"Daniel," Nina began, tucking a strand of hair behind her ear nervously, "Since I'll be staying in town for a while, I've booked a room at a motel in town. It's at the Serenity Inn."

Daniel nodded, his eyes filled with concern. "Are you sure it's safe for you to stay alone there?" he asked, genuine worry lacing his voice.

"I'll be fine," Nina reassured him, trying to sound confident despite the unease that gnawed at her. "I've been on my own for years, remember? Besides, staying close to the investigation might help me stumble upon some leads or witnesses."

"Alright," Daniel relented, though the worry in his eyes didn't fade. "But promise me you'll be cautious and keep your phone on you at all times."

"I promise," she replied, giving him a small smile.

"And I'll call you if anything seems off or if I find anything worth investigating further."

With a shared understanding and unspoken promise to watch out for each other, Nina and Daniel said their goodbyes for the night. Nina made her way to the Serenity Inn, the anticipation of the investigation ahead making it difficult for her to unwind.

As Nina drove back from Daniel's private detective agency, her thoughts drifted back to the past, to the memories of her sister Elle. The weight of their shared experiences and the bond they had formed over the years was ever-present in her mind. She gripped the steering wheel, lost in her thoughts.

After the death of their mother, Elle had taken on the role of caretaker and protector for Nina. It was a responsibility that Elle had willingly shouldered, despite the challenges it presented. Nina was a few years younger than Elle, and the loss of their mother had shaken both of them to their core.

Nina remembered the way Elle had stepped up without hesitation, putting her own dreams and aspirations on hold to ensure that Nina was taken care of. She recalled the late nights they spent talking, Elle offering words of wisdom and encouragement, guiding Nina through the trials and troubles of growing up without their mother.

Elle had always been the strong one, the one who faced adversity with a fierce sense of responsibility. Nina admired her sister's resilience, her ability to carry the weight of their circumstances without ever complaining.

And despite the challenges they faced, Elle had managed to keep a sense of humor and a playful spirit alive within their home.

Tears welled up in Nina's eyes as she thought about the love and sacrifices her sister had made for her. She missed Elle deeply – her presence, her laughter, her unwavering support. The ache of loss was a constant companion, a reminder of the void that Elle's absence had left behind.

Nina wiped away a tear and took a deep breath. She knew that she had to keep moving forward, just as Elle would have wanted. She would carry her sister's memory with her, cherishing the lessons she had learned from her and drawing strength from the love they shared.

Nina pulled her car to a stop in front of the Serenity Inn, a small but charming lodging nestled within the bounds of the town. The soft glow of streetlights illuminated the surroundings, casting a warm ambiance that was characteristic of Serenity Falls. She turned off the engine and took a moment to appreciate the tranquility that enveloped the area.

Stepping out of her car, Nina retrieved her bag from the passenger seat and locked the vehicle. She had been on the road for most of the day, following leads and conducting interviews for the missing cases she was working on. Exhaustion weighed on her, and she looked forward to a quiet and peaceful night's rest.

As she entered the inn, the gentle ding of a bell above the door greeted her. The reception area was cozy and inviting, with warm colors and tasteful decor. The innkeeper, a friendly middle-aged woman, smiled warmly at Nina from behind the front desk.

"Welcome to the Serenity Inn," the innkeeper greeted. "How can I assist you today?"

Nina returned the smile, appreciating the genuine hospitality that seemed to be a trademark of the town. "Hi, I have a reservation under the name Nina Santos."

The innkeeper quickly checked her records and nodded. "Yes, Miss Santos. We have a room reserved for you. It's room number 105. Here's your key."

Nina accepted the key with a nod of gratitude. "Thank you."

"Breakfast is available for room service order,

from 7 to 10 in the morning," the innkeeper added, offering a friendly reminder. "And if you need anything during your stay, don't hesitate to ask."

"I will do that," Nina replied, her tiredness making her appreciative of the innkeeper's thoughtfulness.

With her key in hand, Nina made her way through the sidewalk to the first floor. She found room 105 and unlocked the door, revealing a cozy and well-appointed space. Soft lighting cast a warm glow over the room, and the comfortable bed looked inviting after a long day of work.

Nina placed her bag on the nearby chair and let out a sigh of relief. She walked over to the window and drew back the curtains, allowing the moonlight to filter into the room. The town outside was quiet, and she could hear the gentle rustling of leaves in the breeze.

As she settled into room 105, she couldn't help but let her thoughts drift back to her past with Daniel. They had been so close once, but life had taken them on different journeys. Now, with a shared purpose and a common goal, they were brought back together, and a spark of hope ignited within her.

After a moment of contemplation, Nina decided to take a relaxing shower before settling in for the night. The warm water helped to soothe her weary muscles, and as she stepped out of the shower and wrapped herself in a fluffy towel, she felt a sense of rejuvenation.

Dressed in comfortable pajamas, Nina crawled under the covers of the bed. She reached for the lamp on the nightstand and switched it off, allowing the moonlight to be her only source of illumination. The events of the day had taken a toll on her, and the weight of her sister's disappearance bore heavily on her shoulders. As she closed her eyes, she tried to push away the thoughts of the missing persons' cases and focus on the task at hand.

But just as she was drifting into slumber, a flicker of movement caught her attention. A shadow passed in front of her window, sending a shiver down her spine. Her instincts kicked in, and she quickly sat up, her heart pounding in her chest. Was someone watching her?

Curiosity and unease prompted her to take a closer look. She cautiously tiptoed to the window, careful not to make any noise. Peeking through the curtains, she scanned the area outside. At first glance, she thought she saw a dark figure standing in the parking lot, across the motel, but the distant streetlights and the play of shadows made it hard to discern anything clearly.

"Maybe it's just my mind playing tricks on me,"

she murmured to herself, trying to rationalize the sight. After all, she had been under immense stress, and it wasn't uncommon for the mind to conjure up imaginary figures after a long, emotionally draining day.

Nina took a deep breath, trying to calm her racing heart. She reminded herself that she was safe inside her locked motel room. Nevertheless, she made a mental note to be more cautious during her stay in Serenity Falls.

But when she returned to her bed, she still couldn't shake the feeling of being watched. The darkness outside seemed to hold secrets, and the mystery surrounding the missing persons' cases weighed heavily on her mind. She knew she couldn't afford to let her guard down, not when she was so close to unraveling the truth.

Just as she was about to call it a night, her phone buzzed with a message from Daniel.

Daniel: 'Hey, just wanted to check in. Are you settled in all right?'

Nina: 'Yes, I'm all settled in. Thanks for asking. How about you? Any new leads on the missing persons' cases?'

Daniel: 'Nothing yet, but I'll keep digging. Stay

safe, okay?'

Nina: 'I will. You too. Goodnight, Danny.'

Daniel: 'Goodnight, Nina. See you tomorrow.'

With a small smile, Nina set her phone aside and lay down on the bed, the events of the day playing in her mind like a movie reel. Her determination to find her sister was stronger than ever, and with Daniel's help, she felt more hopeful than she had in a long time.

But neither of them knew then, that their journey would lead them down a treacherous path, riddled with danger and secrets that would test their bond and put their lives on the line. But for now, they had each other, and that was enough to face whatever darkness lay ahead in the pursuit of the truth.

***

CHAPTER 3: DARK WHISPERS

The soft glow of dawn filtered through Vaughn's bedroom window, casting a warm light that gently illuminated the room. He lay awake in bed, his thoughts consumed by the woman he had met only once – Olive. Their brief encounter had left an impression on him that he couldn't shake, and for the past two nights, sleep had eluded him.

With a sigh, Vaughn finally gave in to the restlessness and pushed the covers aside. He swung his legs over the edge of the bed and stood up, feeling an assortment of anticipation and uncertainty. He dressed quickly, his movements guided by a newfound energy that seemed to stem from his desire to see Olive again.

As he walked into the kitchen, Vaughn's mind was preoccupied. He mechanically began preparing breakfast, cracking eggs into a pan and toasting bread.

But as the aroma of the cooking food filled the air, he realized that his appetite was nowhere to be found. The knot of nerves in his stomach seemed to have stolen his hunger.

Pushing his plate away, Vaughn leaned back in his chair and ran a hand through his hair. He knew he couldn't ignore the thoughts that had been plaguing him. He had to see Olive again, even if it meant finding a flimsy excuse to visit her photography studio.

With a newfound reason, Vaughn pushed his chair back and stood up. He grabbed his keys from the counter and headed for the front door. The early morning air was cool and crisp as he stepped outside, his pick-up truck waiting patiently.

He started the engine, the rumble of the vehicle breaking the stillness of the morning. Vaughn's grip tightened on the steering wheel as he navigated the familiar streets of Serenity Falls. In his mind, he replayed their brief conversation, her smile, and the spark of connection that had ignited between them.

Before he knew it, he was pulling up outside Olive's photography studio. The "Open" sign hung on the door seemed like an invitation, and Vaughn's heart raced as he parked the truck. He sat there for a moment, his thoughts a jumble of nerves and anticipation.

Finally, with a deep breath, he climbed out of the truck and walked up to the door. The bell chimed as Vaughn stepped into Olive Adams Photography for the second time that week. He looked around, and his eyes landed on Olive, who was arranging some prints on the counter.

"Hey, Olive," Vaughn greeted with a warm smile. His tall, rugged figure exuded a shadowy charm that drew Olive's immediate attention. Olive looked up, her heart fluttering at the sight of him again. "Hi, Vaughn! Welcome back. How can I help you today?"

"I was wondering if you could take a few headshots for me. My publisher is asking for them," Vaughn explained.

"Of course! I'd be happy to help. We can set up the backdrop right here," Olive replied, leading him to a corner of the studio where she had her photography setup.

As Olive adjusted the lighting in her cozy photo studio, Vaughn sat on a tall stool, a relaxed smile on his face. He was a natural in front of the camera, and she couldn't help but admire his ease and charisma.

"Perfect, Vaughn," she said, her camera clicking away as she captured his striking features. "You're a natural at this."

He chuckled, the sound filling the room like a melodious tune. "Well, you make it easy, Olive," he replied, his eyes locking onto hers. "Your talent as a photographer brings out the best in me."

Her heart skipped a beat at the sincerity in his words. "Thank you," she said, a soft blush tinting her cheeks. "It's not just my skill; it's also the subject that matters. You have an undeniable presence, Vaughn."

As they continued the photoshoot, their conversation flowed effortlessly. They talked about their favorite movies, and shared stories of their travels. Olive learned that Vaughn had a passion for classic literature, and she couldn't help but smile at how animated he became when discussing his favorite authors.

"And what about you, Olive?" Vaughn inquired, genuine interest in his eyes. "What are your go-to books?"

She paused for a moment, considering her response. "I have a soft spot for poetry," she confessed. "Emily Dickinson, Robert Frost, and Sylvia Plath are some of my favorites. Their words have this incredible power to evoke emotions."

Vaughn's eyes sparkled with intrigue. "That's fascinating. I must admit, poetry isn't something I've explored much, but you make me curious to give it a try."

Olive's heart fluttered at the thought of introducing Vaughn to her favorite poets. It felt like they were uncovering new layers of each other with every passing minute, building a connection that went beyond just photography.

As the photoshoot came to an end, Olive felt a surge of excitement and reluctance. She didn't want this moment to end, but she knew there would be more opportunities to spend time with Vaughn as they continued working together on his headshots and possibly other projects.

"Thank you for today, Olive," Vaughn said, standing up from the stool and extending his hand towards her.

The genuine gratitude in his eyes warmed her heart. She took his hand, her fingers brushing against his, sending a jolt of electricity through her.

"The pleasure was all mine, Vaughn," she replied, unable to tear her eyes away from his. "I had a wonderful time getting to know you better."

He leaned in closer, their faces inches apart, and time seemed to slow down as they lingered in the intimate space between them.

"I feel the same way, Olive," he whispered, his breath warm against her skin. "And I hope this is just the beginning of many more moments like this."

Their connection was undeniable, a spark that had ignited from the moment they met. Olive felt like she was on the verge of something extraordinary, something that had the potential to change her life in ways she couldn't yet fathom.

Vaughn hesitated for a moment before taking a deep breath. "Olive, I hope this isn't too forward, but I was wondering if you'd like to go out with me sometime. Maybe dinner, just the two of us."

Surprised and delighted by his request, Olive's heart skipped a beat. She felt a connection with Vaughn that she hadn't felt in a long time, and she was drawn to his intriguing presence.

"I'd love to," Olive replied with a smile. "When were you thinking?"

"How about tonight?" Vaughn suggested. "I'll pick you up at 7, if that works for you."

"That sounds perfect," Olive said, her excitement growing. "Here's my phone number and address so you can find me."

Vaughn took the piece of paper she offered and carefully pocketed it, a grin forming on his lips. "I can't wait for tonight," he said, his eyes locked with hers.

"Me neither," said Olive, her eyes sparkling with sincerity.

As Vaughn walked out of the studio, a sense of contentment settled over him. He had taken a chance, acted on his feelings, and it had led to a meaningful connection. With a renewed spring in his step, he climbed back into his pick-up truck, the memory of their conversation lingering in his mind as he drove away.

*****

Hours went by inside Vaughn's bedroom as he stood in front of his closet, surveying the array of clothes hanging inside. He had a date with Olive, and his excitement was palpable. But with excitement also came a touch of nervousness – he wanted to make a good impression.

He pulled out a couple of shirts, holding them up against himself in front of the mirror. The first was a deep blue, but he shook his head, feeling that it was too casual for the occasion. The second was a plaid pattern in earthy tones, but he discarded it just as quickly. He wanted to look put-together without overdoing it.

With a sigh, Vaughn scanned the hangers once more before his eyes landed on a simple black shirt. He took it off the hanger, the fabric cool against his fingers. Holding it up, he examined it for a moment. The classic style and dark color seemed to fit the mood of the evening – casual yet stylish.

As he changed into the shirt, Vaughn's reflection in the mirror gave him a reassuring nod. The black shirt hugged his frame in all the right ways, and he couldn't help but feel a surge of confidence. He paired it with a comfortable pair of well-fitted jeans, completing the look with his favorite brown boots.

With his outfit chosen, Vaughn turned his attention to his hair. He ran his fingers through the dark strands, giving them a tousled look that he hoped appeared effortlessly cool. A quick glance in the mirror confirmed that he was satisfied with the result.

Next came the aftershave, a subtle but distinct scent that lingered as he sprayed it on his neck. He checked his watch – it was almost time. With a final once-over, Vaughn left his room and headed downstairs.

In the living room, he paused to grab his keys from the table. His heart was racing, as he thought about the evening ahead. The sun had dipped below the horizon, and the sky outside was painted with hues of pink and orange.

Before stepping out, Vaughn took a deep breath, his excitement and determination combining into a sense of purpose. He was about to embark on a new chapter, one that involved getting to know Olive better and allowing himself to open up to the possibility of a deeper connection.

As he walked out the door, Vaughn's hand automatically brushed against his shirt, his fingers grazing the fabric. He felt ready – ready to enjoy the evening, to share stories, and to experience whatever the night had in store. With a final look back at his house, he locked the door and headed toward his truck, his heart beating in time with his steps.

After a quick drive, Vaughn arrived at Olive's doorstep and rang the bell. As he stood there, he couldn't help but feel a flutter of nerves. It had been a while since he had been on a date, especially with someone as intriguing as Olive.

Olive, on the other hand, was a bundle of excitement and nerves as she put the finishing touches on her outfit. She had decided on a flowy, knee-length dress in a vibrant shade of green that brought out the warmth in her eyes. Her dark curls cascaded down her shoulders, and she wore a hint of makeup on her face.

When she finally opened the door to greet Vaughn, a soft gasp escaped her lips. He looked even more handsome than she had remembered, and the sight of him made her heart skip a beat. "Hi," she said, a touch of shyness in her voice.

"Hey," Vaughn replied with a warm smile, taking in the sight of her. "You look absolutely stunning, Olive."

Blushing, she brushed a strand of hair behind her ear. "Thank you. You look pretty great yourself," she replied, trying to suppress her nerves.

"Shall we?" Vaughn gestured towards his vehicle that was parked at the curb.

"We shall," Olive said, her nerves easing slightly as she felt a sense of comfort in Vaughn's presence.

As they made their way, the cool evening breeze swept around them, adding a touch of magic to the night. Once inside Vaughn's truck, he turned on the engine, and the gentle hum filled the space between them.

"Where are we heading for dinner?" Olive asked, trying to ease the tension with conversation.

"There's this charming little restaurant on the outskirts of town," Vaughn replied, a hint of mystery in his voice. "It's one of my favorites."

Olive nodded, her curiosity piqued. "Sounds wonderful. I'm looking forward to it." This was her first official date with Vaughn, and she wanted it to go well. She admired him, fascinated by his aura of mystery, but now that they were on a date, she hoped they could get to know each other on a deeper level.

"So, how's your day been?" Olive asked, trying to ease into the conversation.

Vaughn smiled, his eyes reflecting genuine interest. "It's been good, thanks. Been working on some new writing material," he replied. "And yours?"

Olive leaned back in her seat, a hint of excitement in her voice. "Oh, it's been quite an adventure," she said, recounting her day's journey through Serenity Falls, exploring its scenic beauty and interacting with the friendly locals. "I have to say, this town has a magical charm to it."

As they drove, Vaughn couldn't help but steal glances at Olive, marveling at how easily she seemed to fit into Serenity Falls. He knew she was new to the town, but it felt like she belonged here, like she was a piece of the puzzle that had been missing all along.

Vaughn smiled, his gaze fixed on the road ahead. "Magical charm, huh? That's a perfect way to describe it," he said softly. "It has a way of captivating people, drawing them in and making them stay."

Vaughn couldn't help but feel a connection with Olive as she spoke. It was as if she understood the town's allure on a deeper level, just like he did. He had grown up here, and every nook and cranny held memories and hidden stories.

When they arrived at the restaurant, Olive was immediately charmed by its cozy ambiance, with soft lighting and rustic decor that exuded a warm and inviting atmosphere. The scent of delicious food wafted through the air, making her mouth water in anticipation of the culinary delights that awaited them.

Vaughn held the door open for Olive, and as they entered the restaurant, he couldn't help but notice the curious glances directed their way. People stole glances at them as they walked through the restaurant, and Olive couldn't help but wonder why they were attracting so much attention. Maybe it was because she was new to the town, and Vaughn was a familiar face around here.

She glanced at Vaughn, who seemed to be handling the attention from the other patrons with ease. He smiled reassuringly at Olive, hoping to put her at ease.

"Don't mind them," Vaughn said, trying to sound nonchalant. "Small towns tend to be a bit curious about newcomers." Olive nodded, feeling a bit self-conscious under the gaze of strangers.

"I suppose that's true," she replied, her fingers nervously playing with the edge of her purse.

As they were seated at a cozy corner table, Olive glanced around the restaurant, taking in the warm atmosphere. The aroma of freshly cooked meals and the soft hum of conversations created a sense of comfort. She noticed a faint glimmer of sadness in Vaughn's eyes, but she didn't want to pry. Instead, she decided to steer the conversation toward lighter topics.

"So, Vaughn, what would you recommend from the menu?" Olive asked, picking up her menu and perusing the options.

Vaughn's face brightened, grateful for the change in subject. "Well, their specialty is the grilled salmon. It's always fresh and cooked to perfection," he replied, glancing at the menu himself. "But they also have a fantastic selection of pasta dishes if you prefer something different."

"Grilled salmon sounds great," Olive said with a

smile, closing her menu. "I'll go with that."

Quickly they placed their orders and soon were engaged in light banter. But Olive sensed that there was something troubling Vaughn. She was quick to notice the hint of vulnerability in Vaughn's demeanor, as if he was carrying the weight of something significant on his shoulders. There were moments when his smile faltered, as if he was hiding something beneath the surface. She wondered if he was still recovering from a past heartbreak, but she didn't want to intrude on his personal life. She decided to tread carefully, not wanting to push him into sharing something he wasn't ready for.

Their dinner arrived, and they savored the delicious dishes, savoring not only the food but also the comfort of each other's presence. The conversation flowed easily between them, and Olive found herself enjoying Vaughn's company more and more with each passing moment.

After dessert, Olive decided to take a leap and bring up a slightly personal topic. "You know, Vaughn, I noticed earlier that people seemed curious about us. Is it because you're a well-known figure around here?" she asked, her tone light and inquisitive.

Vaughn's gaze softened, and he paused for a moment before answering. "Well, that might be part of it," he said. "But the truth is, this is my first date since last summer."

Olive's eyes widened in surprise, not expecting such a revelation. "Your first date?" she echoed, trying to process the information. "Since last summer? I had no idea."

Vaughn nodded, a mix of emotions crossing his face. "Yeah, it's been tough," he admitted. "My wife went missing and... it's been hard to move on from that."

Olive's heart sank at the mention of Vaughn's loss. She hadn't known about the tragedy that he had endured. "I'm so sorry to hear that," she said softly.

Vaughn offered her a grateful smile, appreciating her compassion. "It's been a tough journey, but being here with you, it's made me feel like maybe it's time to take a step forward."

Olive felt a rush of emotions, touched by the trust Vaughn had placed in her. She understood that this date was a significant step for him, and she wanted to make it a positive experience. "I'm glad you decided to take that step with me," she said softly. "And I promise, I'll be here to support you in any way I can."

"So, it's been a year since my wife disappeared,"

Vaughn confessed. "She went missing, and despite all the efforts to find her, she was never found."

Olive's heart went out to him, feeling the weight of his pain in every word he spoke. She reached out and gently placed her hand over his, offering a reassuring squeeze. "I can't imagine how difficult that must have been for you," she said softly, her eyes conveying empathy.

"It shattered me," Vaughn admitted, his gaze momentarily distant. "The uncertainty, the constant wondering—it's been a never-ending nightmare. Serenity Falls used to be our home. But now, it feels like a haunting reminder of what I've lost."

Olive could see the heaviness he carried, and yet, she sensed a glimmer of hope in his eyes—a determination to find closure, even amidst the pain.

"I understand the feeling of wanting to escape," she said, choosing her words carefully. "Sometimes, we need to leave behind the places that hold our deepest sorrows to find a new beginning."

Vaughn nodded, his hand still intertwined with hers. "But that's why I've stayed here, you know," he confessed. "This town—it's where my heart and memories lie. Leaving it behind felt like abandoning a part of myself."

Olive leaned in, her voice gentle yet reassuring. "You're not abandoning anything," she said. "You're carrying the love and memories with you wherever you go. Serenity Falls will always be a part of you, no matter where life takes you next."

As they continued to talk, Olive realized that this date was more than just a chance to get to know each other. It was a moment of healing and hope for Vaughn, a chance for him to find solace in the company of someone who cared.

After they finished their meal and stepped back out into the night, Olive leaned against the side of the truck, looking up at the starlit sky. Vaughn joined her, and they stood there in comfortable silence for a moment, taking in the beauty of the moment.

"Thank you for a wonderful evening," Olive finally said, breaking the silence.

"The pleasure was all mine," Vaughn replied, his voice soft. "I had a great time too."

As they stood under the glow of a streetlamp, Olive found herself unable to resist the urge to ask him a question that had been on her mind all evening.

"Can I see you again?" she blurted out, surprised by her own forwardness.

Vaughn's expression softened, and there was a hint of vulnerability in his eyes. "I'd like that," he said, his voice gentle. "I had a wonderful time tonight, and I'd love to get to know you better."

Their eyes locked, and in that moment, they understood each other on a level that went beyond words.

"Well then," Vaughn said, a small smile playing on his lips, "how about we continue this date over coffee? I know a place that makes the best brew in town."

The invitation was too tempting to decline, and Olive found herself nodding eagerly. "I'd love that," she replied, a spark of excitement in her eyes.

With Vaughn at the wheel, they embarked on a short drive through the winding roads of Serenity Falls. Olive couldn't help but feel a sense of anticipation, wondering where this night would lead them. It was as if the mysteries of the town were weaving their own story, guiding their footsteps down a path neither of them could predict.

When they arrived at Vaughn's house, Olive was struck by its cozy charm. It felt like a haven of comfort and creativity, adorned with various artworks and photographs that hinted at Vaughn's artistic soul. The warm, inviting ambiance enveloped her as she stepped inside, and she couldn't help but feel a sense of belonging. "Your house is lovely," Olive remarked, glancing around at the carefully curated space.

Vaughn grinned, his eyes lighting up with pride. "Thank you. I've always believed in surrounding myself with things that inspire me," he said. "Art has a way of making a place feel like home."

Olive nodded in agreement. "Absolutely. It's like you can feel the soul of the artist in every stroke of the brush," she added, her gaze lingering on a particularly captivating painting adorning the wall.

"Please, make yourself at home," Vaughn said, gesturing towards the living room. He disappeared briefly into the kitchen to make coffee. She watched him move around the kitchen with ease, appreciating the simple pleasure of being in his company.

"So, how did you get into photography?" Vaughn asked, returning to the living room with two steaming mugs of coffee.

As they settled comfortably into the living room couch, the aroma of freshly brewed coffee filled the air, enveloping them in its comforting embrace. Olive cradled the warm mug in her hands as she spoke. "Photography has always been a way for me to capture the beauty I see in the world," she explained. "I feel like every moment is fleeting, and through photography, I can preserve those fleeting moments forever."

Vaughn nodded, his eyes locked on hers, as if he could see the depth of her passion. "That's beautiful," he said softly. "You have a true artist's heart."

Blushing slightly, Olive looked away, feeling a mix of shyness and excitement at his compliment. "Thank you," she murmured. "What about you? You mentioned you used to be a writer."

Vaughn's expression turned wistful, a hint of melancholy flickering in his eyes. "Yes, I did," he confirmed. "I used to find inspiration through writing, but lately, the words just haven't come as easily."

Olive sensed that there was more to his story, a deeper layer he wasn't quite ready to share. "Sometimes, creativity goes through phases," she offered. "I'm sure the words will find their way back to you."

He smiled appreciatively, grateful for her understanding. "I hope so," he replied. "Perhaps something will spark that in me."

Olive took a sip of coffee from the steaming mug, savoring the rich flavors that danced on her taste buds. "This is amazing," she said, genuinely impressed. "You weren't kidding about it being the best coffee in town."

Vaughn chuckled, pleased by her reaction. "I'm glad you like it," he replied. "It's a family recipe passed down through generations. I have a bit of a coffee obsession, you could say." Olive grinned, appreciating his passion for the art of brewing the perfect cup. "Well, I must say, I'm impressed with your skills," she said, teasingly raising her cup in a mock toast. "Here's to family secrets and excellent coffee."

"To family secrets and new beginnings," Vaughn added, a glint of mischief in his eyes as he clinked his cup against hers.

They spent the night talking about their dreams, their passions, and their shared love for music. Time seemed to slip away, and before they knew it, the late hours of the night had arrived. "I have to say, Olive," Vaughn began, "I'm really glad we went on this date. I wasn't sure what to expect, but spending time with you tonight has been an absolute joy."

Olive blushed, feeling her heart race a bit. "I feel the same way, Vaughn. It's been a long time since I've had such a great time with someone.

As the clock on the wall struck midnight, Olive stifled a yawn, realizing how late it had gotten. "I should probably be heading home," she said reluctantly.

"Why don't you stay over?" Vaughn suggested. "I don't want this night to end."

"Are you sure it's not an inconvenience?" Olive asked, a touch of hesitance in her voice.

Vaughn shook his head, a warm smile on his lips. "Not at all," he assured her. "I have a spare room, and it's no trouble at all."

Olive felt a wave of relief wash over her as Vaughn's considerate offer sank in. It was a long day, and his kindness made her feel comforted in his presence. With a grateful nod, she accepted his invitation and followed him to the guest room.

As they entered the room, Olive was immediately taken by its charm. The space exuded a cozy, inviting aura, adorned with bookshelves filled with literary treasures and walls adorned with captivating artwork. A hint of vintage allure added a unique touch, making the room feel like a haven of nostalgia.

The soft glow of a bedside lamp illuminated the room, casting gentle shadows that seemed to dance playfully with the artwork on the walls. Olive couldn't help but feel drawn to the ambiance, as if the room itself held a collection of stories and memories from days gone by.

"Wow, this place is amazing," Olive remarked, a genuine appreciation in her voice.

Vaughn smiled warmly. "I'm glad you like it. I've always tried to make it feel like a home away from home for my guests. Not that I have had that many guests at my home in recent times."

"Well, you've certainly succeeded," Olive replied, feeling a sense of ease settle in her heart.

"Oh, there's a spare toothbrush and towels in the bathroom," Vaughn said, trying to be helpful.

"Thank you, that's great," Olive replied, feeling slightly more at ease by his kindness.

As they stood in the doorway of the guest room, Vaughn hesitated for a moment before speaking, "You know, if there's anything you need or if you want to talk about anything, feel free to reach me out. I'm just right outside."

Olive felt touched by his sincerity. "I appreciate that, Vaughn. It's nice to know you're here for me."

"Absolutely. Well, I won't keep you any longer. Have a good night, Olive," Vaughn said, his voice warm and reassuring.

"Good night, Vaughn," Olive replied, feeling comforted by his presence. With that, Vaughn left her to settle into the guest room, closing the door behind him.

Olive felt a sense of relief and gratitude for Vaughn's genuine hospitality. His caring demeanor had lifted the weight of fatigue from her shoulders, making her feel instantly at ease in his home. As she stepped into the bathroom, she admired the clean and tidy space, a reflection of Vaughn's thoughtfulness.

With the toothbrush in hand, Olive began brushing her teeth, replaying the conversations she'd had with Vaughn in her mind. The natural flow of their interaction had left her pleasantly surprised, and she couldn't help but hope that their connection would deepen as they spent more time together.

After her refreshing shower, Olive realized she had forgotten to bring an extra set of clothes. Feeling a bit flustered, she was relieved to find a plush bathrobe hanging on the back of the bathroom door. She wrapped herself in its comforting embrace, thankful for Vaughn's attention to detail.

As she slipped into the inviting bed, the scent of freshly laundered sheets surrounded her, adding to the overall sense of tranquility in the room. Closing her eyes, Olive allowed herself to be embraced by the calmness, reflecting on the events of the night with a contented smile on her lips.

***

CHAPTER 4: THE SILENT HEART

As Olive slowly stirred awake, she was greeted by a delightful aroma that tickled her senses. The inviting scent filled the air, and her stomach rumbled with hunger. Curiosity piqued, she followed her nose, which led her to the kitchen.

To her surprise, Vaughn stood there, looking effortlessly handsome in his pajama pants and a chef's apron. The sight brought a small smile to her lips. "Good morning," she said, her voice still drowsy but filled with appreciation.

Vaughn turned to face her, a warm smile lighting up his face. "Good morning, sleepyhead," he teased gently. "I hope you slept well."

"I did, thank you," Olive replied, her eyes lingering on his casual attire.

As she watched him move gracefully around the kitchen, she couldn't help but feel a sense of connection with him. He was easy to talk to, and their first date had been filled with laughter and genuine conversation. Vaughn seemed like the kind of person who could make anyone feel at ease. "So, how did you learn to cook?" Olive asked, trying to make conversation.

Vaughn chuckled, flipping pancakes with practiced ease. "Well, growing up, my parents were both busy with work, so I had to learn to fend for myself in the kitchen. I started experimenting with different recipes, and over time, I guess I just got better at it."

"That's impressive," Olive said sincerely. "I'm not much of a cook myself, but I'd love to learn someday."

"I'd be happy to cook you, any day." Vaughn replied, glancing at her with a twinkle in his eyes. "I like to dabble in cooking from time to time. I thought I'd surprise you with breakfast. I hope you don't mind."

"Mind? Not at all," she said, feeling a genuine warmth in her heart at his thoughtful gesture. "It smells amazing."

He motioned toward the table. "Please, have a seat. Breakfast will be ready in just a minute."

Olive tiptoed around Vaughn's house, still feeling like an explorer in this new environment. The charming ambiance of the place continued to captivate her, and she couldn't help but admire the tasteful decor that adorned the walls. As she moved around the living room, her eyes were drawn to a set of stairs across the hallway leading to the basement. Curiosity piqued, she contemplated exploring further, but just as she was about to take a step, Vaughn appeared with two trays of delicious-looking food.

"Breakfast is served!" Vaughn announced cheerfully, breaking her train of thought.

Olive smiled and made her way back to the dining area, taking a seat at the table. "This looks amazing, Vaughn. You really didn't have to go through all this trouble."

"It's no trouble at all," Vaughn assured her with a warm grin as he set the trays on the table. "I really enjoy cooking, and I wanted to make sure you had a good breakfast before you head back home."

As they sat down to eat, Olive couldn't help but feel grateful for Vaughn's thoughtfulness. The aroma of the freshly prepared breakfast filled the room, making her stomach growl with anticipation. It was a mix of scrambled eggs with herbs, crispy bacon, and a side of freshly sliced fruits that added a burst of color to the meal.

"Bon appétit," Vaughn said, raising his fork, and Olive followed suit, savoring the delicious flavors.

"This is really good," Olive complimented, smiling appreciatively at Vaughn.

"I'm glad you like it," Vaughn replied, his eyes lighting up with satisfaction. "So, how did you find Serenity Falls so far? Is it living up to its name?"

Olive chuckled, taking a moment to savor the food. "Definitely living up to its name. The town is beautiful, and people are so friendly. I feel like I made the right choice moving here."

"I'm glad to hear that," Vaughn said, genuinely pleased. "Serenity Falls is a wonderful place, and I'm sure you'll enjoy being a part of the community."

They continued to chat and enjoy their meal, the conversation flowing naturally between them. It was evident that they had a connection, despite being relatively new acquaintances. Vaughn shared stories about his time in Serenity Falls, and Olive found herself drawn to his genuine passion for the town and its history.

As breakfast came to an end, Olive couldn't

help but feel grateful for the unexpected turn of events that brought her and Vaughn together. His invitation to stay the night had led to a delightful morning, and she realized that moving to Serenity Falls might be the start of something special – not just in terms of the town but in terms of the people she met, especially Vaughn.

Having just had their first date, they felt a sense of connection and ease around each other, despite being relative strangers not too long ago. It was evident that their bond was growing, and Vaughn's genuine hospitality the night before had only strengthened that connection.

As they sipped their coffee, Olive mentioned, "I really had a wonderful time last night, Vaughn. Thank you for letting me crash at your place."

Vaughn smiled warmly, his eyes meeting hers. "I'm glad you enjoyed yourself. And you're welcome anytime, Olive."

Feeling grateful for his kindness, Olive decided to head back to her house to freshen up and change into a new set of clothes. Vaughn offered to drive her, and she gladly accepted. Upon reaching her home, Olive stood in the doorway with Vaughn as she deliberated into inviting him inside her home.

But before she could say anything, Vaughn gently pulled her closer, his hand finding hers. He looked into her eyes with sincerity, asking, "Do I have your consent?"

Her heart fluttered at his respectful gesture. A smile spread across her face, and she nodded in response, feeling the warmth of his touch. The chemistry between them was undeniable, and in that tender moment, they shared their first kiss, their lips meeting in a gentle and meaningful embrace.

The kiss was soft and sweet, just like the growing affection between them. As they pulled away, they couldn't help but exchange affectionate smiles. Olive turned to go to her bedroom, needing a moment to collect her thoughts, but Vaughn's hand gently caught hers, stopping her.

"Olive," he said, his voice a low whisper, "I don't want to rush things, but I can't deny how I feel when I'm with you."

Her heart raced at his words, and she met his gaze, seeing the sincerity in his eyes. "Vaughn, I feel the same way."

"I really like you, Olive," Vaughn confessed.

"I like you too, Vaughn," Olive replied, her cheeks

flushed.

Without another word, he followed her into her bedroom. Their lips met again, this time with a deeper hunger. The air was thick with tension as they continued to kiss, their bodies drawn together as if by an invisible force.

Their hands roamed over each other's bodies, exploring and caressing. The heat between them grew with every touch, and soon, they were unable to resist the growing need for more.

Olive guided him to her bed, where they collapsed onto the soft mattress. They quickly shed their clothes, their bodies bare and exposed. They kissed hungrily, their hands exploring each other's bodies. The room was filled with their soft moans and gasps as they surrendered to their desire.

Olive's body was fired with arousal as Vaughn's mouth and tongue found her most sensitive spots. She gasped as he sucked and licked her nipples, sending reminders of pleasure through her body. His hands explored her curves, teasing and arousing her even further.

Soon, she could feel his hardness against her, and her heart raced with anticipation. Vaughn's gaze was intense as he stared into her eyes, "May I?"

She pulled him closer, her breath heavy with arousal. Vaughn slowly kissed her again, their bodies pressed against each other.

He positioned himself above her, his cock pressing against her wetness. Slowly, he teased her, rubbing the tip of his cock along her entrance. She moaned softly, her body trembling with need. But even he knew that it was way too soon, so he continued to move against her folds, causing her to grow even wetter. She began to tremble underneath him, and he knew that she was close.

"Olive," he whispered against her ear, his breath hot against her skin. "Tell me you want this."

She moaned softly, her eyes shut as her body writhed in pleasure. Vaughn kissed her deeply, his tongue dancing inside her mouth, he felt her shudder into an intense orgasm. As she gasped, he pulled away and gazed at her beautiful, flushed face. But he wasn't done yet, he smiled as he held her thighs open as he began to kiss and suck on her inner thighs.

As he kissed and nibbled, Olive moaned and trembled, the pleasure building up inside her. She could barely catch her breath as his lips moved closer and closer to her sensitive folds. She gasped as she felt his tongue begin to flick and circle her clit, sending waves of pleasure through her entire body. She could feel her second climax building, and her breathing became shallow and rapid.

"Vaughn," she cried out, her voice trembling. "Please...don't stop."

Her body trembled and shook as the waves of pleasure crashed over her. Her head was spinning, and her vision was blurred as she struggled to catch her breath. She lay there, dazed and exhausted from the intensity of her climax. Vaughn kissed the length of her body as he moved closer to her face.

He then placed a kiss on her lips, his tongue tracing along her lower lip. His eyes burned with passion and desire as he pulled away and looked at her. Olive took a few minutes to catch her breath and when she finally did, she realized something, "Vaughn, did you?"

He grinned, his voice husky with desire, "I did, a few minutes before you did."

"Oh," she whispered.

Vaughn gave her another gentle kiss, then pulled away, staring at her intensely. "I'll take care of the mess," he promised.

She blushed and nodded. "Okay, I'll be in the

shower if you need me."

"Don't take too long, you know I'll need you anyway," he teased, his eyes twinkling.

Olive laughed and playfully shoved him, "Go, before I change my mind."

They shared a final kiss, their bodies pressed together once more. The intensity of their desire for each other was palpable, and it was clear that there was more to come.

As Vaughn left her room, Olive sighed happily. It had been a while since she had been with a man, and it felt good to have someone who respected her boundaries and desires. She knew that Vaughn was different, and that their relationship would only grow stronger.

In the bathroom, Olive turned on the shower, letting the warm water soothe her aching muscles. She closed her eyes and let her thoughts wander. She thought about how lucky she was to have Vaughn in her life.

***

Nina's eyes were heavy with fatigue as she sat at the small table in her motel room, surrounded by stacks of papers and photographs. She had spent the entire night delving into the haunting mysteries of the missing women, trying to piece together any clues that could lead her closer to her sister, Elle. Serenity Falls held more secrets than she had ever imagined, and the weight of uncertainty rested heavily on her shoulders.

When the knock on the door echoed through the room, she jumped in surprise. Rubbing her tired eyes, she called out, "Who is it?"

"It's me, Nina," came the familiar voice of Daniel.

Relief washed over her as she got up and opened the door. There stood Daniel with a gentle smile, holding a tray of breakfast—freshly made waffles, fruits, and two steaming cups of coffee.

"I thought you might need some sustenance after the long night," he said, his eyes filled with concern as he stepped into the room.

Nina's heart warmed at his thoughtfulness. "Thank you, Daniel. You didn't have to do this," she replied, feeling a sense of comfort in his presence.

He placed the tray on the table and pulled out a chair for her. "I know how dedicated you are to finding your sister, but you also need to take care of yourself," he said. "We'll make more progress with clear minds and full stomachs."

She couldn't help but smile at his caring nature. Sitting down at the table, she picked up her fork and took a bite of the waffles. They were delicious, and the taste of home-cooked food reminded her of simpler times. As they ate in companionable silence, Daniel finally broke the quietude, "You know, I've missed this—spending time with you, just like old times."

Nina looked up from the table, meeting his gaze. "I've missed it too, Danny," she admitted, feeling a wave of nostalgia wash over her. "It's strange being back here after all these years. So much has changed, yet some things remain the same."

He nodded, understanding the sentiment. "Yeah, life has a way of taking us on unexpected journeys," he said, his voice soft. "But I'm glad we're on this journey together now."

Their eyes locked, and for a moment, it felt like time had stood still. The years seemed to melt away, leaving them as the two young souls who had once fallen in love. But life had taught them both the art of resilience, and they had grown into different individuals.

"Nina, about us..." Daniel began, his words tentative.

Nina raised her hand, stopping him. "Danny, I

know what you're going to say," she said gently. "It's been a long time, and we've both changed. But I want you to know that I value our friendship more than anything."

He smiled, the concern in his eyes giving way to warmth. "I feel the same way," he replied. "No matter what happens, I'll always be here for you."

Her heart swelled with gratitude. "Thank you, Danny," she said, her voice filled with sincerity. "I couldn't do this without you."

They sat across from each other in silence, the air thick with unresolved emotions and unspoken questions. The breakfast spread remained barely touched as they both seemed lost in their thoughts, each grappling with their own past.

Finally, breaking the silence, Daniel mustered the courage to address the lingering pain that had kept them apart for so long. "But why did you leave? Without even saying goodbye," he asked gently, his eyes searching for answers.

Nina hesitated for a moment, feeling the weight of the past bearing down on her. She knew she couldn't keep this hidden any longer, not from Daniel. "I never really talked about this to anyone ever," she began, her voice tinged with vulnerability. "Me and Elle got into a terrible fight."

Daniel leaned forward, his concern evident. "What happened?" he prodded gently.

"She was dating the good-for-nothing Hector," Nina replied, a hint of bitterness seeping into her words. "Remember that guy?"

Daniel furrowed his brow, trying to recall the person Nina was referring to. "You mean Hector 'Hecky'? The football star back in high school who had to quit school because of his head injury?"

Nina nodded, a touch of pain flickering in her eyes. "Yeah, him. That same night, after graduation, it was just me and him hanging out on the porch. But then he started acting strange, and before I knew it, he tried to choke me."

Shock and anger crossed Daniel's face as he heard the horrifying revelation. "He did what?"

Nina nodded again, her voice trembling with emotion. "I began to yell and scream, and by the time Elle came back out of the house, Hector had backed off. She thought I was making it up because I was jealous of hers and Hector's relationship Can you believe it, my own sister didn't believe me?."

Daniel's heart sank as he tried to process the magnitude of what Nina had experienced.

With a deep breath, Nina continued her painful confession. "That night, I couldn't bear the betrayal. I felt so alone, and I realized that I couldn't stay in Serenity Falls any longer. It was too painful to be there, knowing that Elle didn't trust me, didn't believe me when I needed her the most."

Daniel's heart ached for her, understanding the pain that had driven her away. "You had every right to leave," he assured her, his voice filled with empathy. "I wish I had known, Nina. Maybe I could have done something to help."

"I didn't want anyone to know," Nina admitted, tears welling up in her eyes. "I felt ashamed, like I had done something wrong."

Daniel squeezed her hand gently, offering his support without judgment. "You didn't do anything wrong," he said firmly. "And I believe you, Nina. I always have and I always will. You were many things, but never a liar."

Nina looked into Daniel's eyes, feeling a glimmer of hope that maybe, just maybe, she could heal the wounds of her past that haunted her.

"It means so much to me that you believe me," she whispered, her voice choked with emotion.

"I'll always be here for you, Nina," Daniel said sincerely. "No matter what happens, you can count on me."

Soon, Nina's curiosity got the better of her, and she couldn't resist asking about Hector. "So, whatever happened to that guy?" she inquired, her eyes fixed on Daniel.

Daniel's expression turned solemn, and he hesitated for a moment before answering. "Oh, you don't know?" he replied, his voice tinged with sadness. "Hector went missing."

Nina's eyes widened in shock. "What? When was this?" she asked, concern evident in her voice.

"I don't remember exactly when, but it was like a few months after you left," Daniel explained. "He sort of lost his mind. Well, that's what I heard at the time."

"I can't believe it," Nina whispered, her voice filled with disbelief. "So he must have been the first person to disappear?"

Daniel nodded slowly, his expression grave. "I don't know for sure," he admitted. "It happened years ago, and the only way to find out is by digging through old records at the library."

Nina's determination flared up. "Well, then let's go," she said, her mind already set on the next step of their investigation. She rummaged through her suitcases, searching for the appropriate clothes.

"You mean right now?" Daniel asked, puzzled by her urgency. "It's the weekend, Nina. I highly doubt the library will be open."

She didn't seem deterred. "Trust me, Daniel, it will be open," she insisted, pulling out a pair of jeans and starting to get undressed. Daniel quickly turned away, giving her some privacy.

"I know it's been a while since we were the teenage detectives of Serenity Falls," he mused, trying to lighten the mood. "But sneaking into places was never really our thing, remember?"

Nina chuckled, zipping up her jeans. "Oh, I remember," she said. "But desperate times call for desperate measures, right?"

With a smile, Daniel nodded in agreement. "You're right. You always were the trouble maker out of the two of us," he said, his admiration evident in his eyes.

Nina walked over to the door, holding it open for Daniel. "Exactly, and besides, it's not really sneaking in if we just try the front door," she said playfully.

He couldn't help but laugh at her logic, realizing that her determination was infectious. "You've always had a way of convincing me to do crazy things," he said, following her out of the room.

They headed to the library, their minds focused on the mysteries that awaited them within its walls. As they approached the library, Nina's heart raced with anticipation. She was determined to find any piece of information that might lead them to answers. The glass doors of the library loomed ahead, and she reached for the handle, hoping against hope that it wouldn't be locked.

To her surprise and relief, the door creaked open, granting them access. "See, I told you it would be open," Nina whispered, a hint of triumph in her voice.

Daniel smirked, shaking his head in amusement. "You really do have a way with things, don't you?" he said, following her inside.

They spent hours poring over old archives, searching for any trace of the first person who had vanished. As the day wore on, their excitement grew, knowing they were getting closer to unraveling the town's secrets.

"Look at this," Nina said, pointing to an old newspaper article. "It mentions a suicide fifteen years ago, around the time we finished high school."

Daniel leaned in to read the article, and his eyes widened in surprise. "This could be it," he said, his voice hushed with excitement.

Nina and Daniel exchanged glances, their hearts pounding in unison. They knew they were onto something big.

Her curiosity piqued, Nina leaned in closer, her eyes scanning the text for any clues. "The article mentions that Hector was last seen by his mother, near the waterfall," she pointed out. "That's not too far from where we used to hang out, right?"

Daniel's gaze met hers, and he nodded solemnly. "Yeah, it's the same place. We used to go there all the time."

"Why did we never hear about this back then?" Nina wondered aloud, her mind racing with possibilities. "It seems like such a significant event."

Daniel let out a sigh, his fingers absentmindedly tracing the edge of the newspaper. "I don't know," he admitted. "Maybe it got overshadowed by something else happening around the same time. Or maybe it was just swept under the rug."

Nina frowned, a sense of unease settling in. "Do you think there's a connection between Hector and the other missing persons' cases?" she asked, her eyes searching his for answers.

"It's hard to say," Daniel replied, his brow furrowed in thought. "But there's definitely something strange going on in this town. And if there's even a slight chance that Hector's case is connected to the others, we need to look into it."

Nina nodded in agreement, her determination growing stronger. "I think we should talk to people who were around during that time," she suggested. "Maybe they can shed some light on what happened to Hector."

Daniel flashed her a small, appreciative smile. "Great idea," he said. "I'll start asking around, see if anyone remembers anything."

"We're getting closer, Daniel," Nina said, staring at the old newspaper article. "I can feel it."

***

CHAPTER 5: THE PHOTOGRAPH

The sun was just beginning to cast its warm glow over Serenity Falls as Olive rose from her bed, the soft light filtering through the curtains. With a stretch and a yawn, she pushed herself to start her day. Each morning held a sense of anticipation, a canvas yet to be painted with the colors of her work and the experiences of the day.

Her morning routine was a comforting ritual that set the tone for her creativity. She slipped into a loose-fitting blouse and a pair of jeans, her fingers dancing over the delicate necklace that adorned her neck. She brushed her wavy hair and let it cascade naturally around her shoulders, building up over her own unfiltered beauty.

Stepping into the kitchen, she set the kettle on the stove, its gentle hum accompanied by the soft sounds of birdsong outside. She selected a small succulent from the windowsill and placed it on the table, a touch of nature's green to infuse her space with life.

As the water heated up, Olive glanced out of her window, taking in the serene beauty of the town. A smile curved her lips as she thought about the day ahead – capturing moments, weaving stories through her lens, and discovering the hidden beauty in the ordinary.

With a steaming cup of coffee in hand, she left her house, the familiar jingle of keys in her pocket. The town was still waking up, its streets slowly coming to life as shopkeepers opened their doors and residents began their routines. The local cafe was a short walk away, it's comforting aroma drawing her in. She greeted the barista with a warm smile, exchanging pleasantries as he prepared her usual order.

With a warm cinnamon roll in hand, Olive continued her walk to her photography studio. Upon reaching her studio, she unlocked the door and stepped inside. The soft morning light flooded through the windows, casting a warm and inviting glow. Her heart swelled with pride as she took in the space – the shelves lined with framed photographs, the cozy sitting area with plush cushions, and the neatly arranged workstations.

Olive's fingers brushed over the various props she

had collected over the years – vintage cameras, delicate fabrics, and intricate trinkets that added depth to her compositions. She placed her coffee on the table, the steam rising as she took a moment to savor the aroma.

With a sense of purpose, she began arranging the room, pulling back curtains to allow more sunlight in, and setting up the backdrop for her first shoot of the day. The quiet hum of her favorite instrumental music filled the air, enveloping her in an atmosphere of focus and creativity.

Soon Olive's hands were immersed in the magic of photography as she meticulously developed photographs in her cozy studio. Suddenly, her phone rang, interrupting the serene atmosphere. She wiped her hands on a cloth and hurriedly stepped out of the darkroom to answer the call.

"Hello?" Olive greeted, her heart racing with curiosity.

"Is this Olive?" a voice inquired on the other end.

"Yes, speaking," Olive confirmed, wondering who could be calling her.

"Hello?" Olive said, her heart fluttering with curiosity.

"Hi this is Marcus, the personal assistant to Mayor Alvarez." came the voice on the other end, slightly hurried and professional.

Her mind raced, wondering why the Mayor's assistant would be calling her. "Yes, Marcus. How can I help you?" she replied, trying to maintain composure.

"Well, we have a bit of a situation," Marcus explained, his tone a mix of urgency and relief as he continued, "We're in need of a skilled wedding photographer for the Mayor's daughter's wedding, which is happening in less than a week. Unfortunately, our previous photographer backed out at the last minute."

Olive's eyes widened at the sudden opportunity. Being the wedding photographer for the Mayor's daughter was not something she ever imagined. "I'm flattered you thought of me, but why me?" she asked, curiosity piqued.

Marcus chuckled softly, as if he was about to let her in on a secret. "Well, I saw your online portfolio, and your talent truly shines through your work. You have this way of capturing emotions in the most genuine manner. We want someone who can make this day memorable for the Mayor's daughter and her soon-to-be spouse."

A blush crept up on Olive's cheeks, touched by the compliment. "Thank you. I'd be honored to do it."

"Great!" Marcus exclaimed. "I'll set up a meeting for you with the Mayor and his daughter at their home. Is today afternoon convenient for you?"

"Absolutely," she replied, her excitement growing.
"Perfect. See you today at 3 PM then," Marcus said cheerfully before ending the call.

The chance to photograph the Mayor's daughter's wedding was both thrilling and nerve-wracking. She couldn't wait to meet them and be part of such an important moment in their lives.

Olive went back inside the dark room when her phone buzzed, indicating a new message. Her heart skipped a beat as she opened the text, finding Vaughn's name on the screen.

Vaughn: 'Hey, how's your day going?'

Olive: 'Pretty spectacular.'

She texted back, trying to sound nonchalant, but her excitement couldn't be hidden. Then, Vaughn surprised her with a question that caught her off guard.

Vaughn: 'Do you have a date for the Mayor's

daughter's wedding?'

A mix of confusion and curiosity filled Olive's mind. How did he know about that?

Olive: 'How did you know?'

She texted back, wondering if he had somehow stumbled upon her plans.

Vaughn: 'Well, a little birdie told the Mayor that there was a local photographer in town available to save the day.'

Olive couldn't help but smile at his playful response.

Olive: 'Oh, is that little bird you?'

Vaughn: 'Guilty as charged! Come with me to the wedding as my date, and I'll tell you all about it.'

Their conversation continued, flowing effortlessly as they teased and flirted with each other. Before long, Olive found herself agreeing to be Vaughn's date for the wedding, and the excitement of the upcoming event was now accompanied by a newfound anticipation of spending time with him.

The time ticked away, and Olive soon found

herself in front of the Mayor's grand residence, her camera bag slung over her shoulder. She was greeted by Marcus, who ushered her inside where she saw the Mayor and a radiant young woman, presumably his daughter, sitting in the elegant living room.

"Olive, meet Mayor Alvarez and his daughter, Amanda," Marcus introduced with a warm smile.

Olive shook their hands, feeling a mixture of excitement and slight nervousness. "It's lovely to meet you both," she said sincerely.

"Likewise," Mayor Alvarez replied warmly. "Marcus spoke highly of your work. We're grateful you could step in on such short notice."

Amanda beamed at Olive. "I've seen your photographs, and they're amazing. I'm really excited to have you capture our special day."

When they sat down, the mayor's tone sounded slightly anxious as he explained the situation. "Well, my daughter's wedding is less than a week away, and our original photographer just backed out unexpectedly. It's been a real mess, and I need someone reliable to capture those precious moments. I've heard wonderful things about your photography, and I was hoping you could save the day for us."

Olive's heart went out to the mayor, understanding the importance of capturing such special memories. "Of course, I'd be more than happy to help! I'll do my best to make sure your daughter's wedding is beautifully documented. Just let me know all the details, and I'll be there with my camera ready!"

Relief washed over the mayor's voice. "Thank you, Olive. You have no idea how much this means to us. I'll have Marcus send you all the necessary information right away. Looking forward to working with you!"

"Likewise, Mayor Alvarez. I'll be eagerly waiting for the details. Don't worry; your daughter's wedding will be a day to remember, and I'll ensure every moment is captured with love and care," Olive assured him warmly.

Olive felt a warm sense of relief as the conversation between her and Amanda flowed effortlessly. She sensed that Amanda and her father were truly kind-hearted souls. They were discussing all the little details of the upcoming wedding, and as they chatted, Olive's vision for the photography started to form vividly in her mind. It was going to be a magical event, one that would be etched in their memories forever.

"So, Olive," Amanda said with a smile, "tell me more about your ideas for the photography. We really want this day to be special, and your work seems to capture emotions so beautifully."

Olive blushed a little but felt a surge of excitement. "Thank you, Amanda. I believe that a wedding is about capturing not just the poses but also the essence of love and happiness. I want to freeze those precious moments that you'll look back on and cherish for a lifetime."

Amanda's eyes sparkled with enthusiasm. "Oh, I love that! It's exactly what we want—genuine, heartfelt moments captured forever."

"Absolutely," Olive replied, feeling a sense of connection with Amanda. "I'd love to take some candid shots, too, to capture the raw emotions and the joy of your friends and family. Those are the ones that often become the most cherished memories."

The Mayor, who had been listening quietly, chimed in, "I couldn't agree more. Those candid moments have a way of bringing back the magic of the day, even years down the road."

Olive nodded, grateful for their understanding and support. "I'm really looking forward to being a part of your special day and preserving all these beautiful moments for you."

Amanda reached out and squeezed Olive's hand gently. "We're so glad we found you. I can already tell you'll make this day even more extraordinary."

As they continued to talk about the wedding plans, Olive couldn't help but feel that fate had brought them together. The connection she felt with Amanda and her father reassured her that this was going to be an unforgettable experience for everyone involved. She couldn't wait to capture their love and happiness, creating a timeless tale of romance and excitement through her lens.

Little did she realize that this invitation would lead to an unforgettable evening full of romance, thrills, and unexpected twists that would forever change the course of their lives.

****

As the clock struck late evening, Nina found herself standing outside Daniel's office, her heart pounding with anticipation. Tonight was special; Daniel had called her urgently, whispering sweet promises of good news he couldn't disclose over the phone. The thrill of what he had to say sent a shiver of excitement down her spine.

Inside, Daniel's office was dimly lit, but the warmth of his smile illuminated the room as he welcomed Nina. "I've got something incredible for you, Nina," he said, a glimmer of excitement in his eyes.

Nina's heart fluttered with curiosity and joy. "Tell me, Daniel. What's the news?"

Daniel's eyes sparkled as he revealed, "I managed to work my magic on the Deputy Chief at the police station. We're going to get a look at the official case files of Elle."

Nina couldn't believe her ears, her elation growing with each passing second. She wrapped her arms around him in a tight, awkward hug, unable to contain her happiness. "Oh, Daniel, that's amazing! You're incredible!"

He chuckled, his arms gently embracing her. "I knew how much you needed this, Nina. But we have to go now."

Daniel steered the car toward the nearby police station, and as they cruised along, an unusual hush enveloped them. Nina's mind was a jumbled mess, swirling with thoughts about what she might uncover in Elle's case files. She couldn't help but feel anxious, and the quietness of the moment only intensified her unease.

Finally, unable to bear the silence any longer, Nina

turned to Daniel and asked, "Do you think we'll find something useful at the police station? I mean, Elle was my sister, but there's so much we don't know about what happened to her."

Daniel glanced at Nina, his eyes filled with empathy, and replied, "I can't say for sure, but it's worth a shot. We'll do everything we can to get to the bottom of this, Nina. I promise."

Nina nodded, appreciating Daniel's unwavering support. She was grateful to have him by her side during this difficult time. The rest of the drive was quiet, but somehow, Nina felt a sense of reassurance knowing that Daniel was there for her.

Once they arrived at the police station, Daniel parked the car and turned to Nina. "Are you ready for this?" he asked gently, his hand reaching for hers.

Taking a deep breath, Nina nodded, giving his hand a reassuring squeeze. "Yes, I have to know the truth, no matter how painful it might be."

Daniel smiled softly, his eyes locking with hers. "Then let's do this."

Nina and Daniel stepped into the police station, the familiar scent of justice and tension filling the air. The desk officer, a stern but friendly face, welcomed them warmly and guided them to the office of the deputy chief. To Nina's surprise, it turned out to be none other than Daniel's eldest brother, the deputy chief himself.

"Oh, hey there, Nina!" Daniel's brother grinned, offering a friendly handshake. "Long time no see! How's life treating you?"

Nina smiled back, relieved to find a familiar face amidst the seriousness of a police station. "Hey, Chief! Life's been a rollercoaster, but I'm hanging in there. How about you?"

"Oh, you know how it is, busy as ever," the deputy chief replied, his gaze shifting between Daniel and Nina.

Daniel glanced at Nina briefly before clearing his throat. "Well, Chief, we've stumbled upon something that might interest you. We've got some information about the recent string of mysterious incidents in town, and we thought it might be worth sharing with you."

Nina and Daniel exchanged nervous glances, standing in front of Deputy Chief Turner. His eyes glimmered with intrigue, and he leaned in, eager to hear their story. "You've got my undivided attention. Spill the beans," he urged.

Daniel remained resolute, shaking his head with a knowing smile. "A deal's a deal, my friend. You first, then we'll lay it all out for you."

Chief Turner chuckled, respecting their determination. "Fair enough. Follow me, you two," he gestured, leading them through the dimly lit corridors towards the heavily guarded evidence room.

"Twenty minutes, and no more," he warned, using his keycard to grant them access.

"Thank you brother," Daniel acknowledged warmly, stepping inside with Nina. The deputy chief, not wanting to miss anything, accompanied them into the room. He pointed to a dusty corner of the shelves where the evidence box they sought stood alone.

In the dimly lit evidence room, an electric charge filled the air, sending shivers down Nina's spine. Her heart raced with a mix of fear and anticipation. Beside her, Daniel treaded carefully, his every step echoing the thundering beats of his heart, as if he were about to unveil a long-buried secret.

"Daniel, be careful," Nina urged in a hushed tone, her voice barely above a whisper. "We're about to open a Pandora's box."

Daniel nodded, his eyes locked on the weathered

container before them. The dusty box bore the cryptic label "Case no 1577," holding within it the remnants of Nina's beloved sister, Elle. It was all that remained of her, a silent testimony to a haunting past.

As they reached for the box's lid, the deputy chief, an astute and observant presence, stood nearby, intrigued by the unfolding drama. "Take your time," he encouraged, his eyes reflecting the gravity of the moment.

Nina's fingers brushed against the grime-coated surface, feeling a connection to the sister she had lost. Memories flooded back – laughter, tears, and sisterly love. She swallowed hard, mustering the strength to confront the past.

With a creak, the lid finally gave way, revealing a trove of evidence, fragments of the life Elle had lived. Pictures, letters, and objects that held meaning only to her. Each item held a story, a puzzle piece to reconstruct the life that had been stolen.

Nina and Daniel huddled together, meticulously sifting through the evidence box that held crucial pieces of the puzzling case. As they delved deeper, Nina's eyes locked onto an initial report file, her heart sinking as she read the words: "Prime suspect, the husband Vaughn Knight claimed that he was in the house all night." She couldn't believe what she was seeing - the prime suspect was none other than Elle's own husband, Vaughn.

'Elle, was married?' Nina felt her own voice whisper in her mind. But she didn't realize that she had said it out loud.

Deputy Turner, approached Nina at that moment. "I actually went to high school with Vaughn," he revealed, his voice tinged with surprise.

Nina's curiosity couldn't be contained, and she couldn't help but ask, "What was he like back then? Was he a nerd or something?"

A chuckle escaped Deputy Turner's lips as he reminisced about the past. "Nerd? No way. Vaughn was the prom king that year," he disclosed, shaking his head at the unexpected twist of fate.

Meanwhile, Daniel made a discovery of his own - an old, weathered photograph of Elle and Vaughn on their wedding day. They both looked radiantly happy, their smiles infectious. The sight tugged at Nina's heartstrings, leaving her torn between the evidence and the memory of what seemed like a blissful union. How could he have possibly done such a thing to his wife?

Nina gazed at Deputy Turner, her eyes filled with concern. "Why wasn't Vaughn arrested then? It's always the husband in most of these missing wife cases."

With a heavy sigh, Deputy Turner leaned against the wall. "Believe me, we tried. But there wasn't a single piece of evidence that pointed to him. Vaughn seemed genuinely devastated by his wife's disappearance. He loved her deeply, and we couldn't find anything to suggest otherwise."

Daniel, who had been listening intently, chimed in, "But that doesn't mean he's innocent, right?"

Deputy Turner shook his head. "No, it doesn't. But we can't arrest someone without evidence or reasonable doubt. It's frustrating, I know."

Nina bit her lip, contemplating the situation. "Where is he now?" she finally asked.

"He's still here, in Serenity Falls," Deputy Turner replied. "We're keeping a close eye on him, just in case he slips up."

Nina looked at him, worry etched on his face. "Do you think he's dangerous?"

Deputy Turner shrugged. "I don't know, but in cases like these, you never really know for sure, do you?"

Deputy Turner gave them a bit of extra time in the evidence room before finally letting them go. As they settled back into the car, Nina turned to Daniel, her heart heavy with worry.

"I have to find a way to talk to Vaughn," Nina confessed, her fingers nervously fidgeting with the hem of her shirt.

Daniel glanced at her with concern, "I understand you want answers, but it might not be safe. We can't be sure if Vaughn is somehow involved in all of this. We need solid proof before we put ourselves in danger and risk him running away."

Nina nodded, biting her lip in contemplation. "You're right. I just can't shake the feeling that he knows something important. And if he's innocent, he deserves to know what's going on too."

Daniel placed a comforting hand on her shoulder, his voice gentle, "I know it's hard, but we have to be cautious. Our investigation is just beginning, and we need to be smart about every move we make."

Nina sighed, leaning her head against the window, "I just wish there was a way to figure this out without putting anyone else at risk."

"We'll figure it out, Nina," Daniel said with a

tender touch on her shoulder, offering reassurance. "But promise me you won't go and confront him alone, okay?"

Nina looked into Daniel's eyes, feeling the warmth of his concern. "I... I promise," she replied, her voice wavering slightly. "It's just hard not to, you know?"

Daniel gently cupped her face in his hands, his gaze unwavering. "I know it's tough, but we're in this together. I won't let anything happen to you. We'll face this challenge as a team."

Nina took a deep breath, finding solace in Daniel's unwavering support. "Thank you," she whispered, her heart beating faster at the thought of having him by her side.

Daniel smiled, his touch a comforting anchor for her fears. "Always, Nina. No matter what happens, I'll be right here with you."

***

CHAPTER 6: LOVE TESTED

Olive bid her farewell to Mayor Alvarez and his daughter Amanda after their meeting at their elegant home. The discussion had revolved around Amanda's upcoming wedding, and Olive was paid in advance for her photography services to capture the precious moments of the event.

As Olive stepped out of the grand house, a light spring breeze brushed against her cheeks, carrying with it a sense of anticipation and possibility. Her heart danced with joy as she realized the significance of this opportunity – her first big photography event. The thought of capturing such a special moment for Amanda and her fiancé filled her with a mixture of excitement and determination.

Her steps quickened as she made her way to her car, her thoughts already drifting to the creative ideas she could bring to life through her lens. Her heart raced with excitement as she left the mayor's residence, the meeting having gone better than she could have ever hoped. She knew she couldn't wait any longer to see Vaughn, her pulse quickening at the thought of him. Determined to surprise him, she hopped into her car and drove to his house, a nervous yet eager smile playing on her lips. Her steps quickened as she made her way to her car, her thoughts already drifting to the creative ideas she could bring to life through her lens.

Upon arriving, she spotted Vaughn outside, tinkering with his pickup truck in the driveway. "Hey, stranger," she called out, her voice light with anticipation.

Vaughn looked up, his eyes widening in pleasant surprise as he saw Olive standing there, looking more radiant than ever. "Olive! What are you doing here?" he asked, setting aside his tools and walking over to her.

"I couldn't wait to see you," she replied, her cheeks flushing with a mix of bashfulness and desire. "Today has been amazing, and I wanted to share it with you."

His smile melted her heart, and they found themselves wrapped in each other's arms. Their love was undeniable, a magnetic force that drew them closer with every passing moment.

"I'm so proud of you, Olive," Vaughn said, his voice filled with admiration. "You're incredible, and you deserve all the success that comes your way."

Her heart swelled at his words, feeling a sense of belonging in his embrace. "Thank you, Vaughn. It means the world to me to have your support."

The chemistry between them was electric, igniting a fire that had been smoldering between them for far too long. She gazed into Vaughn's eyes, overcome by the desire to taste his lips again. Their hands moved on their own, exploring each other's bodies, their kisses growing more passionate by the second.

Before they knew it, they found themselves inside the house, their clothes scattered along the hallway floor as they stumbled into Vaughn's bedroom, still connected at the lips.

Olive lay naked on Vaughn's bed, her bare breasts and pink nipples on full display, her hair fanned out on the pillow. Vaughn kneeled before her, his head between her legs as he feasted on her pussy, making her moan with pleasure. His tongue ran up and down her slit, her clit in his mouth, the tip of his tongue flicking it back and forth.

Olive couldn't take it anymore. She grabbed him by the hair, pulling his face upwards, his mouth covered in her juices. They met in a hungry kiss, his hand cupping her breasts, his thumb teasing her nipple.

"I need to be inside you, Olive," Vaughn said, his voice low with lust.

"Yes, please," she gasped, "I want to feel you inside me."

Vaughn positioned himself above Olive, his cock sliding into her wet pussy, his strong, muscular body moving in perfect sync with hers. Olive's moans filled the room as their lovemaking continued, the heat between them growing more intense with every thrust. She wrapped her legs around him, pulling him in deeper, her hips gyrating as he drove himself inside her.

Vaughn could feel his climax building up, the sensations overpowering him. He drove into her one last time, the intensity of the orgasm taking over. Olive held him close, feeling her own orgasm wash over her. She moaned as he kissed her neck, still inside her, his body quaking from the pleasure.

As they lay together, basking in the afterglow, Olive knew that this was just the beginning of their thrilling romance, one filled with passion, and endless possibilities.

Vaughn leaned in once more and brushed his lips

against Olive's. Their kiss held a raw passion and tenderness, and in that moment, the world around them ceased to exist. For both of them, their hearts belonged to one another.

Their lips parted, but their gazes remained locked, revealing a depth of emotion that words could barely express. Vaughn's voice, husky with desire, broke the silence, "Are you hungry?" he asked, a playful glint in his eyes.

Olive couldn't help but chuckle softly, her eyes sparkling with affection. "Starving," she replied, feigning exasperation but secretly relishing every second of their playful banter.

With a smirk, Vaughn rose from his seat and extended his hand toward her, a silent invitation to embark on a little adventure together. "Then, my lady, let's satisfy those cravings," he said with a mischievous grin.

Olive didn't hesitate for a moment as she clasped his hand with her own, her fingers naturally intertwining with his. The spark between them was undeniable, and she was eager to see where this adventure would take them. Her heart raced with anticipation as they set off on this thrilling journey together.

Pausing for a moment, Olive glanced around the room, realizing she hadn't brought her clothes with her. She couldn't help but inquire, "Um, Vaughn, where are my clothes?"

Vaughn leaned in, his warm breath gently brushing against her ear as he whispered, "You don't need clothes when you're with me." His words sent shivers down her neck, and a blush crept up her cheeks. He had a way of making her feel desired and cherished all at once.

A teasing smile played on Olive's lips as she responded, "Is that so?" Her heart pounded in her chest, the excitement of the unknown coursing through her veins. Vaughn had awakened a daring side of her she never knew existed, and she was eager to embrace it.

With a spark in her eyes and butterflies in her stomach, she eagerly joined Vaughn as they strolled into the kitchen, their bodies free from any restraints of clothing.

Vaughn, wearing only a chef's apron, looked utterly charming and captivating. Olive couldn't help but feel a magnetic pull toward him. Her eyes followed his every move as he skillfully prepared pasta, the aroma filling the air and adding to the enchanting atmosphere.

Their flirty banter and playful teasing filled the kitchen like sweet melodies. "So, Chef Vaughn, are you an expert in the kitchen as well as in other areas?" Olive teased with a wink, feeling the adrenaline of their boldness flowing through her veins.

Vaughn's smile widened, a mischievous glint in his eyes. "Oh, you have no idea, Olive. Cooking is just one of my many talents," he replied, his voice low and husky, sending shivers down her spine.

As the pasta cooked, Vaughn couldn't resist stealing glances at Olive's alluring figure. He was drawn to her in a way he couldn't explain. "You know, you're distracting me with your beauty," he teased, using the opportunity to flirt shamelessly.

Olive blushed, feeling both embarrassed and thrilled by his compliments. "Well, you're not so bad yourself, Chef Vaughn. You make cooking look irresistibly sexy," she retorted playfully, enjoying their flirtatious exchange.

The air between them crackled with tension, their attraction undeniable. Olive felt alive, embracing the daring side of herself that Vaughn had awakened. With a knowing smile, she decided to take the lead, stepping closer to him, their bodies almost touching.

Vaughn's eyes darkened, and his heart pounded as

he felt Olive's closeness. He couldn't resist reaching out to brush a strand of hair away from her face, his touch gentle and electrifying. "You're something else, Olive," he whispered, his voice husky with desire.

"And you, Vaughn, are one of a kind," Olive replied, her breath hitching slightly at the intensity of the moment.

And even when the pasta bubbled and cooked to perfection, Olive and Vaughn couldn't help but steal glances at each other, a magnetic attraction silently pulling them closer. The air around them seemed to crackle with excitement, and they knew something special was brewing.

With playful grins and a spark in their eyes, they came up with a unique idea to enjoy their meal. "Why don't we make this dinner a bit more fun?" Vaughn suggested, his voice tinged with flirtatious charm.

Olive's heart skipped a beat, and she eagerly agreed, "Oh, yes! Let's make it an intimate pasta feast."

They set the table with candles, creating a cozy ambiance that felt like their little world. As they sat down, their knees brushed against each other, and a delightful shiver ran down Olive's spine. They couldn't deny the chemistry between them any longer.

"Okay, let's savor these flavors together," Vaughn said, picking up a forkful of pasta and offering it to Olive with a teasing grin.

She giggled, leaning closer, and took the bite from his fork. "Mmm, delicious!" she exclaimed, her eyes never leaving his.

"Your turn," Olive said, scooping up a forkful of pasta and lifting it to Vaughn's lips. Their faces were inches apart, and she could feel his warm breath against her cheek.

He winked and opened his mouth to receive the offering. "Wow, that's amazing," he remarked, his gaze locked on hers.

As the dinner progressed, their flirty banter and stolen glances only intensified. Vaughn couldn't resist playfully wiping away a speck of sauce from Olive's cheek, using his finger to savor the taste himself.

Olive blushed, her heart pounding, and she decided to up the ante. "Oh, is that how it's going to be?" she teased, dipping her finger into the sauce and drawing a line on Vaughn's cheek. "Now we're even."

Vaughn chuckled, enjoying the playful game they were in. "Fair enough," he replied, reaching for a napkin to clean up the sauce.

But Olive stops him and holds his hand, as she leaned forward and seductively licks the sauce from his cheek. The movement is bold and intimate, sending a thrilling jolt straight to Vaughn's core.

A wave of passion hits them both as their eyes meet. Olive could feel a strong connection between them, and she knew this was going somewhere. She was so turned on by his sensual nature and the fact that he was also vulnerable and sweet. She wanted to know all of him.

Olive licked the sauce off her finger, her eyes never leaving Vaughn's. She watched as a dark look crept into his eyes, the tension between them palpable. "I love how you taste," she said in a low, sultry tone, her voice dripping with seduction.

Vaughn chuckled, feeling slightly overwhelmed and yet more turned on than he's ever been in his life. He couldn't deny it any longer. He wanted Olive with an intensity that took his breath away.

"I can't get enough of you," he whispered, his voice a deep growl of desire.

Olive smiled, feeling her pulse quickening and her heart pounding as she knew the chemistry between them was about to reach a whole new level. She could feel the heat radiating off his body as he stood up to pull her into his embrace.

She pressed her body close to his, molding against him like she'd been made for him. They melted into each other, lips crashing together and tongues tasting each other's hunger.

They kissed, their passion burning through them like a wildfire. There was no hesitation as Vaughn's fingers slid down to Olive's butt and pulled her closer, pressing her soft body against him. She reciprocated by holding on to his strong shoulders and lifting herself up on tiptoe to deepen their kiss.

As the kiss grew more intense, the flame of desire within them ignited, their need to have each other outweighing all other thoughts. In a moment of pure animalistic desire, Vaughn held Olive by her hips and lifted her up. Her legs wrapped around his waist by their own involuntary response. She could feel the head of his cock rubbing against her sensitive clit. The pleasure sent a wave of lust through her veins.

She felt herself slipping away as he carried her into the bedroom and placed her on the bed. And then without warning, he plunged into her like he was claiming her as his. He entered her slowly at first, feeling her warmth envelope his throbbing erection. And then with each thrust, he increased his tempo, until they were moving in unison as one.

Olive had never felt such intensity before, she moaned as she scratched his back with her nails. "Vaughn... you're so fucking hot," she whispered, looking him in the eyes, their connection undeniable.

Vaughn kissed her as he increased his pace even more, he wanted to claim every inch of her body as his. They kissed as if they were devouring each other. Their tongues tangled as they reached a point of no return. Their bodies moving together like two perfect puzzle pieces, all thoughts, all worries fading away, leaving only the raw, primal desire. They came together as one, an orgasm like none they'd ever felt before. They were consumed by a hunger, their need for each other undeniable.

The pleasure was intense and raw, as they came crashing down. The release of the tension and energy built up in them over the past few weeks was overwhelming. They were consumed by a storm of passion, lust, and desire. They couldn't get enough of each other.

They fell asleep in each other's arms, a smile on both their faces.

***

Olive stirred in her sleep, gradually becoming aware of her surroundings. As her eyes fluttered open, she found herself in unfamiliar territory – Vaughn's bedroom. A contented smile curved her lips as she recalled the events of the previous night. Slowly, the memories of the previous night flooded back, the laughter, the shared stories, and the tender moments that had brought her here.

Opening her eyes, she turned her gaze to her surroundings, taking in the details of Vaughn's room. The room was infused with a sense of him – the rustic wooden furniture, the warm color palette, and the subtle scent that lingered in the air. She couldn't help but smile, feeling a sense of contentment and belonging in this moment.

And then, her gaze shifted to her side, where Vaughn lay next to her, still lost in sleep. His features were softened by the morning light, his tousled hair falling gently across his forehead. The rise and fall of his chest with each breath was a reassuring rhythm that matched the calm she felt within.

As Olive watched him, a surge of warmth washed over her. In the intimacy of this moment, she realized how much she cherished the connection they shared. It wasn't just about physical attraction – it was the deep bond they had formed, the understanding that went beyond words, and the unspoken promise of support and companionship.

Careful not to disturb him, Olive shifted slightly

closer, her fingers instinctively reaching out to brush a lock of hair away from his face. A gentle smile played on her lips as she thought about the journey that had led her to this point – from escaping a suffocating past to discovering a new beginning, one intertwined with Vaughn's presence.

The soft sound of his breathing was a soothing melody that resonated in the quiet room. She admired the strong lines of his features, the way his lips curved slightly even in sleep. And in that moment, she realized how much she wanted to share her life, her dreams, and her future with him.

Not wanting to disturb his rest, Olive carefully slid out of bed, making sure not to make a sound. Their night together had been intense, leaving her in need of fresh underwear.

She tiptoed across the room, her movements fluid and gentle. The floorboards beneath her feet seemed to cooperate, not creaking as she moved. Spotting Vaughn's flannel shirt nearby, she playfully slipped it on, enveloping herself in his scent – a sweet reminder of their passionate lovemaking. Blushing at the memory, she thought it might be time to find the laundry room in the basement.

She quickly grabbed her clothes off the floor and rushed towards the creaky stairs, she couldn't help but feel a mix of nervousness and excitement. She hoped Vaughn would join her on this laundry mission. After all, she loved these little moments of togetherness that felt like a thrilling adventure.

But she was blissfully unaware, that this seemingly ordinary task would lead to a startling discovery. In the dimly lit basement, amidst the scent of detergent and musty air, Olive's eyes fell upon a peculiar sight.

"What on earth is this?" she whispered to herself, her heart pounding in her chest. There, in front of her, was a large board on the wall, that was adorned with pictures of women. The sight sent shivers down her spine, and her mind raced with questions and fear.

Olive took a step back, only to be surprised by Vaughn standing silently behind her. His sudden appearance startled her, and she jumped a little. "What are you doing down here, Olive?" Vaughn asked with a worried look on his face. He glanced at the murder board she had been studying.

Her eyes widened with concern as she motioned towards the board. "Vaughn, what is this? What does it all mean?"

Vaughn's expression grew somber as he hesitated before walking over to join her. "I should've told you earlier," he admitted, his voice filled with remorse.

But Olive was already retreating, putting distance between them. He reached out to her, pleading, "Olive, please let me explain."

"Oh my God! Let me go!" Olive exclaimed, feeling overwhelmed. Without waiting for Vaughn's explanation, she rushed out of the house, in her half-naked state, and hurriedly got into her car.

As she drove away, emotions churned inside her, unsure of what to make of the situation and the secrets that had now come to light. Vaughn's words echoed in her mind, and she knew she couldn't ignore them. But she needed time to process everything before facing him again.

Back in the basement, Vaughn's emotions swirled into a storm of fury, consuming him entirely. He smashed and shattered, unleashing the storm within him upon the surroundings.

The echoes of destruction resonated through the walls, reflecting the turbulence in Vaughn's heart. In that moment of intense emotion, he felt like a tornado, tearing apart everything in its path. The room bore witness to his inner struggle, the pain and frustration manifesting in every broken piece.

In the midst of the wreckage, Vaughn's breaths came in ragged bursts, matching the rhythm of his pounding heart. Little did he know that Olive's heart was also in turmoil, torn between the love she held for Vaughn and the fear of being hurt again.

***

CHAPTER 7: THE SILENT WHISPERS

The days had stretched into a quiet rhythm, a contrast to the whirlwind of emotions Olive had experienced recently. After the intimate moments she had shared with Vaughn, she found herself needing some space to process her feelings and thoughts. She had chosen to retreat into the cocoon of her solitude, a place where she could reflect without distraction.

As the sun streamed in through the window of her cozy living room, Olive sat on the couch with a cup of tea cradled in her hands. Her gaze lingered on the small garden outside, the vibrant colors of the flowers offering a sense of peacefulness. She was lost in her thoughts, contemplating the new path she was on and the challenges she had overcome.

And yet, every time the phone lit up, Olive's heart

raced with a mix of fear and longing. She knew she couldn't ignore Vaughn forever, but she wasn't ready to face him yet. Their last encounter had left her heartbroken and confused, and she needed time to sort out her feelings.

In the privacy of her house, memories of their time together played like a movie in her mind. She recalled the laughter they shared, the tender moments that made her feel alive, and the passionate kisses that sent shivers down her legs. But along with the sweet memories, painful doubts gnawed at her.

What if opening her heart to Vaughn again meant inviting more heartache? What if he couldn't understand the fears that held her back?

But more importantly, why did he have a board filled with photos of women in his basement? Olive knew she had to confront her fears eventually, but she couldn't bring herself to take that leap of faith just yet.

Outside her window, the world seemed to go on without a care. Birds sang in the trees, and the sun painted the sky with vibrant hues. But within the confines of her home, Olive felt stuck in a storm of emotions.

Vaughn's persistence only deepened her internal struggle. She wanted to pick up the phone and pour out her heart to him, but she also knew that their problems couldn't be solved with a simple conversation. It would take more than words to bridge the gap between them.

Late one evening, Olive found herself cozied up on her couch, trying to lose herself in a book to forget about everything. But just as she settled in, the doorbell rang suddenly, startling her out of her thoughts.

Olive glanced towards the front door, her heart skipping a beat when she realized who it might be. Vaughn. She hesitated, her fingers gripping her book a little tighter. The thought of facing him, of explaining her need for space, was both overwhelming and necessary.

After a deep breath, Olive set her book down and approached the windows. She peered through the curtains, her breath catching in her throat when she saw his silhouette standing on the porch.

"Olive, please open up," Vaughn's voice pleaded from the other side.

"He's persistent," she mumbled, as she silently walked back to her couch.

Olive wrapped herself in a soft blanket and hoped

that her silence would make him leave. Soon enough, her phone lit up with a text message from Vaughn.

Vaughn: Are you okay? I've been so worried.

Olive wasn't planning on giving him the satisfaction but soon she found herself responding to texts.

Olive: Why won't you give up, Vaughn? We can't just pretend like nothing happened.

Vaughn: I know I messed up, Olive. I should've been honest with you from the start. But I was scared, scared of losing you.

Olive: But you did hurt me, Vaughn. It's not easy to just forget a board full of women's faces.

Vaughn: Olive, Please I never wanted to hurt you. I thought keeping things hidden was for the best, but now I see it only caused more pain. I promise, from now on, I'll be truthful with you.

Olive: It's not just about honesty, Vaughn. Trust is broken too. How can I trust you again after all this?

Vaughn: I know trust takes time to rebuild, and I'm ready to do whatever it takes to earn yours back.

Overwhelmed, Olive turned off her phone and allowed herself to cry, the weight of their serious conversation sinking in. She knew deep down that she still loved Vaughn, but regaining trust wouldn't be easy.

The hours seemed to stretch on endlessly, each minute marked by the rhythmic ticking of the clock on the wall. Olive remained on the couch, her thoughts swirling in a storm of emotions. Memories of her past relationship resurfaced like ghosts from the shadows, haunting her with their familiar touch. But this time, she refused to succumb to their pull.

The weight of her past mistakes bore down on her shoulders, and for a moment, it felt as though she was trapped in a cycle that she couldn't escape. The ache in her chest intensified, a painful reminder of the heartbreak she had endured. But as the minutes turned into hours, a sense of determination began to bloom within her.

Olive had been down this road before – a path lined with pain and toxic patterns. She had allowed herself to be consumed by someone who claimed to care, only to realize that their intentions were far from genuine. This time, she vowed to break free from the chains that had bound her for so long.

With a deep breath, Olive pushed herself up from the couch. Her fingers clenched into fists, a physical manifestation of her resolve to take control of her own life. She paced back and forth across the room, her steps echoing with each decision she was making in that moment. Memories of laughter intertwined with tears, of promises made and shattered, flashed before her eyes.

But as the hours passed, Olive's anxiety began to transform into a simmering anger – not just at her past, but at herself for allowing it to happen. The cycle had to end, and it had to end now.

Olive's steps were purposeful as she left the living room and entered her quaint kitchen. The sun streamed through the window, casting a warm glow over the neatly arranged counters and appliances. She paused for a moment, taking in the familiarity of her surroundings and the sense of calm that her home exuded.

With a soft exhale, Olive pulled open the fridge door, the cool air brushing against her skin. She glanced at the shelves, her mind wandering as she considered her options.

As she glanced into her nearly empty fridge, she spotted a rotting orange, which she promptly threw away in the overflowing garbage bin. Realizing she needed to restock her supplies, she decided to call the local grocery store for a home delivery.

With a hopeful smile on her face, she dialed the number and was greeted by a friendly voice from the grocery store.

"Hello, thank you for calling Fresh Mart. How can we help you today?" the cheerful voice said.

"Oh, hi! I'd like to place an order for some groceries, please," Olive replied.

"Of course! We're here to assist you. What would you like to order?" the grocery store asked. Thankfully, they offered this convenient service, and she was relieved she wouldn't have to leave the comfort of her home.

"Okay, here's my list: I need lots of fruits, bread, cereal, pasta, tomatoes, onions, garlic, chicken, a pack of light beer and cheese," Olive said, feeling a little better already.

"Great! That sounds like a fantastic selection. We'll make sure to pack everything fresh and deliver it straight to your doorstep," the store assured her.

"Oh, that's wonderful. Thank you so much!" Olive exclaimed with gratitude.

"It's our pleasure to help you out. Is there anything else you'd like to add to your order?" the friendly voice asked.

As Olive thought for a moment, she remembered something she'd been craving lately. "Oh, yes! Can you also include some chocolate chip cookies? They're my guilty pleasure," she admitted with a light-hearted chuckle.

"Absolutely! Consider it done. Anything else?" the store asked, happy to accommodate Olive's request.

"Hmm, let me think. Oh, how about a bunch of fresh flowers? They always brighten up the room and my mood!" Olive suggested, feeling more and more at ease.

"Great idea! Flowers do have a magical touch. We'll add a beautiful bouquet to your order," the grocery store confirmed.

"Thank you so much for your help. You've made my day," Olive said, genuinely grateful for the thoughtful assistance.

"It's our pleasure to serve you. Your order will be on its way shortly. Take care and have a wonderful day!" the grocery store replied warmly.

As Olive hung up the phone, she couldn't help but feel grateful for the grocery store's kindness. With her order on the way, she knew she could now focus on taking care of herself and leaving behind the past. And who knows, maybe a little snack marathon with those chocolate chip cookies could lead to a delightful change in her mood.

Minutes had passed, and Olive lay on the couch once more. But this time, her heart felt lighter, her mind more at peace. The memories of her past relationship were still there, but they no longer held the same power over her. She had chosen to confront her emotions, to face the pain head-on, and to emerge from the other side stronger than ever.

After an hour or so of waiting, the soft chime of the doorbell broke the silence that had settled in Olive's home. Her curiosity piqued, she moved towards the door and hesitated for a moment before peeking through the small peephole. On the other side stood the same young girl she had encountered at the grocery store during her very first shopping trip in town.

Recognizing her instantly, Olive's lips curved into a warm smile. She remembered their brief but pleasant interaction at the store, where the girl had shared some local insights and even offered assistance with grocery shopping. Now, it seemed like fate had brought them back together.

With a sense of anticipation, Olive unlocked the door and swung it open to reveal the young girl standing there, holding a bag.

"Hey there," Olive greeted, her smile widening as their eyes met. "You must be the one with my grocery order, right?"

The girl's face lit up with recognition as well, and she nodded eagerly. "Yeah, that's me! I hope I got everything right."

Olive's gaze shifted to the bag in the girl's hands, and she chuckled. "Well, there's only one way to find out, right? Come on in." She stepped aside to allow the girl to enter, closing the door behind her.

As the girl carefully placed the bag on the kitchen counter, Olive's eyes scanned the items within. It was as if a piece of her daily life had been delivered to her doorstep – fruits, vegetables, pantry staples, and even a bouquet of fresh flowers that added a splash of color to her kitchen.

Olive turned to the girl, gratitude shining in her eyes. "Thank you so much for doing this. You have no idea how much I appreciate it."

The girl waved off her thanks with a casual smile. "Oh, it's no problem at all. Just doing my job."

Olive couldn't help but be touched by the sense of friendship that seemed to be a part of Serenity Falls. It was a stark contrast to the isolation she had experienced in her past. She found herself drawn to the authenticity of this town and its people. "Well, I'm truly grateful," Olive reiterated, sincerity lacing her words. "By the way, I never got to ask your name the other day."

The girl's smile turned into a friendly grin. "I'm Layla. Nice to officially meet you."

"Layla," Olive repeated, committing the name to memory. "I'm Olive. It's really nice to meet you too."

Layla kindly offered to help Olive unpack the groceries and restack the pantry. They chatted as they worked, and Olive couldn't help but find Layla's company delightful. "Thanks for lending a hand. You're a real lifesaver," Olive said gratefully.

"No problem at all. I'm happy to help," Layla replied with a cheerful grin. "Plus, it's nice to spend time with you, Olive."

Once the groceries were brought inside, Layla handed Olive the bill with a warm smile. Olive, always prompt with her responsibilities, settled the payment with a grin. "Here you go, Layla. All paid!" Olive said cheerfully, handing back the receipt.

Layla nodded, her eyes sparkling mischievously. "You know, Olive, if you keep buying all these groceries, you'll need to open a mini-mart right in your living room!"

Olive chuckled, playfully rolling her eyes. "Oh, Layla, you're probably right! But I can't resist trying out new recipes and treating myself to some guilty pleasures once in a while."

As they moved towards the kitchen, Layla couldn't help but tease Olive a bit more. "Well, then I expect a grand opening invitation for Olive's Food Haven!"

"Oh, absolutely! You'll be my first guest, Layla, and you'll get a lifetime discount!" Olive responded, pretending to be all business-like.

Layla laughed, pretending to swoon. "Oh, you're too kind! I'll be your most loyal customer, Olive."

They both burst into giggles, sharing a light-hearted moment. As they continued chatting and unpacking the groceries, Olive noticed Layla's eyes flickering to a particular item in the bag.

"Oh, don't even think about it," Olive said, wagging her finger. "Those chocolate chip cookies are off-limits, Layla. They're my secret stash for emergency cravings."

Layla feigned innocence, batting her eyelashes. "I was just admiring the packaging, I swear!"

"I've seen that look before," Olive teased. "You've got a sweet tooth that rivals mine."

With the groceries finally sorted, Olive offered Layla a seat at the dining table. "Would you like a drink before you head out, Layla? I can whip up my famous iced tea in no time!"

Layla grinned, settling into the chair. "Your iced tea is famous, huh? Then I must try it! Surprise me, Olive."

And so, Olive hurriedly prepared her signature iced tea, a concoction that had earned her praise from friends and family alike.

Olive poured out two glasses, and they sat down at the cozy kitchen table. "So, tell me more about yourself, Layla," Olive inquired warmly.

Layla took a sip of the drink before sharing, "Well, I live with my grandmother. My dad passed away when I was young, so it's just the two of us."

"I'm sorry to hear that," Olive said with genuine sympathy. "But it's lovely that you and your grandmother have each other."

"Yeah, we're really close," Layla replied, her eyes lighting up. "She's like my best friend."

Olive smiled, happy to see Layla's enthusiasm. "It's wonderful to have someone like that in your life. Family is so important," she remarked.

"Definitely," Layla agreed. "And what about you, Olive? Do you live alone?"

"Yeah, it's just me in this big old house," Olive chuckled. "I haven't had the chance to make many friends since I moved here."

"Well, now you have one!" Layla exclaimed, raising her glass as if to toast. "I'm your friend, Olive!"

Olive laughed, touched by Layla's warmth. "Thank you, Layla. I'm really glad we met."

"Me too!" Layla said happily. "We're going to have lots of fun together, I can tell."

As they chatted more about their lives and shared some funny stories, Olive couldn't help but feel a sense of excitement. The air buzzed with excitement, and Olive's heart skipped a beat. She couldn't believe how this chance meeting with Layla had turned into something so enjoyable.

Layla leaned forward, her eyes shining with mischief, and said, "You won't believe what happened to me last week. I accidentally sent a text meant for my crush to my boss! Can you imagine the embarrassment?"

Olive burst into laughter, clutching her stomach. "Oh no! What did your boss say?"

"He replied, 'I appreciate your dedication to your work, but I think this message was meant for someone else.' I wanted to crawl under my bed and hide forever!" Layla replied, blushing.

"Wow, that's something!" Olive chuckled. "But hey, at least you put your feelings out there, right? That takes some guts!"

They shared more funny mishaps and embarrassing moments, bonding over their shared sense of humor. As they laughed, Olive's heart warmed to Layla's easygoing and vivacious nature. She couldn't remember the last time she had such a delightful time with someone.

As the minutes passed, Layla suddenly exclaimed, "Woah, look at the time!" Her eyes flicked to her wristwatch, an old-looking piece, possibly a hand-me-down.

"I have to get back to work; my boss must be wondering where I am," Layla added, rising from the chair.

Olive grinned and replied, "Alright, off you go! Don't let them catch you slacking!"

Layla chuckled, "Oh, I won't. See you later, Olive!" She waved and bid her goodbye before heading out the door.

With Layla's departure, Olive found herself back in the kitchen, and a sense of relief washed over her—a mood she hadn't experienced in days. Deciding to cook a roast, she prepped the chicken, seasoned it, and carefully placed it in the oven. Setting the timer, she excused herself to the bathroom, where she drew a soothing bath.

After the bath, she slipped into her coziest clothes and returned to the kitchen. The aroma of the roasted chicken filled the air, and she turned off the oven before using her oven gloves to take the perfectly cooked chicken out.

Carving a few succulent pieces, she arranged them on a dinner plate. To complement the dish, she sliced two pieces of sourdough bread, toasted them until they were golden and crispy, and added some fresh, juicy tomatoes to her plate. With her culinary masterpiece ready, she made her way to the dining table, feeling the anticipation of savoring the meal.

As she sat down, she noticed the bouquet of flowers she had purchased earlier, beautifully adorning the center of the table. A smile tugged at her lips as she thought about Layla, the new friend she had made that day. It dawned on Olive that Layla must have kindly placed the flowers in water while she wasn't looking. This gesture warmed her heart and added to the sense of comfort that surrounded her.

With a contented sigh, Olive savored every delicious bite, feeling grateful for the unexpected bond she had formed and the simple joys that life had brought her way that evening.

Later that evening, as Olive lay in bed, her thoughts drifted to Vaughn. She hoped that their love could endure any challenges that came their way, just like the characters in the romance thrillers she adored.

***

In another part of the town, inside a dimly lit motel room, Nina lay sprawled on the lumpy and uncomfortable bed, her mind plagued by haunting memories of Elle. The recollections flooded back vividly, like an old movie reel playing on repeat. But one particular night stood out the most, etched into her memory as if it had just happened yesterday.

It was the night when Hector, Elle's boyfriend, had lost control, his hands wrapping around Nina's throat, attempting to choke the truth out of her. As the horrifying scene played out in her mind once again, she could still hear Elle's furious voice echoing in her ears, accusing her of being a liar. "Hector would never do that," Elle had vehemently shouted, refusing to believe the darkness that lurked beneath his surface.

The nightmare had a tight grip on Nina's subconscious, refusing to let go. She tossed and turned restlessly, the sheets tangled around her, as if mirroring the turmoil within her heart. The room felt suffocating, and beads of sweat formed on her forehead, betraying the intensity of her fear.

As the first light of dawn began to seep through the curtains, Nina's eyes snapped open. Her chest heaved with each ragged breath, and she struggled to shake off the lingering unease. It was then that she heard a soft knock on her door.

"Nina? Its me." came Daniel's gentle voice from outside the room.

Nina rushed to open the door, "Hey, good morning."

Daniel noticed the sweat beads on Nina's temple. "You okay?" He had sensed her unease, and concern filled his eyes as he stepped inside with fresh coffee and breakfast.

Nina forced a weak smile, trying to mask the terror that still clung to her. "Just a nightmare," she replied, her voice shaky as she sat back on the bed.

Daniel put down the food at the table and sat down beside her on the bed, offering a reassuring presence. "Do you want to talk about it?"

Nina hesitated for a moment before opening up to him. She recounted the harrowing memories that had tormented her in the night, the fear of Hector and the pain of losing her trust on Elle. Daniel listened attentively, his eyes filled with empathy.

"It's not your fault, Nina," he said softly, taking her hand in his. "Sometimes, people refuse to see the truth, even if it's right in front of them. You did the right thing by speaking up, even if it cost you so much."

Tears welled up in Nina's eyes, and she leaned into Daniel's comforting embrace. In his arms, she found solace and warmth, a sanctuary from the storm of emotions that raged inside her.

"Hey, I have something that will cheer you up," Daniel said softly as he comforted her. Nina looked up at him, her eyes searching for a glimmer of hope. "What is it? Did you find something else?"

"No, but guess who is going to the Mayor's daughter's wedding tomorrow?" Daniel asked with a smile.

"Who?" Nina inquired, curious about the sudden change of topic.

"Us, we are going," Daniel replied, his eyes shining with excitement.

"Come on, Daniel, you know I hate weddings. That's something that has never changed since high school," Nina said, pulling away gently. She walked over to the table and took a sip of the coffee he had brought for her.

"But guess who else is going?" Daniel continued, following her to the table, holding his coffee cup. "Vaughn."

Nina's eyes widened in surprise, and a hint of intrigue danced across her face. "Wow, now you're talking. That's the perfect setting to ambush him into a confession. I only wish I had some time to do some recon. Perhaps following him?"

"Nina, no! You promised me you'll stay away from him," Daniel pleaded. "For now, he's the only suspect we have."

"Fine," Nina acquiesced, rolling her eyes playfully. "I'm starving, let's eat."

They settled down at the table, their minds still entangled in thoughts of the wedding and the elusive Vaughn. The air crackled with tension and the excitement of the chase. Daniel knew that Nina's determination was unwavering, and he admired her passion for justice.

After Daniel left, a restless Nina paced in her dimly lit motel room, unable to shake her racing thoughts. She had made a solemn promise to Daniel, vowing not to meet her brother-in-law Vaughn. But curiosity gnawed at her heart, and temptation got the best of her.

"Just a quick Google search," she whispered, trying to ease her conscience as she grabbed her laptop from the bag and plopped down on the cozy bed.

The glow of the laptop screen flickered across her face as Nina hesitated for a moment, her fingers dancing over the keyboard. Her heart pounded in her chest, torn between loyalty and the need to uncover the truth. With a deep breath, she surrendered to the allure of the forbidden search.

With determination, she typed in 'Vaughn Knight.' The search results loaded, and Nina's eyes scanned the snippets of information before her. It showed numerous individuals with the same name, so she added 'Vaughn Knight in Serenity Falls.' Suddenly, a relevant link appeared on the screen. It was Vaughn Knight's official website! There, his picture caught her eye.

In Serenity Falls, Vaughn was known as an author of romantic thrillers. Nina scrutinized his photo, wondering if he could be capable of murdering his wife.

"But appearances can be deceiving," she thought, knowing all too well that some murderers appear perfectly ordinary. Still, something about him seemed different, and she couldn't resist digging deeper into his life and his books.

Minutes stretched into what felt like hours, and Nina found herself immersed in Vaughn's online presence. Nina had eagerly downloaded all four of Vaughn Knight's books. To her amazement, one of them had already been turned into a movie.

"Wow, he must be fucking loaded," she mused, considering Elle's insurance money unnecessary, thereby crossing off money from the list of motives.

Once the books were safely stored on her device, Nina wasted no time in immersing herself in the world

Vaughn had crafted with his words. She curled up on the bed, her surroundings fading away as she delved into the first story. The glow of her tablet illuminated her face as she turned the virtual pages, ready to experience the depths of his storytelling.

As she delved deeper, she discovered that Vaughn's writing was as captivating as she had imagined. The narrative was rich with details, each sentence woven carefully to create a vivid tapestry of emotions, settings, and characters. His words painted a world that felt both eerie and enthralling.

However, as the plot unfolded, Nina's initial fascination began to blend with a sense of unease. The story was taking a darker turn than she had anticipated. A romantic couple in the narrative seemed to be gradually unraveling, their love transforming into something far more sinister. Nina's heart quickened with every chilling revelation.

Every murder described in the book sent shivers down her spine. The details were gruesome, the atmosphere thick with tension and foreboding. It was a stark contrast to the Vaughn she imagined – the kind and gentle man who had been a pillar of support for the community during the toughest times of his life.

Nina found herself engrossed in the story, unable to tear herself away even as the shadows of the plot grew darker. Vaughn's storytelling prowess was undeniable, and yet she couldn't shake off the growing discomfort that settled in the pit of her stomach. She began to wonder about the inspiration behind such a tale.

Hours passed by, the world outside growing dim as she continued to read. By the time she finished the first book, her mind was a swirl of emotions – admiration for Vaughn's skill, curiosity about the origins of his dark narratives, and an underlying sense of concern for the underlying themes he explored.

Setting her laptop aside, Nina sat back on the couch, deep in thought. She knew that fiction often mirrored the complexities of its creator's mind, and Vaughn's stories seemed to hold a piece of him that she hadn't encountered before. She wondered if he used his writing as an outlet for his thoughts and experiences.

"There's no way he could be innocent," she concluded, her mind racing with suspicion. That was when Nina made up her mind- it was probably time that she meet Vaughn Knight, her brother-in-law, for the very first time.

***

CHAPTER 8: HIDDEN IN THE DARK

Throughout the day, Nina found herself consumed by a growing sense of unease. The words from Vaughn's books lingered in her mind, and she couldn't shake the feeling that there was more to him than met the eye. Fueled by curiosity and a desire to understand, she decided to take matters into her own hands.

From her car, Nina trailed her brother-in-law's every move. She kept a safe distance, her heart pounding as she discreetly captured his actions on camera. It was an unusual role for her, the role of an investigator, but she was determined to uncover any hidden truths.

As Vaughn moved through his day, Nina watched with a keen eye. She documented his interactions, his destinations, and the subtle nuances of his behavior.

With each passing moment, her intrigue deepened – there was something about his actions that didn't quite align with the man she thought she knew.

One peculiar pattern emerged – Vaughn repeatedly drove past a particular photography studio. This detail was like a puzzle piece that didn't fit. Why would he keep returning to that place? What connection did he have to it? The more she thought about it, the more determined she became to get to the bottom of this mystery.

Driven by curiosity, she mustered the courage to enter the studio. Peering from outside, she caught sight of a captivating dark-haired woman within. Her heart fluttered with mixed emotions, as she couldn't help but wonder if this alluring stranger might be Vaughn's next target. The thought sent shivers down her spine.

In Nina's mind, there was already a haunting link between Vaughn and the women who had gone missing in their town. Swallowing her apprehension, she pushed open the door and stepped inside. The bell above the door chimed softly, announcing her arrival. The studio was bathed in soft, warm lighting, creating an atmosphere that contrasted with the tension bubbling within her.

Her eyes scanned the room and fell upon the subject of her curiosity – a strikingly beautiful woman engrossed in her work. The woman's fingers moved deftly over a camera, adjusting settings and capturing moments frozen in time. The air was charged with creativity and purpose, a stark contrast to the doubts swirling within Nina's mind.

In that moment, the woman looked up from her camera and met Nina's gaze. Their eyes locked for a brief moment, a silent exchange that conveyed a myriad of emotions. There was curiosity in the woman's eyes – a question of who this newcomer was – and there was something else, something deeper that Nina couldn't quite decipher.

Caught off guard, Nina quickly averted her gaze, her heart pounding. She felt like an intruder, invading a space that wasn't meant for her. Suddenly she sensed a knot in her stomach as she awkwardly tried to initiate a conversation.

"I used to live here, fifteen years ago," Nina shared, feeling a wave of nostalgia sweep over her.

The woman's eyes lit up with curiosity. "Oh, must be nice to walk down memory lane again," she replied, her voice tinged with friendliness. "So, what can I do for you today?"

Nina hesitated for a moment, but she knew she had to press forward. If she could save even one life, it would be a victory worth fighting for. "I'm Nina, Nina Santos," she introduced herself, extending her business card to the woman. "I am a journalist looking into the disappearances in this town."

The woman's surprise was evident, her eyebrows raising slightly. "Disappearances? This is the first time I'm hearing of it," she said, her tone tinged with concern.

Nina let out a heavy sigh, knowing she was about to reveal unsettling truths. "Well, consider this conversation, a heads up. People go missing here, almost every summer," she disclosed, her voice tinged with sadness and determination.

The woman's eyes widened, as she asked, "You mean women?" her voice trembling slightly.

Nina nodded gravely, sensing that the woman's suspicion was rising. There was more to her than met the eye, and Nina knew that there was something that she wasn't revealing.

The woman's expression shifted, and she seemed to be contemplating something. "I... I had no idea," she stammered, trying to regain her composure.

Nina could see the fear and uncertainty in the lady's eyes, and it only fueled her resolve to get to the bottom of these mysterious disappearances. "It's essential to shed light on this matter and find out what's really happening," she said firmly, the weight of her responsibility as a journalist settling on her shoulders.

The woman took a deep breath, composing herself. "If there's anything I can do to help, please let me know," she offered, a hint of vulnerability in her voice.

Nina nodded appreciatively, the initial tension between them starting to ease. "I'll keep that in mind," she replied, grateful for any assistance she could get.

Nina noticed how the woman fidgeted with the business card, clearly anxious. "Well, you've got my number now. If anything strange comes up, don't hesitate to give me a call," Nina assured her.

The woman nodded, still feeling uneasy as Nina turned to leave, her steps hurried and purposeful. The door closed softly behind her as she stepped out onto the sidewalk, the sound of the bell's ring still resonating in her ears. The encounter had left her with a mixture of emotions – unease, curiosity, and a growing sense of determination. She knew she had stumbled upon something significant, and her gut feeling urged her to trust her instincts.

With each step she took away from the studio, her

thoughts raced. She couldn't ignore the possibility that she had just discovered Vaughn's next target, especially considering the chilling nature of his books and her own suspicions about his recent behavior. She remembered the victims described in his novels – the intricate details of their lives, their habits, their passions – and a tremble ran down her back.

The cool breeze ruffled her hair, offering a momentary distraction from the intensity of her thoughts. But she couldn't escape the weight of what she felt she needed to do next. Her determination to protect those around her was unwavering, and if that meant keeping an eye on Vaughn, then so be it.

Her phone buzzed in her pocket, and she pulled it out to see a message from Daniel. He was asking about her day and whether she had made any progress on her outfit for the wedding. She hesitated for a moment, her fingers hovering over the keyboard. Then, she typed a quick response, "Not yet, but I'm onto something. Let's meet up at the venue."

As she sent the message, she couldn't help but wonder if Daniel would understand her growing unease and her need to pursue this lead. She knew she was treading on thin ice, venturing into a realm of potential danger, but she couldn't ignore her gut feeling. There was a fire within her, a determination to get to the truth, even if it meant confronting the darkness that might lie ahead.

As Nina walked away from the photography studio, her thoughts shifted from her recent encounter to the upcoming event – the Mayor's daughter's wedding. She realized with a jolt that she had nothing appropriate to wear for such an occasion. Her wardrobe consisted mainly of casual attire and work-related outfits. She needed something elegant and fitting for the grand celebration.

Turning on her heel, she headed towards a nearby thrift store. She pushed open the glass door, stepping into a world of vintage treasures and hidden gems. The store was filled with an array of clothing racks, each holding stories from the past waiting to be discovered.

Nina browsed through the racks, her fingers grazing over various fabrics and styles. She pulled out a few dresses, examining them under the store's dim lighting. A floral print dress caught her eye, but it didn't quite fit the formal vibe she was aiming for. As she continued her search, her heart skipped a beat when her fingers brushed against a fabric that felt exquisite – a rich, black cocktail dress with delicate lace detailing.

She carefully pulled the dress from the rack, holding it up to the light. The dress was stunning, a perfect blend of elegance and sophistication. The lace gracefully adorned the neckline and sleeves, while the fitted silhouette promised to flatter her figure. It was as if the dress had been waiting for her all along.

With the dress in hand, Nina headed towards the fitting rooms, her excitement growing. She slipped into the dress, her reflection in the mirror confirming that it was indeed a fantastic find. It fit her like a glove, enhancing her curves and making her feel confident.

As she admired herself in the mirror, the thought of the price tag crossed her mind. Thrift stores often held the allure of affordability, but she knew she still had to be mindful of her budget. With a determined expression, she carefully placed the dress back on its hanger and headed to the front of the store.

The shopkeeper, an older woman with a friendly smile, greeted Nina as she approached the counter. "Did you find something you liked, dear?" she asked.

Nina nodded, offering the hanger with the black dress. "Yes, this dress is perfect. Is it for sale?"

The shopkeeper inspected the dress, her eyes lingering on the lace detailing. "Ah, a fine choice, my dear. That's a special piece. How about I give it to you for $40?"

Nina hesitated, knowing that she had to stick to her budget. She summoned her bargaining skills and mustered a polite smile. "Could we do $30?"

The shopkeeper chuckled, clearly enjoying the negotiation. After a brief back-and-forth, they settled on a price of $35. Nina felt a sense of accomplishment as she handed over the money. With the exquisite black cocktail dress in her possession, she walked out of the thrift store with a mix of excitement and contentment.

*****

Olive's day at work seemed like it would be a breeze, but everything changed when a journalist stepped into her store. Clutching the journalist's card in her hand, Olive's thoughts drifted to the memory of Vaughn's murder board. The images of missing women, connected by an intricate web of strings and pins, had left an indelible impression on her mind. She had tried to push aside the doubts and suspicions that had crept into her thoughts, but encountering the journalist, had stirred those feelings once again.

Could Vaughn truly be innocent, as he claimed? Was he the caring, genuine man she had come to know, or was there a darker side lurking beneath the surface? Olive's heart ached with the weight of uncertainty. She desperately wanted to believe in him, to believe in their connection, but the doubt had taken root and was spreading like a shadow.

With a heavy sigh, Olive placed the journalist's

card inside her bag. She knew she couldn't ignore her intuition any longer. She needed to confront Vaughn about the questions that plagued her mind. The truth, no matter how painful, needed to be unveiled.

Olive's thoughts shifted from her doubts and uncertainties to the upcoming event—the wedding of the mayor's daughter. It was an occasion that held significance not only for the mayor's family but also for Olive herself, as it marked her first proper photography assignment since her arrival in the town.

With a sense of determination, Olive pushed aside the lingering doubts that had clouded her mind and focused on the task at hand. She had packed a simple yet elegant navy-blue knee-length dress that she had brought from home. Its classic design exuded a timeless charm that would blend in seamlessly with the wedding's ambiance.

As the soft strains of music played from her studio speakers, Olive's fingers moved deftly as she applied her makeup with precision. The soft hues accentuated her features without overpowering her natural beauty. Her dark hair cascaded in loose waves around her shoulders, framing her face in an ethereal glow.

The gentle rhythm of her heart began to shift, replacing her earlier unease with a flicker of excitement. She was stepping into a world that was entirely different from her own—a world of celebrations, smiles, and unity. The thought of capturing these moments through her lens rekindled her passion for photography, reminding her why she had chosen this path in the first place.

As she slipped into her dress, the fabric hugged her curves delicately, exuding a sense of confidence and grace. With a final glance in the mirror, Olive was pleased with her appearance. She had chosen simplicity, letting her natural radiance shine through.

The evening air held a hint of excitement as Olive gathered her equipment and locked up her studio. The town was already buzzing with preparations for the wedding, and the atmosphere was infectious. She took a deep breath, inhaling the anticipation and joy that seemed to permeate the very air around her.

As she made her way to the venue, Olive's thoughts were momentarily occupied with the task ahead. She had different things to occupy her mind tonight—a beautiful occasion to capture, moments of joy to freeze in time. And amidst it all, she was determined to uncover the truth about Vaughn and confront the lingering doubts that had been haunting her.

With her camera in hand and a renewed sense of

purpose, Olive stepped into the venue, ready to weave her magic through her lens and tell the story of a day filled with love and celebration.

As she readied her gear, memories of her recent move flickered through her mind. The quaint town had initially appeared welcoming, but as days passed, an air of mystery had enveloped it. The residents seemed to harbor secrets, and every street whispered untold tales. Yet, she couldn't let her curiosity consume her now. Tonight, she had a job to do.

***

The wedding venue was a sight to behold. The Mayor's beautiful home had been transformed into a breathtaking scene of celebration, adorned with intricate decorations and elegant floral arrangements. The air was filled with an electric buzz of excitement as guests and family members bustled about, making sure every detail was perfect for the impending ceremony.

Olive arrived at the venue several hours before the ceremony was set to begin. The golden rays of the setting sun cast a warm glow over the scene, enhancing the beauty of the surroundings. She walked up the grand pathway that led to the entrance, her camera slung over her shoulder, ready to capture all the precious moments of the big day.

The aroma of freshly cut flowers wafted through the air, mingling with the soft laughter and cheerful conversations of the guests. The sound of music floated from a nearby area where the band was setting up, adding a melodic backdrop to the atmosphere of anticipation.

Olive couldn't help but feel a flutter of excitement herself. This was her opportunity to showcase her skills, to capture the raw emotions and candid moments that made weddings so special. As a budding photographer, she thrived on these occasions, finding inspiration in her camera lens and the stories it could tell.

Walking through the venue, Olive observed the careful attention to detail that had gone into creating a picture-perfect setting. From the elegantly decorated tables to the exquisite floral centerpieces, every element had been meticulously planned to create an enchanting ambiance.

Inside the house, the atmosphere buzzed with a contagious energy. As Olive stepped through the threshold, she found herself in a whirlwind of activity and anticipation. The interior was elegantly adorned, with soft, muted colors and delicate floral arrangements that complemented the joyful ambiance.

Soon Olive spotted a group of bridesmaids

gathered inside a room, their laughter and chatter filling the air. They were surrounded by an array of elegant dresses, jewelry, and cosmetics, all carefully arranged in preparation for the momentous occasion.

Amanda, the radiant bride, was at the center of it all. Dressed in her stunning bridal gown, she emanated an aura of excitement and nervous anticipation. Her eyes sparkled with joy as her bridesmaids fussed over her, ensuring that every detail was perfect for her walk down the aisle.

Olive quietly approached the group, her camera ready to capture the candid moments that unfolded before her. She admired the friendship between Amanda and her bridesmaids, the shared laughter, and the heartfelt exchanges that showcased the genuine bond they shared. Olive greeted them with a warm smile, and Amanda's eyes sparkled with happiness when she saw her photographer.

"Olive, I'm so glad you're here to capture all these special moments," Amanda said, her voice filled with joy.

"Oh, Amanda, it's an honor to be part of your big day," Olive replied, feeling a sense of warmth in her heart.

As the bridesmaids helped Amanda adjust her

stunning wedding gown, the room was filled with laughter and chatter. Olive skillfully captured each smile, every touch, and the love that radiated between Amanda and her friends.

"Is everything going smoothly so far?" Olive asked, adjusting her camera settings.

"Yes, absolutely," Amanda replied, a touch of excitement and nervousness in her voice. "I can't believe it's finally happening!"

"Don't worry, Amanda, you look stunning, and everything will be perfect," Olive reassured her with a reassuring smile.

Amanda's eyes met Olive's, and she squeezed her hand appreciatively. "Thank you for being here with me today."

With a practiced eye, Olive began to frame shots in her mind—candid smiles, stolen glances, the intricate details of the bride's dress, and the anticipation etched on the faces of the bridesmaids. She moved around discreetly, capturing the pre-wedding jitters and joyful interactions that unfolded before her.

The outdoor area where the ceremony was to take place, buzzed with excitement. Olive adjusted her camera lens, taking in the enchanting atmosphere. And soon, the much-anticipated moment had arrived—the wedding ceremony itself, that symbolizes the commitment between Amanda Alvarez and Orlando Morgan.

The garden had transformed into a dreamy wonderland, was adorned with an array of fragrant flowers that released their delicate scents into the air. Twinkling fairy lights were delicately woven among the blooms, creating a magical ambiance that seemed straight out of a fairy tale. The sound of soft music wafted through the air, adding to the romantic atmosphere that enveloped the space.

Rows of pristine white chairs were neatly arranged, their elegant simplicity serving as the backdrop for the union of two hearts. Every detail had been meticulously planned, from the flower-laden arch that framed the altar to the delicate petals strewn along the aisle.

The atmosphere was charged with excitement and an overwhelming sense of joy as family and friends gathered to witness this beautiful union. The sun cast a warm glow over the scene, illuminating the garden with its golden light.

As the guests took their seats, their faces radiated with happiness and anticipation. Amanda's bridesmaids donned stunning dresses in shades of pastel, and Orlando's groomsmen looked dapper in their suits. It was a charming scene that perfectly encapsulated the love and support that surrounded the couple on their special day.

At the front of the aisle, the altar stood adorned with more flowers, that showcased the beauty that blossomed when two souls found each other. The gentle breeze carried the scent of the flowers, adding a touch of nature's own blessing to the ceremony.

As the soft melody of a piano filled the air, a sense of anticipation and joy swelled among the guests gathered in the garden. The vibrant hues of blooming flowers formed a natural tapestry, contrasting beautifully with the elegant white chairs that lined the aisle.

At the entrance of the garden, Mayor Alvarez, his heart brimming with pride and emotion, took his daughter Amanda's arm. Her smile was radiant, a reflection of the happiness that had enveloped her on this momentous day. Her wedding gown flowed gracefully as she walked, a vision of grace and beauty.

The guests' eyes were drawn to the sight of Amanda and her father making their way down the aisle. The gentle breeze played with Amanda's veil, creating an almost surreal effect as it fluttered behind her. Every step she took brought her closer to the love of her life, Orlando, who stood at the altar, his eyes locked onto hers.

Orlando, looking dashing in his sleek suit, radiated a mix of excitement and nerves as he awaited Amanda's arrival. His gaze never wavered from the path she walked, and his smile grew wider with each step she took. Their connection was intense, an unspoken understanding that surpassed any amount of words.

Mayor Alvarez guided his daughter toward Orlando, their journey symbolic of the trust and love that had been nurtured throughout Amanda's life. As they reached the altar, he gently placed Amanda's hand into Orlando's, a gesture that spoke volumes of his faith in their future together.

The ceremony started, and the officiant, his smile radiating warmth, began to speak tenderly about love and commitment. During the ceremony, Olive skillfully moved gracefully around the periphery, capturing every precious moment without causing any distractions. Her camera lens immortalized the love shared between the couple and the tears of happiness shed by their loved ones.

Amanda and Orlando gazed into each other's eyes, their hearts beating faster as they exchanged their heartfelt vows.

"Orlando, from the moment we met, I knew there was something special between us. You've brought so much joy and love into my life, and I promise to stand by your side through thick and thin, supporting you in all your endeavors."

"Amanda, you are my rock, my everything. You've shown me what true love is, and I promise to cherish you every day, making you laugh when you're sad and being there for you no matter what life throws our way."

The guests sat in awe, witnessing the love between Amanda and Orlando, and their eyes sparkled with joy as they listened to the beautiful promises made by the couple.

Amanda's eyes glistened with tears of happiness as she responded, "And I vow to make you smile, to be your confidante and your partner in every adventure, because with you, Orlando, I feel complete."

Orlando gently wiped away a tear from her cheek, whispering, "You already complete me, Amanda. I promise to always be your shoulder to lean on, to stand strong with you as we face the world together."

The guests looked on, captivated by the love shared between Amanda and Orlando. As they exchanged rings, a deep sense of unity and devotion enveloped the couple.

After the rings were exchanged, the officiant pronounced them husband and wife. The gathered crowd of guests erupted into a chorus of cheers and applause, their joy filling the garden with an electrifying energy. Orlando couldn't resist leaning in to steal a sweet kiss from his new bride, sealing their vows with love.

As the newlyweds turned to face their guests, the garden seemed to glow with an otherworldly radiance. The soft light of the setting sun cast a warm, golden hue over everything, creating an atmosphere that was both enchanting and magical.

In the midst of capturing the moment, a sudden gust of wind sent a chill throughout Olive's body. She couldn't shake the feeling that someone was watching her, lurking in the shadows. Shaking off the bizarre sensation, she focused on her work, capturing the heartfelt smiles and happy tears.

After the ceremony had concluded, Amanda and Orlando stole a precious moment away from the delighted crowd. Hand in hand, they walked along a secluded path that wandered through the garden, the soft rustling of leaves accompanying their steps. The sun painted a warm, golden glow across the scene, casting a romantic aura around them.

As they walked, Amanda couldn't help but steal

glances at her newlywed husband. His eyes held an affectionate light, and she felt a sense of completeness that warmed her heart. Orlando's gaze was fixed on her, his love and admiration evident in his expression. They paused by a blooming rosebush, its petals a vibrant shade of red, a symbol of their love's blossoming.

Orlando gently lifted a rose from the bush and presented it to Amanda with a smile. She accepted the delicate gift, her eyes sparkling with gratitude and joy. "I can't believe we're finally married," she said, her voice soft and filled with emotion.

He leaned in, his lips brushing against her forehead in a tender kiss. "I've dreamed of this moment for so long," Orlando replied, his voice carrying the weight of his own emotions.

They stood together, enveloped in a cocoon of love and serenity, sharing a few more quiet moments before the bustling energy of the reception beckoned them back. With intertwined fingers, they turned to rejoin the celebration, knowing that their journey as husband and wife had only just begun.

Back at the reception, the atmosphere was alive with music, laughter, and the clinking of glasses. The reception took place at the estate under a vast outdoor tent. Amanda and Orlando were greeted with warm embraces and congratulations from their friends and family. Their smiles radiated a happiness that was contagious, as they moved through the crowd, taking the time to engage with each guest.

Olive wandered around, capturing candid moments with her camera, when she spotted Vaughn. He appeared dashing in a three-piece suit. As their eyes met, Vaughn made his way over to Olive, and they engaged in a conversation.

"Hey, Olive," Vaughn greeted her with a warm smile.

"Hi, Vaughn," Olive replied, trying to keep her composure despite the memories that flooded back.

"Hey," he said softly, his voice carrying a hint of worry. "I've been trying to reach you. Are you okay?"

Olive offered a faint smile, though her eyes held a touch of apprehension. "Yeah, I'm okay."

It had been a while since they last saw each other. The memory of Olive running away from Vaughn's basement, filled with pictures of women pinned to a board, still haunted her. Vaughn sensed her unease and attempted to explain himself.

"Olive, I want to talk about what happened," he

began.

But before he could say more, Olive interjected softly, "I can't, Vaughn. Not now. I'm working."

Feeling overwhelmed, she excused herself and moved away from the conversation, seeking a moment alone to gather her thoughts and emotions. Vaughn watched her go, his heart heavy with regret for the past and uncertainty about their future.

Vaughn stood among the crowd, his stare was suddenly fixated on a stunning woman with auburn locks, who stood just a few steps away. It seemed as though she was glancing back at him too. A strange sensation washed over him, a feeling of familiarity. As he approached her cautiously, he couldn't shake off the thought that she bore an uncanny resemblance to his wife, Elle.

"Excuse me," Vaughn said softly, trying not to startle her. "I couldn't help but notice... you look remarkably like someone I know."

The woman's eyes met his, a spark of recognition flickering in them. "Do I now? And who might this person be?" she asked, her voice gentle and warm.

Vaughn's heart raced, unsure if he should share the details. However, he found himself drawn to her, compelled to confide in a stranger. "Her name is Elle. My wife, actually."

Her expression softened, and she offered a small, understanding smile. "Your wife must be a beautiful woman, then."

Vaughn nodded, his mind buzzing with questions. "Yes, she was."

"I'm so sorry to hear that," she replied, a touch of sadness in her eyes.

"It's alright," Vaughn said, his emotions beginning to stir. "I still miss her every day, though."

Her genuine empathy brought a sense of comfort to Vaughn, as if he could share his pain with her without judgment. "Sometimes, I feel like I see her in random places, in other people. It's strange."

She nodded in understanding. "Grief works in mysterious ways. We often find fragments of those we've lost in the most unexpected moments."

Vaughn felt a connection with her, something he hadn't felt in a long time. "Thank you for listening," he said gratefully.

"What happened to your wife?" she inquired, her

voice gentle but filled with intrigue.

Vaughn hesitated for a moment, the memories of last summer still haunting him. "My wife went missing," he finally replied, his tone tinged with sadness.

The woman's eyes widened with interest. "And what did the police say about it?" she asked, genuinely concerned.

"Nothing much," Vaughn sighed, "they're still investigating. But it's been months, and I fear it might turn into a cold case."

Understanding his pain, the woman nodded empathetically. "That must be incredibly tough for you," she said softly.

Vaughn managed a weak smile, appreciating her compassion. "It's been a nightmare," he admitted.

The woman's demeanor shifted suddenly, her tone becoming more direct. "So, did you do it?" she asked, her eyes piercing into his soul.

Vaughn was taken aback by the blunt question, feeling a mixture of shock and offense. "Excuse me?" he stammered, disbelief etched across his face.

Undeterred, the woman leaned back, crossing her arms as she maintained her intense gaze. "Did you kill your wife?" she repeated, unapologetically blunt.

Astonished, he stammered out an indignant response, "What the fuck?" He couldn't believe a stranger would accuse him of such a thing.

But the woman didn't back down; she persisted with her probing questions. Vaughn attempted to leave the uncomfortable conversation, but she followed him outside the tent, determined to get answers.

"Tell me the truth, Vaughn. Did you kill her? And what about the other missing women? Did you have something to do with them too?" she accused, referring to the other unsolved cases.

Frustrated and taken aback, Vaughn turned around to confront her. "Look, lady, you have no idea what you're talking about," he retorted, feeling unjustly accused.

The revelation that followed left Vaughn speechless. Nina revealed her identity, and he was shocked to learn that she was his sister-in-law, Elle's younger sister. Vaughn remembered Elle mentioning that she had a sister who had run away from home years ago, but he had no idea it was Nina.

"Nina?" he uttered, disbelief written all over his face.

"Yeah, that's me," Nina responded bitterly, raising her arm in despair. "I'm your freaking sister-in-law."

Vaughn's mind raced with a mixture of emotions - surprise, guilt, and confusion. He didn't know how to respond to this unexpected connection with Nina. The accusations and the sudden revelation had thrown him off balance, and he realized he needed to handle the situation delicately.

"I swear, Nina, I had nothing to do with Elle's disappearance or the other missing women," Vaughn said earnestly, trying to reassure her. "I loved Elle, and I always have. All this time, I've been searching for her."

But Nina remained composed, her expression unwavering. "I'm sorry, but I've learned to trust my instincts," she replied calmly. "There's something about you that doesn't add up. I need to know the truth."

Vaughn couldn't believe what he was hearing. "How could you even think that?" he retorted, his voice tinged with anger. "I loved my wife! I would never harm her or anyone else!"

Vaughn felt a surge of frustration, but he also sensed that his sister-in-law wasn't just trying to provoke him. There was genuine concern in her eyes, as strange as the situation was. Taking a deep breath, he decided to open up, hoping that by sharing his side of the story, he could finally put these suspicions to rest.

"Look, I understand that I might appear suspicious," Vaughn began, his voice softer now. "But I loved your sister, more than anything. She was my whole world. The day she went missing, we had an argument, and she stormed out. I haven't seen her since."

Nina listened intently, her guarded demeanor slowly softening. "And you didn't follow her, or try to find her?"

"I did," Vaughn admitted. "I searched everywhere, asked around, and even hired a private investigator. But there were no leads. It's like she vanished without a trace."

From her vantage point, Olive's eyes caught sight of a commotion not far away. Her heart skipped a beat when she recognized Vaughn's form engaged in a heated argument with a woman. The tension in the air was palpable, their gestures animated and their voices raised.

Instinctively, Olive's initial reaction was to rush toward them, to intervene or at least understand what was happening. But as a photographer, she knew the importance of capturing moments—both joyous and tense—that told a story. With her camera in hand, she hesitated, realizing that this could be an important moment to document.

Suppressing the urge to intervene, Olive made a conscious decision to stay back and capture the unfolding scene through her lens. She adjusted the settings on her camera and focused her gaze on Vaughn and the mysterious woman. The fiery exchange seemed to be laden with emotions, the woman's gestures expressive as she spoke, while Vaughn's stance radiated a mix of frustration and determination.

As the argument continued, Olive's camera clicked discreetly, capturing the raw intensity of the moment. The tension and conflict were laid bare in the photographs she was capturing. With each click of the shutter, Olive felt a sense of detachment from the situation, allowing her to focus on her role as an observer and documentarian.

Eventually, the argument seemed to reach a point of culmination, and the woman turned and walked away with a parting glance over her shoulder. Vaughn stood there for a moment, his expression a mix of emotions. Olive continued to capture these moments, recognizing that this might be an essential stage in their story.

With the altercation over, Olive finally lowered her camera, her heart racing. She knew that she couldn't stay in the shadows forever; eventually, she would need to address the situation with Vaughn. But for now, she chose to let the images she had captured speak for themselves.

***

The wedding celebration continued into the night, with laughter, dancing, and heartfelt toasts to the future of Amanda and Orlando. They made sure to spend time with each of their guests, thanking them for being part of their special day. The love and support from their friends and family filled their hearts with warmth.

As the evening progressed, Amanda and Orlando found themselves at the center of the dance floor, swaying to a romantic melody. Their bodies moved in sync, their eyes locked on each other as if they were the only two people in the room.

With every twirl and dip, their connection grew stronger. The love that had brought them together was celebrated by their loved ones, and the joy of their union filled the space around them. The stars above seemed to shine a little brighter that night, as if they were offering their blessings to the newlyweds.

As the night came to a close, Amanda and Orlando shared a final dance, their arms wrapped around each other in a sweet embrace.

The song played on, and in that moment, time seemed to stand still. They held each other close, cherishing the memories they had created on this magical day.

And when the night sky spread its velvety blanket dotted with stars, Orlando and Amanda stepped out of the reception hall, their hearts still filled with the warmth of the love they had just celebrated. The air was cool and crisp, a gentle breeze rustling through the trees. They paused at the edge of the path, turning to look back at the place where their journey as husband and wife had officially begun.

The reception venue was now illuminated by multi-colored fairy lights that danced in the darkness, casting a soft and enchanting glow. Laughter and music still echoed in the distance, a reminder of the joyful moments they had shared with their loved ones. Amanda's hand found its way into Orlando's, their fingers intertwining as they exchanged a knowing smile.

"It was a perfect day," Amanda whispered, her voice carrying the magic of the evening.

Orlando nodded, his gaze fixed on her. "And it's just the beginning," he replied, his eyes holding a promise of a lifetime ahead.

They turned away from the venue, heading towards Orlando's car that awaited them. The soft purr of the engine seemed to resonate with their own heartbeat, a symbol of the journey they were embarking upon.

"I couldn't have asked for a more perfect day," Amanda said, leaning against Orlando's shoulder as they walked towards their car.

"Agreed," he replied, pressing a gentle kiss on her forehead. "But you know, the best part is that our love story is just beginning."

Amanda looked up at him, her eyes shining with love, "And I can't wait to see where this story takes us, Orlando."

Orlando opened the door for Amanda, and she slid into the passenger seat with a graceful smile.

As Orlando took his place behind the steering wheel, they shared a moment of quiet anticipation. The engine roared to life, and the car began to move, carrying them away from the celebration. The world outside the windows seemed to blur into a canvas of darkness, a fitting backdrop to their thoughts and emotions.

Orlando stole a glance at Amanda, his heart swelling with gratitude for the woman beside him. "Are you ready for this adventure, Mrs. Morgan?" he asked, his tone filled with affection.

Amanda's gaze met his, her eyes shimmering with a mixture of happiness and excitement. "More than ready," she replied, her voice steady and resolute.

***

CHAPTER 9: THE DAY AFTER

The morning after their beautiful wedding, Orlando opened his eyes to find the bed empty beside him. Instantly, a flicker of confusion and a tinge of worry set in, pulling at his heart like an invisible thread. He stretched his arms and stifled a yawn, assuming that Amanda might have risen early to start the day.

With hopeful anticipation, Orlando swung his legs over the side of the bed and stood up, his bare feet meeting the cool floor. He glanced around the room, half-expecting to catch a glimpse of her somewhere nearby. However, as moments turned into minutes, it became evident that Amanda was not within their shared space.

A furrow formed on Orlando's forehead as he stepped out of the bedroom, his pace quickening with each passing second. He navigated through the house, moving from room to room, his senses heightened in his search for his beloved wife. The usually familiar surroundings now seemed to carry an air of mystery, as if they held the secret to her whereabouts.

The living room remained silent, devoid of any sign of her presence. The kitchen, too, stood empty, the countertop neatly arranged as if waiting for her touch. The worry that had initially stirred within him now blossomed into a more pronounced feeling. He reached for his phone, dialing her number with growing urgency. However, it went unanswered, the call sent straight to voicemail.

His thoughts raced as he considered the possibilities. Could she have gone for a morning walk? Or perhaps there was an unexpected errand that required her attention? As he stepped outside onto the porch, the fresh morning air greeted him, carrying with it a sense of unease. The world outside seemed to hold no answers, leaving Orlando in a state of uncertainty.

As he re-entered the house, his steps were more measured, his mind working to piece together the puzzle. He couldn't shake off the feeling that something was amiss. A distant memory surfaced, reminding him of the vows they had exchanged just yesterday—the promise to stand by each other's side through thick and thin. With renewed determination, Orlando realized that he couldn't let his worry consume him. He needed to find her, to assure himself that she was safe and sound.

With a steadying breath, he picked up his phone again, his fingers typing out a quick message to her. "Amanda, where are you? Everything okay?" He hit send and held his breath, waiting for the telltale sound of her reply. As the seconds ticked by, he hoped that their love and the connection they shared would bridge the distance between them, reassuring him that she was just a message away.

Panic started to creep in as he reached for his phone and dialed her number. He pressed the phone to his ear, listening intently for the familiar ringtone, but all he got was an automated voice telling him that the number he dialed was unreachable. His heart sank, and he felt a tight knot forming in his stomach. Where could she be?

With a mix of fear and desperation, he decided to call the Mayor – his new father-in-law. He could feel his pulse quickening as he listened to the ringing tone on the other end. Finally, after what seemed like an eternity, Mayor Alvarez's voice crackled through the line.

"Orlando, is everything alright?" Mayor Alvarez's concerned voice filled the air.

Orlando's throat felt tight, but he managed to

speak. "Mayor Alvarez, I... I can't find her. She's not here, and her phone is unreachable."

There was a brief pause on the other end, and Orlando could almost picture the Mayor's worried expression. "Stay at the house, Orlando. I'm on my way over. We'll figure this out together."

Hanging up, Orlando felt a mixture of relief and anticipation. He paced around the house, his thoughts racing. What could have happened? A million scenarios played out in his mind, each one more terrifying than the last. He knew he had to stay strong, for her, and for himself.

Within moments, the faint sound of a car engine reached Orlando's ears, drawing his attention to the window. He peered out, his gaze fixing on the driveway as a vehicle came to a stop. His heart quickened as he recognized the figure stepping out – Mayor Alvarez, followed closely by a face he knew all too well – Deputy Turner. A wave of puzzlement washed over him, furrowing his brows in a mixture of confusion and concern. Why would the deputy be accompanying the mayor, and what could bring them to his doorstep?

Orlando's mind raced, thoughts intertwining as he tried to make sense of the unexpected visit. He scanned the scene before him, the knot of uncertainty in his chest growing tighter. He watched as Mayor Alvarez exchanged a few words with Deputy Turner, their demeanor carrying a sense of seriousness that didn't escape his notice.

Orlando opened the door just as Mayor Alvarez and Deputy Turner reached the porch. The Mayor's face was a mix of concern and determination, while Deputy Turner's expression was unreadable as usual.

"Orlando, we're going to do everything we can to find her," Mayor Alvarez said firmly, placing a reassuring hand on Orlando's shoulder.

Orlando nodded, his throat still tight with worry. "Thank you, Mayor."

Deputy Turner finally spoke, his voice calm and measured. "We're going to need some information from you. When was the last time you saw her? Did she mention anything to you? Any possible reason she might have left?"

Orlando had recounted to Deputy Turner the details of the previous night when he and Amanda had gone to bed. They were together, as usual. The connection between them was undeniable, and the warmth of their togetherness was something Orlando cherished. Their shared laughter and whispered promises filled the air, creating a bubble of love that wrapped around them.

Deputy Turner, a diligent and seasoned officer, took it upon himself to investigate the situation. He combed through the surroundings, his trained eyes picking up on the subtlest of clues. It wasn't long before he noticed the absence of Orlando's car from the garage. His curiosity piqued, he turned to Orlando and asked with a furrowed brow, "Where's your car, Orlando?"

Orlando's shock was palpable. His eyes widened as he realized that something might be amiss. "I don't know," he stammered, his voice tinged with worry. "We came back from the wedding last night, and I distinctly remember parking the car in the garage."

Deputy Turner, with a reassuring tone, offered a possible explanation. "Amanda might have gone out to run some errands, maybe to get groceries or something. Don't jump to conclusions just yet." He could see the anxiety in Orlando's eyes and hoped to alleviate some of his distress.

With a sense of responsibility, Deputy Turner reached for his radio and called dispatch. His voice was steady and professional as he explained the situation and requested a patrol of the area. The dispatcher acknowledged his request, promising to keep an eye out for any sign of Amanda or Orlando's car.

As they waited in the cozy living room, the tension was palpable. Orlando fidgeted, his thoughts racing with worry for Amanda's safety. The silence was broken when Mayor Alvarez, placed his hands over Orlando's shoulders.

"Orlando, how are you holding up?" Mayor Alvarez's voice was kind, his presence a calming influence in the room.

Orlando managed a weak smile. "I'm worried sick, Mayor. Amanda and I have never been apart like this without letting each other know."

Mayor Alvarez placed a reassuring hand on Orlando's shoulder. "We'll find her, Orlando. This is a tight-knit community, and there are eyes and ears everywhere. Deputy Turner is doing everything he can."

In the midst of the tense atmosphere, a sudden crackle pierced the air, and Deputy Turner's radio buzzed to life. The voice of dispatch filtered through, carrying a mix of urgency and information. The words hit the room like a jolt – Amanda's car had been discovered abandoned in a nearby parking lot. The collective tension that had gripped the space was replaced by a rush of relief, a shared breath held collectively now released.

The news brought a fleeting moment of breather, a glimmer of hope that Amanda's whereabouts might be closer to resolution. Yet, as quickly as the relief settled in, it gave way to a fresh wave of concerns that crashed over them. Questions arose – Why was her car abandoned? Where was Amanda now? The room buzzed with renewed speculation, anxiety, and a collective desire to find answers.

Deputy Turner's expression shifted, his brows furrowing as he processed the information. His eyes met Orlando's, a silent acknowledgment that their situation had evolved yet again. The presence of the mayor and his new son-in-law now carried a sense of urgency, a need for immediate action to unravel the mystery surrounding Amanda's disappearance.

Orlando's voice trembled as he asked, "What does this mean, Deputy?"

Deputy Turner exchanged a meaningful glance with Mayor Alvarez before responding. "It means we need to start a thorough investigation, Orlando. We'll find out where Amanda is, no matter what it takes."

As the evening shadows deepened, a sudden crackle shattered the quiet, filling the room with Deputy Turner's resolute voice. Through the radio's static, his instructions rang out, directing his fellow patrol officers to methodically sweep through the parking lot. Each word was imbued with a sense of urgency, a call to action that resonated deeply with every member of the team.

The stillness of the room was replaced by a palpable energy, an unspoken understanding that time was of the essence.

The weight of the situation hung heavy, propelling everyone outside into motion. With every step the officers took, the determination to find Amanda only grew stronger, a shared purpose binding them together.

Patrol officers fanned out, their flashlights piercing the gathering darkness. Every corner, every shadow was meticulously inspected, each searching eye seeking any trace of Amanda's presence. The crunch of footsteps on gravel, the soft hum of radios, and the rustle of leaves in the wind created a symphony of focused efforts.

The urgency of the moment fueled their resolve, driving them to examine every inch of the parking lot and its surrounding perimeter with meticulous care. A collective determination to bring Amanda home safe pushed them forward, dispelling any weariness that threatened to settle in. In the middle of the search, time seemed to stand still, each passing second an affirmation of their commitment to the task at hand.

Back at Orlando's house, the air was thick with anticipation as they waited for updates over the radio. A collective tension hung in the room, a mixture of hope and apprehension mingling within the officers' voices.

When the radio crackled to life once more, their words carried a weight of both resignation and sorrow.

Through the radio waves, the officers conveyed their findings to Deputy Turner, their voices a melancholia of disappointment. Despite their exhaustive search, Amanda was still missing. Their reports painted a vivid picture of their efforts – the thorough inspection of every nook and cranny, the meticulous scrutiny of surroundings – all resulting in the same disheartening conclusion: Amanda was nowhere to be found.

Her car, a silent witness to her disappearance, had been left unlocked, sitting there in the lot, its gas tank emptied. The ignition held the keys, a perceptible reminder of a drive that halted abruptly. But Amanda's presence, once vibrant and full of life, had seemingly vanished.

Deputy Turner's expression tightened, his brow furrowing with worry and confusion. He exchanged glances with Mayor Alvarez and Orlando, the gravity of the situation pressing heavily upon them all. This was far from an ordinary missing person's case; it was as if Amanda had vanished into thin air, leaving behind only unanswered questions.

Turning towards Orlando, Deputy Turner cleared his throat, the weight of his words mirrored in his eyes. "Orlando," he began, his voice calm but tinged with concern, "we've searched the area thoroughly, but there's no trace of Amanda. Her car ran out of gas, keys still in the ignition, but no sign of her belongings. It's possible that she's... missing."

Orlando's eyes widened in shock, the news hitting him like a tidal wave. He took a step back, his mind struggling to process the sudden turn of events.

"I can't believe this," Orlando muttered, his voice barely above a whisper. "She was just here, and now... she's gone?"

Deputy Turner nodded gravely, his features etched with a mixture of empathy and determination. "We're going to do everything we can to find her, Orlando. We'll start a search party, expand our efforts. But we need to act fast."

But soon, tension filled the air like an unspoken truth. Mayor Alvarez, with a mix of anguish and anger in his eyes, confronted Orlando about his daughter's sudden disappearance. Deputy Chief Turner stood beside the mayor, a stern expression on his face as he awaited Orlando's response.

"I swear, Mayor Alvarez, I have no idea where Amanda is," Orlando insisted, his voice trembling with emotion. "We had a beautiful wedding yesterday, and everything seemed perfect. But this morning, she was just gone."

Mayor Alvarez's jaw tightened, and he shook his head. "You expect us to believe that? You two were the last ones seen together last night. What happened after the wedding?"

Orlando ran his fingers through his hair, trying to collect his thoughts. "We celebrated at the reception, danced, and laughed together. But as soon as we got home, Amanda seemed a bit distant. I thought she might have been tired from all the wedding stress, so I didn't think much of it. We said goodnight and went straight to bed, and that was it."

Deputy Chief Turner crossed his arms, studying Orlando's face carefully. "And you didn't hear or see anything suspicious during the night? No unexpected visitors, noises, or strange occurrences?"

"No, nothing," Orlando replied, frustration evident in his voice. "I woke up alone, and when I couldn't find her, I texted her, but there was no reply."

Mayor Alvarez glanced at Deputy Chief Turner before turning his attention back to Orlando. "Son, you have to understand the gravity of this situation. My daughter is missing, and you were the last person with her. We need answers, and we need them now."

"I want to help, Mayor Alvarez. I love Amanda, and I would never do anything to hurt her," Orlando said, his eyes welling up with tears. "Please, let me assist in finding her."

The mayor's expression softened slightly, and he sighed heavily. "Alright."

A wave of relief washed over Orlando.

"But," the mayor continued, "you will need to come down to the station with Deputy Turner, where the police will interview you in greater detail."

"But, Mayor, that's not necessary!" Deputy Chief Turner interjected. "We have everything we need from him already."

"I don't care, Turner," Mayor Alvarez said. "I want to know if anything suspicious happened the night before, or if Orlando is lying in any way."

"That's ridiculous! I told you what happened, and I have nothing to hide!" Orlando said, his frustration and anxiety rising.

"Mayor Alvarez is right," Deputy Turner replied. "Please come down to the station to give your statement.

Orlando stood in silence as Mayor Alvarez and Deputy Chief Turner made their way to the door, leaving him alone in the living room. He found himself standing in silence, his gaze fixed on the doorway through which the visitors had just departed. The living room was now empty, leaving him alone with his thoughts. Collapsing onto the couch, he allowed himself to sink into its soft cushions, his head hanging low. The weight of the situation pressed heavily on his chest.

His heart drummed in his ears, its rhythm muddled and disoriented. The tension in the room seemed to have a life of its own, wrapping around him like a suffocating embrace. With a heavy exhale, he released the breath he hadn't realized he'd been holding, as if he was finally letting go of some of the burden.

Lifting his head a moment later, his weary eyes shifted to the mantel that adorned the space above the fireplace. It was a place of prominence, a spot reserved for cherished memories and captured moments frozen in time. And there, amidst the carefully arranged trinkets, stood a photograph of Amanda.

Time seemed to stand still as his gaze locked onto her image. It was a simple photograph, capturing her radiant smile and the sparkle in her eyes. The kind of smile that could brighten even the darkest corners of his world. But now, as he stared at her frozen likeness, a chill swept through him, prickling at his skin like icy fingers.

Amanda, where are you? The thought whispered through his mind like a haunting refrain. It was a question that had plagued him since the moment she had disappeared. The memories of their laughter, their shared dreams, and the warmth of her presence flooded his thoughts. Each memory was a bittersweet reminder of what he was missing, of the uncertainty that had replaced the joy they had once known.

Instinctively, he walked over to the mantle and reached out a trembling hand, his fingertips grazing the edge of the photograph. For a moment, he imagined he could feel her there, as if the very essence of her lingered in the room. His chest tightened, a mixture of longing and frustration washing over him.

As he withdrew his hand, he let his fingers linger against his lips, a gesture born from a deep-rooted need to hold onto her memory. The photograph remained before him, a silent witness to the ache in his heart. He knew he couldn't rest until he had answers, until he could unravel the mystery of her disappearance.

"I'm not staying here while they interrogate me! They're just going to accuse me of kidnapping Amanda. I need to get away from this place!" Orlando whispered to himself. "I'm going to find her!"

The room was quiet, save for the distant sounds of the city filtering through the windows. The photograph was a reminder that he couldn't stand still, that he couldn't let himself be consumed by uncertainty.

***

Daniel sat in his dimly lit private detective agency office, his fingers tapping idly on the mahogany desk. His mind was a labyrinth of thoughts, each path leading to the same unsettling destination—the growing number of missing women in his town. The local authorities seemed overwhelmed, and his gut told him there was a connection waiting to be unraveled.

His pondering was abruptly shattered by the jarring ring of his phone. He snatched it up, a frown etching across his face at the unfamiliar number. Before he could speak, a weird silence hung on the line. Suspicion tugged at him, and he was ready to disconnect when a voice, hushed and tense, cut through the quiet.

"Daniel Turner, my wife is missing."

His heart quickened at the urgency in the voice. This was the call he'd been both expecting and dreading. The call that would lead him into the heart of another puzzle, another life in confusion.

"Tell me more," he responded, his hand instinctively reaching for a pen and notepad, his senses sharpening.

The voice on the other end sounded shaky but resolute. "Can you come and meet me at my home? I don't think I am allowed to say anything over the phone."

His pen poised above the pad, Daniel nodded, his lips moving in silent agreement. "Alright, send me your address. I'll be there."

The caller hung up without another word, leaving Daniel staring at the phone for a brief moment. A few seconds later, a text notification popped up, revealing the location. He didn't need to cross-reference it to know whose address it was. Orlando Morgan—the new son-in-law of the Mayor. Daniel's mind clicked into overdrive. There was only one reason Orlando would be contacting him like this. Amanda Alvarez was missing.

Daniel's mind drifted back to the moment Amanda had walked into his office, a whirlwind of determination and concern. Her request had caught him off guard, her fervor igniting a spark of familiarity. Their history together lent an air of solidarity to their present encounter. As their eyes met, memories resurfaced from years gone by, when he had been a part of her father's mayoral campaign. A smile played at the corners of Daniel's lips as he recalled the amusing moments they had shared during those campaign days. Amanda's fire had remained unchanged, her spirited personality intact.

"Daniel Turner, the detective," Amanda had quipped, her eyes sparkling with amusement as she took in his office.

He had leaned back in his chair, offering a playful grin. "Amanda Alvarez, the mayor's daughter. To what do I owe the pleasure?"

Their conversation had flowed effortlessly, the years apart melting away as they reminisced about the ups and downs of her father's mayoral election trail. Amanda's determination to make a difference had resonated with him then, just as it did now.

"I need your help," Amanda had said, her expression serious as she recounted the unsettling series of events in their town – a string of disappearances that had left everyone on edge.

Daniel's eyebrows had furrowed, concern replacing his initial amusement. "You think they are related?"

Amanda's nod had been resolute, her gaze unwavering. "Yes. I've been researching, digging into each case. There's a pattern, Daniel. Something's not right here."

Now, months later, as he sat alone in his office, with Amanda's face etched in his memory, Daniel couldn't help but marvel at the twists and turns that life brought. From campaign trails to missing person cases, their paths had converged once more

Daniel's heart raced as he dialed Nina's number. The phone rang only a couple of times before she answered, her voice carrying a hint of curiosity, "Yeah?"

"It happened again," Daniel blurted out, his words tumbling over each other in his haste to explain the situation.

Nina's voice crackled with disbelief, "What?

Again?"

His grip tightening on the phone, Daniel nodded as if she could see him. "Yes, I can't believe it either. But I need you here with me. Get dressed, I'm coming to pick you up."

Nina's mind raced to grasp the situation. These unexpected twists seemed to be never-ending lately. She could almost see Daniel's determined expression, his brow furrowed in worry, even though they were miles apart.

"Okay, give me a few minutes," Nina replied, already mentally sorting through her suitcase for something suitable to wear for whatever awaited them this time.

At the motel, Nina carefully selected her outfit, ensuring every detail was just right. She folded her clothes with precision and packed her trusty camera and notepad into her bag. The excitement in her heart made her hands tremble slightly as she double-checked everything. She glanced at the watch on her wrist and realized that she was now waiting for Daniel.

Nina's thoughts were interrupted by the sound of a car pulling up outside the motel. She glanced out the window and saw Daniel's familiar car, engine running and headlights illuminating the night.

Stepping outside, Nina met Daniel's worried gaze as he leaned over to open the passenger door for her. She slid into the seat, and he gave her a quick, reassuring smile before pulling away from the curb.

"Hey, Nina," he said, his voice a comforting melody.

"Hi, Daniel," she replied, trying to sound casual but failing to hide her excitement.

He looked handsome in a casual shirt and jeans, a stark contrast to the rugged charm he usually exuded. They had been through so much together in the past few days, uncovering secrets that had led them to this moment.

The drive was silent at first, each lost in their thoughts, until Nina couldn't bear the silence any longer. "Do we even know who is missing?"

Daniel sighed, his grip on the steering wheel tightening. "Not yet. We best wait before we jump in to conclusions."

Nina nodded, a mixture of anxiety and determination settling in her chest. She reached over and squeezed Daniel's hand, the warmth of their connection providing a brief relief from the uncertainty that lay ahead.

As the city lights streaked by outside the car windows, Nina couldn't help but feel that they were hurtling towards something bigger than either of them could imagine. But one thing was for sure – as long as they faced it together, they could overcome anything.

***

Nina and Daniel drove up to a quaint cottage, where the evening sky was tinted in hues of deep blue. A gentle breeze whispered through the trees, imbuing the air with a sense of urgency. Orlando's towering silhouette stood against the soft glow emanating from within the cottage. As he swung the door open, his demeanor carried a subdued urgency, inviting them to enter.

With purposeful steps, they crossed into the cottage's interior, the door closing behind them with a faint, reassuring click. The warm ambiance enveloped them, casting soft shadows that danced upon the walls. The atmosphere hummed with a mix of concern and determination, a silent understanding hanging in the air like a shared secret.

Orlando's gaze locked onto Daniel's as he approached, a mix of anxiety and determination playing in his eyes. "Mr. Turner, thank you for coming."

Daniel offered a curt nod, extending his hand.

"Call me Daniel. I assume you want to talk about Amanda?"

Orlando's grip was firm as they shook hands. "Yes, she's been missing for two days now. The police are looking into it, but I have a feeling they're not taking it as seriously as they should."

Orlando tilted his head as his gaze shifted from Daniel to the woman standing before him. His curiosity danced in his eyes like a flickering flame. "Who is this?" he inquired, his voice a melody of intrigue.

Daniel, standing beside the woman, flashed a charming smile. "Orlando, meet Nina, she is my… associate" he introduced,

Orlando led them to the cozy sitting room, the air thick with an undercurrent of worry. Settling onto a plush sofa, he exhaled deeply, his broad shoulders visibly tense, his dark eyes mirroring the gravity of the situation. Orlando had ascended from being the Mayor's security detail to becoming the Head of Security, and his reputation preceded him. Stories of a man whose mere presence commanded respect had reached Daniel's ears, and now, in this critical moment, they found themselves in his presence, the reality of the situation hitting home.

As Daniel sat in the cozy living room sofa, Orlando gestured towards Nina. "Please, have a seat. Can I offer you something to drink? Coffee, perhaps?"

Nina accepted the offer with a nod and settled onto the sofa, her gaze wandering around the room as if taking in the details of Orlando's life. "Coffee sounds perfect, thank you."

Orlando headed toward the small, well-equipped kitchen adjoining the living room. The sound of cups clinking and the aroma of freshly brewed coffee soon enveloped the room,

Nina's heart clenched as she studied Orlando's anguished expression. It was hard to believe that she had been celebrating their joyous wedding just the night before. The laughter, the dancing - it all seemed like a distant memory compared to the grim reality of his missing wife.

Orlando returned with a tray holding three steaming cups of coffee. He placed them on the coffee table, in front of them and took a seat.

Daniel cleared his throat, breaking the heavy silence. "Orlando, we're here to help. We'll do whatever we can to find her."

Orlando's gaze shifted to Daniel, a mixture of

gratitude and desperation in his eyes. "I appreciate that, Daniel. Every moment feels like an eternity."

Daniel shifted uncomfortably in his seat, his posture strained, and his mind was already racing through the details. "Tell me about the last time you saw her. Any unusual behavior?"

Orlando sank into a nearby armchair, running a hand through his dark hair. "No, of course not. I woke up and she was gone. The police found my car abandoned in a parking lot, but there were no signs of her"

Daniel's pen danced across his notepad as he jotted down the information. "Have you noticed anything strange leading up to her disappearance?"

Orlando hesitated, his gaze dropping for a moment before meeting Daniel's again. "There were some strange phone calls, hushed conversations. She was always secretive about it, and I didn't want to pry."

Daniel's curiosity deepened. "Do you have any idea who might want to harm her or any enemies she might have?"

Orlando's expression darkened, his voice tinged with bitterness. "Her family didn't approve of our marriage. They thought I wasn't good enough for her.

Could be someone from her past, someone trying to get back at her."

Nina's eyes flitted between the two men, absorbing the gravity of the situation. She sipped her coffee, its warmth a stark contrast to the chill that seemed to have settled in the room. Orlando's pain was palpable, his worry etched across his features. She had seen a different side of him earlier, a softer, more open side, and it was disconcerting to witness this vulnerability now.

Daniel's pen continued to dance on the notepad, his focus unyielding. "We'll look into her background, see if we can find any leads from her past. It might help us piece together what happened."

Orlando nodded, his gaze shifting from Daniel to Nina. "Nina, do you have any experience in this kind of investigation?"

Nina's heart raced at the sudden attention, her eyes meeting Orlando's. "I've worked on similar cases before, helping gather information and connecting dots."

Daniel looked between them, his lips curling into a faint smile. "Nina's sharp, Orlando. She's resourceful, and I trust her instincts."

Orlando's eyes bore into Nina's for a moment. "Good, we need all the help we can get."

As the conversation delved deeper into strategy and plans, the tension began to recede away, replaced by a sense of unity. In this dimly lit room, the three of them forged an alliance, driven by the common goal of finding Amanda and unveiling the truth behind her disappearance.

Hours slipped by, the night deepening outside the cottage. They discussed leads, possible connections, and ways to dig deeper into Amanda's life. The flickering candlelight cast shadows on the walls, the air heavy with determination.

***

CHAPTER 10: THE PAST IS IN THE FUTURE

The daylight gushed through the windows of Olive's photography studio, casting a warm glow over her workspace. Her computer screen displayed a series of captivating images—Amanda and Orlando's radiant smiles, their families' tears of joy, and the intimate moments that had unfolded during the wedding ceremony. The atmosphere of love and celebration seemed like a distant memory as Olive lost herself in the process of editing, her thoughts consumed by her work.

But as her fingers deftly moved over the keyboard, her focus shifted when the familiar ding of her phone's notification disrupted the quiet hum of the studio. She glanced at the screen and her heart sank as she read the headline: "Mayor's Daughter Missing: Newlywed Husband Under Suspicion."

A sense of unease settled over Olive as she clicked on the article and scanned the details. Amanda, the woman whose wedding she had so joyfully captured, had vanished without a trace. The small town of Serenity Falls was now enveloped in a cloud of fear and anxiety. The local police had honed in on Amanda's husband, Orlando, as a person of interest. Olive's mind raced, trying to reconcile the joyful scenes she had witnessed just days ago with the grim reality of Amanda's disappearance.

As Olive continued to read, she felt a mix of emotions. Confusion, disbelief, and concern swirled within her. The article detailed the frantic search efforts, the emotional pleas from Amanda's family, and the growing suspicions directed at Orlando. The weight of the situation was heavy, and Olive found herself grappling with a mix of sympathy for Amanda's loved ones and an unsettling curiosity about the truth behind the disappearance.

Setting aside her editing work, Olive leaned back in her chair, her thoughts a whirlwind of possibilities. She remembered the way Amanda had looked on her wedding day, the happiness that radiated from her as she exchanged vows with Orlando. Now, that happiness was overshadowed by uncertainty and fear.

Olive's instincts as a photographer told her that there was more to this story than met the eye. She couldn't help but wonder if her photographs held any clues or insights into the events leading up to Amanda's disappearance. The camera had a way of capturing not only smiles and laughter but also the unspoken emotions that lingered beneath the surface.

With a determined expression, Olive opened a folder containing all of the wedding photographs and began to sift through them once again. She was no detective, but she believed that sometimes, the answers to the most baffling mysteries could be found in the most unexpected places.

Olive's eyes scanned the rows of wedding photographs on her computer screen, each image capturing a moment of joy, love, and celebration. Her finger moved the mouse as she clicked through the shots, one by one. And then, as if guided by fate, her finger stopped. A single image appeared on the screen—a candid shot from the wedding reception. It was Vaughn, looking dapper in his suit, engaged in what seemed like a heated argument with a woman clad in black.

Curiosity piqued, Olive's heart raced as she zoomed in on the woman's face, her features now clear and unmistakable. Recognition hit her like a jolt. It was the same woman who had visited her studio—the journalist. The realization sent a shiver down Olive's spine, connecting dots she hadn't even known were there.

Her mind whirred with questions. What was the journalist doing at the wedding? Why was she arguing with Vaughn? And most importantly, how did she fit into the puzzle of Amanda's disappearance? The shrill ring of her phone echoed through her studio, shattering the stillness of the room. Olive's heart skipped a beat as she hastily reached for the phone on her desk. With a sigh, she swiped the screen and brought it to her ear.

"Hello?" she greeted cautiously, her voice laced with a hint of anxiety.

"Miss Adams?" came the voice on the other end, a blend of official authority and urgency. "This is Deputy Turner from the Serenity Falls Police Department."

Olive's heart rate quickened at the mention of the police department. She gripped the phone a bit tighter, her mind racing through possibilities.

"We're currently investigating the disappearance of Amanda Alvarez, and we're requesting all attendees from the wedding to come in for questioning," Deputy Turner explained. "We're hoping to gather statements and gather any information that might aid in our investigation."

reluctance evident in his tone.

Deputy Turner had been reluctantly thrust into cooperation with the Federal Bureau of Investigation. Afterall it was the Mayor's daughter who had gone missing, and the situation demanded an all-hands-on-deck approach. He left the observation room, his steps heavy as he walked into the interrogation room. His gaze met Olive's, and for a moment, she saw a flicker of sympathy in his eyes. He took the seat opposite her, placing a notepad and pen on the table in front of him. The silence in the room was intense, the weight of the situation hanging heavy in the air.

"Thank you for coming in, Miss…?" he began, waiting for her to fill in the blank.

"Olive. Olive Adams," she replied, her voice a tad shaky.

"Miss Adams," Deputy Turner began, his voice softening just a touch, "I know this is a difficult time, but we need your help to find the Mayor's daughter. Can you tell us anything that might be relevant to the investigation?"

Olive's eyes moved away from the notepad, locking onto Deputy Turner's steady gaze. Inside her, a storm of emotions stirred—fear and doubt, but also a resolute urge to help in any way she could. Memories of her chilling run-in with Vaughn Knight and the board filled with women's pictures that he hid in his basement surged back. Yet, what if her instincts were misguided? Swallowing her apprehension, she mustered the courage to speak.

"I wasn't really close to Amanda," Olive began, her voice tremulous. "I was just the wedding photographer."

Deputy Turner leaned forward slightly, his brows furrowing. "Every piece counts, Olive. Even seemingly small details can often lead us closer to the truth."

Olive's head bobbed gently, her fingers softly skimming the edge of the table, as if coaxing her scattered thoughts to settle. The room around her felt heavy with questions, each one begging for an answer she wasn't entirely sure she had.

"Well, um," she began, her voice a hesitant murmur, "I did notice something a bit odd back then. It was during the reception, you know. I happened to catch sight of Vaughn and a woman. They were having this... well, a really heated argument. Right there, near the garden."

Deputy Turner leaned forward, his brows knitted in keen interest. "A woman, you say? Can you give me a bit more about her?" His tone was both gentle and probing, a mixture of understanding and curiosity.

Olive took a moment, her eyes drifting upwards as she sifted through the memory, trying to conjure every detail she could. "She had this tan complexion, you know, like she'd been kissed by the sun. And her hair, it was that deep brunette shade. Average height, I think," she mused, her lips curving slightly as if she could still see the scene unfold before her. "Oh, and she was wearing this striking black cocktail dress. You couldn't have missed it, really, especially against the backdrop of the wedding."

Deputy Turner's pen danced across his notepad as he jotted down her words, his gaze unwavering on Olive. "Did you catch any of their conversation?" he inquired gently, as if guiding her through a delicate topic.

Olive's brow furrowed in concentration. "Bits and pieces, maybe," she replied, a tiny furrow forming between her brows. "I remember hearing her voice rise, like she was angry about something. And Vaughn, well, he looked frustrated, I guess. It was hard to catch every word, though."

The deputy nodded thoughtfully, his expression a mix of contemplation and appreciation. "Thank you, Olive. You've been a big help. These details might just piece together a puzzle we're trying to solve."

She offered a small, uncertain smile, relief mingling with the remnants of anxiety. "I hope it helps, Deputy. I mean, if there's anything else I remember, I'll let you know."

He rose from his seat, his tall frame casting a reassuring shadow over her. "I appreciate that, Olive. We're just trying to figure out what happened that day." His voice was warm, a steady presence amid the uncertainty that hung in the air. "If you remember anything else, don't hesitate to reach out."

Olive nodded, feeling a sense of relief wash over her. As she stepped back outside, she couldn't help but ponder the mystery that had gripped the town. She might not have realized it yet, but her simple statement could hold a clue, a piece to the puzzle that would lead to the truth behind Amanda's disappearance.

After leaving the police station, Olive swiftly slid into her car and drove away. Night had descended, and she hurried back to her house. Once inside, she settled onto her couch, her head sinking into her hands as she attempted to reconstruct the tumultuous events of the wedding.

Feeling the need to clear her mind, Olive decided to indulge in a long, relaxing bath. She entered the bathroom, ran the water until it was steaming, and then shed her clothes before slipping into the tub.

Submerging herself underwater, she held her breath for a moment. And then, as if a lightning bolt had struck her, the realization hit her like a tidal wave. She had the phone number of the strange woman from the wedding picture. Gasping for air, she shot to the surface, wrapping a towel around herself before dashing out of the bathroom, her wet footprints marking her path.

With her heart racing, she rummaged through her purse that lay on the living room couch. She upended it, its contents spilling out haphazardly. Amid the mess, a business card fluttered to the ground. Trembling, Olive picked it up and turned it over, her phone clutched tightly in her other hand. She dialed the number listed on the card, her fingers dancing nervously over the buttons.

A woman's voice answered after a few rings. "Nina Santos."

"Nina, it's me, Olive. I'm not sure if you remember me, but you came into my shop a few days ago."

Nina's voice held a hint of curiosity. "You'll need to jog my memory a bit."

"I'm the one who owns the photography studio."

Recognition dawned in Nina's voice. "Oh, right.

Olive. What can I do for you?"

Olive's urgency spilled into her words. "Can we meet? It's about Amanda."

There was a moment of silence on the other end. "Sure, but you'll have to narrow it down. What's this about?"

"Could we talk in person? There's a cafe next to my studio. Could you meet me there?"

Nina's response was swift. "Alright, I'll be there. Give me a bit."

Relief flooded through Olive. "Thank you, Nina. I appreciate it."

After ending the call, Olive exhaled slowly, her mind racing with the newfound pieces of the puzzle. Each revelation seemed to bring her closer to untangling the mystery that had enveloped Amanda's disappearance. Meeting Nina felt like the next logical step in shedding light on the truth that was buried beneath layers of uncertainty.

With a mix of anticipation and anxiety swirling in her chest, Olive glanced at the clock. Patience would be her ally now; she needed to wait for the right time. The cafe, a neutral ground, would soon become the backdrop for the conversation that might unveil the missing pieces of the puzzle.

Drawing another steadying breath, Olive focused on the task at hand. She swiftly gathered herself, exchanging her current attire for something comfortable yet presentable. A few brush strokes through her hair and a final check in the mirror ensured she was ready to face what lay ahead.

As she stood before the mirror, her heart continued its erratic dance, a blend of apprehension and hope. The journey she had embarked upon was laden with uncertainties, but there was a determination in her gaze—a resolve to find the truth.

Grabbing her car keys from the table, Olive's steps carried her purposefully towards the door. The weight of the moment was not lost on her; every step she took was a step towards unravelling the mystery that had gripped Serenity Falls.

The engine roared to life as Olive slid into the driver's seat. The road ahead felt both familiar and unknown, a metaphor for the path she was forging in her pursuit of answers. Each turn of the wheel brought her closer to the rendezvous that held the promise of revelations.

The night air was crisp as Olive drove to the

cafe. The streets were illuminated by the soft glow of streetlights, and the distant hum of city life created a soothing backdrop to her racing thoughts. Pulling into a parking spot near the cafe, she took a deep breath before stepping out of her car.

Walking into the cafe, Olive's gaze swept over the cozy interior. Warm lighting bathed the space in a welcoming glow, creating an atmosphere of comfort that contrasted the uncertainties clouding her mind. Determined to focus on the task at hand, she made her way to a quiet corner table and settled into the cushioned seat.

As she glanced around, her attention was caught by the waitress who was moving gracefully between the tables. Catching the waitress's eye, Olive offered a small smile before beckoning her over. "Good evening," she greeted, her voice laced with a blend of anticipation and nerves. "Could I please have some warm sweet tea?"

The waitress, a friendly and welcoming presence, nodded with a warm smile. "Of course, coming right up," she replied before turning to make her way to the counter to prepare Olive's order.

While she waited, Olive took in her surroundings. The cafe's ambiance wrapped around her like a familiar embrace, its soft lighting and gentle hum of conversations soothing her senses. It was the perfect setting for a conversation that held the promise of uncovering truths.

Minutes later, the waitress returned, a tray in hand. Placing the cup of sweet tea on the table, she also set down a plate of cookies. "Here you go," she said, her tone friendly as she met Olive's gaze. "I thought you might enjoy these with your tea."

Olive's lips curved into a grateful smile, touched by the thoughtful gesture. "Thank you," she replied, her voice sincere. "That's very kind of you."

The waitress's smile widened. "You're welcome. Enjoy your tea and cookies. If you need anything else, don't hesitate to ask."

"Will do," Olive assured her, her gratitude evident in her eyes.

With a nod, the waitress moved on to attend to other patrons, leaving Olive to her thoughts. She lifted the cup of sweet tea, its surface, warm against her fingertips. The taste of the sugary concoction was a welcome distraction, momentarily soothing her nerves.

As she sipped on her hot tea and nibbled on the cookies, Olive watched the world outside the window. People walked by in pairs and groups, their laughter and conversations adding to the atmosphere of the night. The city's energy was both familiar and distant, a reflection of the thoughts swirling in Olive's mind.

Time seemed to stretch as Olive sat there, lost in her own contemplation. She imagined the upcoming conversation with Nina, wondering what secrets might be unveiled, what truths might be shared. The glass window offered a view into the lives of others, a glimpse into their own stories, and it somehow made Olive feel connected to the world around her.

As the minutes ticked by, Olive's sweet tea grew colder, forgotten on the table. The cookies had disappeared, leaving only a few crumbs behind. With each passing moment, her nerves and anticipation intertwined, creating a tense but exhilarating sensation.

Olive's gaze remained unwavering, her attention fixated on the cafe's entrance. With every tick of the clock, her anticipation seemed to intensify, creating a flutter of both hope and uncertainty within her chest. And then, as if orchestrated by fate itself, a familiar figure entered the café, her steps purposeful and accompanied by a man. The sight of Nina's presence felt like a beacon of light, illuminating the room and casting aside the shadows of doubt.

With measured steps, Nina and the man approached Olive's table, their expressions a reflection of the complex emotions swirling in the air. As they took their seats, Olive's heart raced, as a merger of curiosity and apprehension weaved around them.

Nina's gaze met Olive's, her eyes a balance of understanding and determination. "Hey, Olive," she greeted, her voice carrying the weight of their shared purpose. "I'm glad you could make it."

Olive managed a smile, the knots of tension in her chest easing slightly in the presence of her newfound ally. "Of course, thank you for meeting me."

Nina initiated the introductions. "This is my friend Daniel; he's a private investigator. We're working together to find Amanda."

Olive was taken aback. "Oh," she managed to utter, her surprise evident. "Are you working alongside the police?"

Nina smiled as she beckoned the waitress over. "No, we're hired privately by Amanda's husband, Orlando Morgan."

Understanding dawned on Olive. "I see," she nodded, absorbing the information. "I think I might know who's behind all the disappearances."

Nina and Daniel exchanged a serious glance.

"Who?" Nina inquired.

Olive leaned in and whispered her revelation. "Vaughn Knight."

Daniel's gaze bore into her. "What makes you believe that?"

Glancing around cautiously, Olive leaned back slightly. "For starters, I stumbled upon a board filled with pictures of women, down in his basement."

Nina's eyes widened in shock. "Wait! You've been inside his house? What were you thinking? He could very well be involved in all these women's disappearances, including his own wife's."

Olive fidgeted, nervously scratching the table's edge. "I know that now. The moment I saw the murder board, I got out of there."

Nina's expression softened, her concern evident. Just then, the waitress arrived at their table. "Can I take your order, please?"

Nina didn't waste any time. "Coffee, and make it endless," she requested before turning back to the conversation.

Daniel directed his attention to Olive. "Does

Vaughn know that you've seen his...," his voice dropped to a hush, "...murder board?"

A pallor washed over Olive's face as she nodded slowly. Concern etched on her features, Nina sighed, "This is risky, Olive. You need protection."

Olive met their eyes, a mixture of fear and determination swirling within her gaze. In the midst of this tangled web of secrets and danger, she had taken a leap that had led her into the heart of the mystery.

As the weight of the situation pressed down on Olive, she felt her anxiety rising. Memories flooded her mind, particularly one instance that had left a deep mark on her.

It was a mundane morning, much like any other. Suddenly, there were sharp knocks on her apartment door. A voice demanded, "Olive Adams, open up. This is the Police." Panic clenched her heart as she rushed to the door, only to have armed officers storm in and search her apartment.

She remembered the fear that had gripped her as they combed through her personal space, her pleas falling on deaf ears. The memory was etched with the feeling of helplessness as they had found something incriminating. "Found it!" someone had exclaimed, and her world had shattered. She was arrested for drug possession, a crime she hadn't committed.

"Olive? Olive?" Daniel's voice pulled her back to the present, back to the cafe.

Olive's chest heaved as she fought to steady her breathing, her hands trembling. "Nina, please," she implored, her voice shaky. "What do I do now?"

Before long, the attentive waitress arrived at their table, bearing two steaming cups of coffee and an additional plate of cookies. The aroma of freshly brewed coffee wafted through the air, intertwining with the delicate scent of the cookies. The trio's attention was momentarily diverted from their weighty conversation as the treats were presented before them.

Daniel's eyes lit up with unanticipated delight as he caught sight of the plate of cookies. "Oh, cookies," he exclaimed with genuine enthusiasm, his fingers reaching for one with almost childlike eagerness. In a swift motion, he seized a cookie and wasted no time taking a hearty bite, a look of sheer satisfaction spreading across his face.

Nina chuckled softly at Daniel's response, her amusement evident. "Well, it seems like the cookies have your seal of approval," she remarked with a playful glint in her eyes.

Daniel's grin widened as he managed to swallow his mouthful. "Absolutely," he confirmed between bites, his enjoyment of the treat apparent. Both Daniel and Nina exchanged a glance laden with understanding.

Olive's gaze remained fixed on Nina, a blend of desperation and uncertainty in her eyes. The weight of the situation hung heavily in the air, as if the answer to her question held the key to an intricate puzzle. "Nina," she began, her voice carrying a mixture of longing and vulnerability, "what do I do now?"

A shared glance passed between Daniel and Nina, a silent exchange of empathy and understanding that spoke volumes. Their collective thoughts seemed to converge in that moment, shaping the guidance they were about to offer. Nina's expression softened, her resolve unwavering as she met Olive's gaze. She let out a sigh, realizing the gravity of the situation they were all facing.

Leaning in slightly, Nina's voice held a tone of frankness, the weight of her words not escaping her. "If Vaughn is somehow involved in all this, there's a chance he might come after you. You could be the perfect bait to catch him."

The reality of the situation settled heavily upon Olive's shoulders, the weight of it all pressing down on her. She found herself torn between her desire for answers and the need to keep herself safe.

"Bait?" Olive stammered, confusion written across her face. "What do you mean?"

Nina leaned forward again, her eyes intense as they bore into Olive's. "It means we're going to have to be roommates."

Olive's brows furrowed, trying to process the unexpected proposition. "Roommates? But why?"

Daniel leaned forward, his voice gentle but serious. "If Vaughn believes you have information about his activities, he might try to get close to you. And we'll be ready to catch him when he does."

Olive's mind whirred, caught between the danger of being involved and the potential to finally uncover the truth. She glanced from Nina to Daniel, feeling a mix of fear and determination. The café's warm ambiance seemed worlds away from the looming threat, but she knew she had to make a decision.

Nina's eyes softened as she studied Olive's expression. "I know this isn't easy, Olive. But if you want to help find Amanda and put an end to this nightmare, we need to take risks."

Olive's heart raced, her thoughts a whirlwind of uncertainty. But beneath it all, a spark of courage ignited. With a deep breath, she met Nina's gaze, her voice resolute. "Okay, then. Let's do it. I'm in."

***

CHAPTER 11: A TRAP IS LAID

In an interrogation room at the Serenity Falls Police Department, Vaughn Knight found himself seated across from Deputy Turner and FBI Special Agent Marks. The room's atmosphere was tense, charged with unspoken accusations. Vaughn's arms were folded as he faced the familiar figure of Deputy Turner, his high school classmate. Agent Marks, however, was more of a mystery, lurking in the background like a shadow with probing eyes fixed on Vaughn.

The silence in the room was broken only by the faint hum of the air conditioning and the muted shuffling of papers. Vaughn's gaze shifted between the two men, an unspoken tension bridging the gap between them. The questions that loomed over his head were as palpable as the air he breathed, hanging there, waiting to be addressed.

Deputy Turner cut to the chase. "Vaughn, we go way back, don't we? Let's not dance around this. Where were you three nights ago between 11 PM and 6 AM the next morning?"

Vaughn's brow furrowed, his arms remaining defiantly folded. "What's the meaning of this, Turner?"

Agent Marks, his stance casual against the corner wall, chimed in. "Just answer the question, Mr. Knight."

Vaughn held Deputy Turner's gaze, determination in his eyes. "I was at home, alone."

Deputy Turner jotted down the response before pushing further. "Can anyone vouch for your alibi?"

"No," Vaughn replied, a hint of unease creeping into his posture. The chair beneath him suddenly seemed unsteady, as if the very ground beneath him was shifting. "As I said, I was by myself."

Breaking away from the shadows, Agent Marks approached the table, his gaze fixed on Vaughn. Their eyes locked in a silent challenge. "Tell me, Vaughn, what's your connection with Olive Adams?"

Deputy Turner paused in his note-taking, surprised by the directness of Agent Marks. Vaughn, equally taken aback, shot back, "What's it matter to you?"

Agent Marks didn't waver, his tone firm. "Just answer the question."

Vaughn's frustration was palpable as he replied, "Fine. We used to date. We're not together anymore."

A fleeting expression of relief flickered across Agent Marks' face, so subtle that only the observant might catch it. He turned away from Vaughn, retreating back to his corner by the wall, as if the weight of a burden had momentarily lifted from him.

"So, who ended the relationship? Was it her?" Agent Marks inquired, his voice more controlled now.

Vaughn's gaze dropped, his fingers unconsciously tapping against his folded arms. "Yes," he admitted, the admission escaping his lips with a subdued air.

Deputy Turner continued to write, the room's silence punctuated only by the scratch of his pen against paper. As Vaughn's words hung in the air, the tension seemed to thicken, like a storm gathering on the horizon. The questions were far from over, and as the night outside deepened, the shadows within the room held secrets that were yet to be revealed.

The room settled into a heavy silence after Vaughn's last words. He looked from Deputy Turner to Agent Marks, his attempt to read the atmosphere yielding little insight. Frustration was etched across his features, his eyes darting between the two men as he sought answers.

"Turner, why am I here?" Vaughn's voice cut through the quiet, his impatience evident.

Deputy Turner's response seemed almost nonchalant. "We're interviewing all the wedding guests, nothing special going on here."

But just as Vaughn thought he might get some clarity, Agent Marks interjected with a chilling statement. "You are the prime suspect, Mr. Knight."

Vaughn's head snapped towards Agent Marks, his surprise palpable. "What?" he exclaimed, disbelief and anxiety mingling in his voice.

Deputy Turner's expression tightened as he turned his attention back to Agent Marks. He understood the chain of command and the importance of following the lead of a senior officer during an interrogation.

Agent Marks leaned against the wall, his posture casual but his tone serious. "We have a witness who saw you arguing with a woman at the wedding."

Vaughn's mind raced, struggling to reconcile the accusation with his memories of the event. "Witness? I'm sure they must be mistaken. Besides, is it a crime to have an argument, these days?"

Agent Marks remained unyielding. "No, Mr. Knight, she is not mistaken. In fact, didn't your wife go missing last summer as well?"

Vaughn's discomfort was palpable as he absently scratched the back of his neck, a reflexive attempt to ease his rising tension. "Yes," he admitted, his voice quieter now. "She went missing last summer. So why don't you do your fucking job and find her?" His frustration was beginning to bubble over, his emotions roiling under the surface.

Agent Marks held Vaughn's gaze, a calculated silence stretching between them. "We are doing our job, Mr. Knight. And part of that job is to investigate every angle, every possibility."

Vaughn's voice, tinged with a mix of anger and desperation, rose. "Well, you're focusing on the wrong angle, then. I loved Elle. I would never hurt her."

The room seemed to close in around them, the tension nearly palpable. Deputy Turner kept his eyes fixed on his notes, absorbing the exchange.

Agent Marks, his demeanor inscrutable, smiled slightly as he approached the door. Holding it open, he delivered a final command: "Don't leave town." With that, he departed, leaving Vaughn sitting there, his mind a whirlwind of thoughts and emotions.

The weight of the situation bore down on Vaughn like a heavy burden. The realization had sunk in—his status had shifted from an observer to a prime suspect. The echoes of the past were ringing loudly in his ears, a cruel reminder of the time when he had faced similar accusations.

The memories surged forth like a relentless tide, sweeping Vaughn back to the previous summer. His mind became a canvas for those haunting recollections, vivid and unyielding. Each memory was a brushstroke painting a picture of days mired in dark shadows and unresolved questions.

Conversations from those tumultuous times echoed in his thoughts. The harsh sound of his own voice reverberated, a persistent echo that seemed to have etched itself into his memory. "I don't know where Elle is," he had said repeatedly, a plea for them to understand, frustration lacing his words like a bitter undercurrent. The police station had become a grim backdrop to his life, its cold walls and unforgiving atmosphere etching themselves into his psyche.

He remembered the countless hours spent seated across from stern-faced detectives, their questions like a relentless barrage, chipping away at his resolve. He had repeated his innocence like a mantra, hoping that his words would eventually pierce through their skepticism. But suspicion had clung to him like a shadow, darkening the corners of his existence.

Elle, his wife, had vanished from their lives, leaving behind an agonizing emptiness that threatened to consume him whole. The memory of her smile, the sound of her laughter, now seemed like fragments of a distant dream. In the midst of their blissful life, she had disappeared, leaving him with unanswered questions and a heartache that knew no relief.

As Vaughn relived those days, he felt the weight of his own desperation, the ache of not knowing, of being trapped in a turbulence of uncertainty. And now, as he sat once again in an interrogation room, the familiarity of the situation was both haunting and infuriating. The memories served as a constant reminder of the past he had fought to leave behind, yet seemed to be inevitably tied to.

And now, here he was again, the lines between the past and the present blurring. The sense of déjà vu was spooky, a reminder that history had a way of repeating itself. The room felt suffocating, the walls closing in as he grappled with the accusations that had once more come crashing into his life.

Vaughn's fingers clenched into tight fists, his nails digging into his palms as if trying to anchor himself in the present.

His mind raced, caught between the fear of being ensnared in a web of suspicion and the urgency to uncover the truth that had eluded him for so long.

As he sat there, a mix of determination and resignation settled within him. He couldn't let himself be trapped in this cycle again. This time, he needed to take control, to break free from the chains of doubt that threatened to bind him. The memories of his sister's disappearance still haunted him, but he was determined to use those memories as fuel to find answers, to uncover the truth buried beneath the layers of deception.

***

Back at Olive's house, a newfound sense of friendship filled the air. The weight of the impending danger seemed to lighten just a bit in the presence of allies. Olive, Nina, and Daniel had made themselves at home in the spacious dwelling, each claiming a spare room upstairs as their own.

In the living room, the heart of their temporary headquarters, Olive sat on the couch, her gaze fixed on a distant point as her thoughts swirled with a mix of apprehension and determination. The room's stillness was soon interrupted by the arrival of Nina and Daniel.

"I'm absolutely starving," Daniel declared as he stretched his arms overhead. "How about we order in?"

He fished out his phone from his track pants and dialed a number. "Hey, you busy?" he began, his voice carrying a certain energy. "Perfect, listen, we're in the middle of something important. Care to join us? We're setting up a trap for a potential suspect."

Nina and Olive exchanged a glance, curiosity piqued. Daniel continued, "Great. I'll text you the location. Oh, and would you mind picking up some food for us? Pizza, maybe? There are three hungry souls here. Awesome, thanks."

As Daniel hung up, he turned his attention to the two women who were watching him with a mix of amusement and interest. "What's the secret conversation about?" he asked, a sly grin playing on his lips. "Food is en route."

Nina nudged him playfully. "You always manage to work your magic, don't you?"

Daniel shrugged nonchalantly. "Well, good food has a way of making even the tensest situations a bit more bearable."

Olive's lips curled into a small smile, the first genuine one in a while. It was a reminder that in the middle of confusion and uncertainty, moments of normalcy could still be found. As they settled in, awaiting both sustenance and the unfolding of their plan, the house seemed to embrace them in its warmth, offering a temporary respite from the storm that was brewing just outside its walls.

Time seemed to stretch, each second feeling like an eternity, until finally, the doorbell's chime resonated through the house. Every head turned toward the sound, tension filling the air like electricity.

In a quiet yet purposeful movement, Daniel approached the door, casting a cautious glance through the peephole before letting out a subtle sigh of relief. He opened the door to reveal Orlando, standing there with three boxes of pizza, his appearance a stark contrast to his usual polished self.

Orlando's eyes held the weariness of countless sleepless nights, his bloodshot gaze barely concealing the weight he carried. A faint, tired smile played on his lips as he stepped inside. "Come inside," Daniel greeted him, taking the boxes of pizza from his hands.

He gestured toward the dining table, where the aroma of the food mingled with the stillness of the room.

Orlando stumbled slightly as he closed the door behind him, his exhaustion evident in every step.

He nodded toward Nina, who returned the gesture. "Hello, Nina."

Nina nodded back. "Orlando. We appreciate you joining us."

Orlando's gaze then fell on Olive, a brief furrow forming on his forehead. "And who might this be?" he asked, his tone polite yet curious.

Nina took the lead in introducing Olive. "Orlando, this is Olive. She was the photographer at your wedding."

Recognition dawned in Orlando's eyes as he ran a hand through his hair, clearly distressed. "My apologies, Olive. Under the circumstances, my memory has been rather scattered."

Olive managed a small smile, her empathy evident. "I'm so sorry about Amanda."

Orlando's response was a gentle nod, gratitude shining through the tiredness. "Thank you."

Nina's voice held a touch of reassurance. "We'll find her, won't we?"

Orlando's gaze flickered to Nina, a mixture of hope and pain in his eyes. "Yes, we will."

Nina's tone shifted, a hint of lightness returning. "But first, let's tackle this pizza. I don't know about you all, but I'm absolutely famished."

Orlando's mouth felt dry, his stomach churning in response to both hunger and nerves. He hadn't remembered the last time he had eaten a proper meal. With a somewhat strained smile, he followed Nina and Olive into the dining area, where the promise of food and a resemblance of normality awaited.

As they settled around the table, the scent of pizza filling the air, Orlando's thoughts were a whirlwind of emotions. Amid the uncertainty that enveloped them, he found a flicker of hope in this gathering—strangers united by a shared mission.

With a sense of quiet determination, Daniel arranged the pizzas and a couple of beers on the table. As the trio started to indulge in the meal, an awkward silence draped itself over the room like a heavy curtain. The tension in the air was palpable, each bite of food tinged with unease. Olive's anxiety threatened to drown out her appetite as she forced herself to eat, chewing mechanically while her mind raced.

Nina's keen gaze didn't go unnoticed by Olive. Setting her pizza slice aside, Olive tried to put on a brave face. Nina leaned in, her voice gentle but resolute. "Olive, I understand you're scared, but remember, you're not alone in this. There are three of us here, and he won't get anywhere near you."

Orlando turned his attention to Nina, his curiosity evident. "Who are we talking about?"

Before Nina could respond, Daniel, his mouth still full, spoke up. "Vaughn."

Orlando's confusion was clear. "Vaughn? Who's Vaughn?"

Nina signaled for Daniel to pause, silencing him with a raised hand. "Vaughn Knight," she explained, her tone hushed. "He's after Olive. She stumbled upon his murder board."

Orlando nearly choked on his bite of pizza, his face a mix of shock and alarm. "Wait, did you just say 'murder board'?"

Nina gestured for him to lower his voice. "Yes, Olive found evidence that suggests he might be connected to the disappearances."

Orlando's concern was evident as he glanced at Olive, who looked both distressed and determined. Just as Daniel was about to speak up, a ringing phone interrupted the tense atmosphere.

Everyone reached for their phones, but it was Nina's that continued to ring. She answered cautiously, her voice steady. "Hello?"

"Nina, it's Vaughn," a voice came through the line, a mixture of urgency and tension in his tone. "We need to talk."

***

The world around her felt hazy and unfamiliar, and a surge of disorientation coursed through her. A jolt of fear pierced her heart as she realized the extent of her predicament – her body restrained, her wrists bound tightly by unforgiving ropes that dug into her skin, rendering her immobile and helpless.

The room's eerie ambiance only heightened Amanda's growing panic. Her attempts to scream were futile, her voice stifled by the gag, leaving her with nothing but her own racing thoughts. The sensation of vulnerability overwhelmed her as she struggled to comprehend the severity of her situation. Bound, gagged, and trapped in this obscure location, she was at the mercy of an unknown force that had cast her into this nightmare.

The room's faint illumination cast unsettling shadows, accentuating the grim reality of her confinement. Amanda's mind raced, her memories swirling as she desperately tried to piece together how she had ended up in this dire state.

Every breath was labored, fear intensifying with each passing moment. The room was shrouded in darkness, the air heavy with tension. The sound of a door creaking open echoed through the space, causing her heart to race even faster.

As a tall figure emerged from the shadows, Amanda's eyes widened in sheer terror. She strained to see, her mind racing to comprehend the situation. The man's silhouette grew more distinct as he moved closer, a wicked presence that sent shivers down Amanda's spine. Her heart pounded in her chest, the realization of her dire circumstances settling in. She struggled against her restraints, desperate to free herself, but the ropes held firm, cutting into her skin.

With each step he took, the man's features became more visible—a face masked in shadows, a chilling smile that sent waves of terror through Amanda's body. She was trapped, her vulnerability laid bare as he stood before her, a specter of darkness that seemed to consume all hope.

The man's presence loomed over Amanda, his

intentions cloaked in a sinister haze. Her mind raced, desperately searching for a way out, a glimmer of hope. She tried to convey her fear through her eyes, her muffled pleas echoing in the confines of her mind.

The room seemed to close in around her as he leaned in, his chilling smile never wavering. Amanda's heart pounded against her chest, the rhythm of her fear resonating through her veins. She strained against her restraints, her body trembling with a mixture of terror and adrenaline.

As he reached out, his fingers grazed her cheek, a touch that sent a surge of revulsion through her. She turned her head away, her breath hitching as she fought back tears of helplessness. The realization struck her— she was at the mercy of a man whose intentions were as mysterious as they were evil.

The man's voice sliced through the air, low and taunting. "My love, now you will never leave me again."

Her heart raced even faster, her thoughts a tangled web of fear and confusion. Who was he? Why had he taken her? What did he want? The questions swirled within her mind, a whirlwind of terror that threatened to consume her sanity.

With great effort, Amanda forced herself to focus, to find the strength to fight against the despair that threatened to overtake her. She met the man's gaze with a mixture of defiance and desperation, a silent plea for answers, for mercy.

But the man seemed to relish in her vulnerability. He circled around her, his footsteps a haunting echo in the dimly lit room. Her heart pounded with a rhythm of desperation, her fight for survival ignited by an unyielding determination.

In that suffocating darkness, Amanda clung to the memory of her life, her loved ones, her dreams. She knew that she couldn't succumb to the terror, that she needed to find a way to escape this nightmare.

The man cautiously removed the gag from Amanda's mouth, granting her a brief moment of relief from the constriction. Yet, her relief quickly gave way to dread as he approached her with a bowl of porridge. The thick, lumpy mixture looked unappetizing, and Amanda's instincts told her to reject it. She spat out the first spoonful, her eyes filled with defiance and repulsion.

However, the man's reaction was not what she had anticipated. Instead of giving up, he seized her head in a tight grip, his fingers digging into her hair as he held her still. The forcefulness of his grip left Amanda feeling powerless, trapped in his unyielding grasp. She could feel her heart pounding in her chest as anxiety and desperation surged through her.

Despite her struggles and attempts to resist, the man remained resolute. With an unnerving determination, he brought the spoon closer to her lips once more, his grip on her head leaving her no choice but to open her mouth. As much as Amanda fought against it, the man's strength overwhelmed her, and he managed to force-feed her the porridge.

Tears welled up in Amanda's eyes as the mixture slid down her throat, a nauseating blend of helplessness and revulsion settling within her. Her thoughts raced as she grappled with the reality of her situation – trapped, overpowered, and at the mercy of someone who seemed intent on exerting control over every aspect of her existence.

As the man continued to taunt and stare, Amanda's resolve hardened. She would find her way out of this darkness, even if it meant facing the unknown with every ounce of strength she had left.

***

CHAPTER 12: THE MISSING PIECE

Back at Olive's house, Nina's grip on her phone tightened as she exchanged a brief look with Daniel and Olive. Vaughn's unexpected call had thrown them a curveball, but she was prepared.

Taking a deep breath, she replied, her tone measured, "Vaughn, I can talk. But let's make it somewhere public, neutral ground. How about the park by the lake?"

There was a moment of silence on the other end of the line, and then Vaughn's voice came through, "That works. I'll meet you there in thirty minutes."

Nina ended the call and looked at Olive and Daniel. The pressure in the room was deep, combined with a mixture of anticipation and uncertainty. "He agreed to meet at the park by the lake," she informed them.

Orlando leaned in, his expression serious. "Are you sure about this? It might not be safe."

Daniel nodded, his voice steady. "I have my law enforcement contacts on speed dial. We won't put Nina in harm's way."

Nina felt a rush of conflicting emotions. Fear gnawed at the edges of her resolve, but a determination burned even brighter within her. She knew that this meeting could be a critical moment in their search for the truth, a step closer to unraveling the mystery behind Amanda's disappearance and the unsettling secrets that had come to light.

As the time ticked away, the group gathered what they needed and headed to the park. The moon hung high in the sky, casting a silvery glow over the quiet landscape. The park seemed to hold its breath in the stillness of the night, and the dark waters of the lake reflected the mystery that unfolded before them.

They settled in a discreet spot, a safe distance away from the potential meeting point. Olive's heart raced, her fingers fidgeting with a mix of anticipation and nervous energy. She glanced at Nina and Daniel, both of whom offered silent reassurance. The feeling of being part of a team, of individuals who had rallied around a common purpose, was both empowering and humbling.

As the minutes stretched, the air was charged with a quiet tension. The wind rustled through the trees, a soft whisper that seemed to carry the weight of their collective hopes and fears. And then, out of the shadows, Vaughn emerged, his gaze finding Olive's with an intensity that sent shivers down her spine.

The tension in the park was palpable as Vaughn walked towards the group, his eyes flickering over Nina, Olive, Daniel, and then finally resting on Orlando. The shock of seeing Olive with them was evident on his face, but he pushed it aside, focusing his attention on the man before him.

Orlando's stance was defensive, his eyes narrowed as he sized up Vaughn. The two men stood there, locked in a silent exchange, before Vaughn broke the ice. "Orlando, I need you to know that I'm not involved in any of this. I've been under scrutiny by the police, but I have nothing to hide."

Orlando's gaze held a mixture of skepticism and wariness. "The police think otherwise."

Olive, unable to contain her curiosity, interjected, "Vaughn, what about the board with the women's pictures, I found in your basement?"

Vaughn's gaze shifted to Olive, his expression sincere. "That wasn't what it seemed. I've been investigating the disappearances since my wife went missing last summer. I had to dig deep, find connections, try to understand what happened to her."

A heavy silence hung over them as Vaughn's words sank in. The realization that he had been chasing the same answers they sought had a profound impact. The lines between suspicion and alliance blurred, and Nina and Daniel exchanged hesitant glances.

Nina finally spoke, her voice tentative. "So, you're saying you've been trying to uncover the truth all along?"

Vaughn nodded, his eyes unwavering. "Yes. I know how it must look, but everything I did was to find Amanda and shed light on what's happening in this town."

Daniel's skepticism lingered, but he seemed to be considering Vaughn's words carefully. "Why didn't you come forward? Why keep it hidden?"

Vaughn's shoulders sagged under the weight of his confession. "I didn't know whom to trust. The police were investigating me, and I couldn't risk anyone compromising my efforts."

Nina's voice held a mixture of sympathy and hesitation. "If what you're saying is true, then we've all been chasing the same answers."

A moment of understanding seemed to pass between them, the realization that their paths had converged in the quest for truth. Vaughn's sincerity began to chip away at the wall of doubt that had surrounded him.

Finally, Vaughn extended an olive branch, his tone earnest. "I know this is a lot to take in, but if you're willing, I'd like to share what I've found. I believe if we join forces, we might just crack this thing wide open."

Nina and Daniel exchanged another look, then nodded in agreement. The group had come to a crossroads, and it seemed their best chance at finding answers lay in joining forces. Vaughn's invitation to his house, to share his findings, was a pivotal moment.

As they left the park, a sense of unity started to replace the fractures of doubt. The road ahead was uncertain, but they were no longer facing it alone.

The drive from the park to Vaughn's house was divided between two vehicles. Vaughn took his pickup truck, navigating the familiar roads with a sense of quiet contemplation. Meanwhile, Olive, Nina, Orlando, and Daniel piled into Daniel's car, the atmosphere inside a mix of uncertainty and newfound understanding.

As they rolled down the road, Olive's voice broke the silence. "I still can't help but wonder if we can trust him completely."

Orlando turned to her, his eyes reflecting a mixture of empathy and thoughtfulness. "I understand your hesitation. It's not easy to place your faith in someone, especially in situations like these."

Nina chimed in, her voice gentle. "Orlando's right, Olive. But think about it, we're all seeking the same thing. Closure, justice, answers. If Vaughn is genuine about wanting to uncover the truth, then it might be worth giving him a chance."

Orlando nodded in agreement. "I'm the only one here who can relate to this. When a spouse goes missing, suspicion often falls on the other. Even without actual evidence, the weight of suspicion can be suffocating."

Daniel, who had been listening intently, finally spoke up. "And not to mention, we're in a tight spot. We don't have much to go on. Sharing information might be our best option now."

As the car continued down the road, the collective decision to trust Vaughn—even if only partially—began to take root. Their journey had brought them to a point where alliances formed out of necessity, where the need for answers overshadowed lingering doubts.

Soon, the two vehicles arrived at Vaughn's house. The darkness had settled over the town, the house shrouded in a blanket of shadows. It stood as a symbol of secrets waiting to be unveiled, of connections that had yet to be fully understood.

Gathering outside the house, the group exchanged a determined glance before stepping inside. The darkness within seemed almost tangible, like a veil that concealed both answers and dangers. But they were not deterred. Their shared mission had brought them this far, and they were resolved to see it through.

The creaking floorboards beneath their feet echoed in the silence as they made their way down to the basement. The single light bulb illuminated the wooden table, now a focal point of anticipation. Vaughn began to spread his evidence once more, photographs and documents taking shape like pieces of a jigsaw puzzle waiting to be assembled.

Listening intently, the group absorbed every detail, their individual threads of investigation weaving together into a tapestry of revelation. Vaughn's dedication and meticulous research were undeniable. As he spoke, it became clear that their combined efforts had the potential to uncover the truth that had eluded them individually.

Olive's initial unease continued to subside as she observed Vaughn's earnestness and vulnerability. The basement that had once felt ominous now symbolized collaboration and unity. The shifting shadows on the walls seemed to mirror their evolving perspectives—moving from doubt to trust, from skepticism to cooperation.

The night wore on, the passage of time marked only by the soft rustling of paper and the hum of their voices. Vaughn's insights were invaluable, shedding light on pattern they had initially known and it sparked hope. It was a fragile optimism, but it held the power to propel them forward.

Nina leaned forward, her eyes locking onto a particular photograph. "This woman here—Samantha. Her case went cold like the others, but if we connect her timeline to the other disappearances..."

Daniel nodded, his voice thoughtful. "We might be able to establish a pattern that could help us predict the next potential target."

Vaughn's eyes flickered with a mix of satisfaction and determination. "Exactly. That's why I've been gathering all this information. We need to anticipate their moves."

As the night deepened, Vaughn's revelations

began to wind down. The group exchanged weary glances, exhaustion creeping in, but their spirits remained unbroken. The basement was now a sanctuary of shared purpose, the evidence a map that would guide them through the labyrinth of secrets.

"We've come a long way tonight," Orlando said, his voice carrying a note of exhaustion but also resolve. "But we can't forget that our work is just beginning. We need to follow up on these leads, dig deeper into these connections."

Olive's gaze swept across the faces around the table—Nina, Daniel, Vaughn, and Orlando. Their diverse backgrounds, motivations, and skills had converted into a force to be reckoned with. In that moment, they embodied the strength of unity, a force capable of facing the darkness and bringing it to light.

Olive fixed her gaze on Vaughn, a mixture of curiosity and concern etched on her face. "What can you remember about Elle?" she inquired.

The question caught Vaughn off guard. He cleared his throat, his eyes distant with memories, and replied, "She was an amazing human being. We loved each other very much. And when she disappeared, it broke me apart."

Nina turned her attention to Olive, her voice

tinged with a solemn edge. "There's something you should know, Vaughn's wife Elle, was my older sister." The revelation hung heavy in the air, a secret unveiled that connected their paths in unexpected ways. Olive's surprise mirrored that of Orlando's, both absorbing the gravity of the revelation.

Nina continued, her voice carrying a trace of pain. "I left this town many years ago and sadly it wasn't until a few months ago that I found out my sister went missing." As Daniel's fingers gently brushed against her shoulder, a gesture of comfort, Nina found comfort in his presence.

In the dimly lit basement, they all sat around the table, drawn together by a shared quest to uncover the truth behind Serenity Falls' mysterious disappearances. The newspaper clippings and pages before them painted a haunting tapestry of unanswered questions.

Orlando turned to Vaughn, his words laden with empathy. "Hey, I know we don't know each other that well, but I'm sorry about what happened to your wife. My only hope is that we find my Amanda before it's too late."

Vaughn's gaze met Orlando's, and with a determined nod, he affirmed, "We'll find her."

Nina, observing this exchange, leaned in closer to

Vaughn, her voice a hushed whisper. "Can you remember anything odd about my sister? Something she never talked about, maybe from her past?"

Vaughn furrowed his brow, trying to recollect. "We shared everything," he began. "But now that I think about it, she had a faint scar on her abdomen. I never asked her about it, and she never brought it up. I always wondered about it, though."

Nina's eyes widened at the revelation. As far as she knew, her sister hadn't been injured or hospitalized. Her departure from town had left her in the dark about the events that unfolded after her absence. She turned to the group, her gaze encompassing them all. "We lack solid leads, evidence, and witnesses in these cases. My gut tells me the answers lie in the past."

Orlando shook his head, skepticism evident. "What about Amanda? She could be out there somewhere."

Nina's determination shone through her response. "What are we going to do, Orlando? We can't search the whole town aimlessly. We need a strategy."

Daniel's gaze bore into her, understanding her well enough to sense her intentions. "Nina, what's on your mind?"

A smile tugged at the corner of Nina's lips, a hint of mischief in her eyes. "Something a bit illegal." Her words hung in the air, a daring proposition that united them further, binding them in a shared determination to unveil the truth, whatever it took.

Olive blinked, taken aback by Nina's sudden announcement. She exchanged glances with the others, a mixture of curiosity and concern evident on their faces. "What do you mean, something illegal?" Olive asked cautiously, her heart starting to race. "Nina, we're already in deep with this investigation. What is this illegal thing that you have in mind?"

Nina leaned in closer, her voice a hushed whisper. "I mean, we need to find the truth, and sometimes that means bending the rules a little. I have an idea, but we have to be careful and strategic."

Orlando furrowed his brow, uncertainty clouding his expression. "Nina, I get that we're desperate, but we can't just dive into something without considering the consequences."

Nina nodded, her eyes unwavering. "I know, Orlando. But hear me out. I've been researching the disappearances, and I've found a few threads that connect all of the victims to this town. I believe there might be something here that could give us answers."

Daniel sighed, his fingers drumming on the table. "Nina, that still doesn't explain what you mean by 'something illegal.'"

Nina hesitated, her gaze moving from one face to another. "I think we need to look for clues, evidence—anything that might lead us to the truth. We can't rely on the authorities alone. We have to take matters into our own hands. We're going to have to break inside a secure location."

Olive's mind raced as she considered the proposal. The gravity of the situation was clear; lives were at stake, and their town was plagued by a hidden darkness. She glanced at Vaughn, whose expression was a mix of apprehension and determination.

Vaughn's voice was measured as he spoke. "Nina, I understand your urgency, but breaking into any place, is a risky move. We need a solid plan if we're going to do this."

Nina nodded, her eyes bright with conviction. "I've been studying the layout of the building, trying to identify potential entry points and ways to avoid detection. We'll need tools, disguises, and a clear timeline."

Orlando's skepticism softened as he listened to Nina's careful explanation. He exchanged a glance with the others, a silent agreement passing between them. As much as they were hesitant to embrace the idea of breaking the law, the sense of urgency and the desire for answers pushed them to consider it.

Daniel sighed and leaned back in his chair, running a hand through his hair. "Nina, if we're going to do this, we need to make sure we're prepared for any scenario. We can't afford any mistakes."

Nina's gaze locked onto Daniel's, her gratitude evident in her eyes. "Thank you, Daniel. I know this isn't easy, but I truly believe it's the best shot we have."

The group fell into a contemplative silence, the weight of their decision heavy in the air. The lines between right and wrong blurred as they confronted the darkness that had plagued their town for so long. The choices they were about to make would shape their future and the future of those who had been affected by the disappearances.

As the night grew deeper, they huddled together around the wooden table, forming a bond that went beyond mere friendship. They were now a team driven by a shared goal—to uncover the truth, no matter the cost. And as they discussed their plan, the darkness outside seemed to mirror the uncertainty and danger that lay ahead.

***

CHAPTER 13: FINDING HER

The collective resolve of Orlando, Nina, Olive, Daniel, and Vaughn propelled them into an audacious plan—a plan that involved infiltrating the local hospital to unravel the truth that had remained elusive for so long. As they huddled together in a dimly lit room, their faces illuminated by the soft glow of a strategically placed laptop, they went over the details of their daring endeavor.

"We need to be careful," Orlando's voice was a hushed whisper, his eyes glinting with a mixture of determination and worry. "The hospital's security will be tight."

Nina nodded, as her fingers danced over the keyboard, pulling up the hospital's blueprints on the screen. "We'll need to memorize the best entry points and escape routes. And we can't forget about the security cameras." Daniel leaned in, his gaze intense.

Vaughn's jaw was set, his hands clenched into fists. "Once you're inside, you have to be quick and precise. We can't afford any mistakes."

The room fell into a tense silence, the weight of their mission settling upon them. Each member of the group understood the risks involved, yet their shared determination pushed them forward. They knew that this was the only way to uncover the truth and bring an end to the mysteries that had haunted their lives.

With a final nod of agreement, they dispersed, each pair heading to their designated positions, their hearts racing with a mixture of anticipation and trepidation. As the night deepened, the stars above seemed to watch over them, bearing witness to their audacious endeavor.

Inside the hospital, Vaughn's steps were purposeful, his heart pounding with a mix of nerves and determination. He approached the reception desk, his expression carefully composed into a friendly smile that had charmed many before.

"Good evening," he greeted the receptionist, his voice calm and reassuring. "I'm Vaughn Knight," he introduced himself.

The receptionist glanced up from her computer, her tired eyes meeting Vaughn's gaze. She returned the smile, her demeanor a mix of shyness and recognition. "I know who you are, Mr. Knight. What can I do for you today?"

Leaning in slightly, Vaughn's voice dropped to a confidential hush. "I would like to obtain all the hospital records of my wife, Elle Knight."

The request was bold, and the receptionist's eyes widened in shock. She stammered, "Um...I don't have the clearance for something like that. Let me call in my supervisor. Please have a seat."

"No worries at all. Take all the time you need," Vaughn assured her, settling into a chair as the receptionist scurried away from her desk. With an air of calm, he pulled out his phone from his pocket and composed a quick text. 'Phase 1 is a go.'

Orlando sat in the car parked outside the hospital, tension thick in the air around him. His phone vibrated, almost slipping from his grasp before he managed to catch it.

"God help us all." Orlando murmured the sentiment, as Vaughn's text displayed the ominous words. His hands gripping the steering wheel tightly as he counted down the minutes, each second feeling like an eternity. The darkness of the night enveloped him, the quiet anticipation of the mission weighing heavily on his shoulders.

Within the hospital's busy corridors, Nina and Daniel moved with a practiced ease, their steps synchronized and purposeful. The hospital staff bustled around them, their attention focused on their tasks, allowing the duo to slip by unnoticed.

As they navigated the maze-like halls, Nina glanced at Daniel with a mischievous twinkle in her eyes. "You know, this reminds me of our teenage sleuthing days," she whispered, a playful smile tugging at her lips.

Daniel couldn't help but chuckle softly. "Ah, the good old days when you used to drag me into all sorts of trouble."

Nina grinned, her voice dripping with mock innocence. "Hey, it wasn't all my fault. You were always up for an adventure."

He rolled his eyes, a fond expression on his face. "Yeah, well, I've learned my lesson since then."

Their banter was a welcomed distraction, lightening the tension that hung in the air. Despite the gravity of their mission, Nina and Daniel had always shared a companionship that allowed them to find moments of humor even in the direst situations.

As they walked past the emergency doors, a flurry of activity caught their attention. A group of hospital staff rushed through the doors, their urgent voices mingling with the sound of sirens from the ambulance outside.

Nina seized the opportunity. "Quick, now's our chance," she whispered to Daniel, her eyes gleaming with determination.

They slipped through the emergency doors, blending in seamlessly with the crowd of medical professionals. Nina's white coat and Daniel's nurse uniform granted them an air of authority as they moved through the hospital.

The bustling atmosphere around them created the perfect cover for their covert operation. They exchanged a knowing glance, the weight of their mission settling between them. This was their chance to uncover the truth, to piece together the puzzle that had haunted them for so long.

The weight of their disguises seemed to amplify their self-consciousness, but they pressed on. Daniel's brow was moist with sweat as he glanced around, catching the attention of curious gazes.

"I told you I wanted to be the doctor," Daniel muttered under his breath, his voice edged with nervousness. "It's more believable."

Nina, walking a few steps ahead, turned to him with a determined glint in her eyes. "Come on, Danny. It's the 21st century. Women can be doctors, and men can be nurses." Her words were laced with empowerment as she led the way, her confidence a guiding light.

Daniel let out a resigned sigh, realizing the truth in her words. He followed her closely as they ventured deeper into the hospital, their footsteps steady and purposeful. The third floor, where the records were kept, was their destination.

Stepping into the elevator, Nina and Daniel exchanged a quick, knowing glance. The confined space made their hearts race, but they were focused on their mission. Alongside them stood another doctor, his attention completely absorbed by the screen of his phone.

As the elevator began its ascent, the doctor continued scrolling through his device, seemingly oblivious to their presence. The hum of the elevator and the distant chatter of staff provided a subtle cover for their conversation.

Nina leaned toward Daniel, speaking in hushed tones. "So, how's our cover story holding up?"

Daniel managed a small, confident smile. "So far, so good. I think we're blending in."

As the elevator the elevator continued its ascent, Daniel turned his attention to the doctor who was inside with them. With a friendly smile, he decided to strike up a conversation.

"Busy day, huh?" Daniel said, nodding toward the man's phone.

The doctor looked up from his phone, offering a quick smile in return. "Oh, you have no idea. It's been non-stop."

Nina nodded in agreement. "Tell me about it. We just started our shifts, and it already feels like chaos."

The doctor chuckled. "Welcome to the life of a hospital. Are you new here?" he asked, looking at Daniel.

Daniel leaned casually against the wall of the elevator. "Yeah, just joined recently. Trying to find my way around."

The doctor nodded. "Well, you'll get used to it. It's a bit overwhelming at first, but you'll catch on."

The elevator stopped at the second floor, and the

doctor beside them prepared to exit. As he reached for the button to open the doors, Nina subtly maneuvered herself to stand closer to him. In one swift, practiced movement, her fingers grazed his coat pocket, deftly plucking the ID card from within.

The doors opened, and the doctor stepped out, still engrossed in his phone. With a faint smile, Daniel nodded to him, allowing the man to exit without suspicion. As the elevator doors closed once more, Daniel let out a silent sigh of relief.

Nina held up the ID card triumphantly, a glimmer of satisfaction in her eyes. "Got it."

Daniel's smile widened as he gave her a nod of approval. "You always were the master of sleight of hand."

As the elevator reached the third floor, the doors opened out into the hushed expanse of level three. They glanced at each other, a silent acknowledgment of the gravity of their mission.

Stepping out of the elevator, Nina and Daniel found themselves enveloped in the quiet stillness of the hospital after hours. The usual hustle and bustle had given way to a ghostly quietness, a perfect setting for their secret mission. This calmness, however, contrasted sharply with the intensity of their purpose.

As they moved forward, their steps were cautious and calculated, every footfall echoing the weight of their actions. The late hour of the night, had granted them the advantage of isolation—the administration staff had long departed for the day, leaving the hospital shrouded in a cloak of privacy. This backdrop provided the ideal canvas for their next move.

Daniel's nimble fingers danced over his phone's screen as he composed a text message to the group chat. "Phase two is complete," he typed, the words a coded confirmation of their progress. They were synchronized, a team of individuals working in harmony despite the risks that loomed ahead.

Nina moved ahead, her determination propelling her down the corridor. The promise of answers and the urgency of their mission drove her steps. She navigated the quiet halls with a sense of purpose, her gaze flickering over each sign and label until she spotted the door that held the answers they sought—labeled simply as "Records."

Daniel caught up to her swiftly, his presence a reassuring anchor as they stood before the unassuming door. He shared a nod with Nina, his voice a quiet reassurance. "It's now or never, Nina."

Nina's heart raced, a mixture of anticipation and anxiety coursing through her veins. She drew in a deep breath, her fingers clutching the stolen key card tightly. With a steady hand, she approached the door and swiped the card through the electronic lock.

The soft click of the lock releasing was barely audible, but to Nina, it sounded like the echo of progress. With a push, the door swung open, revealing a room bathed in the dim light of fluorescents. The air within held a faint mustiness, and the shelves and cabinets lined with records exuded a sense of historical weight.

As they stepped into the room, the door closing behind them with a soft snick, the gravity of their actions intensified. They were standing on the precipice of revelation, the culmination of their daring plan. The records that lay before them contained the keys to the truth, the patterns, and the secrets that had remained concealed for far too long.

Nina exchanged a quick glance with Daniel, a silent understanding passing between them. The weight of responsibility and anticipation hung heavy in the air, and as they moved toward the rows of cabinets, their quest for answers became profound, a fire burning brighter with each step they took.

Rows upon rows of filing cabinets stretched before them, each containing a piece of the puzzle they sought to unravel. Their task was daunting, their time limited, but their determination burned bright.

Working in tandem, they scanned labels and shuffled through files, seeking the elusive documents that could hold possibly hold the clue to Amanda's disappearance and the pattern of vanishing women. The minutes ticked by as they continued their search, every rustle of paper resonating with a mix of hope and apprehension.

As they delved deeper into the records, unaware of the unfolding events outside the hospital, the shadows of the night seemed to mirror their quest, each hidden corner holding the promise of answers that had long evaded their grasp.

Among the rows of filing cabinets, Nina and Daniel split up to maximize their search efforts. Their fingers grazed the labels on the folders, the anticipation of uncovering hidden truths propelling their every move. They navigated the maze of records, each cabinet a potential treasure trove of information that could unveil the secrets they had been chasing.

Their hushed footsteps echoed in the room, a reminder of the significance of their mission. The fluorescent lights hummed overhead, casting a pale glow on the worn labels and yellowing paper. Every flicker of a folder felt like a step closer to unraveling the enigma that had plagued their thoughts.

Nina's heart raced as she meticulously skimmed through folders, seeking any trace of her sister's name. The years of separation, the grief of not knowing her sister's fate, had fueled her determination. Every paper rustled was a whisper of possibility, a chance to piece together the puzzle of her sister's life.

On the opposite side of the room, Daniel's fingers danced over the edges of files, his eyes scanning each label with fervor. He shared Nina's determination, each folder he encountered fueling his desire to find the missing links, the connections that would make the intricate web of disappearances make sense.

Minutes seemed to pass, time measured only by the sound of shuffling paper and the rustling of their breaths. The room became a sanctuary of hope, a space where past stories were preserved in ink and paper. The search felt endless, the weight of their emotions mingling with the weight of the task they had undertaken.

Then, within the countless records, Nina's fingers brushed against a folder that seemed to resonate with her. The name "Elle Santos" stood out, a beacon of significance. Trembling, she pulled it from its slot, her heart pounding as she opened it to reveal the pages within.

Nina's breath caught as she scanned the contents,

her eyes darting over medical reports, notes, and records. The pieces of her sister's life, long shrouded in mystery, began to take shape. Every page was a glimpse into Elle's journey, a narrative of struggles and triumphs, fears and aspirations.

Across the room, Daniel's voice broke the silence. "Nina!" He held out another folder, his eyes wide with a mixture of urgency and discovery. "I think I've found something too."

Nina joined him, their eyes meeting over the folders they held. The records before them were like breadcrumbs, leading them through the maze of the past. The fragments of information they had long sought were finally falling into place, a mosaic of truth that painted a clearer picture with each page turned.

As their hands met, each clutching a file bearing the name "Elle," a surge of anticipation pulsed between Nina and Daniel. Their whispered voices carried a mix of astonishment and urgency.

"I got Elle Knight," Daniel breathed, his voice a mere murmur of disbelief.

"No way! I got Elle Santos," Nina responded, her voice equally hushed. The uncanny coincidence hung in the air, a testament to the interconnectedness of their lives and their mission.

With their heartbeats quickening, they shared a brief but meaningful glance, understanding the significance of the files they held. The gravity of their discoveries urged them forward. "I think we should get out of here," Daniel urged, the urgency in his tone palpable.

Nina, however, hesitated, her fingers lightly gripping Daniel's arm to stop him. "Wait," she said softly. "Maybe we should take a quick look?"

Daniel considered her suggestion, empathy shining in his eyes. He knew how deeply personal this revelation was for Nina. Elle was her sister, and she deserved to know the truth first. "Okay, but let's be quick," he agreed, his voice a blend of caution and support.

Finding a small desk tucked away in a corner, they placed their files side by side. With a sense of purpose, they hurriedly opened the folders, scanning the contents for the answers they sought. The truth was finally within reach, and their hearts raced as they delved into the secrets held within the pages.

"Look at this, Danny," Nina whispered urgently, her finger pointing at the report. "Elle was admitted for an emergency... but this doesn't make any sense."

Daniel's eyes widened as he read on, the shock

mirrored in his voice. "C-section? She was pregnant?"

Elle Santos's file revealed a startling truth—details of an emergency hospitalization and a subsequent C-section. Nina's gaze remained fixed on the pages, her voice shaking as she continued to reveal the information before her. "Look at the date," she pointed out, a tremor in her words. "This was almost 15 years ago, just a few months after I left."

Daniel's eyes followed her finger, and as they read the details together, the truth hit them like a tidal wave. "The child was given away in a closed adoption process," he read aloud, his voice barely above a whisper.

The realization was staggering. The fragments of Elle's life that had remained shrouded in mystery were now unraveling before their eyes. Nina's shock was palpable, the truth more painful than she could have ever imagined. "No, this can't be real," she gasped, her breath coming in ragged bursts.

Realizing the gravity of their discovery and the potential danger they were in, Daniel's fingers flew over his phone's keyboard. He tapped out a final message to the group chat, "Phase 3 is complete."

With the files swiftly returned to their place, Daniel seized Nina's hand, his grip firm yet gentle as he guided her out of the room. The urgency they felt was mirrored by Orlando, who awaited them in the back alleyway. The shadows of the hospital held their secrets, but they were determined to bring them to light.

Inside the car's safety, the tension and gravity of their recent discoveries seemed to hang heavy. Orlando's voice cut through the silence as he drove without headlights, the darkness a shroud of protection.

"It's about time, guys," Orlando's words echoed the collective relief and anxiety that had been building up. His focus was on the road ahead, navigating through the night as his passengers grappled with the weight of their revelations.

Nina's gaze remained fixed on the passing scenery, her thoughts a whirlwind of emotions. The truth they had uncovered about her sister, the reality of Elle's past that had been concealed, churned in her mind. She was grappling with the enormity of it all, the shock and pain of the revelation still fresh.

As the car swerved around corners, Orlando turned to Daniel, his voice gentle yet firm, "So Vaughn is going to meet us at there, right?"

"Yeah, that's the plan," Daniel answered

Orlando's question about Vaughn meeting them at Olive's place.

"So," Orlando asked, his eyes searching theirs for any signs of success, "Got what we needed?"

Daniel's eyes flickered between the road and Nina's distant gaze. He understood that this wasn't the right time to discuss their findings, not while the weight of the revelation hung heavy in the air. Frustration tinged his voice as he responded, "Let's just get back first, yeah?" His annoyance was a shield, a way to deflect the questions and to give Nina the space she needed to process everything.

Meanwhile, at the hospital's reception area, time seemed to stretch in tandem with the tension that gripped the waiting room. Vaughn's rhythmic humming provided an unwitting soundtrack to the drumming of hearts, the rhythm of their collective anxiety of people who were waiting for other reasons.

The minutes continued their measured march, each second carrying with it the weight of their secret mission. Vaughn maintained a veneer of calm, his face a mask hiding the anticipation that swirled beneath the surface. His poise was a stronghold to the importance of their mission, the hope that this meeting would yield the breakthrough they so desperately sought.

At last, the receptionist reappeared, the click of her heels a signal that the moment of truth had arrived. She was accompanied by a supervisor, an older woman whose presence seemed to fill the room. Vaughn's composure held steady as they engaged in a subdued exchange, their voices kept low to ensure the confidentiality of their conversation.

The supervisor, a middle-aged woman with greying hair, was dressed in a brown cardigan and wore glasses that perched on the bridge of her nose. She carried an air of authority, a demeanor that spoke of years spent navigating the complexities of the medical world.

With a nod from the supervisor, Vaughn rose from his seat, a picture of controlled resolve. "Mr. Knight, why don't we go to my office?" Her voice was steady, an invitation cloaked in professionalism.

Vaughn met her gaze, a subtle agreement passing between them. The journey from the reception area to the supervisor's office was a silent one, each step bringing them closer to the culmination of their plan.

Once inside her office, the supervisor closed the door behind them, shutting out the outside world and cocooning their conversation in a bubble of privacy. The room itself was adorned with framed degrees and medical accolades, that showcased her years of dedication to the field.

Vaughn settled into the offered seat, the tension in the room palpable. In the confined space of the supervisor's office, Vaughn and the middle-aged woman sat across from each other, their unspoken intentions hanging in the air. The room's atmosphere was charged with the weight of their conversation, each word spoken carrying the potential to unravel secrets long kept hidden.

The supervisor's gaze remained steady as she addressed Vaughn's inquiry. "I understand that you're looking for the medical records of your wife?" Her tone was measured, a blend of empathy and professional protocol.

"Yes, that's correct," Vaughn confirmed, his voice holding a mix of determination and desperation.

As Vaughn's words hung between them, the supervisor's expression grew somber. "Mr. Knight, we have hospital policies in place to protect the privacy of all our patients," she explained gently. "I'm afraid that I cannot give you what you are looking for."

A sense of frustration crept into Vaughn's voice as he responded, "But she's my wife. Don't I have the right to access my wife's medical files?"

The supervisor's demeanor remained unwavering. "Unfortunately, no, Mr. Knight. At this point, we can only release that information with a court order or a warrant. Do you have either one of those?"

Vaughn's desperation became palpable as he pleaded his case. "Please, you must understand. She went missing last summer. I have been searching for something, anything that can help me find her."

The supervisor's expression softened, a mix of sympathy and the confines of her professional boundaries. "I'm aware of your predicament and believe me, I'm very sorry, Mr. Knight. There isn't anything that I can do about this."

Defeated, Vaughn slumped in his chair, his frustration mingling with a sense of helplessness. He met the supervisor's gaze, his eyes searching for any hint of understanding. With a determined resolve, he posed a question that cut to the heart of the matter. "But do tell, why wouldn't my wife talk about a scar on her lower abdomen?"

The woman's surprise at the question was evident, her brows furrowing in thought. She took a moment, her eyes meeting Vaughn's with a mixture of realization and unease. "There's only one reason why."

Vaughn's heart raced as he pressed for an answer.

"What is that?" he asked, his voice carrying a tremor of anticipation.

The supervisor held his gaze, her words carrying the weight of truth. "You're a smart man, Mr. Vaughn. You already know why."

Her words hung between them, an undeniable revelation. Vaughn's heart sank as he realized the implications, the truth that had eluded him for so long.

With a heavy sigh, the supervisor leaned back in her chair, her face a mask of concern. "You need to be careful, Mr. Knight," she warned, her voice laced with concern. "It's dangerous to ask questions. Trust me, I've seen people get hurt before."

Vaughn nodded slowly, a combination of acceptance and apprehension. He had come to the hospital seeking answers, but the price of his search was clear. In the confines of the hospital's supervisor's office, Vaughn had found the truth. And the truth was more real than he had ever imagined.

***

Back at the house, Olive's emotions churned like a stormy sea, each wave crashing against her inner turmoil. She had sought solace in a tall glass of alcohol, hoping it would numb the rapid feelings that threatened to overwhelm her. Her friends had left for the hospital, their purpose clear and focused, leaving her in a state of restless contemplation. And now, just when she thought the night couldn't become any more turbulent, an unexpected visitor stood before her door.

The doorbell's chime echoed through the quiet house, jolting her from her thoughts. Her heart raced as she made her way to the entrance, her steps a tad unsteady from the alcohol's influence. An unease settled over her like a heavy cloak, tightening around her chest. The shadows outside played tricks on her mind, intensifying her anxiety.

Taking a deep breath, she mustered the courage to open the door, her eyes meeting those of the visitor. It was a sight she hadn't expected, and it stirred a whirlwind of emotions within her, battling against the numbing effect of the alcohol.

The man before her was one she had hoped to leave behind, a threat from her past that had somehow found its way to Serenity Falls. Her breath hitched as her eyes met his, her past catching up with her present in a way she hadn't anticipated.

"Tony! What are you doing here?" The words tumbled out of Olive's mouth, a mixture of surprise and apprehension. She stumbled backward, her mind racing to process his sudden appearance.

The man's smile was unsettling, a familiar face carrying with it a sense of foreboding. "Oh, thanks for inviting me in, Olive." His words were laced with a sinister edge, sending a shiver down her spine.

As he stepped closer, she struggled to regain her composure. "You need to leave," she managed to assert, her voice trembling as she tried to assert her boundaries.

But he ignored her plea, advancing further into her space. "I was in town," he explained casually, his eyes scanning her surroundings. "I thought I'd drop by."

Olive's heart raced as she continued to step back, her vulnerability contrasted against his audacity. "Please, just leave me alone," she implored, her voice carrying a mix of fear and frustration.

His presence seemed to envelop her, the air thick with an unsettling tension. His fingers grazed her hair as he moved closer, his proximity suffocating. "But I just got here, Olive," he purred, his words a chilling caress against her senses.

His touch sent a shiver down her spine, a cocktail of fear and curiosity swirling within her. Her instincts screamed at her to escape, to put distance between herself and Tony who seemed to hold an undeniable power over her.

His fingers continued to dance through her hair, his touch both intoxicating and alarming. Olive's body tensed as her mind raced, trying to make sense of the situation. Questions tumbled in her thoughts—what did he want? Why was he here? And what was the purpose behind his unsettling actions?

Before she could gather her thoughts and find her voice, the sound of a car pulling up in the neighborhood pierced the air. It was a timely distraction that had him pulling away from her, his fingers retreating like a predator interrupted in its pursuit. Olive's heart pounded in her chest, her breathing uneven as relief washed over her in waves.

His laughter rang out, a chilling sound that taunted and filled the air with an unsettling arrogance. "I'll be seeing you around, my dear," he declared, his words carrying a weight that sent a cold shiver down her throat. The combination of his lingering presence and his cryptic departure left her both intrigued and unnerved.

The door closed behind him, leaving Olive standing in her doorway, her heart pounding. The encounter had left her shaken, questions swirling through her mind like a storm. How had he found her? Why was he here in Serenity Falls?

And as the car pulled away, disappearing into the night, Olive was left with a sense of unease and a realization that her past was catching up faster than she could have ever anticipated.

***

CHAPTER 14: TWISTS AND TURNS

Vaughn's departure from the hospital had left him reeling, his mind a flurry of questions and revelations. The streets outside blurred into streaks of light as he drove recklessly, the engine's roar matching the tumultuous whirl of his thoughts. His grip on the steering wheel tightened and his knuckles turned white, a physical manifestation of the turmoil within him.

The events of the past hours had ignited a storm of emotions and uncertainties. Faces, both familiar and unfamiliar, flickered through his mind like a rapid slideshow, each one raising more questions than answers. The memory of the interrogation room, the weight of Deputy Turner's accusations, and the scrutiny of Agent Marks bore down on him like a heavy burden.

His jaw clenched as he tried to make sense of the tangled web of information he had uncovered.

Amanda's disappearance, the connection to Elle's past, the journalist who happened to be his sister-in-law, and the looming shadow of danger—each thread wove a complex narrative that seemed impossible to untangle. He found himself replaying every interaction, every conversation, searching for clues that might lead him to the truth.

The city lights blurred into streaks of color as he navigated the streets, his focus shifting between the road and the chaos in his mind. The truth, he realized, was like a puzzle scattered across his life—a puzzle he was determined to piece together, no matter the cost. His heart pounded in his chest, a mixture of frustration, determination, and fear driving him forward.

As he sped through the night, his thoughts were a whirlwind of possibilities and uncertainties. The road ahead was uncertain, but one thing was clear: he couldn't let fear or doubt hold him back. The truth was out there, waiting to be unveiled, and he was willing to face whatever challenges came his way to find it.

When Vaughn finally arrived in front of Olive's house, he felt a knot of emotions tightening within him as he stepped outside his vehicle. He slowly walked inside, with his head held low, as he closed the door behind him.

The air inside the room was heavy with anticipation, as if the very walls were privy to the gravity of their shared pursuit. The soft glow of lamps cast a warm ambiance, contrasting the storm that raged within his mind.

His gaze was instinctively drawn to Olive, who lay asleep on one of the couches. In that peaceful repose, she seemed so distant from the chaos that had been unleashed in their lives. Her features were serene, a stark contrast to the turmoil that churned within his own chest. He watched her for a moment, a mixture of protectiveness and vulnerability swelling within him.

The hushed conversation that had been taking place among Daniel, Nina, and Orlando came to an abrupt halt as Vaughn entered. The room's occupants turned their attention to him, their eyes a mix of curiosity and concern. It was as if the air had shifted with his presence, carrying with it an unspoken acknowledgment that they were all caught in the same web of uncertainty.

Nina's voice broke the silence, a call to him that held both urgency and concern. "Vaughn, come here." He complied, taking a seat beside Orlando on the couch. The weight of the hospital's revelations pressed heavily upon him, a cloud of uncertainty that seemed to suffocate any remaining hope.

"What happened at the hospital?" Vaughn inquired, his voice tinged with an undertone of weariness.

Nina's response was a hesitant admission, "Vaughn, it seems that my sister...I mean, it did happen. It's in the hospital records." The gravity of the truth was palpable in her words, the acknowledgment of something long buried.

Vaughn's understanding was swift, a silent agreement. "Elle had a baby, didn't she?" The words hung in the air, a shared realization that spoke volumes without need for further explanation.

"Yes, she did," Nina confirmed softly, her gaze holding the weight of her sister's past.

Vaughn leaned back against the couch, his mind processing the implications of this new revelation. The couch seemed to envelop him, offering a temporary comfort from the weight of his thoughts.

But the conversation continued, each new piece of information like a thread weaving a complex tapestry. Daniel's voice cut through the air, "And that's not all." Vaughn's attention snapped back, his eyes fixing on Daniel.

Daniel's gaze locked onto Vaughn's, his words

carrying the weight of another revelation. "The baby was given away in a closed adoption."

Vaughn's thoughts spiraled, a mix of emotions flooding him. He had never considered the possibility of the baby being alive, a connection to Elle that he hadn't anticipated. "Where is it now?" he questioned, his voice heavy with curiosity and a hint of longing.

Nina's response was laced with the reality of the situation. "Closed adoption, Vaughn. There's no way to know. Those have court orders and seals all over them."

The realization settled over him, a bittersweet acceptance of the unknown. "Well, that clears things up," he muttered, the words tinged with sadness.

But Nina wasn't willing to let the matter rest there. "No, it doesn't. The records don't say who the father was."

Daniel's gaze shifted between Nina and Vaughn as he filled in the gaps. "But there could only be one possible person."

Vaughn's confusion was evident. "What do you mean by that?"

Nina turned to Daniel, her determination evident. "The boy she was dating since high school. The hospital records of her c-section fall around a couple of months after the time I left town."

"But," Daniel interjected, "If it's Hector you mean, he committed suicide several years ago. He jumped off the cliff, his mother was the only witness." The mention of Hector's name hung heavy in the air, his memory casting a shadow over their conversation.

Vaughn's hopes were dashed, the possibility of a lead extinguished. "Well, that's another dead end then," he sighed.

Nina's conviction remained firm, her journalist's instincts guiding her. "No, it's not. If there's anything I've learned in investigative journalism, it's that there are no dead ends. Only new clues, and this is a new one. We need to talk to Hector's mom."

Amidst the tension and conversations that unfolded within the room, Orlando's patience wore thin. The words exchanged between Vaughn, Nina, and Daniel seemed to fall short in providing answers to the burning question that loomed over them all — the whereabouts of Amanda, Orlando's missing wife. His frustration, long simmering, boiled over as he couldn't bear the sense of stagnation any longer.

"But what good does this do?" Orlando's voice rang out, the frustration woven deeply into his words.

"We are nowhere closer to finding Amanda, my wife, in case you forgot about her." The weight of his emotions colored every syllable he uttered, a mix of anger, desperation, and a heartache that only those who had loved and lost could truly understand.

Orlando's abrupt departure cut through the atmosphere, the sound of the front door closing echoing in the room. He left, his steps filled with a palpable sense of urgency and exasperation. The space he left behind seemed to carry the echoes of his words, a reminder that amidst the maze of revelations and emotions, their ultimate goal remained unchanged — to find Amanda, to bring her back home.

Meanwhile, Olive who lay on a nearby couch, caught in the in-between realms of sleep and wakefulness. Her slumber was restless, her mind a battleground of memories and emotions. In her dreams, or perhaps her nightmares, Tony's presence felt all too real, his invasive touch a haunting reminder of a past she had tried to escape. Her unconscious mind replayed the fear and turmoil she had once endured, leaving her to relive the trauma that had marked her.

As the heated discussions continued around her, Olive stirred in her sleep, her brows furrowing in response to the internal turmoil she was experiencing. The past and the present seemed to blur, and she was transported back to a time when fear had been her constant companion.

In Olive's dream, the fabric of time seemed to bend, and she found herself reliving moments from her past. The memories were vivid, playing out like scenes from a movie, each detail etched into her mind.

Flashbacks unveiled the beginning of her nightmarish relationship with Tony. The scenes unfolded in a sequence that felt all too real, each moment leaving a lasting impact on her psyche.

In this dreamscape, Olive found herself back in the hallways of her old apartment building, her footsteps echoing softly on the tiled floor. She stepped into the elevator, her heart skipping a beat as she noticed Tony standing there. His charismatic smile greeted her, and they exchanged polite pleasantries, initiating a conversation that would gradually take on a darker hue.

Over the course of several days, their interactions deepened, each elevator ride accompanied by a bit more laughter and a bit more shared personal information. Tony's charm was undeniable, and his words seemed innocuous, drawing Olive into his orbit. As days turned into weeks, the connection between them grew stronger, fueled by seemingly harmless exchanges. In those innocent encounters, Olive saw nothing more than casual conversation, but for Tony, it was the start of a twisted obsession.

In the dream, Olive recalled the moment when Tony had finally mustered the courage to ask her out. It had been a sunny afternoon, the warm rays of sunlight filtering through the windows as they rode the elevator together. His voice held a hint of nervousness as he spoke, "You know, Olive, I've really enjoyed our chats. I was wondering if you'd like to grab a cup of coffee with me sometime?"

Olive's heart had raced in response, her mind momentarily suspended between curiosity and a cautious reserve. She remembered the way she had weighed his words, the blend of emotions that swirled within her. Her response had come after a brief pause, her lips curving into a hesitant smile as she nodded, "Sure, why not? Coffee sounds nice."

In the dream, the scene shifted, transporting Olive to the bistro cafe where she and Tony had their first official date. The ambiance was warm and inviting, a soft glow enveloping the space as chatter and the clinking of glasses echoed in the background. They sat across from each other, a table set with flickering candles and an air of expectation.

As the evening unfolded, Olive found herself sharing anecdotes, stories, and fragments of her life.

Tony listened attentively, his smile never faltering, as if he was genuinely interested in every word she spoke. Yet, beneath his charismatic demeanor, Olive sensed a current of calculated intention, a hidden agenda that cast a shadow over their conversation.

In the dream, Olive could feel the weight of her uncertainty, the internal struggle between being honest with herself and attempting to give Tony the benefit of the doubt. As the evening progressed, she finally found the courage to express her feelings, her voice gentle but resolute, "Tony, I've enjoyed spending time with you, but I have to be honest. I don't feel a romantic connection between us. I think we might be better off as friends."

Tony's reaction was a masterful display of composure. He nodded, his expression one of understanding and agreement. Inside his mind, however, a plan was already taking shape — a plan to worm his way into her life, to become a permanent fixture, regardless of her feelings.

"I appreciate your honesty, Olive," he replied, his tone measured. "It's important to be on the same page. If friendship is where we're headed, then I'm perfectly fine with that."

In the dream, Olive's heart wavered between relief and suspicion. She had spoken her truth, but there was a nagging feeling that Tony's response wasn't entirely genuine.

In the middle of her dream, Olive was transported to a time she had tried to forget, a continuation of the nightmarish relationship that had haunted her. The scenes unfolded before her like a surreal movie, each moment etching itself into her subconscious.

In the dream, a few days after the unsettling first date, Olive was transported back to her apartment. The atmosphere was tense, a feeling of unease lingering in the air as if the walls themselves held a secret. Her heart raced as an unexpected knock echoed through the space, causing her to jump. She cautiously opened the door, only to be met with a group of stern-looking police officers, their expressions devoid of warmth or explanation.

Before Olive could react, the officers barged into her apartment, their presence dominating the room. She stood frozen, her mind racing to comprehend the sudden intrusion. They moved with a calculated efficiency, searching through her belongings with a thoroughness that sent a chill down her spine. It was as if her personal space was being invaded, the sanctity of her home violated without cause.

As the officers meticulously scoured her apartment, Olive's anxiety intensified. Her eyes darted around the room, her thoughts a chaotic mess of confusion and disbelief. How had her ordinary day turned into this nightmare? What could they possibly be searching for?

In the dream, the energy in the room was intense, the silence broken only by the sound of rustling and shuffling. And then, to her shock and horror, one of the officers emerged from a hidden corner with a small packet of drugs, holding it up for everyone to see.

Olive's heart pounded in her chest, her voice caught in her throat as panic surged through her veins. "Wait, that's not mine!" she protested, her voice desperate and filled with disbelief. But her words seemed to fall on deaf ears, as the officers exchanged knowing glances and continued their search.

In the dream's twisted narrative, Olive's world crumbled around her. The discovery of the packet of drugs had irrevocably altered the course of her life, plunging her into a nightmare from which there seemed to be no escape.

As the officers held up the damning evidence, Olive's protests fell on deaf ears. The weight of their suspicion bore down on her, crushing her spirit with each passing moment. In the midst of her pleas of innocence, they moved with a swift and unyielding determination. The dream painted a vivid picture of her arrest, her hands restrained in cold metal handcuffs, her freedom slipping through her fingers like sand.

In the surreal haze of the dream, Olive was led away from her apartment, her heart racing and her mind a whirlwind of confusion and fear. The world around her seemed to warp and distort, the colors bleeding into one another, creating an almost otherworldly scene. The sound of her own rapid breathing echoed in her ears as her surroundings morphed into a blur of faces, walls, and corridors.

The dream captured the disorienting experience of being escorted to the local police department. Olive's senses were heightened, each detail etched into her memory with an intensity that only dreams could conjure. The harsh lighting of the police station, the clatter of footsteps in the hallway, the distant chatter of officers—it all swirled together, overwhelming her senses and intensifying her feeling of helplessness.

And then, like a phantom from her past, Tony appeared at the police station. He was there, like an unexpected sinister presence that sent chills all over her cold skin. He approached her, his voice a quiet but haunting reassurance. "Don't worry," he whispered urgently. "I'll make this all go away. If anyone asks, tell them you're my girlfriend. You are FBI Special Agent Antony Marks' girlfriend, okay?"

Olive's shock immobilized her, her mind struggling to process the gravity of what he was asking. She nodded, a sense of unreality washing over her as she shifted uncomfortably in her seat. Tony's words were a heavy weight, binding her to a narrative she didn't understand but was forced to play along with.

With a kiss to her forehead that sent shivers down her spine, Tony walked over to the police officers who had arrested her. She could barely hear their heated exchange, the words a distant echo as her anxiety tightened its grip on her mind. Her vision blurred as she struggled to hold onto her surroundings.

As Tony's conversation with the officers continued, a hazy Olive watched as he approached her again, his touch a suffocating embrace around her waist. "Come on, love," he cooed, his voice dripping with false concern. "Let's go home."

Her dream twisted and contorted, weaving a narrative of manipulation and fear. The echoes of that past reality echoed within her mind, a reminder of the darkness she had managed to escape from. And in the present, Olive stirred in her sleep, her subconscious grappling with the lingering scars of her history with Tony.

Olive jolted awake from the haunting clutches of her nightmare, her heart racing and her breath coming in ragged gasps. The lines between reality and the dream blurred momentarily, panic gripping her as she tried to orient herself. Confusion clouded her vision until she realized that she was back in her living room, surrounded by the familiar sights and sounds of her home.

To her surprise, Vaughn was crouched beside her couch, his presence a comforting anchor amidst the tumult of her emotions. His gentle voice reached her ears, his words soothing like a balm for her racing heart. "Hush, it's okay, you had a nightmare," he murmured, his tone offering a semblance of reassurance.

Olive's initial panic subsided, her breathing gradually steadying as she pulled away from his touch. Vaughn respected her need for space, his hands retreating as he allowed her room to collect herself. She glanced around her house, her mind slowly reconciling the dream with reality.

"Where are the others?" Olive's voice trembled slightly as she spoke, her gaze seeking answers in the dimly lit room.

"Nina and Daniel are here inside, freshening up," Vaughn responded, his voice carrying a gentle understanding.

With his presence next to her, Olive managed to sit up, the residual fear of her dream still clinging to her senses. Vaughn maintained a respectful distance, his concern palpable yet restrained. The awkwardness of the situation hung between them, unspoken and understood.

Seeking to shift the focus, Olive pressed forward. "So, what happened at the hospital? What did you find out?" Her curiosity was piqued, and she needed to divert her thoughts from the nightmare that still lingered.

Vaughn took a moment before responding, his gaze meeting hers as he began to recount their findings. "Well," he started, "My wife had a baby when she was a teenager. So now, Nina wants to talk to the then-boyfriend's mother, hoping to find some answers."

"Oh," Olive murmured, absorbing the information. She couldn't help but feel a pang of sympathy for Vaughn. "I'm so sorry you didn't know. If I were in your shoes, I would have wanted to know."

Vaughn's response was quiet, the weight of his emotions evident in his voice. "Yeah."

The living room was filled with a heavy silence, each of them lost in their thoughts and the shared understanding of the complex web of emotions they were entangled in.

Olive's weariness was palpable as she slowly rose from the couch, her gaze resting on Vaughn for a moment. "Well, then, I'll be off to bed now," she announced softly, her voice a mixture of exhaustion and gratitude.

Vaughn nodded, his eyes meeting hers. "Oh, okay. Good night," he responded, his expression a blend of understanding and concern.

With measured steps, Olive made her way towards her bedroom, her thoughts swirling like a storm within her mind. As she stood by the door, her fingers grazing the cool surface, she turned back slightly to face Vaughn. "Thanks for staying," she whispered, her voice carrying a depth of emotion that words couldn't fully convey.

The door closed with a soft click, and Olive found herself enveloped by the solitude of her room. The events of the day, the revelations, and the unsettling memories intertwined, creating a web of emotions that left her feeling both drained and restless.

She allowed herself to sink onto her bed, her mind replaying the encounters and discussions that had unfolded with the others. Vaughn's presence had stirred something within her, a sense of vulnerability and companionship that was unexpected. His pursuit of answers paralleled her own, a shared quest to unravel the mysteries that had entangled their lives.

As the shadows danced on her bedroom walls, Olive couldn't shake the nagging thought that had taken root in her mind. What if Vaughn was truly innocent? What if his motives were driven by a genuine desire to uncover the truth about his wife's disappearance? The implications of this possibility were immense, casting a new light on their collective pursuit.

She wrestled with the thought as the night stretched on, her mind a whirlwind of uncertainties. The lines between suspicion and trust, past and present, blurred in the jumble of her thoughts.

***

In the quietness of one of the spare bedroom, Daniel and Nina lay nestled under the covers, their thoughts intertwined with the events of the day. Comforted by Daniel's arm around her, Nina's voice broke the silence, laden with a sense of contemplation. "Do you ever wonder, Daniel? If I had stayed, if I had been there for her, would she have made a different choice?"

Daniel's eyes remained closed as he held her close, his response gentle yet firm. "Nina, don't burden yourself with the 'what ifs'. You can't blame yourself for everything that's happened. There could have been a number of reasons why Elle made the decisions she did."

Nina sighed softly, her fingers tracing patterns on the fabric of the sheets. The weight of her sister's choices, the unspoken regrets, hung heavy in the air. She shifted slightly, turning to face Daniel, seeking his reassurance in the darkness.

Daniel's eyes blinked open in surprise as he met her gaze. Their eyes locked, and a spark of understanding passed between them. And then, without a word, Nina closed the distance between them, her lips finding his in a soft, lingering kiss.

The moment held a mixture of comfort and tenderness, a silent affirmation of their connection in the middle of the turmoil that surrounded them. As they broke the kiss, Daniel's fingers brushed a strand of hair from Nina's face, his touch tender and reassuring. "Nina, we can't change the past, but I'll always be here for you."

Nina's lips curved into a faint smile, the weight of her thoughts momentarily eased by his presence. "I know, Daniel," she whispered, her voice carrying a blend of gratitude and emotion. "I'm glad you're here with me."

Daniel held her close, his words a quiet murmur. "I will never leave you alone, Nina."

Nina closed her eyes, allowing herself to relax into the warmth of his embrace, the sound of his breathing was a calming sound. Daniel ran his hands over her back, his touch gentle, soothing. She felt safe and protected, the familiarity of his arms an anchor in a sea of uncertainty.

Nina's eyes opened in the darkness, and a wistful smile crossed her lips. "Sometimes, I can still remember the first time we met," she said, her voice tinged with nostalgia.

Daniel smiled in amusement, the memory of that day still vivid in his mind. It was the first day of school, and he had been a shy and awkward child. His mother had walked him to school, holding his hand tightly. When they got to the classroom, his mother had bent down to hug him and tell him that she would come back later to pick him up. But Daniel had refused to let go of her, clinging to her leg and begging her not to leave him.

It was at that moment that a young Nina had stepped in, her tone gentle and encouraging. "You're okay," she said, putting an arm around his shoulders. "I'm Nina. We're going to be friends, and I'm going to help you. Okay?"

Daniel's eyes widened as he realized that it was the same girl who was now in his arms. His heart swelled with emotion, and he pressed a soft kiss to Nina's forehead. Nina was quick enough to pull him towards her as she returned his kiss, her lips capturing his in a passionate embrace.

Daniel's mind spun as the heat between them grew, the air charged with a heady mixture of desire and love. As their bodies moved together in a timeless dance, Nina's gaze locked with his, the depth of her emotions reflected in her eyes.

They lost themselves in the moment, their hearts and souls joined in a perfect harmony, the intensity of their connection bringing tears to Nina's eyes. It was a connection that transcended time and space, a connection that had endured through the years, and would endure long into the future.

Nina's fingers traced the contours of Daniel's face, her touch light and reverent. "I've always loved you, Daniel. Even when we were young."

Daniel's smile widened, his eyes alight with happiness. "And I've always loved you, Nina." He paused for a moment, his expression thoughtful. "But I think you were my first love, even though I didn't realize it at the time."

Nina's expression was one of surprise, but she didn't say anything. Instead, she leaned forward and kissed him again, the depth of her feelings evident in the way her lips lingered against his.

As they pulled apart, Nina's eyes were bright with unshed tears, and she could feel her heart beating rapidly in her chest. It was a bittersweet moment, full of joy and sorrow, and she was filled with an overwhelming sense of gratitude and love for Daniel.

Nina's eyes fluttered shut as she leaned her head against Daniel's shoulder, allowing the memories to wash over her. The first day they met, the first time they held hands, the first time they kissed. She had treasured each moment, holding them close to her heart like a precious secret. And yet, she knew that she had to leave again, once she finds out what happened to her sister. Her life was in California, her apartment, her job, her friends. And even though it was painful, she knew that she had to go back.

But that night, their hands intertwined, fingers fitting perfectly like pieces of a puzzle, as they settled into the quiet embrace of the night. The challenges ahead were daunting, the answers elusive, but in the circle of each other's arms, they found a sense of strength that carried them forward.

***

CHAPTER 15: RACE AGAINST TIME

Olive's senses gradually awakened as she stirred from her sleep, the veil of dreams lifting to the reality of a new day. The unfamiliar sounds of conversation and the inviting aroma of coffee wafted through the air, coaxing her to full wakefulness. With a soft yawn, she rubbed her eyes and pushed herself off the bed, feeling a mix of curiosity and confusion tugging at her.

Stepping out of her room, she found herself in the hallway, the source of the sounds and scents becoming more apparent with each step she took. The warm glow of morning sunlight filtered through the windows, casting a gentle illumination on the scene that greeted her. The air was alive with the chatter of voices, and Olive's senses drank in the comforting familiarity of companionship.

In the living area, the scene unfolded before her eyes. Vaughn stood by the dining table, wearing an apron and a warm smile as he dished out breakfast for Nina and Daniel. The atmosphere was surprisingly relaxed, and Olive couldn't help but marvel at the transformation that had taken place in just a short time.

"Olive!" Vaughn's greeting was cheerful, his voice carrying an air of genuine warmth. "Come and join us for breakfast."

"Good morning, Olive," Nina chimed with a playful grin.

"Did you manage to get some rest?" Vaughn added, concern etching his features.

Daniel raised his coffee cup in a mock salute. "We were just discussing what our day might hold. Care to join us?"

Olive's lips curved into a weak smile, touched by the unexpected gesture. She moved to take a seat at the table, the events of the previous day and the echoes of her nightmare slowly receding to the background. Vaughn was quick to pour her a cup of coffee and serve her a plate of scrambled eggs and toast, his actions reflecting a brand-new attitude.

As the conversation flowed between bites of food,

Olive felt a sense of unity that she hadn't anticipated. They four of them were once divided by doubts and suspicions, now seemed to be forming an unspoken bond. She took a sip of her coffee, appreciating its warmth, before finally voicing her thoughts. "You know, I should get back to work. I haven't opened my studio in a few days."

Daniel nodded in agreement, his expression understanding. "Yeah, you should get on with that. We'll be fine just the three of us."

Nina chimed in, her tone playful. "Don't worry, Olive. We'll continue our investigation and fill you in on any new leads."

Olive couldn't help but smile at their shared determination and unity. The weight of the revelations and uncertainties seemed to lift in the company of her newfound friends.

Vaughn silently observed Olive, noticing the distance in her gaze as she focused more on her coffee than her breakfast. He couldn't help but feel a tinge of concern for her, a desire to provide her with some semblance of comfort amidst the turmoil they were all navigating.

Daniel's suggestion about Vaughn staying back for the day, prompted a fleeting thought in his mind. He considered the possibility, but his resolve remained unwavering. He met Daniel's gaze with a nod, "I appreciate it, but I'm in this with all of you. We'll leave once we're done here."

Nina's departure was a signal for Daniel to follow suit, and they left the room together, leaving Vaughn and Olive alone. Vaughn's eyes followed them for a moment, then turned back to Olive, who was rising from her seat. As she began to move towards her room, his voice stopped her in her tracks.

"Olive," he called softly, and she turned to face him, uncertainty flashing in her eyes. He approached her with a faint smile, a mixture of warmth and sadness in his gaze. "I noticed that you barely touched your breakfast. How about I make some egg sandwiches for lunch? I'll pack them up for you."

Her response touched him in a way he hadn't expected. "I would like that," she replied, her voice carrying a newfound vulnerability. Their eyes locked, a moment of connection that went beyond any the words that were ever spoken. But then, as if a sudden impulse overtook them both, Olive closed the distance between them and wrapped her arms around his shoulders, her lips finding his in an unexpected kiss.

The world seemed to stand still in that fleeting moment, a hint of vulnerability mingling in the air.

Vaughn responded gently, his arms instinctively encircling her waist as he returned the kiss, his own emotions echoing hers.

He returned the gesture with a kiss of his own, his hands gently clasping her waist, feeling her body tremble against his. Her lips were soft, warm, her mouth tasting faintly of coffee, and Vaughn felt a sudden sense of urgency in the way she kissed him. He held her tighter, the world around him fading until it was just the two of them, sharing this moment.

When she finally pulled away, her breath was warm on his cheek, and he could feel the pounding of her heart. She gazed up at him, her expression vulnerable, almost pleading, her lips parted as if searching for the words to speak. He stroked her cheek, feeling a slight dampness under his fingertips, and his heart broke as he realized she had been crying.

"Vaughn..." her voice shook slightly. "I need you."

His eyes searched hers, his hand slipping to the back of her neck, cradling her head gently. Her words, the tone of her voice, stirred something deep within him. He felt the same need, the desire to offer her comfort, to make her feel safe, loved. "I'm here, Olive," he whispered, leaning down to capture her lips with his once more, feeling her melt against him, the tension in her body easing. " And you know that I need you too, more than you realize," he murmured, his voice filled with emotion.

Her hands slid up his chest, gripping his shoulders as if to steady herself, and their mouths moved together with a growing urgency. They were lost in each other, the outside world forgotten. Vaughn felt his heartbeat quicken as her tongue slipped into his mouth, exploring, tasting. His hands moved up her back, caressing her through the thin material of her nightgown, feeling her body arch into his touch.

His mind was a whirlwind of thoughts and feelings, and he knew there was no going back now. This was something more than a simple flirtation or infatuation. She had become so important to him, so essential, and he knew that no matter what happened, he would always be there for her. They would face the world together.

She broke the kiss and rested her forehead against his, their breaths mingling, the air heavy with a charged tension. He stroked her hair gently, gazing at her with a mix of affection and concern.

As they pulled away, their eyes searching each other's, a mixture of surprise and understanding passing between them. Vaughn's voice was soft as he spoke, his fingers gently brushing against her cheek. "Olive, I wasn't expecting expect this today."

Olive's lips curved into a shy smile, her heart pounding as she looked up at him. "Me neither," she admitted, her gaze holding his with a newfound sense of closeness.

Vaughn's smile mirrored hers, a shared understanding between them that transcended words. "But you know what, I don't want us to end before we could even begin," he whispered, his fingers lingering on her cheek for a moment longer.

"Me neither," she echoed, leaning into his touch, her eyes never leaving his.

Vaughn couldn't resist pulling her close again, his arms wrapping around her in a warm embrace. He felt her body relax against his, and he knew they were in this together, no matter what the future held.

The intimate moment between Olive and Vaughn was abruptly interrupted by the sound of approaching footsteps descending the stairs. They separated, each feeling a mix of emotions that they weren't quite ready to articulate. As Daniel reached them, a sense of urgency in his demeanor, the weight of the situation became apparent.

"Vaughn," Daniel's voice was tense, "there's been a development. They've arrested Orlando."

The words hung in the air, shattering the fragile shell of connection that had briefly enveloped Olive and Vaughn. Vaughn's brows furrowed, a mixture of concern and confusion taking over. "What? Why?"

Olive's gasp of shock hung in the air, her eyes widening as her hands instinctively covered her mouth. Vaughn's attention was immediately drawn from the phone to her, and then his eyes shifted to the screen. The room was filled with the unexpected report on the local news, and the news reporter's voice carried a tone of urgency.

Vaughn reached out and snatched the phone from Daniel, his eyes locked on the screen as the news report played. The realization hit him like a punch to the gut, and his jaw clenched in disbelief as he listened to the reporter's words.

"The missing mayor's daughter's case," the reporter's voice echoed in the room, the tension palpable, "finally, the police have made a breakthrough. The mayor's new son-in-law, Orlando Morgan, was arrested by local authorities late last night."

A stunned silence settled over the room as the gravity of the situation sank in. The news report depicted a mugshot of Orlando and it now seemed that he was implicated in the disappearance of the mayor's daughter. Vaughn's mind raced, his thoughts a whirlwind of confusion and realization.

The weight of the news hung heavily in the room as the three of them absorbed the shock of Orlando's arrest. Olive's hands trembled as she lowered them from her mouth, her eyes wide with disbelief. Vaughn clenched his jaw, his expression a mixture of anger and frustration, while Daniel's brows furrowed as he stared at the screen, processing the unexpected turn of events. The news report continued, detailing the alleged charges against Orlando and the unfolding investigation.

Vaughn's voice was laced with disbelief as he spoke, his eyes fixed on the screen, "Orlando? But he was with us just last night."

"Orlando got arrested?" Olive managed to whisper, her voice barely audible over the tumultuous thoughts in her mind, "I can't believe this."

Vaughn shook his head, his fingers tightening around the phone as he watched the news report unfold. "This doesn't make sense," he muttered, his tone laced with disbelief. "Why would they arrest him? What evidence do they have?"

Daniel's eyes were fixed on the screen, his voice tense as he spoke, "We need to find out what's going on. There's got to be more to this."

Olive's thoughts raced, her mind a whirlwind of emotions. The arrest of someone they considered an ally had thrown their plans into disarray. She struggled to make sense of the situation, her mind grappling with the possibility that they might have misjudged Orlando.

Vaughn's grip on the phone loosened as he turned to face Olive and Daniel, determination burning in his eyes. "If they've arrested Orlando, there has to be a reason, but we can't afford to lose focus. Daniel, find out what you can. We're going to pay your brother a surprise visit."

"You're absolutely right. I'll reach out to my contact in the local police," Daniel stated, retrieving his phone from Vaughn's outstretched hand before briskly ascending the stairs.

Vaughn turned back to Olive, his presence comforting as he drew her into his arms. He held her close, his grip firm yet gentle, an unspoken promise of protection. "Promise me you'll stay safe," he implored, his voice laced with genuine concern.

Olive's response was a solemn nod, her heart racing as she breathed in Vaughn's familiar scent, the scent that had come to symbolize safety in the midst of chaos. She embraced him, her arms winding around him tightly, seeking solace in his embrace. "Promise me you'll call me if you're ever in danger," Vaughn's words were a gentle reminder, a pact between them.

Once again, Olive nodded, her commitment unwavering as she held him close, cherishing the connection they shared. Vaughn pulled her away slightly, his gaze fixed on her eyes as he sought the affirmation he needed. "Say the words," he urged, his voice a soft plea in the midst of their charged emotions.

"I promise," Olive whispered, her voice carrying the weight of her determination and the unspoken feelings she held for Vaughn. Their eyes locked for a lingering moment, a silent exchange of understanding and support. Vaughn leaned in and pressed his lips against hers, a tender kiss that conveyed his feelings more eloquently than words ever could.

With one last lingering touch, Vaughn released her and stepped back, his expression a mix of longing and resolve. He turned towards the front door, a deep breath taken before he walked away, leaving Olive standing there, her heart racing, her anxiety mingling with a familiar sense of feeling.

As the door closed behind him, Olive was left with a swirl of emotions. She watched the space he had occupied, her fingers brushing against her lips as if to capture the sensation of his kiss. The weight of their shared promises and the intensity of their connection hung in the air, reminding her of the path they had chosen, the risks they were willing to take, and the truth they were determined to uncover.

***

Vaughn, Daniel, and Nina arrived at the local police department, driven by the urgency to gain insights into Orlando's sudden arrest. The building loomed before them, a place that held both the promise of answers and the weight of officialdom.

In the back seat, Daniel's impatience was evident as he pocketed his phone. "Seems like my own brother has ghosted me," he muttered in frustration. Nina, seated beside him, turned her head to face him, her eyes determined. "All the more reason to meet him face to face."

Vaughn skillfully maneuvered his pickup truck through the streets, his grip on the steering wheel firm as he balanced speed with the need to avoid any unwanted attention. Pulling up to the police station, they were greeted by a chaotic scene—press, cameras, and reporters had gathered, hungry for any updates on the investigation.

Vaughn managed to navigate through the crowd without drawing too much notice and parked the truck a short distance away, away from the probing lenses of the cameras. He pulled his hoodie over his head, and the three of them exited the vehicle, blending into the crowd.

The entrance of the police station was adorned with a microphone and podium, signaling that a statement was imminent. With heartbeats racing, the trio walked among the crowd, inching closer to the focal point. The front doors swung open, and a group of officers, Mayor Alvarez, and a man in a sleek black suit emerged.

Nina's curiosity was piqued by the unfamiliar man, and she turned to Daniel, seeking an explanation. "Who's the man in the suit?" she inquired softly. Daniel's head shook slightly, his expression mirroring his ignorance. Vaughn, however, recognized him as the annoying man who was in the interrogation room with him and Deputy Turner.

The deputy chief of the police department approached the podium, and the disharmony of the reporters quieted momentarily in anticipation. He adjusted the microphone and cleared his throat, his gaze steady as he addressed the cameras. "My name is Derek Turner, and I am the Deputy Chief of the Serenity Falls Police Department," he began, his tone composed yet carrying an air of seriousness. "Late last night, we apprehended and took into custody the prime suspect behind the disappearance of Amanda Alvarez."

The words reverberated through the air, a hush falling over the crowd as the gravity of the statement sank in. Vaughn, Daniel, and Nina exchanged glances, their eyes conveying a mixture of surprise and intrigue. As Deputy Chief Turner continued, their focus intensified, absorbing every detail that could shed light on Orlando's involvement and the case itself.

The Deputy Chief's words held weight, and the tension in the atmosphere was palpable as he concluded, "As of this moment, we are still interrogating the suspect. Any further developments will be shared in the near future."

As Deputy Turner concluded his address, the swarm of reporters encircled him, their questions firing rapidly.

"Deputy Turner, is the suspect Orlando Morgan?"

"What about the disappearance of Amanda? Have you found her?"

"Is this a murder case, Deputy Turner?"

Flustered by the barrage of inquiries, Deputy Turner leaned closer to the microphone, his tone firm. "No comments."

With that, the police officers retreated back into

the building, leaving a flurry of reporters in their wake, scrambling to convey the latest updates to their news stations. Among the confusion, Daniel, Nina, and Vaughn quietly navigated their way to the entrance of the police station.

As they entered the building, a stark contrast to the chaos outside, a sense of purpose guided them. The atmosphere seemed deceptively tranquil, opposing the gravity of the investigation that had led them there.

Approaching the reception desk, Daniel introduced himself. "Hi, I'm Daniel Turner. I'm here to meet with Deputy Turner."

However, their interaction was abruptly interrupted by the man in the black suit, whose presence seemed to command attention. The receptionist shifted uneasily, attempting to explain herself, but the man raised his hand in a dismissive gesture.

Addressing Daniel with a curt tone, he informed them, "Deputy Turner is a busy man. He won't be available to meet with his brother for a couple of weeks."

Vaughn's anger was palpable, his jaw clenching as he fought to maintain his composure. Unwilling to back down, Nina stepped forward, leaning on the reception desk, her gaze unwavering. "Let your boss know that we have information pertaining to the missing women case," she asserted with determination.

The man let out a sardonic chuckle, adjusting his tie with an air of superiority. "He is not my boss," he retorted before locking eyes with Nina, sending a shiver down her spine. "You best leave before I consider placing you all under arrest for obstruction charges."

With a final, chilling gaze, he turned and walked out through the entrance doors, leaving Daniel, Nina, and Vaughn stunned by the encounter. Nina couldn't contain her incredulity.

"Who the fuck does he think he is?" she muttered in disbelief.

Though Daniel remained quiet, the receptionist leaned towards them, her voice barely above a whisper. "That's Special Agent Marks from the FBI. You should probably leave. He's known to be quite intimidating."

As the reality of the situation settled in, the trio exchanged glances, realizing that the scope of their investigation had just taken a significant and potentially dangerous turn.

***

Inside Deputy Turner's office, a tense atmosphere hung in the air. Mayor Alvarez sat across from him, his face etched with frustration and concern. The weight of Amanda's disappearance had taken its toll on him, and he was determined to see justice served, no matter the cost.

Mayor Alvarez had his gaze fixed on Deputy Turner as he asked, "Turner, has Orlando said anything? Have you been able to get any information from him?"

Deputy Turner's expression remained composed, his fingers interlocked on the desk in front of him. "No, Mayor. Orlando has lawyered up. He's invoking his right to an attorney, and as a result, he's not cooperating with our questioning."

The mayor's jaw clenched, his frustration deepening. "Lawyered up? Is he hiding something?"

Deputy Turner leaned forward slightly, his voice measured. "It's a standard legal procedure, Mayor. It doesn't necessarily mean he's guilty. People invoke their right to an attorney for various reasons, even innocent ones. It's a safeguard to ensure a fair legal process."

"Deputy Turner, we can't afford to waste any more time," Mayor Alvarez declared, his voice laced with urgency. "We need answers, and we need them now. I want you to use whatever means necessary to get the truth out of Orlando Morgan."

Deputy Turner's expression remained composed, his gaze steady as he met the mayor's eyes. "Mayor Alvarez, I understand your concern and your desire for swift action. However, we must proceed with caution and adhere to the legal protocols in place."

The mayor's frustration was palpable as he leaned forward, his hands gripping the edge of the desk. "Turner, this is my daughter we're talking about. She's missing, and you have reason to believe Orlando might be involved."

Deputy Turner's tone remained firm yet empathetic. "I understand the gravity of the situation, Mayor. But we must remember that any evidence obtained through forceful interrogation might not hold up in court. If we want a proper conviction that will stand, we need to gather evidence through legal means."

Mayor Alvarez's shoulders sagged as he released a weary sigh. "I know you're right, Turner. It's just... the waiting is agonizing."

"I share your concern, Mayor," Deputy Turner said, his voice softening. "We're doing everything in our power to find Amanda and get to the truth. Our investigators are working tirelessly, and we're pursuing all possible leads."

The mayor's eyes held a mixture of sadness and desperation. "I just want my daughter back, safe and sound."

Deputy Turner nodded in understanding. "I understand, Mayor. We're all committed to bringing Amanda back and uncovering the truth. Let's continue to follow the legal process and gather the necessary evidence. That's our best chance at finding her and ensuring justice is served."

Mayor Alvarez leaned back in his chair, his gaze distant. "You're right, Turner. I just... I'll leave it in your hands."

Deputy Turner's expression softened as he offered a reassuring smile. "We won't stop until we find answers, Mayor. We'll make sure that we do everything in our power to bring Amanda home and bring those responsible to justice."

As Mayor Alvarez stood to leave, his shoulders appeared slightly lighter, as if a burden had been temporarily lifted. The deputy chief's office had been a space for difficult decisions and heated discussions, but Deputy Turner's commitment to following the law and seeking the truth remained unwavering.

When the mayor exited the office, Deputy Turner's gaze turned to the framed photo of his own family on his desk, a silent reminder of the importance of justice and compassion in every decision he made. The pressure to find Amanda was immense, and the legal process had its limitations. Yet, he remained resolute in his commitment to upholding the law while pursuing justice.

***

CHAPTER 16: THE TRUTH UNLEASHED

Summoning all her strength, Olive opened her photography studio, determined to keep her life moving forward despite the ominous events surrounding her. The air held a palpable tension, a reflection of the turmoil that had woven its way into her life. Yet, as she turned the key and pushed open the door, a surge of purpose flowed through her.

As she walked into the studio, her fingers brushed against the edge of her desk, where her camera and equipment were meticulously organized. A sense of familiarity and comfort settled over her, reminding her of the joy that photography had always brought into her life. Inside, the studio exuded an ambiance of creativity and passion. Soft lighting illuminated the carefully arranged frames on the walls, each capturing a moment frozen in time, a story waiting to be told.

Taking a deep breath, Olive moved to the center of the room, her eyes scanning the space around her. She remembered the advice of a mentor long ago, words that had carried her through challenging times: "Your art is your sanctuary, Olive. Let it guide you through the storms."

With those words echoing in her mind, soon she sat in front of her computer as she scrolled through the candid moments captured at Amanda and Orlando's wedding festivities.

The images displayed a couple deeply in love, making it difficult for Olive to reconcile the idea that Orlando could be connected to Amanda's disappearance. As she advanced through the again photos, she stumbled upon the image of Vaughn and Nina engaged in a heated argument. She zoomed in on Nina's face, struck by an uncanny resemblance to someone she thought she recognized but couldn't quite place.

Lost in her thoughts, Olive was snapped back to reality by the chime of the bell above the door. Her heart skipped a beat as her gaze involuntarily turned to the entrance, and there he was: Tony, the embodiment of her nightmares, strolling into her shop. His presence sent a shiver down her spine, his tailored black suit exuding an air of arrogance that seemed to fill the room.

His greeting was filled with false cheer, "Hey Olive, so happy to see you again."

The weight of their shared history pressed down on her, memories of his manipulation and control flooding her mind. She watched as he cast a casual glance around the studio, a sinister smile tugging at the corners of his lips.

He strolled closer, his gaze raking over her with a mixture of amusement and something darker. "You know, Olive, I've been thinking about you. Wondering how you've managed to survive without me."

"Surviving without you has been the best thing that's happened to me," Olive retorted, her voice laced with defiance. She refused to let him see the fear that still lingered within her.

Tony's laughter echoed in the small space, a sound that sent shivers down her spine. "Oh, Olive, you always did have a way with words. But let's not pretend you're over me. I can see it in your eyes."

Her heart raced, anger mingling with a deep-seated dread. She wouldn't let him control her emotions anymore. "You don't know anything about me," she shot back, her voice firm.

He leaned in, with a sinister grin. "Maybe not

everything, but I know enough to know that you can't escape your past, Olive."

Olive's arms involuntarily crossed over her chest, as if seeking protection from his presence. "What are you doing here?" she demanded as she stood up from her chair, her voice quivering with apprehension.

Tony's grin widened, his eyes locking onto hers. "Oh, why? Do I need a reason to see the love of my life?" He laughed as if sharing an inside joke.

Fear pulsated through her veins, but Olive forced herself to stand her ground. "Tony, you need to leave, or else—"

"Or else what, my love?" Tony interrupted, his tone dripping with malice. He took another menacing step closer. "You'll call the police?" His tone turned venomous, reminding her of his connections, "Don't forget, I am the fucking police."

The memory of that day, when he had effortlessly bailed her out of jail, resurfaced in Olive's mind like a relentless tide. Tony's words hung heavy in the air, his menacing tone lacing each syllable with an unsettling chill.

"Did you ever wonder," he asked, a sinister smile curling on his lips, "how those drugs found their way into your apartment?"

The puzzle had gnawed at Olive's thoughts for far too long, a mystery she had tirelessly attempted to piece together. Night after night, she had revisited those events in the corridors of her mind, searching for elusive answers that seemed forever just out of reach. Yet, as Tony's words poured forth, a dreadful realization started to crystallize in her mind. Maybe, just maybe, he held the key to unlocking the truth that had haunted her for so long.

"I planted them," Tony confessed, his laughter ringing with a chilling triumph as he mockingly raised his hands in a twisted impression of celebration.

Olive's eyes widened, her heart pounding as his words pierced through her like a jagged shard of glass. "You what?" she gasped, her voice trembling with a mixture of disbelief and horror.

A dark chuckle escaped Tony's lips, his eyes dancing with an evil gleam. "Yeah, and I even went to the trouble of calling the police on you," he revealed, his laughter a jarring contrast to the gravity of his admission. The weight of his actions, the calculated cruelty, bore down on Olive's soul, leaving her reeling in a storm of emotions.

"You did this to me?" The words hung in the air,

a plea for understanding, a cry for an explanation that might somehow make sense of the nightmare she had endured.

But Tony's response shattered any lingering illusions. "Well, I had to make sure that you weren't leaving me, my love. And right then, I had you in the palm of my hands," he declared, the casualness of his tone underscoring the depth of his obsession.

The memories of that fateful day weighed heavily on Olive's mind, as if the shadows of the past had resurfaced to haunt her once more. The chilling words that Tony spoke brought back the rush of fear and confusion she had experienced when her life had been upended by his disturbing actions. She continued to stare at him, her eyes a mix of disbelief and horror.

"You did all of that just to keep me under your control?" Olive's voice trembled in anger and fear. The pieces of the puzzle were finally coming together, revealing the dark and twisted game that Tony had played with her life.

Tony's laughter echoed in the air, a disturbing symphony of malevolence. "Oh, my dear Olive, you have no idea how much power I have over you. It was exhilarating to watch you struggle, to see the fear in your eyes," he taunted, his eyes gleaming with a sick satisfaction.

A shiver ran down Olive's spine, her heart pounding in her chest. The man before her had manipulated her life, using her innocence and vulnerability as tools in his dangerous game. She felt trapped, as if the walls were closing in around her.

"Tony, you're sick," Olive's voice wavered, a mixture of anger and revulsion in her words. "You ruined my life, you manipulated everything." She mustered all the courage she could, her eyes meeting his with a fierce determination.

Tony's smile widened, a twisted grin that sent a chill down her spine. "Oh, my love, I did it all for us. To ensure that you would never leave me. And now, fate has brought us back together."

Desperation surged within Olive, her mind racing for a way to escape the clutches of the man who had held her life in his hands. She had to get him out of her house, out of her life, before his grip on her tightened once again.

"Tony, please, you need to leave, it's over between us" Olive's voice quivered as she pleaded with him. She had survived so much, fought so hard to reclaim her life, and she wouldn't let him steal her future once more.

His laughter was cold, mocking, as he grabbed her

arm, "You need to listen, Olive. You can't escape from me. No matter how far you might run, I will find you. And when I do, I'll make sure you never have the option to leave me ever again."

Olive felt his fingers close around her arm in a painful grip, his nails digging into her skin. She winced, tears brimming in her eyes. "Please, Tony, you're hurting me."

But he seemed to relish in her discomfort. "Remember, Olive, you're mine. You belong to me," he hissed, his grip tightening further, before he finally released her with a cold smile. "I'll be seeing you around, my love."

As Tony turned to leave, Olive's trembling form sank into her chair, her heart racing as if it was trying to escape her chest. The encounter had left her feeling utterly exposed, a chilling reminder of the dangerous web from which she couldn't seem to break free. Her hands shook as she tried to steady her breathing, her thoughts racing in a chaotic whirlwind.

In a moment of desperation, Olive fumbled to retrieve her phone from her pocket. With trembling fingers, she dialed Vaughn's number, her heart pounding so loudly she was sure he could hear it through the phone. The seconds stretched on, each ring amplifying her anxiety, until finally, his voice broke through, "Hey, you okay?"

The sound of his voice was a lifeline in the midst of her turmoil. It was a reminder that she wasn't alone, that there were people who cared about her safety and well-being. She took a shaky breath, grateful for the connection. "Vaughn," she began, her voice quivering despite her attempts to steady it. "Hey, I was just thinking about you."

Vaughn's response was warm, a mixture of curiosity and concern, "Oh yeah? Where are you now?"

Olive hesitated, momentarily grappling with her emotions before responding, "I'm at the studio. Where are you guys at?"

Vaughn's voice carried a slight pause, as if he was carefully considering his words. "We were at the police station. They wouldn't release any more information about the case. So now we're following up on another lead."

A sinking feeling settled in Olive's chest as she realized that Vaughn was in the middle of a serious investigation and couldn't easily break away to come to her assistance. She didn't want to burden him with her own troubles, especially considering the gravity of the situation he was dealing with.

"Call me when you're done," she replied softly, her voice masking the turmoil within her.

"Yeah, sure. I'll call you back, Olive. Bye," Vaughn responded, the sincerity in his voice still offering her a sense of solace.

"Bye, Vaughn," Olive whispered, her heart heavy as she hung up the phone almost immediately after their exchange.

She took a deep breath, wiping away a stray tear that escaped her eye. In the middle of her anguish, she realized that she needed to find her own way to navigate through the challenges that lay ahead, even if it meant confronting her haunting past and the dark figure that seemed to resurface at the most unexpected moments.

***

In another part of town, a famished Daniel, Nina, and Vaughn found themselves at a busy local diner. The aroma of freshly cooked food greeted them as they stepped inside, the comforting scent temporarily diverting their minds from the tension that had been building throughout the day. The diner was the epitome of small-town charm, with checkered tablecloths, vintage posters adorning the walls, and the low murmur of conversations filling the air.

They slid into a cozy booth, grateful for a moment of respite from their relentless pursuit of answers. A middle-aged waitress, who seemed to know most of the regulars by name, approached them with a warm smile. "Hey there, folks. What can I get you?"

Daniel, rubbing his temples as if to ease away some of the day's stress, looked up and offered a tired smile. "Three cheeseburgers and fries, please. And a coffee for me."

The waitress jotted down the order with practiced efficiency, nodding. "You got it. Coming right up." With a friendly pat on Daniel's shoulder, she strolled away to place their order.

Nina leaned back in her seat, letting out a deep sigh. "I can't believe we hit another dead end at the police station. And that FBI agent? He gave me the creeps."

Vaughn, his jaw tense, leaned forward. "We've come this far, and we can't stop until we find out what's really happening in this town."

Daniel, his fingers tapping rhythmically on the table, nodded in agreement. "Yeah, Vaughn's right. We're dealing with something bigger than we imagined."

As they spoke, their orders arrived, steam rising from the hot plates as the waitress skillfully balanced the trays. She set down the food before them, offering them another encouraging smile. "Here you go, enjoy your meal."

"Thanks," Vaughn and Nina said in unison, while Daniel merely nodded, his appetite seemingly overridden by his concern.

As they dug into their burgers and fries, the atmosphere lightened slightly, the simple act of eating serving as a small distraction from the intense emotions that had been plaguing them. They shared glances, a silent acknowledgment of the bond they had formed through the twists and turns of their investigation.

After a few bites, Nina looked at Vaughn. "So, what's our next move?"

Vaughn wiped his mouth with a napkin, his expression resolute. "We need to find out more about this Orlando guy. His connection to Amanda, his history, everything. If he's really the prime suspect, we need to uncover any potential motives."

Nina nodded thoughtfully. "Agreed. And we shouldn't disregard that FBI agent either. He seems to be involved somehow."

But Daniel had other ideas. "I don't think that's the best approach. Hear me out. The police already have everything they need on Orlando. And the FBI's sudden arrival here is most likely to close all the cold cases of the missing women. Our only real lead right now is in Elle's past."

Vaughn nodded thoughtfully as he considered Daniel's words. "It's a valid point. What's your take on this, Nina?"

Nina took a moment to chew on her fries, contemplating the situation. "My initial instinct was to dig into Elle's past, and that remains important, especially if Orlando is innocent. We can't abandon him, but we also can't overlook the urgency of finding Amanda."

Daniel concurred, "Exactly. We don't have the full picture of what the police and the Mayor know about Orlando, and it's clear they're backing him. I can't blame the Mayor; it's his daughter who's missing."

Nina, now determined, cleaned her fingers with a napkin and pushed her near-empty plate aside. "Alright, we can't let this cycle continue. And as much as I'd love to see justice served for Orlando, we have to prioritize what we know for sure."

Daniel took a final sip of his coffee, placing the

cup back on the table. "Agreed. So, let's recap. We know that a woman has gone missing every summer for the past decade. There are no witnesses, no evidence, just these women vanishing into thin air."

Vaughn acknowledged the importance of their decision. "Elle's case is our best chance to break this pattern. Let's not waste any more time. We need to get moving."

Nina signaled the waitress, raising her hand. "Not until we settle the bill."

The waitress promptly delivered the bill to their table, and Vaughn volunteered to settle it. "Allow me to take care of this one."

Nina readily agreed, secretly appreciating Vaughn's gesture. She was starting to understand why her sister had chosen him as her partner – he exuded consideration, strength, and eloquence. As Vaughn added some extra cash as a tip, the trio stood up and exited the diner. Within minutes, they were back in Vaughn's dependable pick-up truck.

This time, Daniel occupied the passenger seat, gazing out at the open road with a sense of uncertainty. "I never realized how remote these areas outside of town can be."

"You're right," Vaughn acknowledged, his attention on the road ahead. "And if my memory serves me well, Hector used to live in his family's farmhouse, which is a few miles out."

Nina, her gaze fixed on the passing scenery outside her window, found herself lost in contemplation. She hadn't anticipated uncovering elements from her sister's past. A realization hit her: the day Nina had left town, Elle might have been pregnant. The idea that her sister might have been carrying such a secret weighed heavily on her mind.

The remainder of the journey unfolded in silence, punctuated occasionally by Vaughn's absentminded humming. He aimed to concentrate on the road ahead rather than allow his thoughts to linger on Olive. The morning's kiss had conveyed sentiments he'd longed to hear, giving him hope that they were on the path to reconciliation. Yet, Vaughn recognized that they still needed to have an essential conversation.

Gradually, the road transformed into a narrower path, and Vaughn navigated the pick-up truck adeptly through the sandy terrain.

After a few minutes, they stumbled upon a weathered wooden sign bearing the words, "Welcome to Wildwood Horse Ranch -> this way." The words etched onto the signpost marked their imminent arrival at their intended destination.

The worn-down path led them further into the heart of Wildwood Horse Ranch. The landscape had an air of abandonment, and the absence of animals was obvious, as if the ranch had abandoned its horses long ago. The surroundings exuded an eerie stillness, broken only by the soft rustle of leaves in the breeze.

Inside the car, Vaughn, Daniel, and Nina exchanged glances, the tension palpable. The journey had led them to this remote place, a piece of the puzzle they were determined to solve. Vaughn's hands gripped the steering wheel, his knuckles turning pale as he navigated the rugged path. The uncertainty of what lay ahead weighed heavily on their minds.

As they rounded a bend, an aging house emerged in the distance. The structure stood in the middle of the desolate ranch, a silent witness to years gone by. Its wooden walls bore the marks of time, with faded paint and peeling edges. The windows were mostly boarded up, and those that remained intact reflected the sun's warm rays.

A short distance from the house, Vaughn brought the car to a stop, the engine's soft hum the only sound in the stillness. He turned to his companions, his expression serious yet resolute. "We're here," he said, his voice steady despite the unease that tugged at his thoughts.

Nina's gaze swept across the large house, her eyes narrowing as she took in the details. "This place gives me chills," she whispered, her voice carrying a mix of curiosity and unease.

Daniel nodded, his expression contemplative. "You're right. There's something haunting about it. Like it holds the memories of what might have happened here."

Stepping out of the car, their footsteps crunched on the gravel beneath their feet as they approached the porch. A sense of anticipation hung heavy in the air, mingling with the layers of history that enveloped the farm house. Nina, Daniel, and Vaughn exchanged cautious glances as they reached the entrance of the old house.

When they approached the front of the house with cautious steps, their eyes widened at the sight before them. An elderly woman was taking a nap, in a weathered rocking chair, cradling a shotgun in her gnarled hands. Her mane was a cascade of silver-gray hair, and she was clad in a faded nightgown that had seen countless years.

Nina's sharp instincts kicked in, and she quickly raised her hands, signaling Vaughn and Daniel to stop moving. They froze mid-stride, their faces a mix of surprise and caution. Unfortunately, Daniel's foot had barely grazed the front step, and the old wood responded with a sorrowful creak. The sound pierced the quiet air, and the old woman's eyes snapped open.

Startled, she jolted upright in her rocking chair, her gaze locking onto the intruders. "Hold it right there, you thieves," she barked, her voice weathered and raspy. The shotgun she held now pointed unwaveringly in their direction, its barrel an extension of her intent.

Caught in a tense standoff, the trio reacted instinctively, their palms raised toward the heavens in a gesture of surrender. Nina, the closest to the woman, dropped to her knees, her voice tinged with a mix of urgency and fear, "Please, we're not thieves. We mean no harm."

The old woman squinted, assessing them from behind her spectacles, her face etched with skepticism. Time seemed to hang suspended in the balance, the tension palpable as the silence of the ranch enveloped them.

Vaughn's heart raced, his gaze shifting from the stern face of the elderly woman to his companions. Daniel's eyes were wide, his breath held, while Nina's imploring posture carried a hope for understanding.

Daniel's words emerged cautiously, each one chosen with care to avoid agitating the armed matriarch. "We're actually friends of Hector's from high school. Isn't that right, guys?"

Vaughn and Nina's heads bobbed in rapid agreement, an almost comical display of unity in the face of uncertainty. The old woman's skeptical gaze held firm, her brows knitting together as she peered at them from behind her glasses.

"Friends?" Her voice carried a mixture of disbelief and bitterness. "Hector is dead, did you not know that?" Her tone dripped with the conviction that only those who were truly close to Hector would be aware of this fact.

Vaughn stepped in, his voice carrying a blend of empathy and regret, "Yes, we're aware of his passing. We're deeply sorry for your loss."

The old woman's reaction was unexpected. Instead of anger or further resistance, her demeanor shifted, her grip on the shotgun relaxing. She aimed her gaze at Vaughn, her eyes holding a mix of sorrow and longing. "My Hector is gone, he jumped off that darned cliff. I saw it all unfold." The pain in her words was palpable, a testament to the depth of her connection with Hector.

Nina's voice carried a note of desperation as she interjected, her words carrying a plea for understanding. "Please, we're seeking answers. We're not here to cause any harm."

The elderly woman's attention turned to Nina, her eyes scrutinizing her as if searching for a connection. "You remind me of someone," she mumbled, more to herself than to them.

Nina took a tentative step forward, her voice steady as she revealed her identity. "Yes, you must know that someone. I'm Nina, Elle was my sister."

The old woman's expression shifted from curiosity to a mixture of surprise and recognition. Her grip on the shotgun loosened, and she leaned back, her features softening.

As if an epiphany had struck her, the old woman abruptly lowered the shotgun and walked slowly to face the weathered front door. Pushing it open, she signaled them forward. "Well, you three best get inside then."

The once-hostile encounter had taken an unexpected turn, opening the door to the possibility of unraveling the mysteries hidden within the walls of the old farmhouse.

Slowly, still cautious, Nina, Vaughn, and Daniel

lowered their hands. They exchanged bewildered glances before cautiously stepping over the threshold into the old woman's home. Its front door creaked slightly, as if welcoming them to uncover the secrets concealed within its walls. The interior was dimly lit, the warm afternoon sun filtering through the curtains casting long shadows across the worn wooden floor.

The old woman shuffled to a corner, placing the shotgun down gently as if it were a fragile relic. Her gaze settled on Nina, scrutinizing her with a mixture of curiosity and sorrow. "Sit down, sit down," she gestured to the rickety chairs around a table. The trio complied, choosing seats where they could keep an eye on the old woman while also taking in their surroundings.

The room they were in was cluttered with memories of the past, photographs, dusty books, and trinkets that seemed to tell stories of years gone by. The air held a mixture of nostalgia and sadness, as if the room itself was a silent witness to the old woman's grief.

"So," the old woman finally spoke, her voice a mixture of curiosity and skepticism. "You say you were friends with my Hector."

Daniel cleared his throat, a little nervous under the scrutiny of the old woman's gaze. "Yes, we all went to the same high school, right here in Serenity High."

The old woman's eyes softened as she looked at an old, framed picture that sat on the mantle. "My Hector was a very bright kid. I was so proud of my son, for all his achievements."

Nina sensed the old woman's mixed emotions and approached her gently. "We're sorry for your loss, ma'am."

The old woman's smile faltered, her gaze distant as she seemed lost in memories. "Why are you here? What do you want?"

Nina shared a meaningful look with Vaughn and Daniel, then turned her attention back to her. "We're here to find out the truth. About my sister, Elle."

The old woman's eyes widened slightly, and she seemed to consider their words carefully. "Elle..." her voice trailed off, and for a moment, it seemed like she was lost in thought.

Nina saw an opportunity and continued, "Did you ever know that Elle was pregnant?"

The old woman's gaze shifted towards the empty air, her expression conflicted as if revisiting memories long buried. After a moment, she collected herself,

"Where are my manners? Let me get you all some cold ones."

Nina tried to protest, "Oh, no, it's okay, we're not that thirsty..."

But her words fell on deaf ears as the old woman had already begun shuffling towards the kitchen. Vaughn and Daniel exchanged glances, both intrigued and a bit unsure of how this encounter was unfolding.

A few minutes later, the old woman returned with a tray, carrying three glasses of iced lemonade. She placed the tray on the table and gestured for them to sit. "Please, have some. It's a hot day, and I'm sure you could use a refreshment." Her tone was warm, and there was a sense of hospitality about her, as if she was trying to make amends for the initial standoffishness.

Nina and the others exchanged glances but accepted the glasses, each taking a cautious sip. The tangy drink was refreshing, and the gesture, though unexpected, seemed to have softened the old woman's demeanor.

The old woman sat back down, her eyes fixed on the old photograph. "Yes, I knew about Elle's pregnancy," she finally admitted. "She and Hector were going through a difficult time, and she confided in me."

Nina leaned in, her voice gentle, "Ma'am, we're here to uncover the truth about what happened to Elle and the other women who have gone missing. We believe there's something more to it, something beyond the surface."

The old woman's eyes filled with tears, and she nodded. "I know about the disappearances every summer. But I'm just an old woman, and I never had the courage to stop it."

Vaughn spoke, his tone empathetic, "You're not alone in this. Together, we can find out what's really going on, expose the truth, and make sure justice is served for all the women who've suffered."

The old woman's gaze shifted from one face to another, and she seemed to find solace in their determination. "You're brave, much like my Hector was when he stood up for what he believed in. I'll tell you everything I know, but it won't be easy. The truth has a way of revealing things we might wish to keep buried."

As Nina delicately sipped the drink, her keen eyes caught something peculiar floating on the surface. She raised the glass to her eye level, scrutinizing the small white particles that drifted within. A prickle of suspicion danced at the edges of her mind, prompting her to glance around the room. Amidst the conversations and the old woman's hospitality, her gaze was drawn to an oddity near the doorway.

There, stacked neatly against the wall, were a pair of men's boots. They appeared pristine, as if recently cleaned, which struck Nina as out of place. She mustered her thoughts and inquired, "Ma'am, does someone else live here besides you?"

The old woman's distant expression seemed to return to the present moment. She looked at Nina and responded, "Yes, my granddaughter lives here with me." Before further questions could be exchanged, an unexpected turn of events unfolded. Daniel's condition deteriorated suddenly. Holding his head, he groaned in discomfort, his unease evident.

Daniel's groans filled the air, his pain palpable. "Nina, we need to get out of here." His glass slipped from his grasp and shattered on the floor, mirroring his collapse moments later.

Nina's head throbbed, her vision blurring at the edges. "I don't know, Vaughn. Something's not right."

"Nina, what's happening?" Vaughn's voice wavered as he struggled to stay on his feet. He clenched the glass tightly, trying to steady himself, but eventually succumbed to unconsciousness.

Fear and urgency surged within her, and she made a desperate attempt to grab her phone. However, her fingers betrayed her, and the device slipped from her grasp, clattering to the ground.

Nina felt her heart race with alarm, realizing that she was facing the same fate as Daniel and Vaughn. Her instincts kicked in, and as her body began to weaken, she delicately placed her glass back on the table and rose to her feet.

However, her attempt to escape was met with swift retaliation from the old woman, who swiftly grabbed the shotgun and aimed it at Nina.

Desperation and confusion swirled in Nina's mind as she turned to confront the old woman. "Why did you do this to us?" she managed to utter, her voice strained as she felt her consciousness beginning to fade away. But as the words left her lips, the room spun around her, and her legs gave way. Darkness encroached on her vision, and her consciousness slipped away.

The old woman's face bore a mixture of regret and resolve. "I'm sorry, my dear. I have no choice," she spoke, her voice laden with a heavy burden. The weight of her actions and the truth behind them remained shrouded in mystery as the darkness claimed Nina, sealing her consciousness and plunging her into an uncertain void.

***

CHAPTER 17: SILENT WHISPERS NO MORE

Nina's consciousness flickered like a dying candle as her vision blurred, the world around her fading into shadows. The last thing she felt was a heavy drowsiness pulling her down, an instinctive sensation that something was deeply wrong. As her eyes closed, she knew she was helpless, trapped in a web of unknown intentions.

In the hazy borderland between wakefulness and unconsciousness, a flicker of awareness touched her mind. It was as if she was floating in a void, disconnected from her body. Slowly, faint sounds began to reach her ears, distant murmurs like whispers in the wind.

Nina's senses jolted awake as a voice penetrated her groggy state, calling out her name urgently,

"Nina...wake up." As her surroundings gradually came into focus, she found herself covered by the presence of hay, its rough texture beneath her fingertips. In the dim light, faint outlines of long poles emerged from the shadows, bearing an ominous appearance.

Squinting against the darkness, she identified figures suspended on two of the poles—Vaughn and Daniel. They were bound, yet their struggles had led to a small victory as their mouth gags were removed. "Nina, you okay?" Daniel's voice reached her, laden with concern.

Taking in their dilemma, Nina assessed her own situation, discovering she too was bound to a pole. With her remaining strength, she attempted to free herself, but the ropes constricting her limbs resisted her efforts, their coarse texture digging into her skin. Muffled by the cloth gag over her mouth, she managed to express her frustration, "Guys, what the fuck!"

Vaughn exerted his strength against the unforgiving ropes that held him captive, his voice a mixture of frustration and sardonic humor, "In case you were wondering, yes, Hector's mom, fucking spiked our drinks." His muscles strained as he sought to unravel the binding constraints that immobilized him. Next to him, Daniel's determination mirrored Vaughn's as he struggled against his own restraints, the urgent desire for freedom fueling his efforts.

The encompassing darkness cloaked their surroundings, leaving them to rely on their instincts and limited sensory perceptions. The realization gradually dawned on them as Daniel's voice pierced the obscurity, "I think we're in one of their storage houses."

Vaughn's sardonic comment echoed in the air, "You think?! Stop thinking and get to work."

Meanwhile, the complex maze of thoughts inside Nina's mind was intertwined with her physical struggle. She managed to loosen the cloth gag from her mouth, allowing her to voice her concerns, "Guys, there's something going on here. Why would the old lady want to knock us out? And how in the world did she manage to carry three adults from the house to this place?"

As the realization of their perplexing situation settled in, their collective efforts became more focused and purposeful. They strained against the bonds that held them, their bodies aching with the effort.

"We need to get the hell out of here," Nina exclaimed urgently, her voice laced with a mixture of fear and determination. She vigorously tugged at the ropes that bound her feet together, her fingers clawing at the coarse fibers in a desperate attempt to free herself from their confinements. The urgency of the situation compelled her to act quickly, but Vaughn's abrupt interruption redirected their attention.

"Wait, did you guys hear that?" Vaughn interjected, his tone commanding, causing them all to pause their movements. His senses had picked up something beyond their immediate problem. The area fell into a tense stillness, broken only by the pounding of their hearts and the muffled sounds of their breathing. Vaughn's heightened alertness had caught onto something that was happening outside the storage house.

Their collective focus intensified as they strained their ears, attuned to the slightest disturbance in the environment outside. The faintest rustling of leaves, the distant echo of footsteps—every sound became amplified in their ears. And then, in the quiet of the night, a woman's tormented scream pierced through the silence.

The chilling cry seemed to hang in the air, echoing with a raw intensity that sent shivers down their spines. The three of them exchanged alarmed glances, the urgency of their situation now overblown by the threatening screams that echoed around them. The realization that they were not alone in this seemingly isolated place ignited a gush of willpower within them.

"Come on, we need to get out of here," Daniel urged, his voice tight with determination as he struggled with his own bonds.

Driven by a renewed sense of urgency, Nina, Vaughn, and Daniel intensified their efforts to free themselves from their restraints. The urgency to escape was heightened by the echoing cries that pierced the night, each scream a chilling reminder that danger was lurking nearby. They knew they had to act swiftly to avoid whatever danger that might be closing in on them.

Nina's legs, raw and aching, finally managed to loosen the knots around her ankles. With a surge of relief, she wiggled her feet free and then, without hesitation, reached out her leg to help untie Vaughn's ropes. The tension in the room grew as their movements became more frantic, their collective focus solely on the task of freeing themselves.

In the midst of their struggle, the door to the storage house suddenly swung open, spilling an unnerving light into the dim interior. The silhouette of the old woman loomed in the doorway, her figure outlined by the faint glow that seeped in from outside. A mean smile played on her lips as her eyes locked onto the three captives.

"You didn't think it would be that easy, did you?" she taunted, her voice dripping with a mixture of amusement and malice. "My poor Hector, he is such a good boy. But he is always a bit too trusting."

Nina's hands worked even faster, fueled by a mixture of fear and determination. Her fingers fumbled, her breaths coming fast and shallow.

Vaughn's muscles strained as he worked to free his wrists, "There is no fucking way that we're dying in here tonight!" With a final tug, Vaughn's wrists were free, and he wasted no time in moving to help Daniel with his ropes.

Outside, the screams continued, a haunting chorus that seemed to surround them from all directions. Fear and adrenaline fueled their efforts as Vaughn and Daniel finally managed to release Nina from her restraints.

The old woman's cackling laughter echoed through the room as they all struggled to their feet.

"We need to get out of here, now!" Vaughn urged, his voice urgent as he grabbed Nina's hand, leading her towards the open door. Daniel followed closely behind as they rushed into the night, their hearts pounding, their breaths coming in ragged gasps.

As they burst out of the storage house, they were met with a chilling scene. The moon hung in the sky, casting its glow on the wild landscape around them.

But that wasn't the worst part of it all.

***

In the dimly lit basement, Amanda sat on a wooden chair, her wrists tightly bound together by rough ropes. Beside her, a hulking man gently combed her hair, his large fingers moving through the strands with a twisted sense of affection. The cold fear that had settled in her chest began to creep up again as she felt his gaze on her, his eyes holding a disturbing mix of possessiveness and madness.

Tears welled up in Amanda's eyes as she gathered the shreds of her courage and begged once more, her voice quivering, "Please, I'm begging you, let me go. I promise I won't speak a word about this to anyone."

Her plea hung in the air, a fragile hope against the nightmare that had become her reality. The man's grip on her hair tightened momentarily, his fingers digging into her scalp, and a chilling smile curved on his lips. His voice, a low and unsettling murmur, filled the room, "Oh, my dear love, after I'm done with you, you'll never be speaking to anyone else but me."

Amanda's heart pounded wildly, her mind racing to make sense of his words. She knew deep down that escape was unlikely, that the man's intentions were far more sinister than a mere plea for silence.

"Who are you?" she managed to choke out, her voice trembling with a mixture of fear and defiance.

The man's smile widened, revealing a glint of madness in his eyes. "Don't you remember me my love. Don't worry, I'll make sure that you won't ever forget about us."

Amanda's breath caught in her throat, a sick realization washing over her. The man's obsession with her was more disturbing than she had initially grasped. She strained against her bonds, her heart aching with desperation.

The man paused his grooming, his hand still resting on her hair, and looked at her with an intensity that made her shiver. Slowly, he withdrew his hand and placed the comb on a table nearby. His deep voice rumbled through the damp air, "Time for you to get ready."

Amanda's heart pounded in her chest as he turned away, his heavy footsteps carrying him toward a table covered with ominous tools. Ropes, restraints, and other unsettling objects lay strewn across the surface, each one a chilling reminder of her captivity.

Summoning a surge of adrenaline-fueled courage, Amanda seized the moment. With a quick, desperate motion, she pulled her bound wrists apart and slipped them through the loosened ropes. The fibers cut through her skin, but the pain was nothing compared to the urgency of escape.

Ignoring the discomfort, she pushed herself off the wooden chair and willed her trembling legs to carry her toward the stairs that led to the upper floor of the house. Her heart raced in her chest, the sound of her pulse drowning out all other noise. The darkness of the basement seemed to give way to a sliver of light as she reached the top of the staircase.

Gasping for breath, Amanda burst through the basement door, her eyes adjusting to the dimly lit hallway. The hope of escape surged through her veins, giving her newfound strength. Every step she took felt like a step closer to freedom, her fear a constant companion pushing her forward.

She hurried down the hallway, her footsteps echoing in the silence. Shadows danced on the walls, and the house seemed to hold its breath, as if aware of her desperate flight.

Amanda's heart raced as she navigated the twists and turns of the old farmhouse, her breath coming in ragged gasps. The musty smell of old wood and dust filled her nostrils, and she was acutely aware of every creaking floorboard beneath her feet. She had to find a way out, a way to escape the clutches of her captor and the horrors that awaited her.

The old house was a maze of dimly lit corridors and rooms that seemed frozen in time. Dust-covered furniture loomed like silent guards, while faded photographs on the walls whispered stories of days long gone. Amanda's eyes darted around, searching for any sign of an exit, a window, a door, anything.

The sound of heavy footsteps behind her sent warning signs from her brain to her feet, and she knew that the large man was hot on her trail. Panic surged within her, propelling her forward even faster. She spotted a narrow doorway leading to what seemed like the kitchen. She rushed inside, her breath hitching as she realized there was no way out from there.

Frantically, she looked around the kitchen, her eyes scanning the room for anything that could help her. Her gaze fell upon a small window near the back, its glass smeared with years of grime. With renewed determination, she sprinted towards it, her heart pounding in her chest.

The window was stubborn, stuck in its frame from years of neglect. Amanda struggled with it, using all her strength to pry it open. The loud crash of footsteps grew louder, echoing through the house. She could feel his presence getting closer, his heavy breathing like a nightmarish soundtrack to her escape.

Finally, the window gave way, and Amanda pushed herself through the narrow opening. She tumbled out onto the ground, the impact jarring her body. Ignoring the pain, she scrambled to her feet, glancing around to get her bearings. She found herself in a small backyard overgrown with weeds and surrounded by a decaying wooden fence.

Her eyes darted around, searching for a way to escape the enclosed space. She spotted a broken gate at the far end of the yard and dashed towards it. The gate protested with a rusty screech as she forced it open, her heart racing as the possibility of freedom beckoned.

Just as she was about to step through the gate, a powerful hand grabbed her shoulder, yanking her back with a force that sent her crashing to the ground. The large man loomed over her, his eyes ablaze with fury. He had caught up to her, and there was no escape now.

Amanda's chest heaved with fear and desperation, her voice trembling as she cried out, "Please, just let me go. I won't tell anyone. Please!" But his grip only tightened, his fingers digging into her skin. His cold, deranged gaze bore into her, a chilling reminder that she was trapped in a nightmare from which there might be no escape.

The man's grip on Amanda's shoulder tightened

as he dragged her back to the side of the house. In the dim light, she could see three figures standing a few feet away, their presence sending a shiver down her spine. The man tilted his head slightly, his cold gaze shifting from Amanda to the newcomers.

Amanda's heart pounded in her chest as she took in the sight of the three individuals before her. They seemed out of place, as if they were unexpected guests in this twisted scenario. The man's grip on her shoulder felt like a vise, and she knew that any attempt to escape would be pointless.

The strangers exchanged a quick glance, a silent communication passing between them. The energy in the air was thick, each second ticking by like an eternity. Amanda's mind raced, trying to make sense of the situation. Who were these people? Were they also victims of this man's madness, or did they play a darker role?

The man's voice cut through the silence, his tone dripping with a sinister amusement, "Oh, what do we have here? Looks like we've got ourselves some unexpected guests, my love." His grip on Amanda shifted, and she felt searing pain crawl up her arm.

Nina, Daniel, and Vaughn's paths had collided with Amanda and the imposing man in the open area, a ghostly silence settling over them as they sized each other up. Confusion and uncertainty danced in the air, each group trying to make sense of the unfolding scene. Their eyes held a mix of apprehension and curiosity as they stood in this unexpected confrontation.

Amidst this tense scene, the old woman made her reappearance, her shotgun once again wielded with chilling intent. A plea for mercy escaped Nina's lips, her voice tinged with desperation, "Please, don't shoot us. If you let all of us go, we promise you won't see us again." Her words hung in the air, a fragile thread of hope against the backdrop of uncertainty.

However, the large man's resolve seemed unyielding. He voiced his wishes in a mournful tone, "But mother, I want them gone. Now!"

The old woman's loyalty was unwavering, her commitment to her son undeniable. "Of course, my boy," she responded, the shotgun steady in her grip, "I would do anything for you, my special boy."

As the old woman took aim at Nina, the moment hung in the balance, poised to shatter into violence. But then, a sudden interruption fractured the tension. The large man's voice cut through the heavy atmosphere, "Wait!" His eyes fixated on Nina, as if seeing her in a new light. He released Amanda from his grasp, and she fell to the ground, a mixture of pain and relief on her face.

Slowly, the large man began to approach Nina, his steps tentative, his gaze locked onto her. "Elle? Is that really you?" His voice wavered with a mix of disbelief and yearning. The single question held the potential to unravel a cascade of revelations, as the past and present intertwined in ways none of them could have anticipated.

Nina's mind raced at breakneck speed, her heart pounding as she recognized him from afar. It was Hector—time had taken its toll on him, but his identity was unmistakable. The way he moved toward her made her feel as though her heart dropped to her stomach, but it confirmed her shocking suspicion. Hector was alive.

In a frantic attempt to play for time, Nina instinctively tucked her hair behind her ears, subtly altering her appearance to resemble her sister Elle more closely. The hope was that this small trick would buy them the time they desperately needed to make a run for it.

"Hector, yes, it's me," she managed to speak with a trembling voice, hoping her words would resonate and pacify him. As he continued to approach her, she tried to remain composed, her heart racing in her chest. Daniel and Vaughn, flanking Nina on either side, exchanged bewildered glances, left in the dark about her impromptu plan.

Daniel's hushed voice reached Nina, "What are you doing?"

Nina responded just as quietly, her focus unwavering on Hector's advancing form, "He thinks I'm Elle. I have to try to reason with him."

With bated breath, she prepared herself for his proximity. And then, in an instant, Hector was upon her, pulling her into an embrace that took her off guard. She trembled under his hold, doing her best to maintain her disguise.

"I'm sorry I've been away," she stammered, her voice quivering as she navigated this unanticipated turn of events, "But I'm back now, Hector."

Hector's embrace enveloped her, and he inhaled deeply, the familiar scent seemingly confirming his conviction. "I've missed you, Elle," he murmured against her hair, his grip tightening as though he couldn't bear to let her go again. The sensation was both surreal and alarming as Nina fought to keep her composure intact. She found herself engulfed in a role she hadn't anticipated, in the midst of a complex game of identity.

Forcing out, all her courage, Nina cleared her throat and spoke the words that sealed her pretense, "I promise that I won't leave again." Those words held a weight she couldn't fully comprehend—the power to maintain the charade and unravel a deeper understanding of the tangled web they found themselves in.

"Hector, stop!" a voice sliced through the charged atmosphere. It was Hector's mother, standing aghast as she witnessed the unfolding scene before her. Her anguished cry reverberated through the air, carrying a mixture of disbelief and desperation.

"That's not Elle," she shouted, her voice cracking with emotion. Hector's grip on Nina loosened, his confusion evident in his furrowed brow. He turned his attention towards his mother, searching for answers.

With her heart pounding in her chest, Nina seized the fleeting opportunity to gather herself. Hector's mother's revelation had thrown an unexpected curveball into her precarious charade. Her mind raced, scrambling to adapt to this new challenge. In that anxious moment, Hector's confusion was intense, and Nina had to think fast.

"Hector, no, it's me," she pleaded, her voice trembling as she met his confused gaze. Her fingers wrapped around his, desperately trying to bridge the gap that had emerged between them. The fragile threads of her disguise were unraveling, and she knew she needed to regain control of the situation.

"Hector, baby, it's me, Elle," she implored, her grip on his hands tight as she tried to invoke a sense of familiarity and trust.

Hector's gaze flickered between his mother and the woman before him, torn between conflicting truths. He looked at Nina with a mixture of doubt and longing, a battle waged within him as he grappled with the conflicting information.

In the midst of this tense exchange, Vaughn seized a moment to silently approach Amanda, who was lying incapacitated on the ground. His heart raced as he assessed the situation, his determination to rescue her overcoming the overwhelming odds they faced. Gently, he extended a hand towards her, his voice soft yet resolute, "Amanda, I'm going to help you out of here, okay?"

Amanda winced as she shifted, a pained expression crossing her face. Her voice trembled as she replied, "My leg...I think it's broken." Vaughn's heart sank at her words, realizing the extent of the challenges they were up against. He racked his brain for a plan, a way to remove all of them from the dangerous situation they had found themselves in.

His eyes darted around the surroundings, seeking any possible means of escape. The old farmhouse seemed to hold secrets and possibilities within its run-down walls. Vaughn's mind raced, his protective instincts propelling him to devise a strategy that would ensure the safety of everyone involved.

"Don't you dare," the old woman's voice pierced the tension, her shotgun now aimed at Vaughn and Amanda.

Vaughn's hands were raised in a gesture of surrender, his eyes reflecting a mix of caution and urgency. He attempted to defuse the situation, his tone measured, "I was just trying to help. She needs a doctor!"

Hector's attention wavered between his mother's threatening stance and the unfolding drama around him. His gaze fell on Nina, his eyes searching for answers within her expression. Beside her, Daniel stood ready to intervene if Hector made any aggressive moves towards Nina.

"Hector, please, you have to stop your mother," Nina pleaded desperately, her voice laced with urgency, "She is the reason I left you."

Hector turned to face Nina, his features a battleground of emotions. The tension in the air was palpable as the complex web of relationships unraveled before them. "Hector, son, don't believe a word that lying bitch says," his mother interjected, her voice sharp.

Hector's fists clenched at his sides, his patience clearly reaching its limits. He drew a deep breath, his voice steady as he declared, "You always came between me and Elle." His words hung in the air, a declaration of his long-standing frustrations and resentments.

"Enough!" Hector's voice thundered as he surged forward, his determination overpowering his mother's resistance. In a desperate bid to protect his beloved Elle, the old woman grappled with him, a battle of strength and willpower.

Simultaneously, Daniel urgently nudged Nina, his voice laced with urgency, "We need to get out of here, now." Swiftly, he moved towards Vaughn and joined him in assisting Amanda to her feet.

Nina didn't need any more prompting. She sprinted ahead of them, her heart pounding in her chest, her instinct urging her to flee from the danger that surrounded them.

As Nina reached the front of the house, she spared a quick glance back and witnessed the tense struggle between Hector and his mother. The scene was a muddled mix of emotions, their pasts colliding with the present, and Nina knew that she couldn't afford to wait any longer. She turned the corner of the house and saw Vaughn's pickup truck, parked in the same spot when they came in.

Nina swiftly opened the truck door, allowing Daniel and Vaughn to carefully guide Amanda into the back seat. Vaughn dashed towards the driver's side, his heart pounding with urgency. As his fingers fumbled with the car keys still in the ignition, a wave of relief washed over him when the engine roared to life. "Thank God," he breathed, the sound of the engine a comforting reassurance amidst the chaos. With swift determination, he settled into the driver's seat, his mind racing with the need to get them all to safety.

In the back seat, Daniel carefully cradled the unconscious Amanda, his worry etched onto his face. He positioned himself with her, ensuring she was as comfortable as possible despite the dire circumstances. Meanwhile, Vaughn's gaze flickered between the farmhouse and Nina, who remained near the house, seemingly caught in a moment of uncertainty.

"Nina, come on!" Vaughn's voice carried a mix of urgency and concern. He couldn't fathom the idea of leaving her behind, especially not when the danger still loomed. Nina turned to face him, her gaze torn between the haunting past and the present reality. The pull of compassion for Hector battled with the instinct for self-preservation.

With Amanda settled in the back, Daniel anxiously called out, "Come on, we need to move!" Vaughn's gaze flickered to Nina who stood a few paces away, seemingly torn between her impulse to help Hector and the rationality of her friend's pleas.

Vaughn's voice carried a mix of concern and determination, "Nina, we have to go. Please, get in the car."

Nina shifted her gaze to Vaughn, her thoughts torn between the tumultuous reunion playing out before them and her desire to reach out to Hector. The gravity of the situation hung heavy in the air as she contemplated a course of action. She whispered, almost to herself, "What if I can save him?"

Vaughn's expression tightened with concern and urgency, his eyes locking onto Nina's. He shook his head, his voice laced with determination, "Nina, there's no way we're going to let you do that. Hector killed all those women because of his lifelong obsession with Elle. Imagine what he'll do to you. Please, Nina, you need to get in the car. I can't bear to lose the only family I have left. I can't lose you too."

His words resonated with a painful truth, and

Nina felt her resolve waver. As she gazed into Vaughn's eyes, his sincerity touched her. She saw the depth of his concern, the fear of losing yet another person he cared for. Nodding slowly, she whispered, "Okay, you're right."

From the back seat, Daniel's voice broke the moment, impatience evident in his tone. "What's taking so long? We need to get Amanda to a hospital right now." The urgency in his words spurred them into action. Just as they were about to leave, the air was pierced by a deafening gunshot, causing their hearts to race in fear and uncertainty.

Nina's eyes widened, her breath catching in her throat. The gunshot echoed, a chilling reminder of the danger that still lingered. Without hesitation, she scrambled into the car, Vaughn revving the engine as they sped away from the haunting farm house. As the engine roared to life, he accelerated away from the farmhouse, leaving behind the haunting echoes of their ordeal.

***

CHAPTER 18: BACK TO REALITY

Vaughn's pickup truck raced through the night, the engine's roar echoing their desperate escape. Inside the vehicle, a heavy silence prevailed, broken only by the occasional whimper from Amanda. The trauma of their recent suffering still clung to them like a shadow, but amidst the tension, Nina's voice sliced through the quiet.

"Danny," she turned toward Daniel from the passenger seat, her voice determined, "I think I might have my spare phone in my bag. Could you please hand it over to me?"

Daniel reached for the small backpack, handing it to her without a word. As Nina rifled through her bag, her fingers closed around the emergency phone she had tucked away. Their personal phones remained behind at the farmhouse, but this one could still serve its purpose.

With the phone in her hand, Nina dialed 911, her words pouring out in a rapid stream as she relayed the urgent situation. "Hello, 911, what's your emergency?" came the response on the other end.

"Please, you have to send officers to the Wildwood Horse Ranch. That's where the missing women were being held," Nina's words were a torrent of urgency, fueled by frustration and fear.

"I'm sorry, ma'am. You're going to have to repeat that for me, slowly," the operator's voice requested.

Nina's impatience simmered as she repeated herself more deliberately, her words cutting through the tension. "Just send someone. You're welcome," she muttered, ending the call with a frustrated exhale.

"Stupid, fucking, police," she muttered under her breath, her irritation palpable as the truck sped ahead, their destination still uncertain but their determination resolute.

In a matter of minutes, they pulled up at the local hospital's entrance. Nina wasted no time, her urgency propelling her out of the vehicle and into the well-lit hospital lobby. Her voice rang out, sharp and frantic, as she called for assistance. In a matter of seconds, a group of nurses appeared, responding to her distress with quick efficiency.

"Help, we need help here!" Nina's voice carried a sense of desperation as she gestured toward the pickup truck.

The nurses understood the gravity of the situation immediately and rushed outside with a gurney in tow. Daniel and Vaughn sprang into action, their collective strength and determination combining as they gently lifted Amanda and carefully transferred her onto the gurney.

With practiced ease, the nurses took charge, wheeling the gurney into the hospital with Amanda's well-being at the forefront of their minds. The harsh fluorescent lights of the hospital corridor illuminated their path as they followed the medical staff, hopeful for Amanda's recovery.

As Amanda was swiftly wheeled into the emergency room, they found themselves confined to the tense space of the waiting area. Time seemed to crawl as they exchanged anxious glances, their thoughts centered on Amanda's well-being. The sterile white walls and muted sounds of the hospital served as a backdrop to their unease.

Nina's fingers tapped nervously against her thigh

as she took in the surroundings, her gaze shifting between Vaughn and Daniel. "I can't believe what we've just been through," she murmured, her voice heavy with a mix of relief and lingering tension.

Daniel leaned forward, his elbows resting on his knees. His worry-lined face reflected the gravity of the situation. "I know. It's like something out of a nightmare. But Amanda's going to be okay, right?"

Vaughn nodded, his jaw set with determination. "She'll be in good hands here. The hospital staff will do everything they can." He ran a hand through his hair, his gaze distant as if processing everything that had transpired. "We need to stay strong for her."

Nina's gaze met Vaughn's, gratitude shining in her eyes. "You're right."

Daniel's expression mirrored their determination. "Absolutely."

After a few minutes, the door to the emergency bay swung open, and a doctor emerged. His professional demeanor gave him an air of authority as he addressed the trio. "Are you the ones who brought in the missing mayor's daughter?"

"Yes," the answer tumbled out of their mouths in unison, a mixture of worry and hope evident in their voices.

The doctor's expression remained somber as he continued, "I regret to inform you that I'll need to involve the authorities. We have a protocol to follow in such cases."

Daniel, weary but resolute, nodded in understanding. He found a seat among the chairs lined up in the waiting area and sighed heavily. "Go ahead and make the call," he replied, his tone steady, "And please let my brother, Deputy Turner, know that I'll be here waiting for him."

As the doctor retreated back into the emergency room, Nina and Vaughn shared a concerned look. They knew that while Amanda was in capable hands, the situation was far from over. Their gaze shifted to Daniel, who leaned forward in the chair, lost in his own thoughts, his expression a mix of weariness and determination.

Soon after, the waiting room's atmosphere shifted as Deputy Turner walked in, flanked by a couple of uniformed officers. His presence commanded attention, and his stern expression softened slightly upon seeing his brother. His eyes were locked onto Daniel, his younger brother, who stood up from his seat as their gazes met. Despite the weariness that hung heavily on his features, a faint smile curved

Daniel's lips.

"Hey, brother," Daniel greeted, his voice tinged with both exhaustion and relief. "We found Amanda. She's inside, being treated."

Deputy Turner's stern expression softened slightly as he nodded, absorbing the news. His attention then shifted to the two people standing beside Daniel – Nina and Vaughn. His eyebrows furrowed slightly as he regarded them, a hint of curiosity dancing in his eyes. After a moment, he directed his question at Daniel, "And what are they doing here?"

Daniel's smile seemed to grow at his brother's question. "Well, brother, isn't that a conundrum? Because the three of us found Amanda and rescued her."

The deputy's brows rose in surprise. "Rescued her? I need the full story," he prompted, his tone a mix of concern and anticipation. He looked around at the trio, waiting for an explanation that would shed light on the events that had brought them to this point.

Daniel took a deep breath and nodded, his gaze meeting his brother's. "It's been a wild ride, Alex. We were investigating, and it led us to the old Wildwood Horse Ranch."

Daniel briefly recounted the events leading up to their discovery at the farm house. He explained how they stumbled upon Amanda and the distressing series of events that they went through.

Deputy Turner rubbed his forehead, clearly processing the information. "This sounds like a nightmare. But you did the right thing by rescuing her and bringing her to the hospital." He looked at his brother, a mix of worry and pride in his eyes. "Daniel, you've always had a way of finding trouble."

Daniel managed a half-smile, a hint of self-deprecation in his tone. "Yeah, I guess I've got a knack for it."

Nina interjected, "We suspect that Hector's mother too, was involved with the kidnappings, at some capacity."

Deputy Turner's expression darkened further. "Hector has a lot to answer for." He turned to the officers who accompanied him. "Send a team to the farm house immediately. We need to get to the bottom of this."

As the officers hurried to carry out their orders, Deputy Turner turned back to the trio. "Thank you for your bravery in rescuing Amanda and bringing this to our attention." He then looked at Daniel. "I'll check in with the doctors about Amanda. Make sure that she's okay."

Daniel nodded, a mix of relief and exhaustion in his eyes. "Thanks, Derek. I appreciate it."

Nina's eyes met his with a glimmer of hope. "Thank you, Deputy Turner. We just want to make sure no one else gets hurt."

He nodded firmly. "I'll make sure of it. You all did a good thing tonight."

With that, Deputy Turner walked inside the emergency room, leaving Nina, Vaughn, and Daniel in the waiting area, where the weight of the day's events began to settle in as they processed the events that had transpired.

After what felt like an eternity, Deputy Turner emerged. His expression was a mix of weariness and resolve as he approached the group. "Amanda is awake," he informed them, his voice carrying a sense of urgency. "She's been asking to speak with the three of you."

Nina, Vaughn, and Daniel exchanged glances, a mixture of anticipation and concern clouding their eyes. Without a moment's hesitation, they followed Deputy Turner back to the area where Amanda was being treated. The hospital room was sterile and white, a stark contrast to the darkness they had encountered earlier.

Inside, Amanda was propped up on a bed, a mixture of exhaustion and relief etched across her face. When she saw them enter, a weak smile tugged at her lips. "Thank you for finding me," she said, her voice soft but full of gratitude. "I don't know what would have happened if you hadn't."

Daniel approached the bed, his concern evident. "We're just glad you're safe," he said, his voice sincere.

Vaughn nodded in agreement. "We're here for you, Amanda."

Amanda's gaze shifted toward Vaughn, her expression wavering between sadness and resolve. "Vaughn, I need to tell you something."

Vaughn's brows furrowed, his curiosity piqued. "What is it?"

Amanda took a deep breath, her fingers tightening around her covers. "I was the one who asked Daniel to get close to you, to keep an eye on you."

Vaughn's eyes widened in surprise, his jaw slightly agape. "What? Why?"

Amanda's eyes welled up with tears. "I was desperate, Vaughn. I needed to know what was happening in the town, especially when the women started disappearing. I thought Daniel could help me uncover the truth."

Nina was shocked, "You were investigating on your own?"

Amanda nodded weakly. "I felt like I had to do something, that maybe I could find some answers that the police weren't able to."

Vaughn's gaze softened, his anger replaced by compassion. "You should have come to me first. I could have helped."

Amanda's tears spilled over, her voice trembling. "I was scared, Vaughn. I didn't want anyone else to get hurt."

Vaughn reached out and gently wiped away her tears. "We're here for you now, Amanda. You don't have to go through this alone."

Amanda managed a small, grateful smile. "Thank you."

Daniel shifted uncomfortably on his feet. "You're part of our community, Amanda. We wouldn't have done anything differently."

Deputy Turner remained standing by the door, his presence a reminder of the ongoing investigation. "Amanda, I need to ask you a few questions about what happened. Is now a good time?"

Amanda nodded weakly. "Yes, I want to help catch those responsible."

As Deputy Turner leaned forward, his expression a mix of empathy and concern, he began to ask his questions. Amanda's voice trembled as she recounted the horrifying details of her captivity and the people involved. Her eyes held a haunted look as she spoke, the memories still fresh in her mind.

"I... I wanted to surprise Orlando," Amanda's voice wavered slightly, "the day after the wedding. I planned to make him breakfast, so I went to the local supermarket to pick out some stuff." She paused, a shiver of current passing through her as she relived the events. "But when I parked my car in the parking lot, I realized my gas was almost empty."

Deputy Turner nodded, his gaze steady, encouraging her to continue.

Amanda's voice grew softer, her gaze distant. "That's when an old lady with a car came up to me. She offered to help, said she'd drop me to the nearest gas station to pick up some gas and then bring me back to my car."

Her words hung heavy in the air, a stark reminder of the innocence that had been twisted into a nightmare. The deputy's brows furrowed, absorbing the details as he leaned in slightly.

"But when I got inside her car," Amanda's voice quivered, "I was... I was suddenly knocked out. The next thing I remember is waking up in that basement, tied up."

The room was filled with a heavy silence as Amanda's words hung in the air, a stark reminder of the darkness they had all faced. Deputy Turner's gaze never wavered from Amanda's as he listened intently, his expression a mix of concern and determination.

"I can't believe this happened to you, Amanda," he finally said, his voice edged with sympathy. "You went through an unimaginable ordeal."

Amanda's eyes welled up with tears, but she nodded bravely. "There was a large man in the house, he forced fed me and almost every day he combed my hair, like I was his doll or something."

The deputy's tone grew more serious. "We're

going to do everything we can to bring those responsible to justice. Can you remember anything about the old lady who offered to help you?"

Amanda closed her eyes for a moment, her brow furrowing in concentration. "I only caught a glimpse of her before she hit me. She was wearing a shawl, I think, and her eyes... they were cold, distant." She shivered as she recounted the memory.

Deputy Turner jotted down notes, his expression thoughtful. "We'll try to identify her. And the man... did he mention anything about his intentions?"

Amanda's grip on the armrest tightened. "He kept talking about how he wanted me to 'understand' something, that I needed to see the truth. But it was like he was obsessed, like he was trying to control me."

The deputy nodded, his lips pressed into a thin line. "We'll make sure he doesn't get the chance to harm anyone else."

Once the questioning was over, Amanda let out a sigh, as if a weight had been lifted off her shoulders. "I just want this nightmare to end," she said, her eyes filled with a mix of determination and vulnerability.

Deputy Turner gave Amanda a reassuring nod. "We're going to do everything in our power to bring those responsible to justice."

Deputy Chief Turner promised Amanda that he would inform her husband and father about her rescue, offering her a reassuring smile.

As they stepped out of the room and back into the cold corridors of the hospital, Daniel turned to his brother, Deputy Turner. "Can we speak privately for a moment?" he asked, his voice carrying a sense of urgency.

Nina and Vaughn exchanged knowing glances before nodding at Daniel and the deputy. They stepped away, giving the brothers their space.

"What is it?" Deputy Turner asked, his expression concerned.

Daniel took a deep breath before speaking. "Hector was the one was holding Amanda. And I think he's behind all the other missing women as well."

Deputy Turner's brows furrowed in surprise and concern. "But what would be his motive for that?"

Nina chimed in, her voice steady. "When we were escaping from the farm, we overheard Hector and his mother arguing. It seemed like they were fighting about something related to the women. That's when we managed to slip away."

Deputy Turner's lips pressed into a grim line. "I had a feeling there was more to this. We need to get back to that farm, find evidence, and bring them all down."

At that moment, a crackle came through on his radio, and he was radioed by one of his team members who were still at the farmhouse. "Chief, you need to come see this."

Deputy Turner's gaze flickered between Daniel, Nina, and Vaughn. "You three should stay here. It might not be safe."

Nina's voice was firm. "We want to go back with you. We want to help."

Vaughn nodded in agreement. "We're not going to sit around when there's a chance they might still be out there."

Deputy Turner sighed, torn between their determination and their safety. Finally, he relented. "No, the three of you are civilians, go home and rest. That's an order."

With that he left to get to the farm house, leaving Nina, Vaughn, and Daniel standing in the hospital corridor.

***

In a different corner of the town, Olive's anxiety was intense as she paced back and forth in her living room. The past hour had been a whirlwind of worry, her attempts to reach Vaughn and Nina growing increasingly frantic as each call went unanswered, only leading to their voicemail boxes. The silence on the other end of the line was deafening, and her imagination ran wild with all the possible scenarios.

She clutched her phone tightly in her hand, her fingers trembling. The room felt smaller, the walls closing in as uncertainty gnawed at her. She had just begun to trust Vaughn, to open herself up to the possibility of a new chapter in her life, and now this. The fear of losing him surged within her, a feeling she hadn't anticipated.

As her mind raced, a hundred thoughts competing for attention, she forced herself to take a deep breath. She needed to think rationally, to find out what was happening. Maybe there was a logical explanation for their lack of response.

With newfound determination, she dialed Vaughn's number again. She watched the phone ring, her heart pounding in her chest, until finally, it switched to his voicemail. She hung up, frustration building up inside her. She had to keep trying, had to believe that they were okay.

Gathering her resolve, she dialed Nina's number next. The anticipation as the phone rang was almost unbearable. And then, a click as the call connected. Relief washed over her, but it was short-lived as she heard the automated voice informing her that the subscriber she was trying to reach was unavailable. She ended the call, her worry deepening.

Olive's mind raced with possibilities. Were they in danger? Had something happened to them? She considered calling the police, but without concrete information, it might be premature. She needed to stay calm, think logically, and maybe even enlist some help.

Abruptly, the doorbell shattered the tension in Olive's home. Her pulse quickened, and her heart raced as she hurried to the door. Hope surged within her, her mind convinced that Vaughn, Daniel, and Nina had finally returned. She flung the door open with a mixture of relief and anticipation, ready to embrace them.

But her hopes were instantly dashed as she faced a stark reality. Standing before her, with a smile that held an unsettling charm, was Tony. A jolt of shock and fear coursed through her veins, freezing her in place. Her eyes widened, and she felt her breathing stop involuntarily.

Her voice trembled as she managed to speak, her tone laced with unease. "Tony? What are you doing here?"

He leaned casually against the doorframe, his demeanor oozing with confidence. "Hey, Olive. Long time no see."

Olive's mind raced, her heart pounding against her chest. She hadn't expected to see Tony again, not after their last encounter. She stepped back, creating a slight distance between them, her guard firmly up.

"I told you to leave me alone," she said, her voice quivering but resolute.

Tony's smile remained, though there was a coldness in his eyes that sent chills down her spine. "Now, now, Olive. Is that any way to greet an old friend?"

"You're not my friend," she shot back, her voice growing firmer. "I want you to leave right now."

Tony's expression darkened slightly, his facade of charm slipping for a moment. He took a step closer, and Olive's instincts screamed at her to retreat. But she held her ground, her resolve firm.

"I've been thinking about you, Olive," he said, his voice carrying a hint of possessiveness.

"Well, I haven't been thinking about you," Olive retorted, her voice laced with a mixture of anger and fear. "You need to go."

He took another step closer, and Olive's heart raced. She knew she had to stand strong, to show him that she wasn't afraid. But her body betrayed her, trembling slightly under his intense gaze.

"Olive, you and I had something special," Tony said, his tone growing more insistent. "I think it's time we renew that connection."

Olive's voice hardened, her fear giving way to anger. "I don't want anything to do with you, Tony. You need to leave before I call the police."

Tony's smile faltered, replaced by a look of frustration. He took a step forward, his eyes narrowing as he assessed her. "You're making a mistake, Olive. But fine, for now, I'll go."

As he turned and walked away, Olive let out a shaky breath, her heart still racing. Relief washed over her briefly, but her sense of calm was short-lived. Panic gripped her once more as Tony abruptly spun around, a white cloth now clutched tightly in his hands. Before she could react, he lunged towards her, his movements swift and forceful.

Olive's instinct to resist kicked in, and she fought against him, attempting to break free from his grasp. But his strength was overpowering, and his grip on her was unrelenting. In her desperate struggle, she felt the cloth press against her face, its sickly-sweet scent invading her senses.

"No!" she tried to scream, her voice muffled by the cloth that Tony held against her. Fear surged through her veins as her vision began to blur, her consciousness slipping away. She fought against the intruding darkness, but her body betrayed her, growing weak and heavy.

Through the haze, she heard Tony's chilling whisper, his words an uncanny promise that sent a shiver down her spine. "I'll always find you, Olive. I told you, didn't I? I told you that you'll never be able to leave me, ever again."

As the world faded into blackness, Olive's last thoughts were of Vaughn, a desperate hope that he would somehow come and rescue her.

***

Olive's consciousness slowly emerged from the depths of sleep, her eyelids fluttering as she attempted to orient herself. The rhythmic vibrations of the car beneath her served as a reminder that she was on the road. A cascade of throbbing sensations pulsed through her head, creating a discordant symphony with the blaring jazz music that filled the air. The world around her seemed hazy and disoriented, like pieces of a jigsaw puzzle that hadn't yet found their rightful place.

As Olive struggled to regain her senses, she focused on her surroundings. The interior of the car was dimly lit, the neon glow from streetlights outside casting intermittent streaks of light across Tony's face as he drove. She tried to move, but her limbs felt heavy, as if weighed down by an invisible force.

Gathering her strength, Olive tried to speak, her voice coming out as a raspy whisper, "Where... am I?"

Tony glanced at her, a twisted smile playing on his lips. "You're with me, Olive. We're going somewhere safe. Somewhere we can be together, just like old times."

Fear shot through her veins like a bolt of electricity. Memories of their past together flooded her mind – the suffocating control he had over her life, the desperation to escape his grasp, the way he manipulated and threatened her. She knew she couldn't let history repeat itself.

Summoning every ounce of courage, Olive struggled to sit up straight. Her blurred vision focused on the interior of the car, seeking any means of escape. Her eyes landed on the door handle, and a surge of determination overcame her grogginess.

With trembling hands, she reached for the door handle and silently prayed that it wasn't locked. As her fingers closed around the cold metal, she exerted pressure, the door giving a slight creak. Tony glanced at her again, his expression shifting from amusement to alarm as he realized what she was attempting.

"No, Olive!" he shouted, his voice tinged with panic. He swerved the car abruptly, causing her to lose her grip on the door handle. The sudden movement intensified the throbbing in her head, but it also sparked a fire within her. She refused to succumb to Tony's control again.

Desperation fueled her actions. Ignoring the pain, Olive lunged for the door handle once more, this time gripping it with relentless determination. Tony's hand shot out to stop her, his fingers grazing her arm. But the adrenaline coursing through her veins made her stronger.

With a forceful yank, she managed to open the door just as the car screeched to a halt. Olive tumbled out onto the pavement, her body aching from the impact. She could hear Tony's enraged shouts behind her as she scrambled to her feet and stumbled away from the car.

The night air was crisp against her skin, and the sound of traffic in the distance offered a glimmer of hope. Olive's heart pounded as she ran down the sidewalk, her vision still blurry, but her determination clear. She needed to find help, to escape from Tony's clutches once and for all.

"Help, somebody please," Olive screamed but no one heard her.

The echo of her desperate cries seemed to get swallowed by the night, the empty streets offering no solace. Olive's breath came in ragged gasps as fear and adrenaline fueled her flight. Every step felt like a lifeline, a chance to break free from the suffocating grasp of her tormentor.

As she fled into the darkness, her mind raced with thoughts of her friends – Vaughn, Nina, and Daniel. She knew they were out there, fighting against their own challenges. And she was determined to reunite with them, to face the shadows of the past together and forge a brighter future.

Olive's breath came in ragged gasps as she sprinted through the streets, her pulse echoing in her ears. She had managed to put some distance between herself and Tony, but she knew she couldn't let her guard down. Her mind raced, trying to remember the layout of the neighborhood. She needed to find a crowded place, a place where Tony wouldn't dare to follow.

Her heart sank as she realized that she was running out of options. The streets were quiet, and the darkness seemed to swallow her whole. But just as panic threatened to consume her, a familiar sight came into view – a park, illuminated by faint streetlights in the distance.

Without a second thought, Olive veered towards the park, her footsteps pounding against the pavement. The park was shrouded in shadows, and the night seemed to press in around her. But she knew that her best chance of escaping Tony was to blend in with the darkness.

Olive's breath hitched as she entered the park, her eyes scanning the area for any signs of movement. Her heart raced as she realized that she was alone in the scary silence. But just as her fear began to rise, a rustling sound caught her attention from behind. She whirled around, her eyes widening as she saw Tony emerging from the shadows, his face contorted in anger.

"You can't run from me, Olive," he hissed, his voice carrying a dangerous edge. Olive's heart pounded, but she refused to let fear paralyze her. She darted deeper into the park, using the cover of trees and bushes to shield her from Tony's sight.

Her breath came in labored gasps as she weaved through the park, her mind racing for a way out. She knew she needed to stay quiet and move quickly. The darkness was both her ally and her enemy – it hid her, but it also made navigation difficult.

Suddenly, Olive spotted a small structure ahead – a gazebo. It was situated at the center of the park, its silhouette outlined by the faint glow of moonlight. An idea sparked in her mind. If she could reach the gazebo, she might have a chance to hide or even find a way to call for help.

With newfound determination, Olive sprinted towards the gazebo, her heart pounding in her chest. She could hear Tony's footsteps echoing behind her, his enraged shouts growing louder. She pushed herself harder, her muscles burning, and her adrenaline fueling her movement.

As she reached the gazebo, Olive's fingers fumbled in her pocket for her phone. She needed to call for help, to let Vaughn, Nina, and Daniel know that she was in danger. But just as she was about to dial, a hand closed around her wrist, yanking the phone from her grasp.

Olive turned to face Tony, her eyes narrowing as she assessed her options. She was cornered, but she refused to give up without a fight. The two of them stood in tense silence, the darkness enveloping them as they faced each other.

"I told you, Olive," Tony's voice was chillingly calm, "you can't escape from me."

Olive's heart raced as she quickly turned away from Tony and sprinted out of the gazebo. Fear coursed through her veins, giving her the adrenaline she needed to push herself forward. The urgency in her steps mirrored the pounding of her heart. She burst out onto the park lane and continued running, her breaths coming in ragged gasps.

The park lane led her to a busy intersection, the rush hour traffic adding to the chaos of the moment. Olive didn't stop; she ran across the street, her eyes focused on finding safety. She heard Tony's footsteps behind her, his shouts filled with anger and desperation. But she was determined to outrun him.

As she dashed across the street, her heart leaped as she heard the screech of tires. She dared a quick glance back and her heart sank as she saw Tony being struck by an oncoming red pick-up truck. The impact was swift and brutal, and Tony was sent flying in the air.

Olive's breath caught in her throat as the scene unfolded before her eyes. Time seemed to slow down, each moment etching itself into her memory with a surreal clarity. The screech of tires and the sickening thud of impact reverberated through the air, a haunting symphony of chaos and consequences.

Tony's body twisted and tumbled through the air, the collision propelling him like a ragdoll. The world seemed to blur around him as he crashed onto the road, the force of the impact leaving him sprawled and motionless. The pick-up truck screeched to a halt a short distance away, its driver leaping out in shock and disbelief. Olive's heart raced even faster as she recognized the driver – it was Vaughn.

Vaughn quickly got out of the truck, his eyes widening in surprise and concern as he saw Olive standing there, her face a mix of shock and fear. Without a second thought, he rushed towards her, his arms enveloping her in a protective embrace. "Olive, are you okay? What happened?" he asked urgently, his voice laced with worry.

Olive could barely find her voice; she clung to Vaughn as tears streamed down her face. She was safe, she was with him. Nina and Daniel emerged from the truck, their expressions a mix of confusion and concern. The scene had caught the attention of onlookers, and someone had already called the emergency services.

As the sirens wailed in the distance, Olive's tears flowed freely. Vaughn held her close, offering her the solace and comfort she desperately needed. It was a moment of relief, a moment of triumph over the darkness that had threatened to consume her.

Nina and Daniel joined the embrace, forming a protective circle around Olive. The sound of approaching sirens grew louder, a symphony of rescue that would bring an end to this nightmare.

Olive clung to Vaughn, her tears soaking his shirt as relief washed over her. She couldn't believe she had managed to escape from Tony, that he was now lying on the road, his figure illuminated by the flashing lights of the oncoming vehicles. Vaughn held her tightly, his concern evident in his grip.

Nina and Daniel rushed over, their faces a mixture of shock and worry. "Olive, are you okay?" Nina asked, her voice shaking with concern.

"I'm okay now," Olive managed to choke out between sobs. She pulled away from Vaughn slightly, her eyes filled with gratitude as she looked at him. "Thank you for coming."

Vaughn's expression softened, and he brushed a tear from her cheek. "I'm just glad you're okay."

As the sirens of approaching emergency vehicles grew louder, the bystanders who had witnessed the accident began to gather around. Olive took a deep breath, trying to steady her racing heart. She watched as paramedics rushed towards Tony, their urgency evident. Despite the danger he had posed to her, a pang of guilt gnawed at her chest.

Nina wrapped her arms around Olive, offering comfort and support. "It's okay," she whispered, giving her a reassuring squeeze.

Daniel exchanged a worried glance with Vaughn before stepping forward, his gaze on the unfolding scene. The police arrived, cordoning off the area and beginning their investigation. An officer approached the group, asking questions about the incident and taking statements.

As the chaos of the moment unfolded, Olive found herself overwhelmed. She had narrowly escaped a dangerous situation, and now the reality of it all was sinking in. The support of Vaughn, Nina, and Daniel was a lifeline, grounding her in the midst of the turmoil.

The paramedics worked quickly, tending to Tony's injuries before loading him onto a stretcher. Olive watched from a distance, her emotions a mix of relief, fear, and uncertainty. Despite the danger he had posed to her, there was a part of her that couldn't help but feel a sense of pity for him.

The ambulance doors closed, and Tony was whisked away. Olive turned back to her friends, her gaze locking with Vaughn's. "Thank you," she whispered, her voice laden with emotion.

Vaughn's eyes softened, and he pulled her into a comforting hug once more. "You don't have to thank us," he murmured, his words a soothing balm to her frazzled nerves.

As the scene slowly cleared, the group stood together on the crowded sidewalk, a united front against the chaos that had just unfolded.

Nina squeezed Olive's hand, offering a small smile. "Let's get out of here," she suggested gently. "We'll make sure you're safe."

With a nod, Olive allowed herself to be led back to the pickup truck, the familiar presence of her friends providing a sense of comfort. As they drove away from the scene, the weight of the night's events hung heavy in the air, but so did the strength of their friendship and their resilience in the face of adversity.

***

The scene at the old Wildwood Horse Ranch was unreal, the air heavy with a mix of tension and foreboding. Deputy Turner and his team cautiously approached the worn-down farmhouse, their flashlights cutting through the darkness as they scanned the area for any signs of danger.

As they entered the grounds, the beam of Deputy Turner's flashlight illuminated the unsettling sight that lay before them. Hector's lifeless body was sprawled, a look of torment frozen on his face. It was evident that he had choked his own mother to death, their lifeless forms tangled in a final, tragic struggle.

Deputy Turner's gaze shifted to the shotgun that lay a few feet away from them. The muzzle was stained with blood, and it was clear that in her last desperate moments, Hector's mother had managed to pull the trigger, ending both their lives.

The officers carefully examined the scene, collecting evidence and taking photographs. The weight of the tragedy hung heavily in the air as they processed what had transpired. It was a grim testament to the depths of despair that had consumed Hector and the twisted bond he shared with his mother.

Inside the dimly lit house, the air was heavy with a sense of unease as the officers meticulously combed through every corner, driven by the urgency of their mission. Deputy Chief Turner led the way, his face a mask of grim determination. The weight of responsibility bore down on him as he guided his team through the unsettling exploration.

With each step, the tension seemed to escalate, the collective breaths of the officers catching in their throats as they moved further into the shadows. The house held its secrets tightly, an enigmatic puzzle they were determined to solve.

As they entered a narrow hallway, one of the officers called out, "Chief, I've found something here." The others gathered around, their flashlights illuminating the entrance to a concealed cellar beneath a trapdoor.

Deputy Chief Turner's heart sank as he realized what they might be about to uncover. He nodded at the officer, his voice steady despite the gravity of the situation. "Open it."

With cautious precision, the officers lifted the trapdoor, revealing a narrow set of stairs leading down into the darkness below. Their flashlights cut through the blackness, revealing a scene that would forever haunt their memories.

The hidden cellar held rows of makeshift shelves, each one holding a macabre display of human remains. The officers exchanged horrified glances, their breaths catching in their throats. The truth they had suspected for so long was now an undeniable reality, and the magnitude of the horror they were facing sent a shiver down their spines.

Deputy Chief Turner's jaw tightened, his emotions a turbulent mix of anger and grief. He knew that they had stumbled upon the haunting evidence of the disappearances that had plagued their town for years. The faces of the missing women stared back at them, a chilling testament to the darkness that had festered in their midst.

As the officers processed the grim scene before them, Deputy Turner's mind raced. The weight of the truth settled heavily on his shoulders, and he knew that their work was far from over. This discovery marked the beginning of a relentless pursuit of justice, a fight to ensure that the lives lost would not be in vain.

He took a deep breath, his voice firm as he addressed his team. "We need to document everything here, gather as much evidence as possible. This is a critical moment, and we owe it to the victims and their families to see this through to the end."

As the officers got to work, their determination

was unwavering. The cellar held the chilling answers they had sought for years, and now it was their responsibility to bring those responsible to justice and provide closure to the families who had waited for so long.

Deputy Turner's heart was heavy as he looked at the remains, each one a tragic story of lives cut short and families left grieving. He knew that the town would be scarred by these events for a long time, but he was determined to ensure that justice would be served and closure would be found for the families affected.

Outside the farmhouse, the moon cast a haunting glow on the scene, as if nature itself was mourning the lives lost within those walls. Deputy Turner took a moment to collect his thoughts, his heart heavy with the weight of the darkness he had uncovered.

As he turned away from the house, he was resolved to bring an end to this chapter of Serenity Falls' history. The truth had been uncovered, and now it was time to heal, to rebuild, and to ensure that the memories of those lost would be honored by the town's resilience and the pursuit of a better future.

***

CHAPTER 19: BURYING THE PAST

The town of Serenity Falls was caught in a whirlwind of emotions as the news of Amanda's rescue resounded through the community. The air was thick with a mix of relief and tension, a blend of hope and nervousness that colored every interaction and conversation. Local residents gathered around televisions and radios, their eyes glued to the screens as the news channels broadcasted updates on Amanda's dramatic rescue operation.

The headlines splashed across newspapers and websites told the story: "Missing Woman Amanda Alvarez Found Alive: Police Rescue in Dramatic Operation." The town collectively exhaled, grateful that one life had been spared from the horrors that had plagued Serenity Falls.

In the newsroom of the local station, reporters

discussed the case's twists and turns. "It's been a shocking turn of events," one anchor remarked, adjusting her glasses. "After weeks of uncertainty, Amanda Alvarez has been rescued. The police's swift action has certainly captured the town's attention."

As the news report played, the camera panned to Deputy Chief Turner, who stood in front of the police station surrounded by cameras and microphones. "We're pleased to report that Amanda Alvarez has been found and rescued," Deputy Turner announced, his demeanor exuding authority. "Our dedicated team worked tirelessly to solve this case and bring her home safely."

Meanwhile, at a local coffee shop, residents gathered to discuss the latest developments. "Can you believe they found Amanda?" one woman exclaimed, sipping her latte.

"Thank goodness she's safe," another replied, her eyes glued to the news coverage on the large TV screen. "But it's strange how the deputy chief is taking all the credit."

The conversation turned to Orlando Morgan, who had been released from his arrest following Amanda's rescue. The news report briefly touched on his release, and the anchor mentioned that there had been a lack of evidence to tie him to the disappearance.

Back at the police station, Orlando was seen walking out, his face a mix of relief and exhaustion. Reporters swarmed around him, bombarding him with questions. "Mr. Morgan, how do you feel now that you've been released?" one reporter shouted.

Orlando paused for a moment, his gaze steady as he addressed the crowd. "I'm grateful for the support of my family and friends during this difficult time," he said, his voice measured. "I had faith that the truth would come to light, and I'm relieved that Amanda is safe."

But even as the relief washed over them, there remained an undercurrent of tension. The knowledge that Amanda's ordeal was just one piece of a much larger puzzle cast a shadow over the town. The cold cases of the missing women that had haunted their community for years had finally been cracked open.

Reports of the police solving these cold cases began to circulate, unveiling the grim truth that had been hidden beneath the surface. The remains of the missing women were discovered at the Wildwood Horse Ranch, a revelation that sent shockwaves throughout Serenity Falls. The local news outlets released brief statements: "Police Uncover Remains of Missing Women at Wildwood Horse Ranch: Ongoing Investigations."

As the community grappled with the shock of these revelations, Deputy Chief Turner and his team were hard at work, piecing together the evidence and ensuring that justice would be served. The police's dedication to bringing closure to the families of the victims was unwavering, and their efforts were met with a mixture of gratitude and anticipation.

Nina, Daniel, and Vaughn watched the news coverage from Nina's living room. "Can you believe Turner is acting like he cracked the case?" Vaughn muttered, his frustration evident.

Nina clenched her fist, her eyes narrowing as she watched Deputy Turner speaking to the reporters. "He's taking credit for something he didn't even do," she said, her tone incredulous.

Daniel shook his head, his jaw clenched. "This is outrageous. We were the ones who found the farmhouse and helped Amanda."

As the news report continued, Amanda was shown being interviewed from her hospital room. "I'm just grateful to be safe and back with my family," she said, her voice quivering with emotion. "I want to thank everyone who supported us during this time."

The coverage shifted to the investigation's ongoing efforts to identify and apprehend the individuals responsible for the kidnappings. "Our investigation remains active, and we are determined to bring those responsible to justice," Deputy Turner stated confidently.

Outside the police station, protestors held signs demanding transparency and accountability. "Give credit where credit is due!" one sign read.

Nina, Daniel, and Vaughn sat in the cozy living room, the flickering glow of the TV casting a warm light around them. Amanda's rescue had brought a collective sigh of relief to the group, even though Deputy Chief Turner had taken the credit for it. Despite the injustice, they found solace in the fact that Amanda was safe.

Vaughn had Olive nestled up against him on the couch. Her face was pale, and her eyes carried the weight of the recent events. The accident had shaken her, and she hadn't spoken a word since. He gently stroked her hair, his concern evident in his eyes. He had been relieved when she was found safe and sound, but now he was worried about the toll the trauma had taken on her.

Nina sat across from them in an armchair, her fingers tapping thoughtfully on the armrest. She exchanged a glance with Daniel, her worry for Olive unspoken but deeply felt. The events of the past few days had been harrowing, and it was clear that Olive was grappling with the aftermath.

After a while, Nina turned to Daniel, her voice lowered. "We should ask your brother about Agent Marks. Why was he out on the road? It doesn't make sense."

Daniel nodded, his expression serious. "You're right. I'll talk to him today. We need to know what he was doing there."

As they spoke, Vaughn noticed Olive stir on the couch. He shifted his gaze to her, concern etched on his face. "Olive," he said softly, "Are you okay?"

Olive looked up at Vaughn, her eyes glassy but filled with gratitude. She managed a small nod, not yet ready to speak about the ordeal she had just endured.

Nina leaned forward, her voice gentle. "Olive, we're here for you. If you need to talk or if there's anything we can do, just let us know."

Olive managed a weak smile, touched by their support. She appreciated their understanding, even if she wasn't ready to share the details just yet.

A knock on the door interrupted their conversation, and Vaughn got up to answer it. It was a uniformed police officer, there to deliver a message. "Deputy Turner sent me to inform you that Agent Marks is at the local hospital. He's okay, just a bit banged up from the accident."

Nina's eyebrows furrowed, the pieces of the puzzle coming together in her mind. She turned to Daniel, her voice low. "This is our chance. You need to talk to your brother about Agent Marks. Find out what he was doing on that road."

Daniel nodded, his determination renewed. "I'll do it. I'll head to my brother now and get some answers."

He turned to Vaughn and Olive, his tone reassuring. "I'm sure everything is fine, but we just need to make sure."

Vaughn nodded, his arm wrapped protectively around Olive. He looked up at Daniel, his voice steady. "Be careful, Daniel. We don't know who or what we're dealing with here."

With a firm nod, Daniel left to confront his brother, leaving the others behind to anxiously wait for his return.

***

A short while later, Daniel walked into the police

station with a sense of purpose. He had his suspicions about Agent Marks, and he was determined to find out the truth. He found his brother, Deputy Turner, in his office and knocked on the door.

Deputy Turner looked up from his paperwork, a surprised expression on his face. "Daniel? What are you doing here?"

"I need to talk to you about something important," Daniel replied, his tone serious.

Deputy Turner motioned for his brother to take a seat. "Alright, what's on your mind?"

Daniel leaned forward, his eyes focused. "I want to know more about Agent Marks and what he was doing on the road when he was hit by Vaughn's truck."

Deputy Turner sighed and leaned back in his chair. "Look, Daniel, Agent Marks was on the road by accident. He didn't look before crossing and got hit. It's as simple as that."

But Daniel's suspicion remained. "I find it hard to believe that an FBI agent would be so careless. There's something more to this."

His brother sighed again, running a hand through his hair. "I understand your concerns, but sometimes accidents do happen."

"Accidents or not, I want to know if there's something he's not telling us," Daniel insisted. "Did you recover any personal effects from the scene of the accident?"

Deputy Turner raised an eyebrow, his curiosity piqued. "Personal effects? Why does that matter?"

"Just answer the question," Daniel pressed.

Deputy Turner nodded to his assistant, who left the office and returned moments later with a clear plastic evidence bag. He handed it to Deputy Turner, who examined its contents.

"Nothing out of the ordinary," Deputy Turner said, his brow furrowed as he listed the items. "Keys, wallet, two phones..."

Daniel's eyes narrowed when he heard "two phones." He interrupted his brother, "Wait a minute, two phones?"

Deputy Turner glanced at the phones on the table and then back at his brother. "Well, it's not unusual these days. But let's take a look at it anyway."

He carefully pulled out the two phones and placed them side by side. Daniel picked one up and examined it. "This one is Olive's phone."

Deputy Turner's expression turned from confusion to surprise. "Olive Adams, the photographer? Why on earth would he have her phone?"

"That's exactly what I'm trying to figure out," Daniel said, his voice tense. "We found Olive that night on the street. She seemed to have been running from something."

Deputy Turner leaned back in his chair, lost in thought. "Where is she now?"

"At home," Daniel replied.

Deputy Turner stood up, his demeanor now serious. "Alright, I'm coming with you. Take me to her."

As they left the police station together, the truth was beginning to unravel. Both brothers were determined to get to the bottom of the mystery, to uncover the connections between Agent Marks, Olive's phone, and the events that had taken place.

The atmosphere in Olive's living room was tense as Daniel and Deputy Turner entered. Vaughn and Nina were already there, and Olive was nestled on the couch with Vaughn's protective arms around her. Deputy Turner found a seat on the coffee table in front of them, his expression a mix of concern and determination.

"Olive," Deputy Turner began gently, "I know this has been a traumatic experience for you, and we're here to help. We need to understand what happened, and we need your cooperation."

Olive's gaze was distant, her eyes reflecting the haunting memories that had been consuming her. For a few moments, she didn't respond. Vaughn tightened his grip around her, offering silent support.

After a few minutes, Olive slowly opened her eyes and sat upright. Her voice was shaky as she spoke, "I... I can't believe what happened. It's like a nightmare."

Deputy Turner leaned forward slightly, his tone empathetic, "I understand that this is difficult, Olive. But we need to know the truth. Can you tell us what you remember?"

Olive took a deep breath, her hands trembling. "Tony... he came to my house. He forced his way in... said he wouldn't let me go. He drugged me and... I woke up in his car."

Deputy Turner's brows furrowed, his jaw tensing

as he listened intently. "Go on."

"We were driving, and he told me he wouldn't let me leave him again," Olive's voice trembled, tears forming in her eyes. "I managed to escape when he got out of the car. I ran into the park, and he followed me. I was so scared..."

Deputy Turner's eyes remained locked on Olive's face, his heart aching for her. "I promise you, Olive, that you're safe now. We're here to protect you. But we need to know more about Tony, about why he was after you."

Olive wiped away her tears, a mixture of fear and determination in her eyes. "I... I don't know everything. But he was always so possessive, so controlling, all the while I stayed at his apartment. He said he would never let me go, that he would make me love him again."

Deputy Turner nodded, his voice soothing, "I understand. We'll get all the information we need from you. We'll make sure you're safe and that Tony won't be able to harm you again."

Vaughn gave Olive's shoulder a reassuring squeeze, his eyes filled with a mixture of concern and affection. "We're here for you, Olive."

Nina added her support, her voice gentle, "You're

not alone in this. We're all with you."

Deputy Turner leaned a bit closer, his expression unwavering, "And I promise you, we won't let anything happen to you. But to help us, we need to understand why Tony was so obsessed with you. If there's anything you're not telling us, now's the time to speak up."

Olive took a shaky breath, her gaze meeting Deputy Turner's determined eyes. She could sense the sincerity in his words, and slowly, the weight on her shoulders felt a bit lighter. "There's something... something about my past, something I've been trying to forget. Tony knew about it, and he used it to control me."

Deputy Turner's expression remained resolute, "Whatever it is, Olive, you can trust us. We'll uncover the truth and make sure justice is served."

In the safety of Olive's living room, bathed in the soft glow of the lamplight, the air was heavy with the weight of her confessions. The room was filled with a tense silence as she finally gathered the courage to share her past with Vaughn, Nina, and Deputy Turner.

Olive's voice wavered as she recounted her story, her hands clenching and unclenching in her lap. "Tony and I, we lived in the same apartment building, back in New York. We went on one date, just one, and then everything changed. The next thing I knew, I was being arrested in my own apartment for drug possession. Tony was there at the police station, and he used his influence to get me out."

Deputy Turner's brow furrowed, his eyes narrowing as he listened intently. "He helped you out? How did you end up at his place?"

Olive's voice cracked with emotion, "He said he would help me, that he was an FBI agent and he could make everything go away. He took me to his home, and over the next few days, he moved all my things from my apartment into his. He even made me give up my lease." Her gaze dropped, and she continued in a whisper, "I felt trapped, Deputy Turner. He promised me that he would protect me from going to jail."

Nina's eyes widened, and she exchanged a worried glance with Vaughn. Olive's story was more sinister than they could have imagined.

"But then... then things started to change," Olive continued, her voice trembling. "He became controlling, wouldn't let me leave the apartment without him. For three months, I lived in fear, planning my escape every single day."

Deputy Turner's jaw clenched, anger and concern visible on his face. "That's when you decided to run?"

Olive nodded, her eyes welling up with tears. "Yes, one day he left for an assignment out of town, and I saw my chance. I packed my things and left without telling him. I came here to Serenity Falls, hoping I could start over."

Vaughn's grip on Olive's hand tightened, his voice full of compassion, "You've been through so much, Olive."

Nina placed a comforting hand on Olive's shoulder, her voice gentle, "You're incredibly strong, and you're not alone in this anymore."

Deputy Turner leaned forward, his expression determined, "Olive, thank you for sharing your story. It was crucial for us to understand the whole picture. We're here to help you, and we'll make sure Tony doesn't get away with what he's done."

Olive wiped away her tears, a mixture of relief and vulnerability in her eyes. "I just want my life back."

Deputy Turner's gaze never wavered, his voice firm, "We'll make sure that happens. Tony won't be able to hurt you again."

Olive's words hung heavy in the air as she recounted her harrowing experience with Tony. The room was filled with a mixture of shock, anger, and empathy from those gathered around her. She took a deep breath and continued her story, her voice growing stronger with each word.

"After I left, I thought I could start anew here in Serenity Falls. I wanted to escape from his control, from the fear he had implanted in me," Olive's gaze was resolute, her hands gripping the edge of the couch. "But somehow, he tracked me down. He found me, and I've been living in constant fear since then."

Nina's eyes flashed with anger, "That's insane, how could he manipulate the system like that?"

Olive's expression grew weary, "He's an FBI agent, he knows how to bend things to his advantage. He used his authority to make me believe I had no way out."

Vaughn's grip around Olive tightened, his voice filled with a mixture of protectiveness and anger, "You're safe now, Olive. We won't let him hurt you anymore."

Deputy Turner leaned forward, his gaze unwavering, "We're going to put a stop to this, Olive. Agent Marks won't get away with what he's done."

Olive nodded, her eyes showing a glimmer of hope. "Thank you all for being here for me."

***

In the hospital room, the sunlight filtered through the window, casting a warm glow over Agent Marks as he sat on the edge of the bed, dressed and ready to be discharged. A soft knock on the door preceded the entrance of Deputy Turner and a couple of officers. A friendly grin lit up Deputy Turner's face as he walked in, his fellow officers following suit.

"Well, well, look who's finally getting out of here," Deputy Turner quipped, his tone lighthearted as he extended a hand towards Agent Marks.

Agent Marks chuckled, shaking Deputy Turner's hand firmly. "Seems like I can't catch a break. First, I get hit by a car, and now you guys are here to ruin my peaceful hospital stay."

The officers shared a chuckle as they greeted Agent Marks, exchanging pleasantries and light banter. The doctor, an older woman with a warm smile, joined the group. "I see we have some friendly visitors," she said, addressing Deputy Turner and the officers.

Deputy Turner nodded with a grin. "Just making sure our friend here is on the mend."

The doctor laughed, giving Agent Marks a playful nudge. "Well, he's in good hands. I'm about to discharge him, so you can take him off our hands."

Agent Marks mock-sighed. "Oh, the sympathy is overwhelming."

The doctor winked at him. "Don't worry, you're free to go. Just follow the prescribed medication and rest well."

As the doctor went over the discharge instructions, the atmosphere in the room remained light-hearted. Laughter and camaraderie filled the space, overshadowing the seriousness of Agent Marks' recent accident.

"You'll have to tell us the secret of your miraculous survival," Deputy Turner teased, "Getting hit by a car and walking out almost unscathed? Impressive."

Agent Marks shrugged, a playful glint in his eyes. "Pure talent, Deputy Turner. It's all about timing and agility."

The officers chuckled, enjoying the friendly banter between their superior and Agent Marks. As the doctor handed Agent Marks the necessary paperwork and prescriptions, she gave him a warm smile. "Take care of yourself, Agent Marks. And if you find yourself in the hospital again, try not to make it a regular occurrence."

Agent Marks saluted her with a grin. "No promises, but I'll do my best."

As the doctor left, Deputy Turner leaned in, a mischievous glint in his eyes. "So, FBI Special Agent Marks, how's it feel to be the first agent in history to be hit by a car on Serenity Falls' streets?"

Agent Marks rolled his eyes, a smirk tugging at his lips. "Oh, come on, Deputy Turner. Just adding some excitement to your quiet little town."

Deputy Turner laughed, patting him on the back. "Well, you definitely managed to do that. We even had a car chase on our roads for once."

As they exchanged banter, Deputy Turner's tone shifted, his expression growing serious. He reached into his pocket and pulled out a piece of paper. He handed it over to Agent Marks, his gaze unwavering. "Take a look at this, Marks."

Agent Marks raised an eyebrow, his eyes scanning the paper. His expression turned to one of surprise as he read the words on it. "A restraining order?"

Deputy Turner's voice was firm, his eyes locked onto Agent Marks'. "Olive Adams filed it against you. She doesn't want you anywhere near her."

Agent Marks scoffed, crumpling the paper in his hand. "She's just being dramatic, Turner. She's overreacting."

Deputy Turner leaned in, his voice low and stern. "Listen carefully, Marks. You come anywhere near her again, in my town, I'll be sure to arrest you. And you know what that means now, don't you? I have to report to your superiors about your performance here in my town. How you severely lacked resources and hardly brought any value to the case. For God's sake, you ended up on the streets, chasing a woman and getting hit by a car." He leaned back, a smug smile tugging at his lips. "You'll be walking into your worst nightmare, Marks. Good luck with that."

Agent Marks glared at Deputy Turner, a mix of frustration and disbelief in his eyes. "You don't know what you're getting yourself into, Turner."

Deputy Turner's smile remained unwavering, his gaze steady. "Oh, I think I do, Agent Marks. I know exactly what I'm doing. I'm standing up to corporate scums like you who think they can do whatever they want."

As Deputy Turner turned to leave the room, a newfound confidence radiated from him. He knew that standing up to Agent Marks might not be easy, but he was determined to protect his town and its people from any threats, no matter how high up the ladder they might be.

***

CHAPTER 20: LOVE CONQUERS ALL

As the days passed, Agent Marks prepared to leave Serenity Falls, his chapter in the small town coming to an end. But now, he found himself facing an unforeseen turn of events that would shatter the life he had known. After his accident and recovery, he knew he had to leave town, but the echoes of his past actions were about to catch up with him.

He packed his belongings and said his goodbyes to those he had crossed paths with during his time there. Some faces carried relief, others curiosity, but most held a mix of emotions that could only be shared by those who had been part of the tumultuous events that unfolded.

Back at FBI headquarters, Agent Marks walked into his office, ready to resume his usual duties. However, his anticipation turned to shock as he found himself summoned to an unexpected meeting.

Senior agents and officials were seated around a table, their expressions stern. Internal affairs was conducting an investigation into his actions surrounding the Serenity Falls case, including allegations of misconduct and connections to criminals.

Agent Ramirez, the lead investigator, looked at Marks with a mix of suspicion and regret. "Agent Anthony Marks, we have evidence suggesting a misuse of authority, questionable decisions, and alliances that raise serious concerns."

Marks remained composed, the weight of the accusations heavy on his shoulders. "I've always done what I believed was necessary to bring criminals to justice."

Agent Ramirez leaned forward, his gaze unwavering. "And sometimes, the lines between justice and personal motives blur."

Sitting across a stern-looking panel, Agent Marks listened as allegations of misuse of authority, ties to criminals, and other misconduct were laid out before him. The internal investigation had unveiled a web of corruption that had gone unnoticed for too long. Agent Marks' world crumbled as he realized the gravity of the accusations against him.

Agent Marks' mind raced, memories and decisions from the past flashing before him like fragments of a shattered mirror. He had walked a fine line, believing that the ends justified the means, that his actions were necessary for the greater good. But now, confronted with the consequences of his choices, he couldn't deny the truth that stared him in the face.

One by one, the committee members questioned him, their voices cutting through the heavy silence of the room. The accusations and evidence left little room for denial. Tony knew that he was standing on the precipice of his downfall, a precipice that he had unknowingly edged closer to with every compromise he had made.

Incarceration was a stark reality that Tony never thought he would face. As he stepped into the prison yard on his first day, he felt the weight of his past catching up with him. In the harsh environment of the prison yard, Tony's freedom had been replaced by confinement, and his once comfortable life was now reduced to the stark reality of incarceration. As he took his first steps into the yard, he couldn't shake the feeling of his past catching up with him. The chilling clang of metal doors closing behind him echoed in his ears, a sound that would become all too familiar.

Assigned to a cramped cell, Tony exchanged uneasy glances with his new cellmate, a burly man with a hardened expression. The cell was a stark reminder of the life he now had to endure – a narrow bed, a small desk, and cold, gray walls that seemed to close in on him. His belongings were minimal, a stark contrast to the opulence he had once enjoyed.

In the midst of the tense silence, a prison officer approached, his gaze cold and detached. "You better get used to this, newcomer," the officer grunted, his voice laced with authority. "Rules are simple here: keep your head down, follow orders, and don't make any trouble."

Tony's jaw tightened as he absorbed the officer's words. He was no longer the one in control; he was just another inmate in a system that didn't care about his past or his privileged background. His once confident demeanor had been replaced by a sense of vulnerability he had never experienced before.

Nightfall brought with it a chilling darkness, both inside and outside the prison walls. In the dimly lit cell, Tony lay on his cot, his thoughts racing. The sounds of distant conversations and footsteps echoed through the corridors, a haunting reminder of the world he had entered.

The morning sun had barely risen when chaos

erupted within the prison walls. Tony found himself caught in the crossfire of a violent altercation between inmates, the air thick with tension and aggression. In the midst of the turmoil, he was cornered by a group of convicts, their faces twisted in malice as they closed in on him. Fear coursed through Tony's veins, his heart racing as he realized the danger he was in.

Among the shouts and threats that filled the air, the glint of a knife caught his eye. Time seemed to slow as he watched the blade gleam in the harsh light. Before he could react, a searing pain lanced through his side, the impact of the weapon sinking into his flesh. The shock of the moment rendered him momentarily paralyzed, the agony radiating through his body.

As he struggled to keep his feet, the words of one of the inmates pierced through the chaos, a chilling whisper in his ear, "Die, you fucking pig."

The gravity of his situation hit Tony like a tidal wave, his thoughts racing as his vision blurred. The world around him spun in a disorienting dance, the sounds of the altercation a distant buzz in his ears.

Fighting to stay conscious, Tony's thoughts became a whirlwind of memories and regrets. Deputy Turner's warnings echoed in his mind, a stark reminder of the choices he had made and the consequences that had come crashing down on him. The internal investigation, the web of corruption he had been entangled in, and the shadows that had consumed his life – they all converged in a haunting symphony.

In those final seconds, as darkness threatened to overtake him, Tony's thoughts turned to Olive, the woman he had loved and lost. Her face flashed before his eyes, a bittersweet reminder of the happiness he had once known. And as his grip on consciousness wavered, he clung to that image, finding a moment of consolation in the last moments of his life.

***

After the horrific events that unfolded, Amanda's story took an unexpected turn. Her rescue from the farmhouse had been a turning point, freeing her from the clutches of darkness and bringing her back to her family. The days that followed were filled with tearful reunions, joyful embraces, and heartfelt apologies.

Mayor Alvarez, Amanda's father, had initially suspected Orlando, Amanda's husband, of being involved in her disappearance. The weight of suspicion had strained their relationship, leaving both father and son-in-law wounded by the distrust that hung in the air.

However, the truth began to unravel as the investigation progressed. Evidence pointed away from Orlando and towards the actual culprits who had held

Amanda captive. The Mayor's heartache was twofold — his daughter's suffering and the realization that he had doubted the man who loved her.

In a private meeting, Amanda's father and Orlando found themselves face to face. The room was heavy with tension, the weight of their emotions palpable. Mayor Alvarez spoke first, his voice laced with regret, "Orlando, I owe you an apology. I should have never doubted you, especially after all that you've done for Amanda."

Orlando's gaze met the Mayor's, a mixture of pain and forgiveness in his eyes. "Mayor Alvarez, I understand your concern for Amanda. I would have done anything to bring her back to safety, even if it meant facing suspicion."

The Mayor nodded, his expression reflecting the turmoil within him. "Amanda told me everything — about your support, your determination to find her, and your unrelenting love. I see now that I was wrong to doubt you."

Tears welled up in Orlando's eyes as he accepted the apology with grace. "All that matters is that Amanda is safe and back with her family."

Mayor Alvarez extended a hand towards Orlando, their differences and suspicions slowly dissipating. "I should have said this long back. Orlando, welcome to the family. You've proven yourself to be the man Amanda loves and the one who stood by her side in her darkest hour."

The handshake was a symbolic bridge, mending the divide that had formed between them. From that moment on, Orlando became an integral part of Amanda's life and her father's inner circle.

In the weeks that followed, Amanda's recovery was a gradual process. Her family surrounded her with solid support, helping her piece together her life and regain a sense of normalcy. Orlando's presence was a constant comfort, a reminder of the love that had never wavered even in the face of adversity.

As for Amanda's father, he dedicated himself to advocating for justice and change. The events surrounding Amanda's kidnapping prompted him to increase resources for missing persons cases and improve the town's safety measures. He turned his sorrow into action, ensuring that no family would have to endure what he had to go through.

***

The town of Serenity Falls witnessed a transformation – not only in the lives of the individuals directly impacted by the events but also in its collective spirit. The community came together, supporting one another through difficult times and celebrating the triumph of love and resilience.

Daniel found himself at the center of the town's attention, acknowledged by the mayor as a local hero for his role in solving the case and revealing the truth that had eluded them all.

Standing before a gathered crowd in the heart of Serenity Falls, Daniel felt a mix of emotions surging within him. The mayor's words reverberated through the air, recognition and gratitude etched into every syllable. "Ladies and gentlemen," the mayor began, his voice carrying a weight of sincerity, "we gather here today not only to celebrate the conclusion of a long and arduous investigation, but to acknowledge the bravery and determination of one individual who played a key role in uncovering the truth."

Daniel's heart swelled with a sense of pride, and he exchanged a glance with Nina and Vaughn, who stood by his side as a united front. The mayor continued, "In the midst of darkness, there emerged a beacon of hope – a young man who refused to turn a blind eye, who dared to challenge the status quo, and who persisted until justice prevailed."

As the mayor's speech continued, recounting the events that had transpired and the courage Daniel had exhibited, a swell of emotions filled the crowd. The town's residents nodded in agreement, their expressions reflecting a mix of relief and gratitude. The weight of suspicion that had hung over Serenity Falls for years was finally lifted, replaced by a sense of unity and healing.

After the mayor's speech, Daniel found himself approached by various townspeople, offering words of thanks and admiration. Among them was the mayor himself, who extended a hand to shake Daniel's. "You've brought closure to this town, son," the mayor said, his voice genuine. "Your actions have shown us that the power to bring about change lies within us all."

Daniel nodded, humbled by the recognition. "Thank you, Mayor Alvarez. But I couldn't have done it alone. I had the support of my friends and the community behind me."

The mayor's gaze held a mixture of pride and sincerity. "Indeed, Daniel. The strength of a community lies in its unity, and you've reminded us of that. Serenity Falls owes you a debt of gratitude."

As the crowd gradually dispersed, leaving the town square behind, Daniel reflected on the journey that had brought him here. The community began to heal as the cloud of suspicion lifted, and they could finally find closure for the years of unanswered questions.

***

Nina's stay in Serenity Falls extended longer than she had initially anticipated. Despite the challenges and heartaches she had encountered, her childhood town had grown on her.

One afternoon, she sat in the worn-out leather chair across from Daniel's cluttered desk in his private detective office. The sun cast a warm glow through the window, illuminating the room's vintage decor and the scattered case files that filled every available space.

"So, how's life as a full-fledged detective hero treating you?" Nina asked, a playful grin on her face.

Daniel leaned back in his chair, a tired but content expression on his face. "It's definitely more exciting than my old desk job, that's for sure. But also a lot more chaotic."

Nina chuckled. "Well, chaos suits you."

They spoke about solved cases, crazy clients, and the unpredictable nature of their work. Despite the sometimes-grim subject matter, they found humor in the absurdity of the situations they encountered.

After a while, the conversation shifted to a more serious tone. Nina looked at Daniel with a thoughtful expression. "You know, I never really thanked you properly for everything you've done. For helping me find Elle, for being there when I needed someone the most."

Daniel's expression softened. "You don't have to thank me, Nina. I'm just glad I could help. And besides, that's what friends are for."

Nina nodded, a grateful smile on her lips. "Well, I'm lucky to have a friend like you."

As they continued talking, Nina's thoughts inevitably turned to her imminent departure. She knew she had to return to California, to her life and job there. She had come to Serenity Falls to find answers, and she had found so much more—friendship, closure, and a chance to heal.

The gravity of the moment hung in the air, and Nina's voice held a trace of melancholy. "You know, Danny, soon I'm gonna have to get back to California, to my life there. But part of me wishes I could stay longer, to continue being a part of this community."

Daniel's expression mirrored her sentiment, a mix of both acceptance and reluctance. "I understand, Nina. You have responsibilities and commitments back there. But remember, Serenity Falls will always welcome you back."

Nina offered a grateful smile, her eyes reflecting the bond they had formed. "And who knows? Maybe our paths will cross again someday."

***

Vaughn's latest book, "Shattered Hearts and Silent Whispers," had struck a chord with readers nationwide. It chronicled his journey, both the darkness he had faced and the light he had found through it all. The book's success was a demonstration to the power of resilience, healing, and the strength of love that defied all odds.

In a cozy, book-lined room, Vaughn sat across from an interviewer, a warm smile on his face as they delved into the journey that had led to his book, "Shattered Hearts and Silent Whispers."

The interviewer leaned forward, her voice a blend of curiosity and admiration. "Vaughn, your book has touched the hearts of so many readers. Can you share with us what inspired you to write such a powerful story?"

Vaughn's gaze held a mixture of reflection and determination. "Well, it all began with the events that unfolded in Serenity Falls. The darkness that had shrouded the town for years needed to be brought to light, and I felt a responsibility to tell that story. But beyond that, it was a story of resilience, of individuals coming together to face their fears and find hope."

The interviewer nodded, clearly intrigued. "And the title, 'Shattered Hearts and Silent Whispers'—it's quite evocative. Could you tell us more about the significance behind it?"

Vaughn's expression turned contemplative. "Certainly. 'Shattered Hearts' symbolizes the pain and trauma that the characters endured—Amanda, Nina, Daniel, and so many others. It speaks to the brokenness that comes from loss and suffering. 'Silent Whispers,' on the other hand, represents the hidden truths, the secrets that are often too painful to voice aloud. The book explores the journey of uncovering those whispers, of finding the strength to speak up and seek justice."

The interviewer leaned in, captivated by his words. "And the characters in your book—they're so vivid, so real. How did you approach bringing them to life?"

Vaughn's eyes sparkled with passion. "Every character in the book is a blend of inspiration from real people and the imagination that comes with storytelling. Each of them represents a facet of the human experience—pain, hope, fear, and love. I wanted readers to connect with them on a personal level, to see themselves in their struggles and triumphs."

As the conversation continued, Vaughn eloquently shared the journey of writing "Shattered Hearts and Silent Whispers," weaving in his personal connection to the story and the profound impact that the events had on his life. He spoke of the friendships that had formed, the resilience that had emerged, and the way the town of Serenity Falls had found its way back to light.

As the interview came to an end, the interviewer leaned back with a satisfied smile. "Thank you, Vaughn, for sharing your insights and your journey with us. Your book has truly touched the hearts of many."

Vaughn's gratitude shone in his eyes as he nodded. "Thank you. It's been a privilege to be part of this journey, to witness the strength of the human spirit in the face of adversity."

And just as the interview wrapped up, the interviewer leaned in with a curious smile. "One last question, Vaughn. We've heard a lot about the strength of relationships in your book. Is there a special someone in your life right now?"

Vaughn's eyes sparkled, a hint of a smile playing on his lips. He took a moment to gather his thoughts, then looked back at the interviewer. "Well, you know, life has a way of surprising us. And I've come to realize that love and connections can come when you least expect them. So, to answer your question, let's just say... there might be someone."

The interviewer's eyebrows raised, clearly intrigued. "Care to share any details?"

Vaughn's smile widened, a mixture of playfulness and warmth in his expression. "I think I'll leave that up to the imagination for now. But I can say that I've learned from the experiences of the characters in 'Shattered Hearts and Silent Whispers.' Love is a journey, and sometimes, the best things in life happen when we let go of expectations and allow ourselves to be open to the possibilities."

With those parting words, Vaughn's book continued to resonate with readers, reminding them of the power of resilience, the healing of community, and the enduring strength of love that could guide even the most shattered hearts back to the light.

***

But perhaps the most profound transformation was witnessed in Olive. Freed from the clutches of a toxic relationship, she embraced her independence with fervor. Her photography studio thrived, and her work captured the essence of life's moments in ways that resonated deeply with her clients. Her heart, once shattered, found solace in her newfound strength.

The crisp morning sun cast a warm glow across Olive's photography studio, painting the room in shades of gold and amber. As she moved around, adjusting the lighting for an upcoming photoshoot, a contented smile graced her lips.

The studio had become more than just a space to capture images; it was a witness to her resilience and rebirth. Olive and Vaughn rekindled their connection, the trials they had faced only bringing them closer.

Vaughn, leaning against a wall, observed her with a mixture of pride and adoration. He admired how Olive had transformed the studio from a dream into a reality, infusing it with her unique vision and creative energy.

"Everything looks amazing, Olive," he commented, his voice a soft murmur.

Olive turned to him, her eyes sparkling. "Thanks, Vaughn. It's been quite a journey, hasn't it?"

He nodded, the memories of their shared struggles and triumphs etched into his mind. "Definitely. But we made it through."

They shared a knowing smile, their eyes locking in

a silent exchange that conveyed volumes. The trials they had faced individually and as a couple had only strengthened their bond.

A few months had passed since the chaotic events surrounding Amanda's rescue and the uncovering of Agent Marks' sinister intentions. Olive had been through a whirlwind of emotions, but her spirit had emerged unbreakable. Vaughn's unwavering support had been a constant, helping her navigate the aftermath of her past trauma.

Her photography had taken on a new life, capturing moments of joy, love, and resilience. The clients who walked through her studio doors were met with warmth and understanding, making them feel at ease in front of her lens.

As they continued to chat, Olive's gaze wandered to the photographs adorning the studio walls – candid shots capturing genuine smiles, couples lost in tender moments, and families united in love. Each image told a story, a reflection of the beauty she saw in the world.

***

As the investigation of the cold cases reached its dramatic conclusion, a sincere sense of closure settled over Serenity Falls. In the wake of the revelations that had shaken Serenity Falls to its core, Deputy Turner's unwavering dedication and commitment to upholding the law had not gone unnoticed. His meticulous efforts in solving the cases, while ensuring that proper protocol was followed, had garnered the respect and admiration of both his fellow officers and the community at large.

One day, as the sun cast a warm glow over the town, a ceremony was held at the Serenity Falls Police Department. The atmosphere was charged with a mix of pride and excitement as Deputy Turner stood before a gathering of his colleagues, community members, and local officials.

Mayor Alvarez, standing at the podium, spoke with conviction. "Today, we recognize the exceptional leadership and dedication of one of our own. Deputy Turner's unwavering commitment to justice and his exemplary work in solving the cold cases that have haunted our town for years have not only brought closure to many families but have also restored our faith in the law enforcement system."

Applause and cheers filled the air as Deputy Turner stepped forward to accept his new role. His eyes shone with a mixture of gratitude and determination. The mayor continued, "It is with great pride that I announce the promotion of Deputy Turner to the position of Police Captain. In this new role, he will continue to lead our department with integrity, ensuring that Serenity Falls remains a safe haven for all."

As the badge of a Police Captain was pinned onto Deputy Turner's uniform, the weight of his new responsibilities settled in. He glanced around at his colleagues and friends, feeling a surge of both honor and duty. His journey, marked by challenges and triumphs, had led him to this pivotal moment—a moment of recognition for the tireless efforts he had put into upholding justice and safeguarding the community.

With a firm handshake from the mayor and the supportive nods of his fellow officers, Captain Turner embraced his new role with a renewed sense of purpose. As the ceremony concluded and the crowd dispersed, he couldn't help but reflect on how far he had come, and the impact that his commitment to the truth had made on the town he cherished.

Under the leadership of Captain Turner, the police meticulously gathered evidence, ensuring that the remains of the missing women were properly identified and returned to their grieving families. The town collectively mourned the lives lost, finally able to say their goodbyes and offer some resemblance of peace to the victims' loved ones.

***

At the cemetery grounds, Vaughn and Nina

stood together in front of Elle's tombstone, a simple marker bearing her name, "Elle Santos, Beloved Wife and Sister." The simplicity of the inscription held within it a world of memories, a lifetime of shared moments, and a love that had endured through countless trials.

The weight of their shared history, the pain of loss, and the journey they had undertaken hung heavy in the air. As the wind rustled the leaves and the sun cast a warm glow, emotions swelled within them.

Nina's tears flowed freely as she gazed at the tombstone, memories flooding back. Vaughn's steady presence beside her offered a source of strength, a reminder that they were not alone in their grief. He gently placed a comforting hand on her shoulder, his touch a silent reassurance that they were in this together.

"She would have been proud of us, you know," Vaughn murmured softly, his voice laced with both sadness and determination. "We did what we needed to do, for her and for the others."

Nina nodded, her voice choked with emotion. "I just wish she could be here to see it, to know that justice was finally served."

Their shared silence spoke volumes, an unspoken

understanding passing between them. After a moment, Vaughn gently guided Nina away from the tombstone, leading her to a quiet spot where they sat on one of the benches.

Vaughn asked Nina the question that had been burning in his mind, ever since the night they escaped from the farmhouse. "Nina, why did you hesitate?"

Nina smiled, a hint of melancholy in her eyes. She had been hoping to avoid discussing this particular topic. "Whatever do you mean?"

"You know exactly what I mean," Vaughn persisted.

With a sigh, Nina finally relented. "Fine. I was hoping that you'd forget about it. But since you're asking… I don't know, Vaughn. At that moment, all I could think about was Hector. How his twisted obsession with Elle led him down this path. And it all happened after I left town. Part of me felt responsible for not staying, for not being there to prevent this. I guess I just wanted to make things right, in some way. I thought if I could get through to Hector, maybe…"

Vaughn shook his head, firmly disagreeing. "Nina, it wasn't your fault. These things, they happen on their own, regardless of what we do or don't do. Hector was a broken person, and he made his own choices. You leaving town wasn't the cause of all this."

Nina blinked back tears, touched by Vaughn's words. "Thank you, Vaughn. It's just hard not to second-guess everything, especially when you're faced with something so dark and twisted."

Vaughn reached out and gently placed a hand on hers. "I get it. We all have our demons to wrestle with. But we're here now, trying to make things right. And that's what counts."

For a moment, they sat in companionable silence, the weight of their shared experiences heavy in the air. Finally, Nina managed a small smile. "How about some coffee?"

Vaughn chuckled, the tension in the moment easing. "Yeah, I could definitely use some coffee right about now."

Later that evening, at a local diner, Vaughn and Nina sat across from each other, their hands wrapped around warm cups of coffee. The cozy atmosphere of the diner provided a comforting backdrop to their bittersweet conversation.

Nina took a sip of her coffee before breaking the silence. "I can't believe it's been months already."

Vaughn nodded, his gaze gentle as he looked at her. "Time flies when you're... not having fun?"

Nina chuckled softly. "No, actually, I've had a great time here, Vaughn. It's been healing, being around people who care about me, who support me."

Vaughn smiled, his eyes reflecting the genuine happiness he felt for her. "I'm glad you found some comfort here."

Their conversation shifted to memories they had shared, the moments that had brought them closer together. They talked about the challenges they had faced, the mysteries they had unraveled, and the bond that had formed between them.

As their conversation came to a natural pause, Nina looked at Vaughn with a mixture of gratitude and sadness. "I promise I'll visit. I'll come back and see you."

Vaughn reached across the table and gently squeezed her hand. "We'll be waiting for you."

The moment was bittersweet, a mix of longing and acceptance. They both knew that life had its own plans, that Nina had her own journey to continue. But the connections they had forged during her time in Serenity Falls would remain strong.

Hours later, as Nina boarded a plane back to California, she carried with her a renewed sense of purpose and a heart full of cherished memories. Sitting by the window seat of the airplane, Nina gazed out at the landscape below as it slowly shrank into a patchwork of fields and towns. The memories of her time in Serenity Falls were etched vividly in her mind, a tapestry of emotions that ranged from heartache to healing, from uncertainty to newfound clarity.

As the plane taxied on the runway, Nina couldn't help but replay the moments that had shaped her journey. The faces of the friends she had made—Olive, Vaughn, Daniel, and even Orlando—flashed before her eyes. Each of them had played a role in unraveling the mysteries of the past, while also weaving threads of connection that had left an indelible mark on her heart.

The warmth of the community, the serenity of the falls, and the bonds she had forged had all become a part of her story. Serenity Falls had given her the closure she had sought, and in return, she had left a piece of her soul there.

As the plane gained altitude, Nina took a deep breath, feeling a mix of emotions. There was a sadness in leaving behind a place that had brought so much clarity, but also a sense of gratitude for the experiences that had enriched her life. The memories of late-night conversations, shared laughter, and the quiet moments of introspection would forever be cherished.

Nina's fingers lightly touched the necklace she wore—a small pendant shaped like a heart. It had been a gift from Olive, a symbol of their friendship and the strength they had found in each other. She closed her eyes, letting the memories wash over her once more, carrying with them the lessons she had learned, the wounds that had healed, and the friendships that would endure.

As the plane soared through the sky, Nina looked forward to the path ahead, carrying with her the lessons she had learned in Serenity Falls. It wasn't just a place on the map; it was a chapter in her life's story, a chapter that had transformed her in ways she had never anticipated. With a renewed sense of purpose and a heart full of cherished memories, she was ready to face the horizon that awaited her.

With her heart heavy but hopeful, Nina bid farewell to Serenity Falls and returned to her life in California. She continued her work in journalism, capturing the beauty and stories of the world around her. Her time in the small town had shaped her perspective and fueled her passion for telling stories through her writing.

***

Months later, in a cold Serenity Falls, as the winter sun began its descent, Olive and Vaughn found themselves sitting side by side on the porch of their shared home. The air was crisp, carrying a hint of chill that was softened by the cozy blankets draped around them. The garden around them had transformed, the vibrant blooms of spring and summer replaced by the serene beauty of winter.

The scent of blooming flowers may have faded with the colder months, but the memory lingered, and it was as if nature itself was taking a restorative pause, preparing for the eventual rebirth of spring.

Olive leaned against the porch railing, a contented sigh escaping her lips. She gazed out at the tranquil scene before them – the snow-covered ground, the trees standing tall and proud despite the cold, and the subtle hues of the setting sun painting the sky in a mesmerizing display of colors.

"Isn't it beautiful?" she mused, her voice soft as she turned her head to Vaughn.

He nodded, a warm smile tugging at his lips. "Absolutely. There's something magical about winter, isn't there? It's like nature's way of reminding us that even in stillness, there's a sense of wonder."

Olive's eyes sparkled as she looked at him. "You always find the poetry in everything, don't you?"

Vaughn chuckled, his gaze lingering on her. "I suppose I do. But you've also taught me to see the beauty in the ordinary."

They sat in companionable silence, each lost in their own thoughts as they watched the sun dip below the horizon. The evening's calmness wrapped around them like a comforting embrace, a moment of respite from the chaos and darkness they had faced together.

"It's been quite a journey, hasn't it?" Olive said softly, her voice carrying a mixture of reflection and gratitude.

Vaughn turned to Olive, his eyes filled with a mixture of gratitude and admiration. "You know, I never imagined that we'd be here – together, stronger than ever."

Olive intertwined her fingers with his, leaning her head against his shoulder. "Life has a funny way of surprising us, doesn't it?"

He chuckled softly. "That it does. But I wouldn't change a thing."

Their conversation drifted into comfortable silence, the soft rustling of leaves and the distant chirping of crickets creating a serene ambiance.

"Vaughn," Olive spoke softly, breaking the silence.

He looked down at her, his eyes gentle and attentive. "What is it, Olive?"

She took a deep breath, her gaze unwavering. "I just want you to know how much your support meant to me. You've been my rock through all of this, and I'll forever be grateful."

Vaughn smiled, his touch warm as he lifted her chin to meet her eyes. "Olive, you're the strongest person I know. I'm just honored to be by your side, witnessing your journey to healing and happiness."

Their lips met in a tender kiss, sealing their unspoken commitment to each other's well-being and growth.

Olive turned her other hand to grab his arm, a gesture that felt both familiar and comforting. "I wouldn't change a thing about it. The pain, the challenges, all of it led us here."

Vaughn's gaze met hers, his eyes filled with a depth of emotion that words couldn't fully convey. "And here is exactly where I want to be."

Soon the evening deepened into night, the stars

began to twinkle in the velvety sky. Olive and Vaughn remained on the porch, wrapped in their blankets and each other's presence. In the midst of the winter's quiet, they found a sense of peace and renewal, a promise of brighter days ahead. The scars of their past had faded into the background, replaced by the promise of a future built on strength, resilience, and the unbreakable bond they had forged.

And as the pages turned, the town of Serenity Falls emerged from its tumultuous history stronger and united. The stories of those who had faced their fears, confronted their pasts, and fought for justice intertwined, leaving behind a legacy of resilience, friendship, and the enduring power of the human spirit.

*** THE END***

ABOUT THE AUTHOR

Kathy Winslower has been a reader all along—of the stories she reads and of the stories she tells. Her characters are old friends, with all their flaws, hopes, and goodness. Writing is how she sees the world, how she struggles with love, loss, and the intense moments that define us.

As a child, she wrote stories in dog-eared notebooks, never imagining that one day she would be publishing them for the world. She writes from the heart and gives us stories that linger long after the final page is closed.

Kathy resides in London with her fabulous son and her beautiful cat, drawing inspiration from life itself, chance meetings, and the simple pleasure of a well-brewed cuppa.